WHEN GUNS ROAR

Siobhan Dunmoore Book 6

TASK FORCE LUCKNER

AUDACES FORTUNA JUVAT

Eric Thomson

When the Guns Roar
Copyright 2019 Eric Thomson
First paperback printing October 2019
This edition May 2023

Published in Canada
By Sanddiver Books Inc.
ISBN: 978-1-989314-18-0

Sanddiver
Books Inc

— One —

"That assemblage of spare parts has to be the Shrehari forward operating base my drones picked up." Lieutenant Shanna Nishino's hologram looked up at Siobhan Dunmoore, sitting in the throne-like command chair at the heart of *Iolanthe*'s combat information center. "It appears lightly armed by our standards and isn't hosting any ships at the moment. As my favorite obachan would say, a carp on a cutting board. We paid particular attention to the planet's Lagrangian points, in case the boneheads know about us and are running silent hoping to spring an ambush, but found nothing. However, based on the emissions signature, there's someone home, and they put a half dozen satellites in geosynchronous orbit as a rudimentary surveillance constellation."

"Confirmed," Chief Petty Officer Third Class Marti Yens, *Iolanthe*'s sensor chief said. "And if we can see it, then it's a given *Fennec*'s eyes aren't telling lies, since they're at least twenty percent better than ours."

"Make that thirty percent, Chief," Nishino, *Fennec*'s captain, replied with more than a hint of pride in her voice.

"Eyes aren't telling lies?" Lieutenant Commander Thorin Sirico, *Iolanthe*'s combat systems officer, cocked an eyebrow at Yens. "When did you take up the fine art of poesy?"

"Everyone needs a hobby, sir," Yens replied, unrepentant. "And I'll accept thirty percent, Lieutenant. Those new long-range sensors are amazing."

The Q-ship and her diminutive consort, one of Task Force Luckner's two sloop-sized scouts, had come out of hyperspace as close to the dead planet as they could while remaining within the wartime safety envelope. They were now running silent, albeit with an undetectable laser comlink joining them while looking for the enemy battle group calling the hastily constructed orbital station home.

Dunmoore nodded.

"That they are. Let's hope the resident Shrehari battle group isn't stalking Admiral Petras while he's hunting that convoy. Otherwise, it could become messier than planned."

Nishino made a face.

"No kidding."

After weeks of fruitless patrolling as a formation along the frontier, Rear Admiral Kell Petras had finally accepted Dunmoore's suggestion and taken Task Force Luckner well into what was Shrehari space even before the war. There, instead of stalking known interstellar shipping routes, they'd loitered at the heliopause of a star system named Khorsan. According to naval intelligence, it might harbor a forward operating base. Perhaps even the one which supported the strike group *Iolanthe* fought from time to time.

FOBs received regular supply convoys, and every ship crossing the heliopause was forced to drop out of FTL because hyperspace physics severely limited a starship's velocity inside a heliosphere. Passing the heliopause on an inward-bound course at interstellar speeds never ended well. And jumping through interstellar space at in-system speeds meant an endless voyage. Starships were never more vulnerable to ambush than either at the heliopause or their target planet's hyperlimit.

Thanks to a stroke of luck, when they probed Khorsan, the scouts detected an eight ship convoy. Its presence in an otherwise uninhabited system meant it was probably leaving a FOB after resupplying it with ammunition, food, spare parts, and other items essential to waging interstellar war. Five of the vessels were armed freighters, the other three were *Ptar* class escorts, corvettes that stood no chance whatsoever against the Q-ship's guns.

But inexplicably, Petras had ordered *Iolanthe*, his most powerful ship, to reconnoiter the suspected FOB accompanied by *Fennec* instead of putting her at the head of Task Force Luckner's attack phalanx. But Dunmoore could guess why.

Ever since joining Luckner, she had been as cooperative as possible with the demanding admiral, biting her tongue whenever his tactics during their never-ending battle drills ran counter to the experience *Iolanthe*'s crew had gained from raids inside the enemy's sphere. After a few rebuffed attempts at diplomatically suggesting ways to improve performance — always in private, with no one else around to hear — she'd given up.

The task force's mission was to raid enemy commerce, harass their shipping, and cause as much havoc as possible, just as its namesake, Count Felix von Luckner, a famous wet navy commerce raider did during one of Earths' wars centuries ago. Yet Petras insisted on deploying his ships in ways that didn't seem to deviate much from conventional doctrine.

That he didn't want Dunmoore around for his first real try at stalking and destroying a Shrehari convoy wasn't exactly a surprise to most of *Iolanthe*'s people. Or to Lieutenant Nishino, a career chief petty officer commissioned from the ranks early in the war when the Fleet doubled in size and experienced officers were at a premium.

"What are your intentions, sir?" Nishino asked. "We could do a flyby at fairly close range and carry out a detailed scan. With no enemy ships around, the FOB is pretty much a sitting duck."

Commander Ezekiel Holt, *Iolanthe*'s first officer, or rather his hologram, since he was at his station on the bridge, saw an all too familiar gleam appear in Dunmoore's eyes.

"The admiral wants us to scout out this place, Skipper. He didn't indicate we should attack the FOB if it appeared ripe for the picking. That bizarre construct might be lightly armed by our standards, but I'm sure it still packs a punch. Even a flyby should stay out of gun range."

"Are they carrying out active scans, Chief?" Dunmoore asked instead of answering Holt.

"Negative. And I'm not reading anything that might show they're powering up to fight."

"Not unreasonable," Sirico said. "They don't expect hostile ships this deep inside their own space, which means they aren't looking for any."

"And we should take advantage of that." She smiled at her first officer. "Don't you think, Zeke? Imagine the effect on Shrehari morale if we destroy one of their orbital stations and then simply vanish. The battle group based here would need to travel further back for resupply, meaning they'd have less time to spend hunting us. A winning proposition, no?"

The first officer let out a soft sigh, knowing his captain's mind was made up.

"Once again, I find it difficult to argue with your logic, Skipper."

She grinned at Holt.

"To paraphrase the great Horatio Nelson, our fleet will sooner forgive an officer for attacking his enemy than for leaving him alone. When the station's orbital period takes it behind the planet, we will fire thrusters to accelerate and hope their surveillance systems don't spot us. A single pass, then we boost back to the hyperlimit and check out the gas giants before rejoining the task force. One of them must have an automated antimatter fueling station in orbit. We should destroy it as well. *Fennec* will stay out of known effective enemy range at all times."

"I'll ask Astrid to prepare the navigation plot right away."

"And I," Lieutenant Commander Sirico added, rubbing his hands with bloodthirsty glee, "will prepare a firing plan to destroy that monstrosity with a single salvo."

"Best plan on several salvos, Thorin," Dunmoore replied. "It could be tougher than we think. The Shrehari aren't much on esthetics, but they know how to build something solid."

"I'll keep that in mind."

It wasn't long before the CIC's tactical projection lit up, showing a plot that would bring the Q-ship within optimum gun range of the FOB as it swung around the planet on a course to slingshot back toward the hyperlimit. *Fennec* would follow a parallel course, but beyond known enemy weapons range, and record every single detail about the target for Fleet intelligence.

Lieutenant Drost's hologram appeared beside that of the first officer.

"Good work as always." Dunmoore smiled at her. "What about you, Thorin?"

"My fire plan is coordinated with Astrid's plot, sir." Further symbols appeared in the tactical projection, showing the planned firing window.

"*Fennec?*"

"We received your navigator's calculations, Captain, and our own course is laid in to conform with your movements but at a greater distance from the target."

Dunmoore gave the three-dimensional projection of the dead planet and the orbital station one last glance, knowing she was about to cast the die and exceed her orders.

"Since the target no longer has a direct line of sight to our current position, you may fire sublight drives as per the navigation plot and put us on the right course at full acceleration."

"Aye, aye, sir," Drost and Lieutenant Nishino responded in unison.

"And Thorin..."

"Sir?"

"Turn her into the Furious Faerie. There's no sense letting the enemy watch us unmask. They will undoubtedly send word on their subspace net, and I prefer them to think a battlecruiser is attacking and not that dastardly phantom raider they've been chasing for months."

"Aye, aye, Captain."

Moments later, Dunmoore felt the vibration of camouflage plates sliding aside and gun turrets rising from their hidden compartments, transforming a harmless bulk carrier into a deadly warship. A countdown timer appeared on one of the CIC's secondary screens, marking the hours, minutes, and seconds remaining before *Iolanthe* reached optimal engagement range. Or as Sirico would put it if asked, marking how long the Shrehari forward operations base had left to live.

Dunmoore climbed to her feet.

"You have the CIC, Mister Sirico. I'll be in my day cabin."

"Sir." The combat systems officer sprang up. "Shall I send for you five minutes before we reach extreme engagement range?"

"Please do." She glanced at Holt's hologram. "Join me for coffee."

Her day cabin was halfway between the bridge and the CIC, and they arrived simultaneously. Once inside, Holt headed for the urn, picked up two mugs emblazoned with the ship's Furious Faerie crest and filled them while Dunmoore dropped into the chair behind her desk.

"I hope you won't try to talk me out of attacking, Zeke."

He handed her one of the steaming cups.

"Me? Perish the thought. It's too late, anyway. But be prepared for one of Petras' stern talks about managing risk this far from the nearest Commonwealth star system."

"I am." She sighed. "You'd think after working at Special Operations Command HQ, the idea we exist to take greater risks than conventional units would come naturally to him."

"Sure, but losing ships still gets you in front of a board of inquiry. And if there's the slightest hint of preventable error, it turns from a formality into a full-blown inquisition, even for a SOCOM flag officer."

"And he's not experienced enough to understand just how far we can push the envelope. I know." Dunmoore took a sip of the dark brew. "What I fear is that he'll never make the leap, meaning ships such as *Iolanthe* and *Jan Sobieski*, who were built to take the fight deep into enemy space, will be wasted. The Shrehari are running out of steam. I can feel it. Every intelligence digest hints at it. Which means this is the time to hit them below the belt often and hard."

"Such as destroying one of their FOBs and tons of supplies recently delivered but not yet distributed to patrolling ships. As I said, Skipper, I can't fault your logic, but the admiral will try. Especially if we come back damaged enough to need dry dock time." Holt snorted. "I wouldn't be surprised if he considers you a bad influence on the other captains. Petras must already suspect Gregor Pushkin feels more loyalty toward you than toward him."

"But he's also smart enough to know Gregor will do his duty with utmost diligence nonetheless. Lena Corto is the one who worries me."

Holt made a face upon hearing the name of Task Force Luckner's flag captain. "Me as well."

"Lena is desperate for her first star. And she knows the only way to become a commodore when you've spent most of the war in staff appointments and never commanded at the captain rank is by riding an admiral's coattails. And you don't ride coattails that aren't headed up the greasy pole. Dear Lena won't want her boss to make the sort of mistake that'll see him stay a rear admiral for the rest of his career. She's invested too much in him for a change of patrons at this late date. The rule is passed over for promotion ten times, and you retire — at least in peacetime. Her last promotion was a while back, which means she's already been passed over several times. A few more and the moment this war ends, she'll swallow the anchor for good, even if she doesn't want to retire."

"Tick tock."

"Yup. And that sound is getting louder in her ears."

"Meaning Corto won't let Petras take what she considers undue risks. Better to be suspected of excessive prudence than seen as overly aggressive when one comes home with dented starships."

"It has ever been thus, Zeke. Our dear navy will never change, not even under the pressures of interstellar war." She put her mug down. "Speaking of excessive prudence versus naked aggression, how about a few games of chess?"

Holt let out a theatrical groan, but it was mostly feigned. He enjoyed their regular matches, even though she still beat him two times out of three.

"I'll fetch the set."

Five rounds later, Dunmoore glanced at the timer on her cabin's main display. Sirico would call soon. She moved her queen and sat back.

"Checkmate."

Holt sighed.

"I was hoping you wouldn't notice my mistake, but nothing ever gets by you."

Dunmoore grinned at him.

"Cheer up, Zeke. You won two games. That's almost half."

He rounded up the chess pieces and placed them one by one in the antique mahogany case which, when open, also served as the board.

"I suggest we grab a sandwich before returning to our duty stations, Skipper. My stomach is making demands I can't ignore."

"Ditto."

— Two —

"Captain." Lieutenant Commander Sirico jumped up the moment Dunmoore entered the CIC. "I was just about to call you. The boneheads are still quiet. No active scans, no signs they're powering up for a fight, and no ships hiding in plain sight. We're tracking the target on passive. Our weapons systems are ready and waiting on low power standby. It'll take the usual ninety seconds from your command to the first round downrange."

She studied the three-dimensional targeting plot, where a red icon orbited a reasonably accurate facsimile of the rocky, airless world. A pair of blue icons, one larger than the other were moving toward it, their planned course marked by two dotted lines. The larger of them would pass within a few thousand kilometers of the red icon at its closest approach to the planet before using a gravity assist maneuver to slingshot around and head back out toward interstellar space, along with its smaller companion.

Sirico touched his console, and the projection zoomed in on the orbital station, now bracketed by symbols marking the beginning and end of the optimum engagement window.

"Provided they don't detect us until we go up systems, our firing window will allow for way more than three salvos, sir. It's really a question of how much ammo you want to expend. The boneheads are stuck in a predictable orbit. Which means every shot and every missile will be on target."

Dunmoore squinted at the tactical display.

"We might as well give them as little time as possible to react and thereby not empty half of our stocks on a target of opportunity. I think it won't be as tough a nut to crack as our own FOBs. Besides, the admiral might look to the weight of our broadside during a planned operation before our next resupply run, and I'd rather not come up short."

She reached into the hologram and, with a fingertip, narrowed the firing zone.

"There."

Sirico tilted his head as he studied her changes.

"Three salvos it is, Captain. And it gives us enough margin for a fourth."

Major Tatiana Salminen, commanding officer, E Company, 3rd Battalion, Scandia Regiment — *Iolanthe*'s embarked infantry contingent — entered the CIC, no doubt warned by one of the watchkeepers they were on final approach and would soon go to battle stations. She joined Dunmoore and Sirico.

"Captain. Thorin. I gather they haven't spotted us yet. Incredible."

"Not really," Sirico replied. "Space is vast, our hull is dark, Shrehari sensors suck, and our emissions control is tight. Besides, garrison troops of every sapient species share a common failing."

Salminen nodded.

"They become complacent if they never see the enemy."

"Making them prone to dismiss sensor ghosts as an equipment malfunction or a natural phenomenon, especially if they occur frequently," Chief Yens added, "instead of immediately thinking *enemy ship running silent.* Mind you, our orbital station crews aren't much better in that regard, even if our sensor gear is."

Dunmoore took the command chair and glanced at Holt's hologram.

"Put the ship at battle stations."

"Battle stations, aye."

Seconds later, a klaxon sounded, though, under the circumstances, it was mainly a formality. Most of *Iolanthe's* crew members were already at their posts, as Holt's report proved when he declared the ship ready less than three minutes later.

Time seemed to slow, and space expand as they approached the optimum engagement window, making it appear forever out of reach. But the impression was merely an illusion brought on by pre-battle jitters and fear the enemy would detect them before they came out of silent running. No matter how often the Q-ship went into combat, the last moments before they unmasked were always the same. Everyone aboard monitored the countdown timers displayed throughout the ship, bracing themselves as the last sixty seconds ran out.

"Up systems." Dunmoore's order came out in a smoky, almost raspy voice. A new countdown timer appeared, this one to mark the minute and a half until the weapons systems were ready to spew death.

"Shields are up," Sirico reported twenty seconds later.

"Active targeting is on," ten seconds after that. "We should be lighting up the boneheads' threat board brighter than a Founder's Day fireworks show."

"Pucker factor pegged at ten on the meter," Yens rumbled. "If they own puckers. But then, the damn boneheads are galaxy-sized assholes..."

"We're locked on, and the firing program is engaged. Thirty seconds to first rounds downrange."

Dunmoore felt a faint, almost imperceptible vibration run up the soles of her feet — *Iolanthe*'s missile launcher bays opening.

Precisely ninety seconds after she gave the order to go up systems, Dunmoore's ears picked up the characteristic dull thump of launchers ejecting missiles and autoloaders shoving pure copper disks into plasma gun breeches. The CIC's main display, showing a real-time visual of the space between *Iolanthe* and its target, came to life with excruciatingly bright streaks of light.

Hell was descending on the hapless Shrehari forward operating base. With any luck, the first rounds would strike before they could raise shields. And that station didn't look as if it carried the sort of armor protecting permanent orbital installations.

"Their watchkeepers are awake," Yens said seconds before the opening volley splashed against an invisible cocoon enveloping the station, giving life to an ovoid greenish-blue aurora. "Shields are up, and targeting sensors are locking on to us. Countermeasures are taking out our missiles."

A second salvo left *Iolanthe*'s launchers. With the enemy awake and fighting back, the best tactic was saturating their defenses.

"First batch of birds neutralized, though the guns are degrading shields."

The aurora dancing across the cocoon took on a deeper hue as competing energies battled each other.

"For what we are about to receive," Sirico intoned moments before a green glow enveloped *Iolanthe* as the enemy's guns found their mark.   But only the guns. "Fifteen missiles in their first volley. All destroyed."

The Q-ship's thirty quad-barreled close defense calliopes had done their job.

"Enemy guns and launchers are of the same type as those aboard a *Tol* class cruiser, except the FOB has more of them," Yens announced.

Sirico gave off a ferocious chuckle.

"This is where the boneheads' habit of keeping production lines to a minimum will bite them in the ass. We can take what they're chucking twenty-four hours a day long and twice on Sundays. Third salvo away."

"Reluctant to waste heavier ordnance on a FOB? Or don't they make bigger guns?" Holt's hologram glanced up at Dunmoore.

"Considering we're probably the first to attack a Shrehari orbital base, at least in this sector, I doubt anyone can answer that."

Though she'd witnessed the same scene many times before, Dunmoore still watched with something close to awe as an almost continuous stream of plasma connected her ship to the FOB. Its shields crackled and glowed with an increasingly more menacing shade of purple as missiles evaded defensive fire and exploded against them, triggering energy feedback loops capable of damaging emitters.

"Sir, the target is transmitting in code on a Shrehari emergency subspace frequency. The crypto AI thinks it's a distress signal," Chief Day, the CIC communications noncom, reported.

A faint, almost inaudible whine, reached her ears. *Iolanthe*'s shield generators were feeling the strain of sustained enemy fire.

As if he could read his commanding officer's thoughts, Sirico said, "We're going into the blue, Captain, but only a little."

"Second missile salvo, four hits," Yens said. "Enemy shields are flickering."

The FOB's protective energy shell now sparked with deadly deep purple flares, its edges wavering as generators fought to keep out the energy unleashed by four nuclear warheads exploding almost simultaneously.

Moments later, "Third missile salvo, five hits."

With a silent pop, the eerie colors vanished, leaving the orbital station exposed to *Iolanthe*'s large-caliber cannon. The continuous stream of plasma attacked its outer shell with remorseless intensity, at first digging divots in the thick alloy, then punching through to release geysers of flash-frozen air.

The entire CIC crew stared at the main display, mesmerized by the enemy installation's death throes. Then, without warning, a bright light blotted out their view. When it faded, nothing but wreckage remained.

Yens let out a low whistle.

"That never gets old. We either hit their main reactor or a stack of nuclear missiles destined for the resident battle group's ships."

"Check for life signs."

Almost a minute passed before the sensor chief shook her head.

"Nothing."

"Destroy the satellite constellation and make it a clean sweep, Mister Sirico."

Dunmoore briefly wondered how many enemy lives they'd taken, but before she could reflect on the vicissitudes of war, Chief Day raised his hand.

"*Fennec* is calling."

"Put her on."

A holographic projection of Lieutenant Nishino materialized in front of Dunmoore.

"That was spectacular, Captain. Did you take any damage?"

"Probably nothing more than strained shield generators. My chief engineer hasn't reported yet."

"How about I push out to the hyperlimit and make a jump for the innermost gas giant? That way, when you arrive, I'll either be able to point you at the antimatter fueling station right away or tell you it's not there."

"Certainly. In fact, if you find it before we join you and are willing to fire a missile or two, or perhaps even engage in a little target shooting, please indulge yourself."

Dunmoore winked at *Fennec*'s captain.

Nishino's face lit up with a hungry smile.

"Yes, sir. Thank you, sir. I believe my crew will enjoy that. It'll make a nice change from our usual shoot and scoot."

"Then you're free to accelerate out of here."

"On our way. *Fennec*, out."

Dunmoore glanced at Holt's hologram.

"Return the ship to cruising stations. After-action review for the department heads in the conference room in one hour. If you and Renny would care to join me for a cup of coffee when you've finished your own reviews."

"Aye, aye, sir."

She stood.

"You have the CIC, Mister Sirico."

Forty minutes later, a soft chime pulled Dunmoore from her perusal of the ammunition expenditure report. If Admiral Petras counted on using *Iolanthe*'s ammo locker as Task Force Luckner's emergency supply should *Skua*, his replenishment ship, run out before they returned to base, he might be disappointed.

Not that Petras ever mentioned it in so many words, but his flag captain had recently made several comments about *Iolanthe*'s extensive holdings. Never mind that Q-ships carried so much ammo because they fought more often and couldn't be easily replenished underway — not when they were hunting several light-years inside the Shrehari Empire's sphere. It was just another sign of how little Petras and Corto really understood Q-ship operations.

"Enter."

The door slid aside soundlessly to admit Commander Renny Halfen, *Iolanthe*'s bearded chief engineer.

"Captain. I hear there's decent coffee on offer in here." She nodded at the urn.

"Help yourself. Still not getting satisfaction from the engineering crew?"

He let out a disconsolate grunt.

"I've given up trying to teach them how proper coffee should look, smell, and taste. Philistines, the lot of them. Thankfully, being inept with the fine art of coffee making is their sole weakness."

Halfen poured himself a cup and sat in one of the chairs by Dunmoore's desk.

"Before you ask, the shield generators are fine, though a few more engagements of the sort and I'll need to swap out the number two aft starboard unit. We have only one spare left, and so far HQ hasn't seen fit to send us more, even though we've had three on order for several weeks. Field repairs only go so far, and will break at the worst possible moment."

The door chime pealed again before she could reply. This time it was Holt. He headed straight for the urn.

"That was a nice thing you did, giving *Fennec* the chance to break something. I think you might end up being as popular with Shanna Nishino's crew as you are with Gregor Pushkin's."

"Aye." Halfen nodded gravely. "And won't *that* thrill the admiral."

Dunmoore raised a restraining hand.

"Let's not go there, gentlemen. Anything I should know about before we run the after-action review?"

— Three —

The intercom's insistent pinging pulled Admiral of the Fifth Rank Brakal, Imperial Strike Group Khorsan's commanding officer, from a deep sleep. He sat up with an irritated grunt and stabbed at the offending object.

"What?"

"It's Urag, Lord. We received a message from Commander Gra'k." Brakal's face twisted in disgust at hearing his flagship captain pronounce the name of Strike Group Khorsan's chief of staff, whom he'd left behind when he took his ships on patrol to hunt the humans bedeviling this part of the imperial frontier. "Our base is under attack by an enemy battleship."

"A single battleship?" Brakal's lips parted to show yellowing, cracking fangs. "I hope the honorable Gra'k remembers how to fight."

Urag grimaced.

"The base's subspace radio carrier wave is gone, Lord. We are trying to re-establish contact but without success. I fear it came to grief. Is not that demon-spawned phantom we have been seeking for the last turn supposed to be a battleship under the skin? Perhaps it found our lair."

"And our supplies."

Brakal swallowed a string of pungent curses. Gra'k had announced the monthly convoy's arrival a few days ago. If the humans were indeed destroying Khorsan Base, it would force him to withdraw the strike group and head for the nearest permanent station to replenish in a few days. That would leave this area wide open to human depredations. And if they were now bold enough to find and destroy the Deep Space Fleet's support installations inside the imperial sphere, then the war was indeed turning against the Shrehari Empire.

"We will head to Khorsan at best speed. When your navigator finishes plotting our course, you may synchronize our patrol and engage without further permission. Warn the other patrols and tell them to plan on replenishing at Atsang Base. I will issue orders once we know for sure."

A sly grin twisted Brakal's face. "Perhaps we will get lucky and find our phantom loitering in the hopes of ambushing us. He will be aware Gra'k called for help. But even a battleship cannot stand against three *Tol* and three *Ptar*."

As the words left his mouth, Brakal remembered a time, long ago, when a human battleship did just that and made him withdraw before he lost the rest of his force. He had given as good as he got and intelligence reports proved the humans removed the battleship from active service afterward.

Nonetheless, the flame-haired she-wolf's actions in the Cimmeria system had ensured his promotion to a higher rank was delayed until the Admiralty dismissed Strike Group Khorsan's former commanding officer. And if Hralk's inability to contain the phantom and its fellow raiders led to his downfall, what would the admiralty do once he reported Khorsan Base destroyed, along with weeks of supplies?

Urag did not notice his superior's sudden discomfiture. He merely bowed his head.

"As you command, Lord."

The intercom died away, taking Urag's image and voice with it. Sleep interrupted for good, Brakal rose from his bunk, threw off his nightclothes, and pulled on his uniform. He knew with certainty that if and when his ships docked at Atsang or one of the other permanent fleet bases, he would find a missive ordering him to take the next courier headed for Shrehari Prime after turning Strike Group Khorsan over to the most senior officer available.

How often was the same scenario repeating itself throughout the Deep Space Fleet? How often did the leadership of strike groups, assault divisions, and fleets change because commanding admirals did not satisfy the sclerotic imbeciles who could not fathom how one fights an interstellar war against a foe as tenacious as he was irrational?

Nor could they understand how much morale-sapping turmoil each turnover caused, leaving thousands of disaffected senior officers to languish on the empire's core worlds, their experience and talents wasted while less seasoned warriors took over and found themselves outmaneuvered by the damned hairless apes?

Brakal was on his second mug of *tvass* when *Tol Vehar* shifted into otherspace. Now, the only thing he could do was wait until they arrived. Urag would not thank him for fretting on the bridge and annoying the crew. It meant he was practically a prisoner in a day cabin he was beginning to loathe. If only the admiralty had thought of giving Strike Group Khorsan an appropriately appointed flagship. But the home world's growing stinginess was merely another sign this war might no longer be winnable.

**

"Nothing." Menak, *Tol Vehar*'s sensor officer turned to face Brakal. The cruiser and its five companions were at the dead planet's otherspace limit, running with systems dampened. "No emissions signature, no heat signature, and no evidence of the satellite constellation. I only see debris, and I only hear the recording beacon's carrier wave."

Brakal grunted. His worst fears had come true.

"What about the refueling station?"

"I cannot find it nor hear its subspace radio carrier wave."

"Any sign of the attacker?"

"No, Lord. I paid particular attention to the planet's co-orbital points. Something the size of a battleship would appear on visual even if it eludes the sensors altogether."

"Your orders, Lord?" Urag asked.

After a moment of silence, Brakal ran his large, paw-like hand through the ruff of fur running across the top of his skull.

"We will recover the recording beacon, then plot a course for... Where was the monthly convoy headed after dropping off our supplies?"

"Back to Atsang Base. Khorsan was its last stop." Urag replied after a brief pause to consult *Tol Vehar*'s database. "You think the human battleship might pursue it?"

"If I were hunting behind enemy lines that is what I would do after scoring such a victory here. Besides, I suppose Atsang will be Strike Group Khorsan's new home until the admiralty decides what happens, since it is the closest, and we are getting low on several consumables."

But not ammunition, Brakal thought, silently consigning his slippery human opponent to the deepest regions of hell.

"Inform the other patrols they should make for Atsang once they need replenishment, then put us on a course which mimics that of the convoy."

"As you command. When will you inform the admiralty about Khorsan Base's destruction?"

"Once we extract whatever the beacon recorded of the attack. And seeing as how Menak found no threats, take us to what remains of Khorsan Base so we may pick it up. After that, we will check on the refueling station's status before leaving this useless star system."

**

"Surely that thing is the battleship which ambushed us when we were hunting for the phantom," Urag said after they watched a silent replay of the attack from the doomed base's perspective. "The one hiding in the co-orbitals of that accursed moon. What was the planet's name again? Satan's Eye?"

"It *is* the phantom." Brakal thumped the arm of his command chair with a meaty fist. "The same ship we saw threatening Kilia Station under the guise of a corsair. By the demons of the Underworld, do you know what that means, Urag?"

"You will chase him around the Black Hole of Qax, and round the Demon Star, and round the Undying Ion Storm, and through the fires of the Ninth Hell before you give him up," Urag replied in a somber tone, quoting a famous line from one of Shrehari literature's best known revenge stories.

"Hah!" Brakal's lips curled back to reveal his fangs. "A literate flag captain. Will miracles never cease? So I am to be the accursed Captain Qahb and my ship is to become the *Tol Ehqad* is that it?"

"Consider yourself fortunate to command such an educated warrior." Urag glowered at his superior. "Now, picking up the phantom's trail — that will be a true miracle."

"And the longer we wait, the harder it will be. Send one of the *Ptars* — I don't care which one — to check on the refueling station. He can catch up with us. We leave for Atsang at best speed."

"The course is set, and the patrol is synchronized, Lord," Tuku, *Tol Vehar*'s navigator said, glancing over his shoulder at Brakal with his black within black eyes. "May I suggest *Ptar Litk* check on the refueling station? He has the best of the three *Ptar* navigators."

Brakal made a sign of assent.

"So it shall be."

"And your report to the admiralty?" Urag asked.

An irritated growl escaped Brakal's throat.

"It will be ready to send before we reach the otherspace limit."

— Four —

"**U**nkind people who shall remain nameless are speculating that Admiral Petras got lost after letting that convoy slip through his fingers," Ezekiel Holt said the moment Dunmoore's day cabin door slid shut behind them.

They'd been waiting at the rendezvous for almost four days. By now, she and her crew were feeling the strain of both forced inactivity and continuous silent running this deep inside enemy space.

"I hope your first officer's basilisk stare stilled unwarranted speculation. We don't need mutinous humor pervading the ship."

Holt filled two coffee mugs from the urn and handed one to his captain.

"You were once in my shoes, so I'm sure you remember that stilling unkind rumors about unloved senior officers is an impossibility on the same level as controlled time travel."

"True, but we can't allow anyone aboard to think we might conceivably share their opinion of the senior officer in question."

He dropped into one of the chairs facing her desk and raised his cup.

"Don't worry. Anyone who disparages the admiral within my hearing never does so again. But you and I know it's a losing proposition. The only thing my corrective words do is make sure miscreants watch their words in my or your presence. Our people aren't easily fooled, Skipper. Sending us on a recon mission, even though it turned into a punitive expedition, instead of letting *Iolanthe* do what she does best — raid enemy shipping — sticks in your crew's collective craw. And in mine."

"Then everybody better unstick their craws, Zeke." When she saw amusement in Holt's eyes, she glared at him. "Special Operations Command issued orders assigning *Iolanthe* to Task Force Luckner. We will carry out the orders of the flag officer commanding said task force to the best of our abilities, with no mental reservations whatsoever. Is that clear?"

"Perfectly, Captain. And that is precisely the message I've been conveying to the department heads. The cox'n is doing the same with the chiefs and petty officers. He and the divisional chiefs are jacking up any crew member who publicly disparages our current situation. But that doesn't change the way people feel. You included."

Dunmoore let out a heartfelt sigh.

"I know, Zeke."

"How much longer do we wait here before we decide our friends aren't coming to fetch us? Perhaps the admiral ran into something he couldn't handle with three frigates, two destroyers, and a scout, even though one of the frigates could easily be rated as a light cruiser."

She shrugged.

"A week. Ten days. The admiral might be chasing that convoy back to its homeport. Or at least the system's heliopause. I doubt he'll be so foolish as to put himself within reach of a major Shrehari base."

"Unlike a certain frigate captain several years ago." Holt winked at her.

"Yes, and I was damned lucky to bring *Stingray* home with only a handful of casualties. Petras will have read my after-action report and knows we almost perished. What I did then isn't going to be taught in any naval tactics course."

"Indeed." A mischievous smile tugged at Holt's lips. "Much better to blow up enemy FOBs on a whim."

"All right, Mister First Officer. That remark just earned you the right to a drubbing at chess." She reached for the mahogany box.

Holt grimaced in dismay.

"Me and my big mouth."

**

Dunmoore's eyes snapped open before the intercom in her quarters chimed a second time. Instantly awake, she reached out and stabbed the screen.

"Captain here."

"Lieutenant Kremm, sir. I have the watch. Sensors picked up several hyperspace disturbances headed in our direction. Their course is roughly opposite to the one taken by Task Force Luckner."

"Meaning it could be the admiral returning from his pursuit."

"Yes, sir. But it could equally be a Shrehari formation. Word of our destroying the FOB would have reached higher headquarters by now, if only because it stopped reporting."

"If they drop out of hyperspace on top of us, how long do we have?"

"Fifteen to twenty minutes. Should I call battle stations?"

"Yes, but don't go up systems. I'll be in the CIC shortly. Warn *Fennec*."

"Aye, aye, sir."

"Captain, out."

The battle stations klaxon sounded moments later, tearing Iolanthe's off-duty crew members from their sleep or recreational activities. Dunmoore dressed, stepped into her boots, and ran splayed fingers through her graying copper-colored hair.

By the time she entered the CIC, it was fully staffed, with Lieutenant Commander Sirico occupying her chair. He stood the moment one of the watchkeeping petty officers whose station faced the door said, "Captain on deck."

"The hyperspace bubbles are still nearing on an almost perfect intercept course, sir. We make out seven distinct signatures."

"Then it has to be the task force. The chances of it being a Shrehari strike group with the same number of ships as Luckner, headed in our precise direction in interstellar space are infinitesimal." She sat and stared at the tactical projection. "We will, however, stay at battle stations and under silent running."

"Out of precaution, or to show the others how we Q-ship pros make a hole in space, Skipper?" Holt's hologram by her elbow asked. "And yes, the Furious Faerie is at battle stations."

She made a face.

"Both, I suppose."

Dunmoore settled back and called up the ship's log to see if anything noteworthy happened while she was sleeping. Then, she busied herself with the never-ending stream of administrative matters until, almost precisely fifteen minutes after Lieutenant Kremm warned her, Chief Yens raised a hand.

"Seven emergence signatures three hundred thousand kilometers ahead and slightly to starboard." A pause. "The signatures confirm it is Task Force Luckner. One of the ships seems to be leaking more emissions than it did when we last saw them."

Sirico glanced at the passive sensor readout. "Battle damage, perhaps?"

"It's *Tamurlane*," Yens replied, naming one of Luckner's two destroyers. "They're actively scanning."

"The flagship is calling," Kremm announced from the bridge. "On the reserved Luckner subspace frequency and in code."

"Did they see us?" Holt asked no one in particular.

"Not a chance," Sirico replied. "We're as tight as a tick on shore leave after two years in space."

Dunmoore exchanged a glance with her first officer's hologram.

"I suppose we should go up systems and cancel battle stations."

"On it, Skipper. I'd love to be a holographic fly in *Hawkwood*'s CIC as we suddenly appear on their sensors, big as life and twice as mean."

"Open a comlink with the flagship and pipe it to my day cabin. Mister Sirico, you have the CIC."

A few minutes later, Dunmoore sat behind her desk, face composed as the primary display came to life with Rear Admiral Kell Petras' square, bulldog face. In his mid-fifties, bald, with a hooked nose and cauliflower ears, he reminded Dunmoore of nothing so much as an aging colonial prizefighter. Dark eyes beneath beetling brows examined her in silence.

"Sir. I trust you gave that convoy last rites."

He dipped his head in greeting.

"Captain Dunmoore. Showing us how to hide, were you?"

"I prefer running silent in enemy space when I'm in a holding pattern, sir. Did *Tamurlane* suffer a hit? My sensor chief says her emissions signature is stronger than when we parted ways."

"Minor damage. The Shrehari fought back harder than we expected. Two of the freighters and one *Ptar* escaped."

Dunmoore was pleased her expression didn't change at hearing the news. With three frigates and two destroyers under his command, Petras should have wiped out the convoy in the time it took them to cycle their hyperdrives between jumps.

"Still, three freighters and two *Ptars* can no longer serve our enemy's war effort. Congratulations, sir."

"Did you and *Fennec* get a good look at the enemy installation in that star system?"

"Yes, sir. A temporary, wartime forward operations base. It, and the system's automated refueling station also no longer serve the empire."

Petras' right eyebrow shot up as he gave her a hard glare.

"I beg your pardon?"

"My report on the action is ready for your perusal, sir. It came over with the rest of the reports and returns the moment we established a comlink."

"I want to hear an explanation of why you overstepped your orders, Captain. That was supposed to be a recon mission only."

"I deemed the FOB a target of opportunity, sir. Our scans showed no enemy ships in the area, and the base itself was lightly armed compared to our standards. At best, its ordnance equated that of two *Tol* class cruisers. *Fennec* stayed well out of enemy weapons range while *Iolanthe* closed in. We suffered no damage beyond stressing one of our shield emitters, but it was already approaching end of life. Once we fried the FOB's shields, we either scored a direct hit on its reactor or on its anti-ship missile stocks. It exploded, causing one hundred percent casualties and destroying everything the convoy dropped off a few days earlier. I doubt any of the supplies reached the resident strike group's ships before we arrived. On our way out of the system, *Fennec* destroyed the fueling station."

"I see."

Based on the expression in his eyes, Dunmoore figured Petras couldn't quite bring himself to congratulate her nor issue a reprimand for overstepping his orders.

"Sir, losing that FOB will limit enemy activities in this sector by forcing them further back into the empire for resupply. It will also hurt their morale to know we can strike at them far beyond our sphere and cause real damage. Whoever commands the strike group based at that FOB will have some explaining to do, and since intelligence reports more and more senior officers are getting fired for perceived failures, he'll no doubt face the Shrehari admiralty's wrath. It's a winning situation all around for us."

"Perhaps. But what would have happened if the FOB was more heavily armed than you believed? *Iolanthe* is my most powerful ship. Losing her to battle damage would be intolerable."

Dunmoore was again pleased with her ability to keep a bland expression, even though she desperately wanted to ask Petras why he didn't take *Iolanthe* on the convoy hunt if he considered her his most powerful ship. Perhaps none of the enemy vessels would have escaped if the Furious Faerie had been present.

"Sir, *Fennec*'s sensors gave us a good view of the target. It wasn't as big a risk as you might think. We approached unseen until we were within optimum firing range. From start to finish, the fight lasted only a few minutes. We literally overwhelmed them with gun and missile fire."

"And how much of your ammunition stocks did you expend?"

"The number expended and amount remaining is in my report, sir. We still carry more than enough to complete this patrol. In fact, I daresay the frigates and destroyers will run out before we do."

A frown creased Petras' high forehead.

"Did you not think I might count on your capacious ammunition lockers to replenish the rest of the task force so we can stay on station longer?"

"The idea occurred to me, sir. But considering what the loss of that FOB will do to the enemy, especially his morale, I think it was worth every missile we fired."

"You might find me disagreeing once I read your report."

"Understood, sir. What are your orders?"

"We will hold a collective after-action review in three hours via comlink. You're welcome to join in as an observer." He paused and a thoughtful expression crossed his eyes. "In fact, I want you to observe, but please keep any comments for a private discussion between you, me, and Lena."

"Certainly, sir. Thank you."

"We will talk again about that target of opportunity once I read your report. Petras, out."

When the Furious Faerie emblem replaced his face on the main display, Dunmoore sat back and exhaled. Moments later, the door chime pealed.

"Enter."

Holt stuck his head through the open door and grinned.

"Are you still my captain?"

"For now." She waved him in and pointed at a chair. "I know you want a verbatim account and I need to vent just a little."

— Five —

When Dunmoore's face faded from the day cabin's main display, Rear Admiral Kell Petras turned to his flag captain, Lena Corto, who had silently witnessed the exchange from beyond the video pickup's range. Described by many as the archetype of the icy blond, her pale, shoulder-length hair framed a narrow face that was mostly sharp angles. Intense blue eyes beneath brows that seemed almost white stared back at Petras. The calculating wariness that seemed to surround her like a palpable aura struck him again.

"Any comments, Lena?"

"Her reputation as a loose cannon when she's not under a battle group commander's watchful eye holds true, sir. We could have lost both *Iolanthe* and *Fennec* in that ill-considered attack, seeing as how we know so little about Shrehari orbital stations. Dunmoore was lucky it didn't carry heavy guns and multiple missile launchers capable of overwhelming her shields. *Iolanthe* is powerful but hardly invincible."

Corto shook her head.

"I'm sorry, sir, but I still can't understand why Dunmoore was given the Fleet's newest Q-ship and allowed to act with almost no oversight — Admiral

Nagira's patronage notwithstanding. Also, she didn't seem pleased when you told her she could listen in on the after-action review but not comment."

"I noticed nothing."

"Dunmoore kept a straight face, sir, but the eyes rarely lie. I figure she considers our inability to take the entire convoy a failure rather than admit *Stingray*'s success in doing so was a fluke brought on by a combination of fatal enemy mistakes and recklessness on her part."

Petras' smile was devoid of warmth.

"You really don't hold her in high regard, do you, Lena?"

"My feelings toward her aren't particularly relevant, sir. I'm simply not comfortable with patronage appointments. Dunmoore's record shows a pattern of behavior some might consider irresponsible. As you'll recall, many in SOCOM weren't happy with her taking *Iolanthe*. If the attack on the FOB had turned to disaster, it would have reflected on your competence as the task force commander, and we can't allow rash starship captains to jeopardize your command or even worse, your career."

Petras studied Corto in silence. He'd always known she was ambitious, seeking her first star by riding on his coattails. And in truth, she was an intelligent, competent, and hard-working officer, though she wasn't the sort to inspire loyalty, let alone devotion in her subordinates, or a sense of comradeship in her peers. But Corto was nursing a deep-seated grievance ever since the Fleet gave *Iolanthe* to Siobhan Dunmoore.

Corto was convinced she'd been cheated out of her turn to command as a post captain, one of the unwritten prerequisites for promotion to flag rank for officers in the combatant occupational specialties. Yet after spending more than half the war in various staff assignments, including three years as SOCOM's top operational planner, her chances of returning to starship duty were fading, and she knew it. Soon after word came down from Fleet Operations that SOCOM would get *Iolanthe*, Corto had lobbied to become her first commanding officer, but in vain.

"I'm not quite as uncomfortable as you are, Lena. Yes, Dunmoore takes risks, but they seem to pay off more often than not. Besides, if we gloss over the fact she exceeded her orders, Dunmoore is right when she says destroying that FOB will mess with the enemy's morale. She showed them we were willing to sail deep into their sphere and hit them behind the lines, so to speak. Considering how proud the Shrehari are supposed to be, that's a bit of a dent in the old ego."

"Perhaps," Corto replied in a grudging tone after a momentary pause. "May I ask why you forbade Dunmoore from speaking during the after-action review?"

"Because I wish to hear her thoughts privately once she's processed the discussion. Whether or not we agree with her methods, Dunmoore has been doing this longer than the rest of us. If we need to make adjustments, it is better done through properly formulated orders from me than interventions during a hot wash."

Corto nodded once.

"Understood, sir."

Yet Petras read more than understanding in his flag captain's eyes. He saw her carefully hidden resentment at Dunmoore surface for a few seconds before she brought her feelings under control. That brief flash made him belatedly wonder whether Corto's advice he send *Iolanthe* to reconnoiter the Shrehari FOB instead of taking her on the convoy hunt stemmed from sound tactical acumen or something more personal. Dunmoore rejoining the task force with a victory of her own must not be sitting well with Corto.

Petras owed her for the loyalty she'd shown him since reporting for duty at SOCOM HQ. Task Force Luckner would not be a reality without her efforts to help build the case for its creation. The ideal solution, of course, would have been to appoint someone with Q-ship experience as his flag captain, but Dunmoore was the only officer at the right rank since *Iolanthe* was the first of her kind. Besides, he couldn't see her as anyone's chief of staff. She lacked the temperament.

It was bad luck Fleet Operations gave him *Iolanthe* rather than a few of her smaller siblings as he'd requested. But he was now saddled with a resentful flag captain and a starship commander of the same rank chafing at the chains tying her to an admiral. Or could it have been deliberate? If so, why?

"Is something wrong, sir?"

He waved away her question.

"An idle thought just crossed my mind, Lena. Nothing important. Please read Captain Dunmoore's report and pay particular attention to her ammunition expenditure. Find out whether she still carries enough to balance holdings across the task force once we issue *Skua*'s remaining stocks. Based on what *Rooikat*'s recon drone saw of the Atsang star system, it seems to be a major hub. That could mean supply convoys for the entire sector's forward operating bases originate there, not to mention Atsang receiving even larger convoys from the empire's core worlds. The longer we can spend raiding their shipping before we return home, the better. That first hunt merely whetted my appetite."

"Of course, sir. If there's nothing else, I'll get on it now, before the after-action review."

"Thank you, Lena."

When he was alone, Petras called up a visual of *Iolanthe* on his day cabin display and gazed at it. Task Force Luckner's partial victory at the Atsang heliopause along with Dunmoore's daring and entirely successful attack on the enemy FOB was finally opening his eyes to an undeniable fact. *Iolanthe*'s captain knew more about raiding behind enemy lines than all of Luckner's other starship commanders put together.

Worse yet, if Petras was honest with himself, he'd acknowledge Dunmoore had tried counseling him. But he didn't listen, in part because he'd succumbed to Lena's influence. And that was on him.

Petras needed Luckner to prove itself — fast. This was his last command in space as a rear admiral. Either Luckner put him on the vice admirals' list, or he would spend the rest of the war as a two-star working staff jobs before retiring once the hostilities were over. Just like Lena Corto, Petras would soon face the dreaded limit imposed on senior officers who were passed over for promotion year after year.

**

"Thank you for your candid views." Petras met the eyes of each starship commander in turn, or rather the eyes of their holograms sitting around the conference table, except for *Hawkwood*'s captain, Commander Kirti Midura, who was present in the flesh along with Lena Corto. "You've given me much to ponder. We will reconvene once I've digested everything. Until then. Captain Dunmoore, please stay on the link. I want to speak with you and Captain Corto."

Every hologram save for one winked out of existence while Midura excused herself.

"Thoughts, Dunmoore?" When she hesitated, Petras added, "No need for diplomacy. I want — no, I *need* your honest opinion."

Dunmoore gazed at him warily as if searching for a trap.

"I believe the crux of the matter," she replied in a measured tone, "is that we're thinking of Task Force Luckner as a conventional formation which fights the enemy in conventional ways. Before hearing my colleagues speak, I had my suspicions based on the results of our battle drills but never could put my finger on the cause because I'm used to operating alone. Listening just now as someone who wasn't present brought it into focus."

"So what's your solution?" Corto asked.

"I don't know that I can offer an answer as such. My assessment is we face a mindset issue rather than a tactical or doctrinal one. Perhaps captains trained to sail and fight in formation around a flagship don't possess the predatory instincts of commerce raiders."

Dunmoore paused while a vaguely remembered historical tidbit surfaced from the depths of her memory.

"And you do?"

"Yes. I've been operating far from a flagship for years," she replied absently as an idea swam into focus. "Please give me a second."

Corto and Petras exchanged puzzled glances.

"That's it." Dunmoore's face lit up. "Are either of you familiar with the wars of Earth's twentieth century? Specifically, the mid-century global war?"

When neither reacted, she said, "In those days opposing nations fought with ocean-based navies as well as on land. One of those nations used underwater ships to raid convoys. They would send dozens of them out on separate patrols. When one of these submersibles spotted an enemy convoy, it signaled its home base. That home base would warn other submersibles in the general area so they could converge to form what was called a wolf pack which would sink as many ships as it could."

Petras tilted his head to one side and frowned.

"How does this apply to our situation? You said we faced a mindset challenge, not a tactical one."

"Sorry, sir, I'm trying to find the right words. I've only thought of this now."

"Fair enough. Take your time."

Dunmoore nibbled on the inside of her lower lip, eyes narrowed.

"There are two aspects we should consider. One, although we know Atsang is a major shipping hub, locking onto and tracking enemy convoys is more a matter of luck than planning, even if we can keep the planet itself under continuous surveillance by using scout ships' drones. The more dispersed our task force, the more luck we can create."

After a moment, Petras inclined his head.

"Granted, for the sake of discussion."

"Second, operating in a dispersed fashion and grouping only for the kill would force Luckner's starship captains to shed their baked-in notions of how a naval formation operates." She thought for a moment. "As a bonus, they might be more inclined to attack targets of opportunity on their own initiative. That can create interesting second and third-order effects on the enemy's ability to wage war, even though it might only be locally."

"As you did with that FOB?"

Dunmoore allowed herself a faint smile.

"Yes, sir."

"So you're advocating what?" Corto asked in an icy tone. "Controlled anarchy?"

Dunmoore could almost feel her disdain as if it were a living thing.

"Controlled predation of enemy shipping. Luckner's starship commanders need to think like wolves, not well-trained sheepdogs. Become the sort who can smell blood and call their pack mates in for the kill."

She ignored the scornful expression on Corto's face, concentrating instead on an obviously curious Petras.

"How would you create such a wolf pack?" He asked.

"Divide the task force into balanced packets of perhaps two or three ships. Or even single vessels, if you prefer. *Jan Sobieski* and *Iolanthe* are more than capable of operating alone until the wolf pack forms. When I mean balanced, it's on capabilities such as sensor range, speed, subspace radio reach, that sort of thing, not necessarily tonnage or firepower. Seed the packets around a hub such as the Atsang system and wait. When one of them, or perhaps a scout drone spots a convoy heading outward, confirm its course, and call the pack to form. Whichever ships are nearest take the lead to keep watch on the target until everyone catches up. Shrehari convoy doctrine favors cohesion over speed, and that means we will catch them before they reach their destination system. Once they drop out at the heliopause for instance, whichever wolf pack ships get there first attack without waiting for the rest."

"What if only a singleton such as your *Iolanthe* or *Jan Sobieski* gets there in time?" Petras asked. "And for argument's sake, the convoy is ten freighters with five escorts?"

"Then they use the element of surprise to strike as hard as possible before evading retaliation. Even a partial sweep by a single ship can entail consequences on enemy morale and planning beyond the mere loss of hulls and cargo."

"Deploying our ships in penny packets is risky, sir," Corto said. "We stand a chance of being wiped out piecemeal."

"May I send you a historical write-up of the wet navy wolf pack tactics I mentioned?" Dunmoore kept her focus on Petras, acting as if she hadn't heard Corto's objection.

"Please do. Your suggestion is unconventional, to be sure. But I confess I'm intrigued."

"That's because commerce raiding comes under the heading of unconventional warfare, sir. Hit and run rather than set-piece battles. Apparently, it drives the Shrehari insane, and angry sophonts of any species make mistakes."

"Give me time to discuss it with Lena. I'll make my decision by tomorrow. In the meantime, do you have any ideas about how to, as you put it, split Task Force Luckner into balanced packets?"

"Yes, sir."

"We can discuss that tomorrow. You may return to your duties."

— Six —

Amorose Brakal sat in the spare command chair bolted to the deck beside Urag's on *Tol Vehar*'s bridge, watching as Atsang Base grew on the main screen. He knew his fate awaited him in an office at the heart of the large cylinder festooned with countless docking arms. It would not be pleasant for Admiral of the Fifth Rank Brakal, whose naval career was surely over, but he had already resolved to take a different path.

Seconds after the thought crossed his mind, a communication from base operations seemed to confirm it.

"Incoming message for Admiral of the Fifth Rank Brakal from Admiral of the Third Rank Kerhasi, commanding officer of Assault Division Atsang. Admiral Brakal shall report to Admiral Kerhasi's office the moment *Tol Vehar* docks so he might account for his command of Strike Group Khorsan."

The stilted formality of the order conveyed everything he needed to know.

"Send my reply as follows. Admiral of the Fifth Rank Brakal hears and obeys."

Urag turned his head to stare at his commanding officer.

"That was not a friendly greeting between old comrades, Lord."

"It was not meant to. I suppose I should pack my belongings before we dock. If my prediction is correct, Toralk can bring them when he joins me for our voyage home."

"You expect to leave Strike Group Khorsan?"

"Since there no longer is a Khorsan Base, I expect Kerhasi will disband the strike group and reassign its ships to other units."

"Your pardon, Lord, but are you not giving up too quickly?"

Brakal made a dismissive gesture.

"Kerhasi will have received orders from the admiralty. Senior officers who fail may not redeem themselves these days, and I am the first who lost an orbital base because of enemy action. That will be considered an enormous dishonor, especially by those who do not understand this war."

"Besides, at this juncture, I might be able to do more if I hang up my admiral's robes and don those of the imperial lord representing Clan Makkar in the Kraal," he added after a momentary pause.

The Kraal, a legislative assembly where the empire's highest-ranking nobles from ancient families met, existed to keep the governing council and the emperor, or in this case the regent in check. At least theoretically.

"In that case, may I ask something of you, Admiral," a voice said from the shadows behind the command chairs.

Brakal glanced over his shoulder at Regar, the *Tai Kan* political officer assigned to watch for disloyalty aboard *Tol Vehar*. But instead of reporting the crew's disaffection with the imperial government and its handling of the war, Regar had become Brakal's adviser on all matters concerning politics and the empire's secret police, especially its pervasive surveillance network.

"Speak."

"Let me swear an oath of fealty to the Lord of Clan Makkar, then take me with you. I can serve the empire better by staying at your side instead of pretending to spy on Commander Urag's crew. My experience as a *Tai Kan* operative and my contacts in low places will be useful, should you pursue political avenues."

Brakal and Urag exchanged a glance. The latter made a small gesture of assent, encouraging Brakal to accept.

"Do you think an oath of fealty to a clan lord will release you from the *Tai Kan*?"

"No, and I do not, as yet, wish to resign my commission. But Admiral Kerhasi will surely allow you a few personal retainers. He may be in receipt of orders relieving you, but he remains a friend and Warrior Caste brother."

"You know this how?"

"He couched his summons in a way that announces your fate, so you may prepare since an officer relieved of his command is not allowed back aboard his ship."

"And that is why you need Regar," Urag said. "He can read evil signs and dark portents. You might be a superb tactician and naval officer, but in Shredar's darkest corners, especially around the government precinct, you are only a mewling cub. Unless, of course, you intend to retire and manage the Clan Makkar estates while becoming an old man who no longer cares about those who rally behind him."

Brakal jumped to his feet with surprising vigor and pointed at the deck in front of him.

"Come here and drop to one knee, Regar." Once the *Tai Kan* officer did so, Brakal held out his right arm. Regar grasped it just below the elbow while Brakal did the same. "Do you swear to serve Clan Makkar with your body and spirit now and always, lest you forfeit your undying honor?"

"Upon my honor, I swear I will serve the Lords of Clan Makkar until my last breath."

"Arise, Regar, Liegeman of the Makkar." Brakal pulled Regar to his feet. "You might as well pack your belongings too."

**

"Brakal, you sad old rogue." Admiral of the Third Rank Kerhasi rose from behind his desk and reached out to grasp his old friend's forearms in greeting. "Those humans are becoming a true plague. Khorsan Base was not their only victim. They ambushed convoy *Haqqa* One Five at the Atsang heliopause as it returned from Khorsan. Literally on my doorstep. Not your phantom battleship, of course, but a swarm of smaller vessels. We were fortunate two freighters and one *Ptar* escaped destruction. What is happening to us?"

They released each other's arms, and Kerhasi indicated a chair.

"Sit."

"What is happening?" Brakal let loose a bark of humorless laughter as he complied. "We are losing the war."

"Surely it cannot be that bad." Kerhasi nodded toward a sideboard. "*Tvass*?"

"Unless you have something stronger on offer."

"Perhaps later, when what needs saying has been said."

"Then a cup of *tvass* will be fine."

"We can talk about the war after I carry out my orders, unpleasant as they are." Kerhasi served them then sat across from Brakal. "There is no easy way around this.

The admiralty has directed that I relieve you of your command and send you back to Shrehari Prime. As of this moment, you are placed in the reserve of officers and no longer hold any appointment in the Deep Space Fleet, nor do you wield any sort of authority. Once on the homeworld, you will report to Admiral of the Second Rank Zakit. He will no doubt send you to tend your estates."

An amused smile twisted Brakal's ridged face.

"Tend my estates? No. I will take Clan Makkar's seat in the Kraal and see if my peers and I can revive its authority. The council has done enough to damage the empire and jeopardize its future. Our enemy runs rampant deep within our sphere. We should take it as a sign from the gods that we urgently need a course correction before we face collapse."

Kerhasi slapped his knee with delight.

"I feared you might dispute me and we would part as enemies, yet here you are, ready to take on the sclerotic idiots ruining us. You may count on my support if ever I can do anything to help."

"Excellent! Perhaps you could send word to relatives and friends on the homeworld who are acquainted with members of the Kraal and tell them about my intentions."

"Consider it done."

"How will I travel to the homeworld?"

"Aboard the regular courier run. It leaves tomorrow."

"I shall bring two retainers with me. My bodyguard Toralk and Sub-Commander Regar."

Kerhasi tilted his massive head to one side in question.

"Toralk, I remember well. Loyal as the day is long and able to frighten the most savage of miscreants. Who is Regar?"

"Task Force Khorsan's chief *Tai Kan* spy. Since I assume you plan to disband Khorsan and reassign its ships, his departure will not be felt."

"You assume correctly. But a *Tai Kan* officer as a retainer? The universe is truly upside down. Dare I ask?"

"Regar, just as many if not most of us, is unhappy with the conduct of the war. And he feels no great loyalty for his masters. I find him useful."

"I will not stop you from taking him, but you might attract the *Tai Kan*'s wrath when they notice his presence on the homeworld."

"Bugger the *Tai Kan*. They are as much a part of the problem as the council and the admiralty. They also need a good reaming out."

Kerhasi drained his *tvass* mug. "Enough of this swill. We must celebrate. What would you say to a bottle of chilled Zahkar vintage ale?"

"Does a *kroorath* shit in the woods?"

**

"Urag asked that I remind you of his and the crew's loyalty, Lord," Regar said when Brakal entered the guest suite set aside for them in Atsang Base's VIP quarters. "If at a future date, you should call on *Tol Vehar*, they will do their best to respond. Toralk placed your bags in the primary bedroom." Regar pointed at an open door. "Your friendship with Admiral Kerhasi appears as strong as ever."

"And you deduce this how?"

"These are the finest quarters on the station other than Kerhasi's private suite, Lord. Fit for an admiral of the first rank. And the pantry is well stocked. Nothing but Zahkar vintage ale and the finest distilled spirits, imported from Shrehari Prime at great expense. Only a friend offers the best to a comrade returning home in disgrace. He did not object to my being among your personal retainers?"

"No. I explained why, and I told him of my intention to take the clan seat in the Kraal. After hearing of my plans, he offered his assistance."

"Good. You will need the support of every fighting admiral if you are to push out those useless relics polluting the admiralty and the highest levels of government."

"Push out? Are we not getting ahead of ourselves? Let us first see who we can rally to the cause of reform. Perhaps I will not find enough takers."

A cruel smile split Regar's lips.

"Trust me on this, Lord. You will. Start with those unfairly removed from command and sent to the officers' reserve. They will be nursing a grudge that only blood can extinguish, and many of them are members of the Kraal or belong to the four hundred noble clans who claim a seat in the Kraal."

Brakal's eyes narrowed as he studied Regar.

"You have thought much on this matter, it seems."

"Since before the day we first met. I have known for a long time that someone with enough prestige, charisma, and influence needs to arise and end the war before it ends the empire. Remember, before joining *Tol Vehar*, I labored in the bowels of *Tai Kan* headquarters. I saw incontrovertible evidence of our leaders' incompetence and corruption."

"And I am that someone?"

"The gods placed you on this path for a reason and expect that you follow it until victory or death."

— Seven —

Dunmoore's hologram faded away, leaving Corto and Petras alone in the conference room.

"Sir, I hope you're not seriously entertaining her notions. Using tactics devised for underwater combatants five hundred years ago? Ludicrous."

Irritated by her tone, Petras gave Corto a withering glance.

"Did you ever hear the saying only a fool never changes his mind? Or the one that defines insanity? It's doing the same thing over and over and expecting different results? Finding that convoy took too long, and we didn't do a good job taking it. With three frigates and two destroyers, not a single Shrehari ship should have escaped. I can't afford to try again unless we change our mindset and adapt our tactics. We have a finite time on patrol, and SOCOM expects results from our first cruise, not a report stating *Iolanthe* struck terror in the enemy's heart when on detached duty while the rest of Task Force Luckner was muddling around."

A pained expression crossed Corto's face.

"So we didn't make a clean sweep, sir. Yes, we took longer than expected to find our prey, but it was our first actual engagement with the enemy. I wouldn't throw out the tactics we developed at the first sign of difficulties. Besides, the skeptic in me wonders whether this isn't merely Dunmoore's way of getting out from under your control so she can keep acting as she pleases."

Petras shook his head.

"I doubt she's that devious."

"You read her report on the Toboso incident, right? If her actions there don't count as being devious, then my definition of the word is out of sync with yours."

"Imaginative rather than devious, Lena. She did what was necessary for a peculiar situation. I suggest we read what Dunmoore sent us on wolf pack tactics, then think about how we'd adapt them because I'm seeing similarities between the situation in which those underwater combatants operated and our situation. I'll be interested to see if Dunmoore, you, and I come up with similar answers."

Petras saw his flag captain's jaw muscles working, and he knew she was holding back an angry outburst. It made him wonder about the depth of her resentment at *Iolanthe* going to a freshly promoted post captain with three previous wartime commands in space. Corto's first and last ship, an elderly Type 204 frigate by the name *Akula*, had been decommissioned long ago after suffering irreparable damage in the early years of the war.

He nodded at the conference room door.

"You go on ahead, Lena. We'll talk about this after breakfast tomorrow."

"Yes, sir."

Once she left him sitting in splendid solitude at the head of the conference table, Petras switched the main display to a live view of space around his flagship. He searched for *Iolanthe* somewhere off the starboard quarter, wondering once again why SOCOM chose her as

Task Force Luckner's Q-ship. Surely the entire senior staff knew about Lena's disappointment at not being given command.

**

"Why do I think Corto would rather see you burn in the fires of hell?" Holt asked once Dunmoore severed the link with *Hawkwood*. He had quietly watched the entire after-action review from beyond video pickup range. "She held it in, but if her eyes could kill... Petras, on the other hand, was obviously intrigued, which surely didn't help her mood."

"Perhaps there's something to the idea Lena Corto coveted *Iolanthe* and is miffed at SOCOM giving me, a newly promoted post captain, command instead of appointing a more senior officer who worked at SOCOM HQ for the last few years. It can't just be my pouring a dose of reality on their long-held notions about raiding in enemy space as a formation. Or trying to give the admiral advice after we first joined the task force."

Holt let out a humorless bark of laughter.

"Especially after we came back with an orbital station kill to our credit while they let almost half a convoy slip through their fingers. You know, maybe Petras wouldn't listen before because Corto was whispering sweet poison into his ears, but their partial success and our clean sweep might be opening his eyes."

"Let's hope so. In any case, we should hear our answer tomorrow."

"And what if Petras not only rejects the wolf pack idea — or Corto convinces him to do so — but also keeps us within visual range of the flagship from now on?"

"We keep doing our duty, Zeke, as you well know. How about we play mix and match with Task Force Luckner so I can give the admiral a few ideas when we speak again?"

A lazy grin split Holt's face.

"Let me start. *Iolanthe* and *Jan Sobieski* to form the first team."

Dunmoore shook her head.

"Pairing the two newest and most powerful ships?" She rolled her eyes at him. "Please."

"But together, we'd wipe out every bit of shipping in the sector and give the boneheads serious headaches while Petras and Lena play battle group command. Gregor will be crushed you rejected the idea."

"He also knows better," she replied in a dry tone. "If you don't want to take this seriously, I can manage by myself."

Holt raised both hands in surrender.

"I'll be as serious as a case of the Darsivian mange."

Dunmoore made a face at her first officer.

"Ugh. Next time, try a less disgusting simile."

**

"Good morning, Captain." Admiral Petras nodded at Dunmoore's hologram when it materialized in *Hawkwood*'s conference room.

"Good morning, sir," she replied in a bright tone, smiling at her commanding officer. Dunmoore turned virtual eyes on a sour Corto. "Good morning, Lena. I trust both of you slept well."

"Tolerably," Petras replied when he saw Corto wouldn't return Dunmoore's cheerful greeting. "I spent part of the night with visions of semi-feral submersibles dancing in my head. A fascinating era. The statistics are, for their day, staggering. Almost seventy percent of German underwater combatants and crews became casualties, yet they sank over two thousand six hundred merchant ships and almost two hundred warships in less than six years. How did you come across this bit of naval history?"

"When I was first appointed to command *Iolanthe*, I spent a lot of my spare hours researching historical commerce raiders, including those fielded by wet navies. I was trying to familiarize myself with their mindset and the tactics they used, since Q-ships aren't on the curriculum at the Armed Services Academy. I dug up that article on submersible wolf packs along the way. But since *Iolanthe* appeared destined to work alone and the very idea of wolf packs seems unknown in the Commonwealth Navy, I promptly filed it in the back of my memory. That's why the idea didn't occur to me until after I observed your review yesterday."

"I see. Lena and I debated the matter all morning, and we seem unable to agree on the merits of the idea." If Dunmoore felt surprise at Petras' unexpected candor, she kept evidence of it from her expression. "Lena believes the risks of splitting up so we can track down enemy shipping outweigh the benefits, especially if the Shrehari pick up our subspace transmissions and determine approximately where we are. She fears the enemy could pick our ships off one by one, as happened to those submersibles."

"There's no doubt it's riskier than sailing and fighting in formation, sir. Yet the success of the wet navy wolf packs speaks for itself, casualties notwithstanding, and we enjoy an advantage the old submersibles lacked. We can jump to hyperspace and evade the enemy if his warships track the source of our radio signals or come upon individual Task Force Luckner ships before the pack can form. As far as I know, they still need more time to cycle their hyperdrives between jumps than we do.

But space is immense, their sensors aren't as good as ours, we can run silent better than they can, and they already know human ships are operating inside their sphere. I think the biggest issue we will face using wolf pack tactics is getting the message out when one of our ships spots an enemy convoy since it's probable at least some of us will be FTL when it happens. But I may be able to propose a few solutions."

Petras gave his flag captain an involuntary glance as if expecting another round of objections, but she merely sat there, stony-faced.

"They are?"

"Assuming we pair off the ships, they could leapfrog each other on their patrol route, so that one ship in each pair is sublight and able to listen. Another would be to assign a ship as retransmission node, responsible for listening to alerts and ensuring everyone in Luckner acknowledges them. It would stay sublight in the center of the patrol area until every unit confirms, then join the pack at the appropriate coordinates."

Petras rubbed his square chin with a rough hand.

"Interesting. I prefer your second idea. Who would you appoint as the node?"

"Whichever ship has the most powerful subspace radio array. But for our purposes, any of them would do. Perhaps cycling ships through retransmission node duty would be best for morale and give everyone a chance to hone hunting skills."

"If we intend on following this path, then I suggest *Hawkwood* be the node," Corto said, breaking her silence. "The flagship has a subspace array as powerful as any, including *Iolanthe*. Besides, we shouldn't be patrolling, we should be controlling."

Dunmoore inclined her head.

"Good point, Lena. It parallels wet navy practices, seeing as how the submersible wolf packs were directed from a shore-based operations center rather than one of the units at sea."

Corto scowled at Dunmoore's easy use of her first name.

"I still think splitting up the task force is too much of a risk, Admiral, but if that is your choice, staying sublight until all ships are vectored on an enemy target seems best."

"I choose to do so. What are your recommendations for dispersing the task force, Lena?"

"Sorry, sir. Give me a moment to think it over."

Petras turned to Dunmoore.

"Siobhan?"

A flash of surprise crossed her eyes. He'd never used her first name before now.

"Sir, if you intend to keep *Hawkwood* as the node, then *Skua* should stay with the flag. That leaves an odd number of ships. I propose we pair a scout each with *Jan Sobieski* and *Tamurlane* since they're the strongest after my ship and the flag, and team up the remaining two frigates. *Iolanthe* would be a singleton, but she's also powerful enough to operate alone."

"Interesting choices. Thoughts, Lena?"

Corto shrugged.

"We're talking six of one, a half dozen of the other, sir," she replied in a grudging tone. "The pairings make sense, and I expected Captain Dunmoore would propose *Iolanthe* patrol on her own."

"Four packets." Petras rubbed his chin again. "Okay. Lena, please work out the protocols to assemble the wolf pack from the moment one of our ships spots an enemy convoy. I'm sure Siobhan will be happy to help."

"Target area, sir?" Corto asked, her sullen expression making it obvious she'd never approach Dunmoore for even an iota of help.

"The outskirts of the Atsang system, now that we've established it as a hub of sorts for this sector. We'll place the patrols astride the probable shipping lanes leading to suspected outlying bases and to the heart of the empire."

"Yes, sir. What about rules of engagement if a pair's senior officer believes the pack will not form in time to intercept a target?"

Petras glanced at Dunmoore, who kept a bland face as she bit back her instinctive answer to the question. But he had noticed the flash in her eyes, as his next words proved.

"They may engage at their discretion." When he saw disapproval in Corto's face, he added, "None of our captains are reckless enough to take on more than they can handle this far from the nearest starbase."

Corto eyed Dunmoore's hologram again, clearly struggling to swallow a biting retort. Perhaps a reminder of *Stingray*'s former captain doing precisely that and returning home on a combination of hope and prayer when she should have perished in the enemy-occupied Cimmeria system.

"Yes, sir."

"All right." Petras tapped the tabletop with the extended fingers of both hands. "If something else comes to mind, Siobhan, call me. Otherwise, stand by for orders. Thank you both."

**

Holt clapped his hands without making the slightest bit of noise when the insignia of the Furious Faerie replaced Petras on the day cabin's main display.

"And another victory for our Siobhan." His roguish grin, combined with the patch covering an eye ruined years ago, gave *Iolanthe*'s first officer the aura of an elegant pirate in naval uniform.

She made a dubious face.

"Let's wait until we see results before calling it a victory."

"At least you convinced Petras to try rather than continue patrolling as a formation, which is a win in itself. And if he racks up the kills thanks to wolf pack tactics, Corto won't be his favorite captain anymore. In fact, by the crabby look on her face, I'd say she's already feeling less love. Who knows? If this gets him a third star, maybe it'll earn you your first."

Dunmoore waved away the idea.

"I haven't done enough HQ staff jobs for promotion to flag rank. The last time I rode a desk was as a lieutenant before the war."

"Working for Admiral Nagira, if I recall correctly. But that's not a hard rule, Skipper, only a convention to help guide promotion boards. Should the grand admiral wish to make you a commodore, then it'll happen, and I'm pretty sure Admiral Nagira breaks bread with him several times a week."

"Could we stop fantasizing about a dazzling future for little old me and war game a few wolf pack scenarios? I think *our* admiral will have an epiphany within the next day and look to *Iolanthe* as his anchor."

"So long as it doesn't involve chess."

— Eight —

Brakal, flanked by Regar and Toralk, stood atop the military spaceport's observation tower and gazed down at Shredar, the imperial capital, in the distance. Its ancient stone buildings seemed to sulk beneath a blanket of low, gray clouds, the sort that would release a primal deluge capable of turning dust into a sticky, nauseating slime. Even the financial district's modern metal and glass towers appeared drab and careworn under a dull, late afternoon sky that gave everything a sick, greenish hue. The oppressive atmosphere suited Brakal's dark mood.

His eyes were inevitably drawn to the imperial palace at the heart of the government district, Shredar's Forbidden Quarter perched on a flat-topped rise marking the city's center. There, those who started this war and were most assuredly losing it lived in isolated splendor, divorced from the consequences of their decisions.

Though the child emperor and his mother, who acted as regent, were considered untouchable under both the law and ancestral customs unless they lost the favor of the gods, no such taboo covered the members of the governing council. They could be removed and punished for treason.   And those same ancestral customs protecting the imperial family allowed for a *kho'sahra*, a military dictator, to take the council's place and rule the empire if its future was under threat.

Brakal could conceive of no greater peril than that of a slow, agonizing defeat at the hands of increasingly bold human commanders equipped with ships outclassing any design produced by Deep Space Fleet construction yards.

The war might have been winnable early on if the council and its pet admirals had stuck to limited goals, but even at this late date, they still did not understand what he had realized long ago.   By attacking the human Commonwealth unprovoked, the empire woke up a sleeping giant.   That giant needed many turns to muster his full strength, but he was now striding toward Shrehari Prime, looking for vengeance in the form of a victory which would humiliate the empire.

Such humiliation would cause no end of social unrest, especially among the subject species, and could even threaten the child emperor's legitimacy in the eyes of his people.   Many dynasties had fallen during the empire's long history because of decisions damaging to the Shrehari people's collective sense of honor.   Every such fall came with brutal civil strife.   And what could the empire's citizens consider more dishonorable than succumbing to a species still regarded as weak and contemptible by most Shrehari, even long after they had proved the contrary?

Toralk's gruff voice broke through his brooding thoughts.

"The estate car is almost here, Lord."

"Hmm?"

Brakal's eyes turned to the serpentine slash in the dense vegetation which surrounded the spaceport like a broad, living wall, one that offered better protection from intruders than any perimeter fence. He quickly picked up what Toralk saw from a greater distance. One of Clan Makkar's ground vehicles, a black, boxy, slightly menacing armored car adorned with the clan's double dragon crest floating on an antigrav cushion.

Brakal would have preferred to fly home from the spaceport, but a council grown fearful of its enemies banned private aircraft in and around the capital. That the decree insulted clan lords loyal to the empire escaped their timid souls.

"We should go, Lord," Toralk said. "Cold ale and roasted meat await us at the manor."

Brakal turned to his chief retainer and curled up a lip.

"And so they do. I suppose I should thank the gods Clan Makkar's estates are within reasonable ground travel distance. Your belly will howl in surrender soon enough."

"Seniority among those who sit in the Kraal has its privileges," Regar murmured. "Not that I would dare complain. After the insipid rations served aboard that cursed courier, I too long for real food."

"Always thinking with your stomachs — when it isn't your loins," Brakal grumbled. He gestured at the lift doors behind them. "Come and follow your sworn liege..."

"Instantly and without reservations, even if your orders take us to the Ninth Hell."

Brakal clapped Regar on the shoulder.

"Only the sons of whores wallowing in their own filth at the heart of the Forbidden Quarter are destined for the Ninth Hell, my *Tai Kan* spy."

When they climbed into the roomy car, Brakal felt surprise at seeing Anag, the Clan Makkar estate manager at the controls. The family of the grizzled former

Imperial Ground Forces underofficer had served the clan for generations in the same way as the faithful Toralk and his family.

Brakal reached out and grasped the man's arm in greeting.

"You honor me, Anag."

"I honor and protect you, Lord, mostly from yourself." Anag gave Toralk a knowing look. "Better I bring you home than a hapless youngling who has not yet felt the full fury of your bad moods."

"Hah! You think I return full of rage at my dismissal from active duty? Nothing could be further from the truth."

"He has a plan," Toralk said in a somber tone conveying dread.

"Anag, this is Regar. Though he might look as if he was a shifty, treacherous *Tai Kan* insect, Regar served in the Deep Space Fleet before he became a spy. Now he serves me as a sworn retainer, though he still holds his appointment in the *Tai Kan*. Regar, my friend Anag has been taking care of the Clan Makkar estates here in Shredar and out in the countryside since before the war."

The two warriors eyed each other for a few moments, then Regar inclined his head.

"Well met, Anag. Am I right in thinking you once wore the Imperial Armed Forces uniform?"

"Imperial Assault Troops. Thirty turns."

"That is what I thought."

Brakal gestured at Anag.

"Take us home, but cut through the city. I want to bask in its mood."

"Then you might feel the urge to bathe afterward. The city's mood is dark, if not downright filthy," the estate manager replied once they were in motion. "Though the council and its *Tai Kan* minions do their best to suppress the truth, news of our losses against a foe gaining in strength invariably escapes. It would astonish you to know how many in Shredar wonder whether time has come to negotiate a peace with honor rather than continue hemorrhaging lives and ships for no gain."

Anag glanced over his shoulder only to see a ferocious smile twisting Brakal's features.

"A plan you said, Toralk? Why am I suddenly fearful our lord wishes to swim in the muck of imperial politics?"

"Your lord wishes to cleanse imperial politics of its muck, you miscreant," Brakal growled.

A sound of dismay escaped Anag's barrel chest.

"It is even worse than I feared after receiving word of your involuntary return."

"When did the Kraal last meet?"

"You know as well as I. It has been many turns. The military lords have been absent. Or most of them were until they lost their commands. Many of the civilian lords have so far not felt enough pain from this endless war to challenge the council. That, or they do not want to attract undue *Tai Kan* attention. We know Council Leader Mishtak uses those infernal spies as his personal enforcers."

"Indeed," Regar said. "*Tai Kan* Director Yatron resides in Mishtak's pocket. When the great cleansing starts, Yatron must be on or near the top of the arrest list. First Deputy Director Kroesh will be happy to take over and work for whoever replaces Mishtak."

When Anag gave Regar an incredulous glance, Brakal roared with laughter.

"And now you understand why I accepted an infernal spy's oath of fealty to Clan Makkar. Surely enough lords are on Shrehari Prime so the Kraal may meet as per the Rules."

"No doubt," Anag replied. "And those who are offworld can be summoned. The question is, how many can we rouse from their torpor and assemble in the Forbidden Quarter."

"Or set free from their fear of retribution," Regar added. "Troops under admiralty control, which is the same as saying under Mishtak's control, guard the Quarter, backed by a regiment of *Tai Kan*."

"Not anymore." Anag glanced over his shoulder again. "The Forbidden Quarter is now entirely guarded by uniformed *Tai Kan* troops."

"Then it is worse than I thought."

"Bah." Brakal made a rude gesture. "Bugger the lot of them. We lords of the empire need not meet in the Forbidden Quarter. The Rules specify no particular location. In fact, historical lore claims the lords met in the Jakrang before there was such a thing as a Forbidden Quarter."

"The Jakrang is nothing but ruins," Anag said.

"They still use it for operatic performances. I saw a brilliant staging of *Akuh and Mylota* there before the war. It even featured live animals. Sitting on stone benches polished by millions of Shrehari rear ends over the last five thousand turns and under a sunny sky should cheer up even the most morose of my peers."

Brakal glanced through the polarized window and lost his good mood as they entered the worst of the capital's slums.

"If you want true ruins with no use to anyone, then I would say this qualifies. Am I dreaming, or are there more beggars than ever?"

Downtrodden, disheveled Shrehari males and females — the poorest of the poor in a city never short of those disfavored, unemployed, or wretched, watched the ground car glide over the ancient cobblestones through eyes shining with deprivation, envy, and anger.

"You are not dreaming, Lord," Anag replied. "The war has been hardest on the lower castes. Tax increases to build more ships drove many small farmers and manufacturers into bankruptcy. And the council does not seem to care. Another turn or two and we may face a critical mass of dispossessed ready for a bloody revolution. It is the same everywhere on the homeworld. Even your noble peers are feeling pinched by Mishtak's taxes, though he has been careful to avoid alienating them so far. Of course, the usual rumors of tax money vanishing into various pockets instead of paying for the war effort run rampant."

"And that is why the Kraal must reassert its control over the empire's affairs. Before Mishtak turns us all into beggars, hoping we will be easier to please."

Anag signified his agreement with a mournful grunt.

"Preferably before human banners gently wave in the breeze atop the Forbidden Quarter's palaces."

They left the slum behind as the car took them into a more prosperous section of Shredar, nearer to the seat of government and the imperial palace. Though its inhabitants seemed less deprived, Brakal saw a not dissimilar gleam of envy and anger in the black within black eyes watching a clan lord's car waft by.

When they entered the Field of Honor, a broad plaza paved in pink granite fronting the ornate ceremonial entrance to the Forbidden Quarter, Brakal let out a derisive snort.

"Mishtak may be craven, but he is no fool. The Field of Honor seems guarded by at least twice as many troops as before."

"Three times," Regar said, "and if I am not mistaken, those uniformed *Tai Kan* are wearing armor and carrying functional power weapons. Director Yatron must have ordered a recruitment drive. I do not recall the Shredar regiment being strong enough to field so many sentries day and night. The Great Demons only know how many patrol within the Quarter's walls. Could it be the council no longer trusts our glorious Imperial Ground Forces?"

"Will you visit the admiralty?" Anag asked when he spied the red-tiled roof of the military headquarters above the walls.

"I do not wish to speak with anyone there and will not pollute my ears with whatever those puss-filled pimples wish to say. Since I no longer hold a military appointment, my sole status is that of clan lord and member of the Kraal. It means I will only consider accepting an invitation issued by an admiral of the first rank."

A sly smile appeared on Regar's face.

"In other words, you will not report to Admiral of the Second Rank Zakit upon arrival in Shredar."

"Certainly not." Brakal's lip curled up in a snarl. "An insect such as Zakit cannot issue orders to a clan lord. Those idiots should have thought twice about placing me in the reserve of officers *before* I arrived on Shrehari Prime."

A deep, rumbling guffaw erupted from Anag's throat.

"For a reason that escapes me at the moment, I think you will make an excellent politician, Lord Brakal."

— Nine —

The intercom's gentle peal pulled Dunmoore from her contemplation of early First Migration War naval tactics. She placed her reader on the desk and touched the controls.

"Captain here."

"Kremm, sir. I have the watch. We intercepted a message from *Fennec* to the flag. They picked up a convoy leaving Atsang orbit on visual and are tracking it to the hyperlimit so they can determine its course. At *Fennec*'s current distance from the planet, the visuals are twelve hours old, so it's a given the boneheads are FTL by now."

Dunmoore called up the intelligence they'd accumulated on Atsang, silently cursing Lena Corto. She'd convinced Petras that sending FTL recon drones to the planet's hyperlimit so they could obtain almost real-time data on enemy movements would be an unacceptable risk. It left them looking at an FTL capable enemy with equipment limited by light speed physics.

"I'll wager they're almost at the heliopause, ready to drop out of FTL for the transition to interstellar space. But where?"

Dunmoore tapped the desktop with gloved fingers. Task Force Luckner had been loitering on the edge of the Atsang system for the last five days, each wolf pack element sailing astride potential shipping lanes to outlying Shrehari bases.

"I acknowledged receipt of *Fennec*'s transmission and alerted the CIC to be on the lookout."

"Thank you, Theo. Was there anything else?"

"No, sir."

"Dunmoore, out."

She sat back in her chair and stared at the star map covering part of one bulkhead. Her wolf pack proposal based on wet navy tactics from five hundred years ago was about to face the only valid test of ideas — cold, harsh reality — and suddenly, she didn't quite know how to feel. Hunting alone was a vastly different proposition, one with no need for coordination.

Find prey and chase it unto death. Dunmoore would be happy to nip at that convoy by herself, taking a ship or three every time it dropped out of FTL and chase the survivors until she found herself within a few thousand kilometers of an orbital base's guns.

Sharing the chase and the kill with other starships whose captains and crews, through no fault of their own, didn't have a predatory mindset, still seemed unnatural. Yet, a part of her knew the only way for a hunting formation of Task Force Luckner's sort to succeed was transforming each frigate, each destroyer, and each scout into smaller versions of *Iolanthe*. Gregor Pushkin had discovered his inner cut-throat long ago and now commanded a ship built to punish the enemy. But his colleagues hadn't lived through *Stingray*'s wild adventures, far from an admiral's gaze or a battle group's support.

With nothing else to do while *Iolanthe* ran silent, she picked up her reader and immersed herself again in the violence of humanity's diaspora among the stars, as much to find nuggets of wisdom as to pass the time. Almost precisely three hours later, the intercom pulled her back to the present.

"Yes?"

"Sirico, sir. *Fennec* sent a confirmed FTL vector for the convoy. *Jan Sobieski* and *Rooikat* are closest to where it should drop out of hyperspace at the heliopause, which would be on the general heading to a suspected outpost in the Lorgh system, just over four light-years from our current location. We confirmed receipt to the flag."

She heard a muffled voice over the link, stilling Sirico's next words. After a few moments, he said, "*Jan Sobieski* and *Rooikat* spotted the convoy dropping out of FTL. They're too distant for an ambush. Captain Pushkin figures by the time they get there, it'll have spooled up and jumped again. He'll calculate their course, then send *Rooikat* to sniff out and follow their hyperspace bubble while waiting for orders from the flag."

Dunmoore silently shook her head. That was another of Corto's so-called improvements on the wolf pack plan. Task Force Luckner, minus the tracking ship would come together before the chase, instead of letting each pair of ships join in as fast as it could, allowing the pack to form organically.

How she talked Petras into it, Dunmoore couldn't fathom. They should receive those orders in just about forty-five minutes, once *Jan Sobieski* confirmed the convoy's heading. But since *Iolanthe* was furthest from her former first officer's ship, the situation called for a brief jump. It would put them in a better position to join the others once Petras called the pack together.

"Thank you, Thorin. Bridge, this is the captain."

"Officer of the watch, sir."

"Execute FTL jump Sobieski."

As a precaution, Lieutenant Drost had prepared contingency navigation plots leading to whichever packet was closest to an enemy convoy crossing the heliopause. Naturally, she named the plans after the senior ship in each pair.

"Aye, aye, sir."

A few seconds later, the jump klaxon blared throughout the ship, warning everyone aboard to sit or grab hold of a bulkhead, so the disorientation from crossing into hyperspace didn't knock them on their rear ends. Thirty seconds after that, Dunmoore felt the familiar but thankfully brief jump nausea twist her innards before they settled again.

The door chime rang, and Holt poked his head through when it opened.

"I understand Gregor has first dibs. Or would if we were doing this right."

"I'm sure he's as annoyed as anyone at waiting for orders from the flag instead of putting that magnificent pocket cruiser of his to good use right away. At least *Rooikat* is on the loose."

Holt stepped in.

"If I didn't know any better, I'd say that sounded a tad bitter."

She sighed.

"If I actually cared about making Task Force Luckner the most successful commerce raiding formation in human history, I suppose it might be worthwhile proposing Lena and I swap places so she doesn't whisper stupidities in the admiral's ear."

A horrified expression replaced Holt's earlier good humor.

"No. Don't even joke about it. She hasn't driven a starship in what? Eight years? And her last command was pretty small compared to the Furious Faerie. Corto couldn't fight *Iolanthe* properly, let alone competently lead the Fleet's quirkiest crew. It would be a complete waste of potential."

"All true, but if the admiral still won't let his newest, most powerful ships run at full capacity because he can't stop listening to his flag captain, what's the point of us being here? Both Gregor and I could do more on our own."

"Wow. First a hint of bitterness, now a shadow of disloyalty. You *are* off your feed." When he saw her eyes harden, Holt raised both hands in surrender. "It was a joke, Skipper. I realize you'd never be disloyal, but please don't make your feelings about the task force's success or lack thereof known to anyone other than yours truly."

"No worries. I'm just afraid this might turn into a clusterfuck. Half measures generally do. They're one of the reasons the First Migration War ran up casualties in the hundreds of millions. If it weren't for this Lena-inspired nonsense, Astrid would be standing by her plotter, ready to send us on a pursuit the moment either *Jan Sobieski* or *Rooikat* confirm the enemy's vector. Instead, we're waiting for the flag to collect us in an orderly gaggle."

A pained expression crossed Holt's face.

"You aren't just off your feed. You're royally pissed off, aren't you? Orderly gaggle? That would be hilarious if it weren't for the class five ion storm I see stirring in your eyes."

"Gregor should be hard on that convoy's tail now, not later. Considering what I managed with *Stingray* and the fact *Jan Sobieski* is essentially twice as powerful as the old girl was, not letting him slip his leash is almost criminal."

**

"The flag is asking why we went FTL without waiting for orders, Captain."

Dunmoore bit back the first question that came to mind. The flag, or the flag captain?

"Let them know we did so to speed up the wolf pack's formation."

"Aye, aye, sir." If Chief Day noticed his captain's mood, he showed no sign.

"*Jan Sobieski* sees us, sir," Chief Yens said, raising a hand to attract Dunmoore's attention. "She's painting us with a communications laser."

"Comms, please return the favor and open a link. Pipe it to my command chair, in case Captain Pushkin wishes to speak with me."

"Aye, aye, sir. At current separation, it's one and a half seconds each way."

"Thank you."

Laser comms moved at the speed of light, meaning a three-second round trip delay between *Iolanthe* and *Jan Sobieski*. Subspace radio would have been instantaneous, but anyone could listen in provided they were on the right frequency and capable of decrypting transmissions. Perhaps Gregor wanted a private conversation with his former captain and mentor.

Almost a minute passed, then Pushkin's face appeared on the display embedded in her command chair's arm. Dunmoore raised its electronic privacy shield so no one could overhear them, though she could still hear the rest of the CIC.

"Good afternoon, Skipper. I'm in my cocoon. We can talk privately."

"Hi, Gregor. I'm in my cone of silence as well. What's up?"

Three seconds passed.

"Any chance of you twisting the admiral's arm and sending both of us after *Rooikat* and the convoy. When I spoke with Darcey Hauck a few minutes ago, *Rooikat*'s sensors showed the convoy turning on a course that doesn't lead to any outlying star system, and they'll jump shortly."

"So they're not headed for Lorgh?"

"Doesn't seem so. At least not directly."

Dunmoore thought for a moment.

"You and Darcey figure they plan on making a dogleg a few light-years out to shake any potential hunters? Could well be. Sometimes the bastards learn faster than we expect. I suppose it's worth trying — if I can catch *Hawkwood* before she goes FTL inbound for our location. Wait one." Dunmoore touched her chair's control surface. "Get me the admiral on subspace and pipe it to my chair."

"Aye, aye, sir."

"Why did Petras backtrack on fully implementing the idea?" Pushkin asked.

"Corto and her obsession with keeping control over the task force, lest any of us does something that'll reflect badly on the admiral, what else?"

"Sir," Chief Day interjected. "I have the admiral on subspace."

Petras' angular features replaced those of her former first officer.

"What is it, Siobhan? We're about to go FTL for the rendezvous."

"Sir, it appears the convoy took a heading that doesn't lead directly to one of the enemy-held star systems, and I fear they might already be adapting their tactics after your attack. At this point, they're going FTL in fifteen minutes at most and should be on their intended hyperspace course. If the convoy plans on tacking two or three light-years out, we could easily lose it. I was hoping you might allow *Iolanthe* and *Jan Sobieski* to join *Rooikat* in chasing them down while Luckner assembles. We three have the best sensor suites of any ships and can leapfrog each other to stay in contact. Besides, *Iolanthe* and *Jan Sobieski* can do a lot of damage if we catch them tacking and keep the bastards sublight until you arrive with the rest of the task force."

Dunmoore bit her tongue before adding a comment about flexibility in the face of enemy plans being one advantage of well-executed wolf pack tactics. But reminding Petras he'd succumbed to his flag captain's blandishments again wouldn't help her cause.

A frown creased his admiral's forehead.

"I wish someone thought of this possibility beforehand, but I suppose there's no helping it now."

Dunmoore's ears picked up a muffled voice over the comlink. Corto protesting? Petras glanced over his shoulder as the audio cut out. When he turned back, she noticed a spark of irritation in his hooded eyes.

"Go. Don't take chances and stay in touch. I'd rather you waited for the rest of Luckner if there's a risk you or the others might suffer damage."

"Thank you, sir."

"Petras, out."

She glanced down at Pushkin.

"Your navigator and mine need to talk. We're joining Darcey. And unless there are other matters you wish to discuss in private, we'll use the subspace channel. Even though they're only three seconds, these delays are irritating."

After the expected pause, a delighted smile appeared on Pushkin's face.

"Yes, sir! Subspace it is. *Jan Sobieski*, out."

— Ten —

"**B**rakal, one of us at last." An older Shrehari of the Warrior Caste rose from his rough-hewn chair to greet Strike Force Khorsan's former commanding admiral. He studied his friend and fellow Kraal member through black within black eyes deeply set in an angular, ridged skull polished to a deep amber by decades beneath combat helmets.

"Vagh." Brakal gripped the retired general's arms in a comradely greeting. "You still look ready to chew up the best the humans can throw at us."

"Bah." Vagh waved away Brakal's words as he dropped back into his chair. "Sit. I recognize Toralk lurking by the door, but who is your other shadow?"

A feral smile split Brakal's face.

"Regar, of the *Tai Kan*. Sworn to Clan Makkar."

"What?" Vagh stared across the tightly packed lower town tavern at the smiling spy. "One of them sworn to a Warrior Caste lord? Will wonders never cease?"

Laughter rumbled up Brakal's throat.

"Kerhasi said as much when I told him."

"Another who will soon join the inactive reserve of officers, no doubt. It seems Trage is determined to replace anyone capable of winning against the humans,"

Vagh replied, naming the Imperial Armed Forces' commander-in-chief.

Brakal took the foaming mug of ale proffered by one of the tavern's aproned waiters and took an appreciative sip before letting out a deep sigh.

"Excellent stuff." He placed the mug between them. "I fear winning is no longer a realistic outcome, my friend. Trage is flailing around, dismissing field commanders at the slightest hint of failure because he no longer knows what else he can do. The humans are beating us. They adapt and plan new ways faster than our sclerotic admiralty can wipe its collective hind end."

Vagh let out a sad grunt.

"And they are persistent. Trage dismissed Kokurag and me because we could not extinguish every sign of human resistance in the Cimmeria system. Never mind it has not, so far interfered with our war effort. But Trage and his useless operations staff cannot comprehend such a goal requires more ships capable of keeping smugglers from resupplying human combat units which, instead of dwindling during all these turns since we occupied the planet, are growing in strength. Our replacements will fare even worse — they do not enjoy the benefit of our experience keeping resistance to a mere irritant."

"It is the same everywhere." Brakal took another gulp of ale. "In every star system we occupy. And now they invade our space, carrying out raids that are well beyond irritating. The gods are turning against us. Let me tell you why I am here instead of commanding a strike group."

When Brakal fell silent after a long tale of frustration and woe, Vagh made a gesture of dismay.

"I am but a soldier, yet even I know they build better ships and build them faster than we can. If one of theirs is capable of destroying an orbital base, then yes, we face disaster. Perhaps not soon, perhaps not to the degree we might fear, however..." Vagh let his words hang.

"However, indeed. And in the interval, the empire will continue bleeding until the common people rise in revolt. Too much taxation, most of it unfair, too many dead, most of them from ordinary citizen clans and too many promises of victory proved false by the enemy. Perhaps the ruling dynasty deserves to be overthrown, as many have throughout history, for failing to preserve our honor and losing favor with the gods. Although blaming the child emperor is futile. No, it is the council which deserves our wrath. It dragged us into this futile war without end."

"Agreed." Vagh drained his mug and thumped it on the table, signaling he wished a refill. "And I daresay you will find most of us dismissed by Trage for not winning an unachievable victory agree with your views."

"No doubt." Brakal's lip curled up. "Yet grumbling among ourselves in taverns is also futile. I seek not only the admirals, generals and other officers unfairly dismissed. I also seek those who sit in the Kraal, or would if that august body deigned to carry out its ancestral duties, such as stifling the emperor's and the council's worst impulses."

"So this is why you sought me out so soon after your return."

Two fresh mugs of ale appeared as if by magic. Brakal raised one of them in salute.

"You are merely the first, Vagh. Join me, and we will each speak with others who wore the imperial uniform and whose clans claim seats in the Kraal. Once we bring those of Warrior Caste to our side, we will reach out and cajole the civilian lords until the four hundred clans come together and stand against the council. It is the only way. We must stop our empire's lifeblood from leeching out into the galaxy until nothing but a husk remains for the humans and our subject races to pick over."

Vagh studied Brakal in silence for a few moments.

"What do you intend once the Kraal votes to dissolve Mishtak's government? Replace it with a new band of thieves? We clan lords cannot sit on the council, nor can members of the military services even if they are in the inactive officers' reserve and not under military discipline." When Vagh saw Brakal bare his fangs, he glanced around the room to make sure no one was listening. "By the demons of the Underworld, you intend to name a *kho'sahra* and set up a military dictatorship which would rule in the emperor's name, am I correct?"

"Is there a better solution to end this war with honor, extricate us from human space, and heal the empire?"

Vagh's gesture of assent was grudging.

"We have not seen a *kho'sahra* in the Forbidden Quarter since the days of Emperor Torav the Weak, five hundred turns ago. This would be momentous."

"Yet the common people will cheer."

"It is not the common people's reaction that should worry you."

Brakal's feral smile returned.

"The military will welcome one of their own to replace a council that has failed it and sullied the honor of its members. With them and the people supporting us, everyone else will submit. Mishtak and his fellows command little loyalty, even among the bureaucracy. They will find few who would stand against a popular *kho'sahra* promising an end to the madness of war." He held out his hand. "Are you with me, Vagh?"

The older Shrehari snorted as he reached out to grasp it.

"You speak as if I have something better to do nowadays. Of course, I am with you." After toasting each other, Vagh asked, "Who shall be our *kho'sahra*?"

"I can think of several admirals and generals who would do well, Warrior Caste officers smart enough to surround themselves with honest, capable Shrehari who have a talent for public administration. None of them serve at the admiralty, needless to say. That bunch of superannuated incompetents will not even spend their last turns on the inactive reserve list when we are done."

Vagh eyed Brakal with undisguised suspicion.

"I hope you do not consider me a candidate for the position."

The latter rubbed his angular chin as if lost in thought.

"As a general of the third rank and clan lord, you enjoy sufficient standing, and there will be few generals or admirals of the second rank, let alone of the first rank whom anyone would consider suitable. We will invite most of those to retire once the empire changes its leadership."

Vagh held up a restraining hand.

"Not even in jest, Brakal of the Makkar. I will help you with this, but I will not become the dictator."

"Agreed, Vagh of the Najuk. You would be best placed as deputy commander of the Imperial Ground Forces and oversee our soldiers' withdrawal from human worlds."

A faint air of indignation crossed Vagh's features.

"You would simply hand back what we took?"

"What profit did their star systems bring the empire? How much treasure and how many lives did we waste taking and holding them? So long as we leave a single Shrehari trooper on their soil, this war will continue."

Another grudging assent.

"Understood and accepted."

"The Kraal may decide who will be our *kho'sahra*, though we must make sure it chooses whoever is best for the empire's future. But until it meets, our words are nothing more than farts in an ion storm." When Brakal noticed Vagh's eyes dart over his shoulder, he asked, "What?"

"Your *Tai Kan* pet. He slipped out. Toralk is still at his post."

"Then something alerted him. Your bodyguards?"

"Within sight. Retired troopers, both of them. If Mishtak's spies are imprudent, they will pay with their lives. What shall we do now?"

"Talk to the following, obtain their agreement, and ask that each speaks to another six." Brakal rattled off half a dozen names, forcibly retired admirals and generals who were either clan lords themselves or first-degree relatives of clan lords. He then named six more, saying, "I will speak with them in the next two or three days. The Kraal must meet before the next change of the moons. Tell them we assemble in the Jakrang, far from Mishtak's lair. And if you could ask a friend for reliable troops to guard the Jakrang, so much the better."

"I will find us a full regiment of Assault Infantry." Vagh stood, imitated by two oversized Shrehari in civilian clothing who had been lounging in a booth behind them. "Take care, Brakal. The moment Mishtak hears you are assembling the Kraal, he will be tempted to send his assassins. Unlike Trage, that misbegotten whelp of a diseased whore will order a clan lord's slaying without hesitation. After ruling unopposed for so long, he believes himself untouchable."

"Then we will disabuse him of the notion." Brakal climbed to his feet and gripped Vagh's forearm. "Take care."

He watched his friend and his guards leave by a side door before joining Toralk by the tavern's main entrance.

"Where is Regar?"

"Taking care of someone who showed too much interest in General Vagh and you, Lord."

Brakal let out a thoughtful grunt.

"I suppose he can identify secret police spies more readily than either of us."

"He said we should return to the estate without him if he does not meet us at the car by the time you finished speaking with Vagh."

Toralk touched the holstered weapon on his hip out of reflex, then turned for the exit before Brakal could move ahead of him, and step into the waning afternoon light first.

They found Regar leaning against the boxy vehicle with the double-headed dragon crest on its sides, looking pleased.

"Is General Vagh with us?"

"He is. And the individual you pursued?"

"Stepped into the wrong alley, slipped on some dung, and cracked his skull open as he struck the cobblestones. A sad yet not uncommon occurrence in this area. His body will already have vanished, never to be seen again."

"Was he...?"

"Without a doubt. Since word could not yet be going around telling of your intent to assemble the Kraal, I can only assume either you or the general were being watched simply because you are known as cantankerous, old clan lords with no love for the regime."

A growl rose in Brakal's throat.

"Prudence, my liegeman. I may be cantankerous, but I am still in my prime."

Regar made a gesture of submission that was anything but.

"If you say so, Lord."

— Eleven —

"Nothing." Chief Yens allowed herself a frustrated sigh once the sensors finished searching almost thirty minutes after *Iolanthe* came out of FTL. The three ships had been playing leapfrog for two days, trying to detect the convoy. "Unless they're sailing into the black, the boneheads need to change course just about now."

"Funny you should say that, Marti," Chief Petty Officer Day said, grinning at his friend. "Incoming from *Rooikat* on a repeater, Captain. They caught the enemy convoy tacking six hours ago, while we were in hyperspace. Their new heading is for the Tyva system."

Sirico slapped the arm of his chair.

"I knew it. Astrid owes me a bottle of Glen Arcturus. I told her about the intelligence reports claiming there's a FOB orbiting the system's second planet, but she didn't think the convoy would dogleg back so sharply. Nor does she think intelligence knows a black hole from a pulsar. Navigators." He grinned at Dunmoore. "What can you do, right? They're all about math."

She gave him a pained look which wasn't wholly feigned.

"Gambling? On my ship? Please tell me I misheard."

"Just a friendly wager between shipmates, sir," an unrepentant Sirico replied.

"Nice try. Add *Rooikat*'s info to the tactical projection."

Red icons denoting several enemy ships appeared, along with a dashed red line connecting it to a star system identified as Tyva. Blue icons showed the last known position of Task Force Luckner's other ships, with those presumed to be FTL surrounded by a blueish halo.

Ezekiel Holt's hologram appeared at Dunmoore's elbow.

"What are you thinking, Skipper?"

"Time and distance, Zeke. Ask Astrid to plot a course for Tyva's heliopause, one jump. I want to come out of FTL as close as possible to where that convoy will emerge based on *Rooikat*'s information. It'll be the wolf pack's rendezvous."

"Will do. Stand by."

"Signals, send to *Rooikat*. Remain sublight until *Jan Sobieski* and the flag acknowledge the enemy's new heading and my intentions, which are as follows. *Iolanthe* will make one jump to the Tyva system's heliopause hoping to overtake the enemy and intercepting him before he leaves interstellar space. *Jan Sobieski* will join us as quickly as possible. *Rooikat* shall follow once she completes her retransmission duties. Standby for rendezvous coordinates at the Tyva heliopause."

Chief Day repeated the message verbatim, and upon receiving Dunmoore's approval, encrypted it and pushed it out on the task force subspace frequency.

"*Rooikat* acknowledges."

"Rendezvous coordinates are on the CIC navigation board, Skipper," Holt said shortly afterward. "According to Astrid, if we climb into the upper hyperspace bands even without redlining the drives, we should easily arrive before the convoy, and so should *Jan Sobieski*, provided she receives the message within the next few hours."

"Put us on course and ready to jump, Zeke. Chief Day, push the coordinates out to *Rooikat*."

"Aye, aye, sir," they replied simultaneously.

After a brief interval, just long enough to nudge *Iolanthe* on a new heading, the jump klaxon echoed throughout the ship, warning everyone aboard they would transition to hyperspace in thirty seconds.

Dunmoore could sense the anticipation in the CIC almost as if it were a living entity in its own right. To paraphrase an ancient, pre-diaspora author, the game was indeed afoot. Then, the universe twisted into a gigantic, multicolor pretzel while an invisible hand squeezed her innards mercilessly.

**

"If we push our engines right up to the outermost safety limits, we might get there before *Iolanthe*." Lena Corto looked up from the plot prepared by *Hawkwood*'s navigator. "Or at least almost at the same time. Being able to cut across the convoy's dogleg because we're a day behind Dunmoore is this situation's one saving grace, Admiral. It'll allow you to keep her from overstepping orders in case we can't catch that convoy before it goes FTL inside the heliosphere. The Tyva system's forward operations base might well be a tougher nut than the one she destroyed."

They were in Petras' day cabin, next to the flag bridge, alone and able to speak frankly. Inexplicably irritated by her tone, he wandered over to the sideboard and poured himself a cup of tea from the samovar kept hot twenty-four hours a day by the wardroom steward.

"Why," he asked in a soft tone as he turned to face Corto, "would you assume Dunmoore might commit a rash act, Lena? Although it's early days yet, the wolf pack method is already proving worthwhile, if only in finding suitable targets for our guns compared to patrolling in the usual way."

She stared at him with eyes colder than interstellar space.

"My apologies, sir. I was merely pointing out how useful it would be to form the pack at the earliest opportunity, so our efforts can be better coordinated. Shall I issue orders implementing this navigation plot?"

Petras took a sip of tea while he studied his flag captain, both annoyed and amazed at her growing pettiness. Perhaps she had always been like this but kept it better hidden when she wasn't confronted daily by her frustrated ambitions for one more command at the rank of captain. It could at least partially explain why the navy hadn't deigned to give her another starship since the early years of the war. Someone higher up might have noticed and made a comment in her confidential file.

That sort of thing could be the kiss of death for any chance of advancement, especially if that someone was an admiral of Nagira's caliber — uncompromising, demanding, and intolerant of careerism. In a flash, Petras understood Corto would never wear a commodore's star. Not because she wasn't competent, but because she possessed what some in the navy deemed a lack of character. A flaw that diminished her in comparison with her peers.

"Issue the orders. But we will stay within established safety limits. Task Force Luckner will push into the highest hyperspace band congruent with the safety of its slowest ship. Should *Iolanthe* and *Jan Sobieski* engage the enemy before we reach the rendezvous point, so be it.

The whole point of adopting these tactics is to hit the enemy with whatever we can and as fast as we can, instead of maneuvering to carry out the optimal solution when it might be too late for a clean sweep. Remember, the perfect is the enemy of the good."

"Yes, sir." Corto straightened to attention. "Anything else, sir."

"No."

She left via the door leading to the flag bridge while Petras stared at the navigation plot. He took another sip of tea and exhaled slowly. Did a formation such as Luckner, with next to no staff, no fixed base, and operating as a single entity even need a flag captain?

Every assumption they'd made war gaming a commerce raider formation at SOCOM HQ, every brainstorming session and tactical development proposed as *the* solution to make the enemy squeal in pain didn't seem to fare as well as he'd hoped. As with all things, reality was the final arbiter.

**

"Nothing on sensors," Yens reported a few minutes after *Iolanthe* emerged near where the convoy would cross the Tyva system's heliopause. Provided this was its destination, and the dogleg wasn't another feint aimed at confusing potential pursuers.

"Nothing on our own subspace bands either," Chief Day added from the signals station.

Sirico glanced at Dunmoore over his shoulder.

"Everyone else is probably FTL right now. Perhaps luck will favor us, and we'll enjoy first dibs on the boneheads."

"That's too much to hope for, Thorin. *Jan Sobieski* will show up before the Shrehari." She nibbled on the inside of her lip for a few seconds, then mentally shrugged. "When *Rooikat* drops out of FTL, I'll want her to send a drone inward and find the FOB this convoy is resupplying. If it's another hurriedly built wartime contraption similar to the last one and no enemy ships are hanging around, perhaps the admiral will allow us a stealth attack."

Sirico rubbed his hands with murderous glee.

"That would be splendid. Let's hope fate is smiling on us. We are the bold and as they say, *audaces fortuna juvat*."

"All right." Dunmoore stood and glanced at Holt's hologram. "Keep us at battle stations for now, Zeke. I'll be in my day cabin catching up on ship's business. You have the CIC, Mister Sirico."

"I relieve you, sir."

Yens raised a hand.

"You may wish to hang around, Captain. Sensors picked up a hyperspace bubble coming in our direction. It's not big enough to be a convoy traveling in sync."

"*Jan Sobieski*?"

"Could be."

"And we have an emergence, two hundred thousand kilometers aft." Yens paused for a moment. "It's *Jan Sobieski*."

Dunmoore turned to the signals station.

"Chief Day, link me up with Captain Pushkin."

"Done, sir," he replied moments later.

Gregor Pushkin's face materialized in front of her. "Captain! Please tell me we arrived before the convoy."

"I think we did. Our sensors aren't picking up anything useful and the subspace frequencies, ours and the enemy's, are quiet. The rest of the task force are hopefully FTL for our location by now."

Pushkin nodded in agreement.

"We're not picking anything up other than *Iolanthe*, and then only because you're transmitting, otherwise even our state-of-the-art sensors wouldn't see more than a faint ghost. What are your orders?"

"Stay on your present heading, set up a laser comlink with us, go to silent running, and wait for the convoy to drop out of FTL. Once it does, we'll figure out the best angle of attack."

"Without waiting for the admiral?"

"Without waiting. If the convoy shows up within strike range, we pounce. And once *Rooikat* joins us, I'll send her to take a look inside this star system and find the Shrehari forward operating base. It would be a shame if it was no stronger than the one *Iolanthe* destroyed in the Khorsan system and we wasted the opportunity."

"Because blowing up naval installations deep within the empire will give Shrehari admirals the sort of conniptions that won't stem from mere material loss."

"Precisely. You didn't think our operations were aimed purely at causing physical damage. Repeated defeats inside their sphere will sting the Shrehari sense of honor, and an enemy whose blood is roused inevitably makes mistakes he can't afford."

Pushkin grinned.

"That's the skipper I remember. Funny how attacking the moral dimension seems to be under-appreciated by so many."

"Probably because it can't be measured in ammo expenditure and kills ratios. The naval staff hates things that aren't mathematically provable."

"Though they do seem happy that we front line pigs can't mathematically measure the usefulness of staff officers."

Dunmoore raised a finger and gave him a mock frown.

"Now, now. Don't be so harsh. Someone needs to make sure we deal with our fair share of administrative trivia. But enough persiflage. Time for silent running. We may find ourselves in a target-rich environment before long."

"The laser comlink is up," Chief Day said. "Switching over."

Pushkin's image wavered for a fraction of a second.

"We're powering down," he said.

Shortly after that, Yens nodded.

"Confirmed. She's fading from sensors. And not a moment too soon. I'm picking up multiple hyperspace traces." She paused. "Five."

Dunmoore looked up from Pushkin's image.

"The rest of the task force?"

"Or the convoy sailing in a looser formation than we expect," Sirico replied. "Maybe they decided scattering a bit might make our job of intercepting them more difficult. The convoy was what? Ten armed freighters and five *Ptar* class corvettes? Five traces, three ships per trace — two freighters and one escort. I'd say the math works well enough to satisfy even the most anal-retentive admiral."

"We'll find out soon," Yens said. "I figure ten minutes at most before they drop out of FTL."

"Zeke, put *Iolanthe* on a course matching the hyperspace traces and prepare for a micro-jump to close with the enemy the moment they emerge. You too, Gregor."

"Aye, aye, sir," both replied in unison.

— Twelve —

Toralk appeared in the formal dining room's open doorway as if by magic, startling Brakal who was reading up on the minutiae of Kraal protocol while finishing his breakfast *tvass*. He was sitting alone at a dark, polished table carved from the trunk of a single tree more than ten generations earlier, one able to accommodate twenty guests. The table's lustrous sheen matched that of the waist-high wainscoting covering ancient stone walls.

"Lord, a messenger from Admiral Trage respectfully requests you receive him. He has proper identification. I confirmed it with the admiralty's duty officer."

Brakal grunted.

"Took the poxed whoreson long enough to realize a lord of the empire would only acknowledge the admiralty via an invitation from an admiral of the first rank. Send in the messenger."

"Yes, Lord. Regar is checking him to make sure he carries nothing he should not even as we speak."

Brakal thought it a tad paranoid. Someone such as Trage was cunning enough for an oblique approach if he ever decided on assassination. He would not send a killer openly. But stranger things were happening in Shredar these days.

After a time, Toralk returned, followed by a young, almost arrogantly proud sub-commander wearing the insignia of a senior admiral's aide. Though his head fur was trimmed in the manner of a Warrior Caste member's ruff, he clearly was not one of them. No true warrior would serve a contemptible worm such as Trage.

The sub-commander stomped to a halt three paces in front of the table. He raised a fist in salute.

"Admiral Brakal. Greetings. My name is Kheyl. I serve Admiral of the First Rank Trage."

"You are welcome in my home, Kheyl. What is your business?" Brakal kept a carefully neutral tone, knowing every detail of his interaction with the aide would reach Trage's ears.

"Admiral Trage invites you to visit him at the admiralty for a discussion on matters of common interest."

"Since he shows me honor as clan lord by sending an aide instead of a written summons, I am equally honor-bound to accept. When?"

"This afternoon at the fourteenth hour."

Brakal successfully suppressed a flash of irritation at being given such short notice. It was but another of Trage's games.

"Certainly. Please tell the honorable Trage I shall attend him at the given time. Was there anything else, Sub-Commander Kheyl?"

A rictus that came just short of mocking split the officer's face.

"I must commend your security, Lord of the Makkar. A *Tai Kan* officer? Few of your stature enjoy such deadly competence in their service."

"Regar serves me well, as some who would see me dead found out to their great sorrow. You are dismissed, Sub-Commander."

"By your will, Lord." Kheyl gave him the clenched fist salute again, pivoted on his heels and marched out, trailed by Toralk.

What devilment was that insect with pretensions of adequacy preparing? Brakal scratched his chin, lost in thought. It could not be because he failed to report as ordered upon arrival. Trage knew once he placed an admiral on the inactive reserve list, his civilian rank was the only one that counted.

No, Trage wanted something else. The commander-in-chief of the Imperial Armed Forces was neither a lord from the four hundred noble clans, nor could he claim relatives who sat in the Kraal. But in this incestuous city, gossip traveled fast and always found a receptive ear. And Brakal's criticism of how Trage and his sycophants were handling the war effort was well known among the powerful.

Regar appeared in the open doorway with indecent haste.

"When and where, Lord?"

"At the admiralty on the fourteenth hour today."

"You will attend?"

"Do you see an alternative? Mishtak hears of my efforts assembling the Kraal, and in typical fashion, he orders his minions to solve the problem for him. Yet rejecting Trage's invitation would be taken as an admission of guilt by the council. Cowards that they are, the motherless bastards see their own weaknesses and fears in others, as puny insects do. They will find guilt where they would experience guilt, no matter the truth that honest Shrehari carry out nothing more than their duty to the empire."

Regar inclined his head in submission.

"I will not argue the point since you see things more clearly than most of your peers. May I attend as your aide? Who knows what perils await once you enter the walls of the Forbidden Quarter?"

"You may."

**

Brakal, wearing civilian clothes proper for his status, that is to say, dark and sober, yet exquisitely tailored, walked out into the early afternoon sun and made for his ground car, sitting at the center of a courtyard paved with green-hued flagstones worn smooth by centuries of rain.

His Shredar estate — the clan's primary holdings were half a continent away — was a thousand-turns-old semi-fortified pile of granite blocks seized by one of his ancestors from a hapless supporter of the losing side during the last forcible dynastic change. It had been a bloody affair that almost collapsed his people's star-faring civilization. Fortunately, it happened at a time when the hairless apes from Earth were still confined to their own star system. If another civil war of the sort erupted, but under the guns of human fleets, the empire might dissolve for good. The current dynasty, useless as it was, must stay, but with a new government serving it.

Regar and Toralk, also in civilian clothes, though of a more common cut and quality, waited patiently by the car. Both wore ceremonial knives stuck into the dark blue sashes wrapped around their midriffs, though Brakal knew they hid power weapons on their persons. Neither went anywhere without at least one concealed sidearm, preferably two.

"Are you ready for Shredar's greatest den of iniquity?" Brakal asked in a roaring voice when both straightened to attention. "Where perfumed admirals cavort with low caste whores who call themselves politicians."

"No," Regar replied with a feral grin. "But we will risk our lives and reputations to guard your virginity nonetheless, Lord."

"Then my virginity faces ruin."

With Toralk at the controls, they drove through the estate's open iron gates. Back when it was built, the small castle could protect its inhabitants from angry mobs, roving gangs, and unhappy monarchs. But in an age of power weapons and aerial vehicles, its walls and crenellations seemed quaint.

Though parkland surrounded the main house on all sides, the estate itself had long been hemmed in by the unfortified mansions of those whose families were built on money rather than pedigree. The sort who mindlessly supported Mishtak and his council. Few sent their offspring into the Imperial Armed Forces, and fewer still understood real honor meant knowing when one should acknowledge a foe who could not be bested. But they knew to the last coin how much their coffers held and the amounts they were owed.

And they resented the power of clan lords who claimed a seat in the Kraal.

Soon, however, the wealthy suburb gave way to government buildings, a sprawling complex of low-rise stone, steel, and wood structures that escaped the Forbidden Quarter's walls at least two dynasties ago. Their patina and drab sameness nevertheless pleased Brakal's eyes more than the overly ornate mansions did because they represented the quasi-immutable core of the empire's administration, one which survived wars, civil and other, insurrections, and dynastic upheavals since time immemorial. If he succeeded in removing the council in favor of a *kho'sahra*, it would serve the dictator, whoever he might be, with the same grim efficiency.

They emerged from the complex and drove onto the Field of Honor, aimed straight at the Forbidden Quarter's temple-like ceremonial gate. It was guarded by a platoon of uniformed *Tai Kan*. Toralk stopped the car short of the shimmering force field which barred the way when the starship-grade alloy doors were open. An officer with two troopers at his back approached the vehicle. Their faces were expressionless as if carved from the same dark stone as the government complex buildings.

Brakal opened the passenger compartment window and held out his credentials.

"I am Brakal, Lord of the Makkar. Admiral of the First Rank Trage is expecting me at the admiralty."

The uniformed *Tai Kan* troops stomped to a halt, and the officer raised his clenched fist in salute.

"He is indeed expecting you. May I examine your identification and that of your retainers?"

Brakal allowed him to take the credentials while Toralk and Regar showed theirs. If the officer thought it strange that one of his *Tai Kan* colleagues accompanied a clan lord, he showed no sign. His duty done and the identification cards back in the hands of their owners, the officer waved at one of his troopers. The force field faded away.

"Please go ahead, Lord."

Brakal inclined his head.

"Your courtesy does you honor."

The officer saluted again before taking a step back.

"Huh," Regar grunted once they passed beneath the gate's red-tiled roof. "Part of me was sure Trage would play little bureaucratic games, such as having the guard detail keep us past the appointed time on spurious grounds, or worse yet, unaware of your appointment with the admiral and ready to turn us around. This was unexpectedly civilized and properly done."

"Trage might be cunning, but he is not a fool," Brakal replied with a dismissive gesture. "Playing games with one of the four hundred who sit in the Kraal would do him no favors, and he knows as much."

Contrary to most Shrehari citizens' expectations, the buildings within the Forbidden Quarter's walls resembled those in the government complex, imperial palace included. Drab, unadorned granite structures, none more than five stories high, lined streets crossing each other at precise right angles. Sober metal signs above main doors were the sole indicators of each building's functions, and most of them were the various ministries' headquarters, where top officials held court.

The three-story imperial palace itself sat at the heart of the Forbidden Quarter behind an inner wall high enough to hide all but a sliver of the top floor and the red tile roof. Brakal saw only a few officials on the tree-lined sidewalks, mostly hurrying from one building to another rather than taking a leisurely afternoon stroll. As always, the city within a city reminded him of an insect hive where drones toiled in obscurity and to little effect.

Toralk pulled up in front of the admiralty, which distinguished itself from neighboring ministries by colorful banners hanging over the entrance. Sentries stood on either side of the transparent doors, weapons slung. They watched impassively as Brakal and Regar climbed out of the car.

"Brakal, Lord of Clan Makkar for Admiral of the First Rank Trage," Regar announced using a tone that left no doubt he was an officer in one of the imperial services.

The sentry on the left raised a hand to his mouth and mumbled a few words into the communicator strapped to his wrist. A few seconds later, he barked out a command, and both sentries came to attention.

"You and your aide may enter, Lord. Do you need a guide to Admiral Trage's office?"

A cold rictus briefly uncovered Brakal's yellowing fangs.

"If he still sits in splendor on the top floor, then I know the way."

"He does."

At a hand signal from the sentry, both door panels vanished into the walls.

Brakal and Regar took one of the lifts rather than climb five flights of stairs, and stepped out on what the former privately considered one of Shredar's most opulent whorehouses, a place with enough power to screw every member of the Imperial Armed Forces ten times over on a whim.

Sub-Commander Kheyl intercepted them before they managed more than a few steps down the corridor leading to Trage's inner sanctum.

"The admiral awaits you, Lord Brakal, though your aide must stay in the antechamber. Please follow me."

After indicating where Regar should sit, Kheyl ushered Brakal into an office more substantial than most peasant housing units. An elderly Shrehari male in formal admiral's robes rose from behind a polished stone desk.

Brakal felt more than a bit of shock at Trage's appearance. Compared to how he had looked the last time they met, the commander-in-chief appeared as ancient as a corpse left to dry out in the Karakat desert.

The skin over Trage's skull ridges seemed to have lost its color and taken on the texture of desiccated leather while his neck muscles were nothing more than thin steel cables covered by ancient parchment. Trage's black within black eyes, though still bright were slowly sinking into his skull. But worst of all was the hand he raised in greeting. It reminded Brakal of nothing so much as a dried out *yatakan*'s claw.

"Welcome, Lord of the Makkar."

— Thirteen —

"**E**mergence," Yens called out. "Two freighters, one *Ptar*, one point two million kilometers almost directly ahead." A pause. "Another emergence. Same configuration. One point five million, five degrees to port, eight degrees down."

"Two packets in, three to go." Sirico chortled with delight.

"Correction." Yens nodded at the tactical display. "All five packets came out of FTL ahead of us. Scattered but not too badly. I'm designating the groupings Tangos One through Five. Transmitting designations to *Jan Sobieski*."

Dunmoore, operating on instinct rather than conscious thought, stood, walked over to the three-dimensional projection and reached into it. She touched three enemy icon groupings.

"Ours, starting with the packet labeled Tango One. The others, Tango Four and Tango Five are *Jan Sobieski*'s. Captain Pushkin may decide which will be his first target."

"Acknowledged," Gregor Pushkin replied a few seconds later. "Coordinated jump?"

"Coordinated arrival. Once you've selected your initial target, our navigators—"

"Tango Five."

Dunmoore nodded.

"Tangos One and Five are the first targets. Navigators to sync jumps, so we arrive simultaneously."

"On it, Skipper."

"Us too, sir."

"Good. Thorin, program the missile launchers to fire off a full salvo, one third at each of the Tango One units the moment our systems recover from hyperspace transition. Since we'll be almost at point-blank range, a single flight should be enough to collapse shields. Main guns are to open fire as soon as they acquire targets, again one-third of the barrels on each ship."

"Aye, aye, sir. I'm working on it."

She returned to her command chair and watched video feeds of the oblivious Shrehari convoy packets until Holt's hologram reappeared.

"Navigation is plotted and synced. *Jan Sobieski* will go FTL a few seconds before us. Since both ships are already at battle stations, you can order up systems and jump at your leisure."

"Gregor?"

"Confirmed. We await your command."

"The command is given. Up systems. Start the jump countdown."

Almost immediately, the CIC's status panels lit up as *Iolanthe*'s combat systems came to life. Moments later, the jump klaxon filled Dunmoore's ears with its shrill warning. Thirty seconds to go.

"Any sign of the task force, Chief?"

"Negative, sir. Looks as if we're doing this on our own."

"As we should." Sirico grinned at Dunmoore over his shoulder. "The navy's hottest Q-ship and the first in its newest frigate design working together will turn what might have been a nice day for the boneheads into a demoralizing massacre."

"Perhaps, but them spreading out in packets will make it more challenging for a clean sweep with only two ships. Whoever organized this convoy was thinking."

"Or decided to test a variation on doctrine and got lucky."

Dunmoore's universe twisted itself into a colorful vortex while her stomach made a valiant attempt at escape. Before she could take more than one breath, the vortex spun in the opposite direction, leaving her with an overwhelming urge to vomit. After a few seconds, her senses stabilized, and there they were, clear as day on the optical pickups, seemingly close enough to touch: two armed freighters and a *Ptar* class corvette.

"Missiles away," Sirico announced, voice still sounding faintly strangled by the quick succession of jump and emergence nausea. "I'm opening with main guns."

"Bridge, adjust course to intercept Tango Two. Mister Sirico, target Tango Two the moment our missiles breach Tango One's shields."

"Missile hits on all three targets."

The energy cocoons enveloping the Shrehari vessels surged from green to deep purple in a matter of seconds before they vanished, overwhelmed by the massive release of energy. Almost faster than Dunmoore could process, continuous streams of plasma began eating through armored hulls, creating ever wider black craters. Puffs of crystallized air soon came through numerous breaches.

"They're done for," Sirico said. "I'm targeting missiles on Tango Two."

"Whose *Ptar* is powering up to return the favor," Yens added. "Tango One's *Ptar* is also firing back. More for the honor of the flag than anything else."

A bright light blotted out part of the main display.

"That was the Tango One *Ptar*. Either we hit their launchers just as a brace of birds armed, or we damaged the gun capacitor system. Never gets old, though." Two additional white blossoms joined it before Dunmoore could reply. "Both freighters. Scratch Tango One."

"The Tango Two *Ptar* fired off two dozen missiles." Tiny red icons joined the larger ones in the holographic tactical display. "As did Tango Three's. That should account for at least a third of their loads, if not half. Our second salvo is about to hit Tango Two."

Dunmoore briefly glanced at the defense status board and saw that the Q-ship's ring of anti-missile calliopes was swatting enemy birds away in rapid succession. Two made it through and exploded against her shields, but other than a faint feedback whine, *Iolanthe* shrugged the assault off like the old pro she was.

The Tango Two *Ptar* didn't fare as well. *Iolanthe*'s first missile salvo exploded against its shields almost as one. An observer would miss them cycling from cool green to explosive violet as the generators overloaded if he or she so much as blinked. They popped soundlessly a fraction of a second later, leaving the hapless corvette exposed to the full fury of *Iolanthe*'s large bore main guns. It and the two freighters under its protection didn't last much longer than the Tango One ships.

Sirico let out a ferocious whoop.

"The Furious Faerie's terrible swift sword is as deadly as ever."

"Captain to the bridge. Turn us on an intercept course for Tango Three. Mister Sirico, adjust your fire to the next targets, engage with missiles when ready."

Dunmoore desperately wanted to see how Gregor Pushkin was doing. Though *Jan Sobieski* might be overpowered for a frigate, she still carried nowhere near *Iolanthe*'s weight of ordnance. But her first responsibility was to see her own ship through the engagement.

Chief Petty Officer Day raised his hand.

"The boneheads are shooting off encrypted messages over their emergency subspace channel. Newer code than the latest HQ gave us."

"Missiles away for Tango Three."

"Uh-oh." Yens glanced at Dunmoore. "I'm reading a power spike from the Tango Three ships, sir. Hyperdrives spooling up to jump."

Sirico turned to Yens.

"Without cycling them? Don't they need forty minutes minimum?"

"The senior officer probably decided to risk a Crazy Ivan instead of suffering Tango One and Two's fate, Thorin," Dunmoore said. "This close to Tyva's heliopause, an emergency jump shouldn't throw them that far off or cause extensive structural damage during the transition, unless their drives are badly tuned to begin with. Fire all guns. Let's see if we can interfere with their spool-up."

"Firing now."

"The *Ptar* is engaging our missiles."

Dunmoore's eyes automatically switched to the holographic display where little blue icons were winking out one after the other. Unlike its now-defunct sister ships, the *Ptar* protecting Tango Three enjoyed the benefits of time and distance to successfully thin out the Q-ship's salvo, sparing its packet from a devastating strike.

"Hit on one of Tango Three's freighters." A force field cocoon flared on the main display. "And on the second."

The three ships wavered as their hyperdrives reached full power, though continuous streams of plasma struck each of them, painting their shields with purple auroras. One popped, exposing the freighter's bare hull to *Iolanthe*'s full fury. Almost without thinking, Sirico concentrated every gun that could bear on it.

While the second freighter and the *Ptar* vanished from view as they translated to hyperspace, the packet's third, ill-fated ship wavered convulsively while its engines fought against energy released by the Q-ship's plasma. Then, without warning, the freighter gave birth to a tiny supernova which dissipated almost as quickly as it was born, leaving nothing more than an ever-expanding debris field.

"That's two *Ptars* and five freighters," Sirico said, slumping back into his chair.

"A good haul, Thorin. Well done. Chief, I need to know how *Jan Sobieski* is doing."

"Already on it, Captain," Yens replied. "*Rooikat* just dropped out of FTL."

"Chief Day, send to *Rooikat* — when your drives are cycled, enter the Tyva system, and find that FOB. Deploy recon drones as required. Since the enemy knows we're here, stealth is not necessary beyond normal precautions against detection."

"Aye, aye, sir."

"Captain, it appears *Jan Sobieski* took out Tango Five. I can't find a trace of it. But Tango Four's ships are accelerating away as if the devil was nipping on their heels."

Sirico let out a soft grunt.

"They'll probably try a Crazy Ivan as well once they realize Captain Pushkin won't let go."

"If they escape his ordnance." The main display shifted to show tiny beads of light pursuing three sets of drive nozzles. Yens helpfully outlined the Shrehari ships in red and *Jan Sobieski* in blue. The red outlines abruptly disappeared. "Crazy Ivan it is."

"Still, not bad. Between us, we accounted for ten enemy ships, and our shield generators barely felt the sting of their return fire."

Dunmoore smiled at Sirico.

"The power of tactical surprise, Thorin."

"Sir." Chief Day raised a hand. "*Rooikat* acknowledges. She'll send an FTL recon drone to study the second planet soonest and follow when her drives are ready. Estimated time to departure, twenty-five minutes."

"Thank you. Please link me with Captain Pushkin."

His face swam into focus in front of her moments later.

"Captain!" A broad grin split Pushkin's face. "I hear you accounted for seven enemy ships — two *Ptars* and five freighters. Please pass my congratulations to your gunnery crew."

"You didn't do so badly yourself. Three ships before the rest jumped out on a whim and a prayer."

"I hope the bastards come out of FTL somewhere nasty or better yet, burn up a critical hyperdrive component, leaving them stranded in interstellar space until help arrives. What are your orders?"

Dunmoore shrugged.

"We sit tight until the rest of the task force arrives. There's no point in trying to find the remaining boneheads. If their hyperdrive maintenance was even a bit off, they could be anywhere, and most likely scattered in every direction. I'm sending *Rooikat* to find the FOB. If it's as weakly defended as the one in the Khorsan system, I hope I can convince the admiral we should make it vanish. Losing two bases within a short time, along with a couple of resupply convoys will hit their pride hard."

"Here's hoping the admiral will see it your way. I have enough missiles left for two more heavy engagements."

"I'm a bit better stocked, but since the others didn't expend anything yet on the current battle run, we should be good." She glanced at the tactical display. "We'd best shift to silent running, in case the local strike group shows up before the rest of Luckner."

"Good idea."

"But stay at battle stations."

"That goes without saying. You know, this reminded me a bit of the time *Stingray* ran that convoy into the Cimmeria system before handing Brakal his first major defeat."

She gave him a warm smile.

"It did. Except back then we didn't know where the war was going and whether we'd ever win. I daresay these days, our enemies feel as if they bit off more than they'll ever be able to swallow. And since we both need to hold after-action meetings with our department heads before writing our separate reports for the admiral, as well as our ammunition expenditure reports for the flag captain..." She let her words hang. "Keep a laser link open and when Luckner appears, wait for my word to go up systems."

"Will do, sir. Cheers!"

His image dissolved, leaving her to stare at the tactical display.

"Zeke, after-action review in forty-five minutes. Rig the ship for silent running."

"Aye, aye, sir," the first officer's hologram replied.

— Fourteen —

Trage gestured at the chair in front of his desk. "Sit. You seem to be well, Brakal."

"And you wear the mask of death."

A dismissive gesture.

"Someone with my responsibilities ages faster than others."

Brakal's upper lip curled away from his teeth.

"Especially when you spend half your days explaining to an idiot such as Mishtak that we are losing the damned war he and the other congenital idiots on the governing council started."

"We are *not* losing the war." Trage's clenched fist hit the desktop with a distressingly weak and thoroughly unconvincing smack.

"The humans are operating inside imperial space with impunity and have been doing so for over a turn. Meanwhile, two out of every three raiders we send into their space never returns. If we are not losing the war, then what?" A cruel rictus transformed Brakal's face. "Did you dream up a clever scheme to draw the humans into a trap? Let them gradually penetrate deeper and deeper into our sphere so we may ambush them as they approach the homeworld with a fleet capable of exterminating our race?"

Anger lit up Trage's eyes.

"You forget yourself, Brakal. Even a clan lord who sits in the Kraal cannot address an admiral of the first rank in this manner."

"Bah." Brakal waved away Trage's protest. "I will speak my mind as I see fit. Someone must because it seems most here in the Forbidden Quarter no longer cling to reality. I come from the front lines, Trage. I have been fighting the humans for many turns now and they are not the weak, undisciplined, anarchic primates Mishtak claims. But you see more clearly than he does. Surely you understand that if after so much time we are still far from winning the war, then we are losing it. Perhaps not because of glorious battles but even if it is only through attrition, the humans will, in due course, make paupers of us. And an empire of paupers cannot hold its star systems together for long. The war must end — now. Before Mishtak pushes the empire into a crisis which will topple the dynasty."

"I disagree. So do the council, the regent, and the admirals serving me."

"Only because you dismissed the admirals who experienced defeat at human hands and know final victory is forever beyond our grasp."

A grunt of disbelief escaped Trage's sunken chest.

"Is that what this is about? You being dismissed into the inactive officers' reserve because of failure?"

"No. You did me and the empire a favor. Now I can actually do something more productive than chasing human phantoms between the stars."

"Mishtak and the regent would rather you stay on your estates and leave the conduct of the war in the hands of those not tainted by failure."

"I see. You are warning me off at his orders, no doubt. Why am I not surprised? Mishtak enjoys hiding behind his minions. Surely you know me well enough to understand I do not care what Mishtak and the emperor's mother prefer. I care only about the empire, the ruling dynasty, and their continuing survival."

"Perhaps you should care more about your own survival." Trage's words, intended as menacing, came out in a low hiss followed by convulsive coughing.

"Yours seems in greater question. Are you well?"

When Trage finally recovered, he brushed off Brakal's concern.

"The vicissitudes of old age married to hardship. You were saying you cared about the empire and our ruler? Then do not interfere. Some might consider setting the Kraal against the council during a time of crisis as an act, if not quite of treason, then one of deep disrespect. Perhaps even an attack on the council's honor."

"Take care, Admiral. You step on dangerous ground. The Kraal has always been independent of the council and the emperor. It may act as it wishes in pursuit of the common good."

Suddenly, Brakal felt immensely tired and irritated by Trage and his willingness to let incompetent political creatures such as Mishtak rob him of his honor in return for power and wealth.

"Was there anything else? Or did you invite me merely so you could pass along Mishtak's desire I bugger off into the sunset? If so, please tell that rear echelon fornicator the next time he wishes to threaten me, I shall see his fat arse ushered into *my* presence."

Brakal felt amusement when he saw Trage's already taut leathery skin tighten further at the insults.

"One day, you will go too far. Then Clan Makkar will look for a new lord." Trage waved imperiously at the door. "You may leave."

"See to your health, Admiral." Brakal climbed to his feet. "It would be a shame if you died in office before the war is over. Considering possible successors as commander-in-chief would be even more inept than you are, we might well suffer our greatest losses before the imperial government regains its sanity."

**

Once back in the car's privacy, Brakal recounted his conversation with Trage almost verbatim for Regar and Toralk's benefit.

"It is what we expected," Regar said with a dismissive gesture once Brakal fell silent. "We knew Trage would not offer you a return to active duty as an admiral of any rank. But threatening you, even indirectly, might be evidence Mishtak is worried about the Kraal meeting again after so long and taking him and the council to task for their conduct of the war."

"And so he should be because we will. By the way, I think Trage is dying."

"We are all dying."

Brakal scowled at the *Tai Kan* officer.

"Faster than the rest of us, I mean."

"Infected by the council's moral rot no doubt."

"Where should I take you now, Lord?" Toralk asked. "It is still too early for your meeting with Admiral Edronh."

"We could head directly for the Bloody Lance now and enjoy ourselves," Brakal replied, naming a lower town tavern favored by Deep Space Fleet non-commissioned officers and junior ranks serving at Shredar's military spaceport. "But since we are already here, perhaps I should visit the Kraal's sacred Red Chamber and breathe in its atmosphere at least once before we assemble in the Jakrang instead of the Forbidden Quarter. Take us there."

Toralk guided the Makkar estate car through a grid of avenues and boulevards crossing at perfect right angles until they came to a massive red and gray granite construct on one side of the Forbidden Quarter's central plaza, facing the enclosed imperial palace. A five-level stepped pyramid with a flat roof, the building had been the Kraal's home since time immemorial.

The legislative chamber which took its name from the color of the wall hangings and leather upholstering of four hundred chairs arrayed in a circle around an arena-like speaker's area filled most of the pyramid. Offices for those employed in the Kraal's service occupied the rest.

They stopped by a front door surrounded with carvings of beasts, demons, and gods culled from Shrehari mythology. More fantastic creatures adorned the upper edge of each level, staring down at those who would petition the Kraal.

"Hah." Brakal pointed at a carving as he climbed out of the car. "That is precisely Trage's appearance nowadays."

Regar glanced up and squinted.

"An imp of the Death Bringer? Not entirely inappropriate considering the Deep Space Fleet's growing losses."

Massive bronze doors, each leaf bearing the imperial dragon, silently drew aside at their approach, revealing an elderly Shrehari male in simple dark robes. He bowed his head at the neck.

"Brakal of the Makkar. Welcome to your house and home, honored noble of the four hundred clan lords who make up the Kraal. May your great family's banner forever hang from the Red Chamber's rafters. I am Gvant, Chief Keeper of the Kraal's Records."

Brakal returned the man's bow.

"Well met, Gvant. Your courtesy does you honor."

They stepped into a vast, high-ceilinged, but short corridor adorned with ancient images of long-forgotten battles.

"The north wind brings rumors, Lord Brakal. They say you intend to summon the four hundred and see them sit in the Kraal for the first time in many turns. If so, may I say this is not before time?"

"That is indeed my intent."

"Then what may my staff and I do to bring about this felicitous occasion?"

"Help me with matters of protocol and do what is necessary so the Kraal may legally meet in the Jakrang instead of here."

Gvant's face froze in an expression of disbelief.

"The Jakrang?" But before Brakal could speak, his features regained their mobility and took on a thoughtful air. "May I assume you believe summoning the four hundred to the Red Chamber would entail peril? Not because it is the Red Chamber but because this place is within the Forbidden Quarter?"

Brakal inclined his massive head by way of acknowledgment.

"Your assumptions are correct, Gvant. I must make sure the Kraal assembles in peace, far from forces that might interfere with its ancient rights. Here, within these walls, the council's writ is law. And it has a full *Tai Kan* regiment, if not more, to enforce its will. Out there," Brakal waved at the hallway's polished stone walls, "those who respect the Kraal's freedom can watch over our safety with troops sworn to the empire, not the council."

Gvant bowed again.

"I understand, Lord Brakal, and will assist in any way possible so the Kraal may assemble in the Jakrang. Mishtak's council has ruled for too long with no oversight by those whose interest in the empire's welfare runs deeper than that of politicians because they understand blood and tradition. Since the Kraal has not met in over six turns and you are the first of the four hundred to call it up, the honor of speaker is yours until it elects one. Should you wish it, of course."

Brakal bared his fangs.

"I wish it."

"So I shall write it in the records. When will you stand before the Kraal?"

"In one full change of the moons. Let the exact date be given once every one of the four hundred acknowledges their duty to attend."

"A wise choice. Since we Keepers of the Records act on the speaker's behalf, rest assured we will prepare that which needs preparing. Give us the final time and day, and we will turn the Jakrang into an open-air version of the Red Chamber. In the meantime, I am at your disposal for any matter of procedure and protocol."

"Then I will avail myself of your knowledge. But at this moment, I would breathe in the Red Chamber's atmosphere."

"Certainly." Gvant gestured toward a massive set of carved doors dominating the short corridor. "If you would follow me, Lord Brakal."

**

"I feel satisfyingly refreshed," Brakal said with an air of contentment as he climbed into the car. "Though I entered the Red Chamber before as a spectator, this was my first time as a member, and for some mystical reason, the ghosts of those clan lords who sat and deliberated in there over the ages spoke to my soul. It was as if they approved of my quest."

"Then they would be the only beings, living or dead, within the Forbidden Quarter's walls who do so," Regar replied, settling across from Brakal in the passenger compartment. His lips curled up in a smile. "Present company excepted."

"There are more, though they do not know it yet. Take us to the Bloody Lance, Toralk. Admiral Edronh will soon make his way there to meet me."

"One question. Why did you tell Gvant you would call the Kraal together in one full change of the moons? I thought you wished to do so the instant you found enough supporters. Misdirection?"

"Precisely. If I can assemble the four hundred in under a full change, I will take my enemies by surprise. You are not the only one with a devious mind, Regar."

"It pleases me to hear you say so."

A mass of gray clouds moved in as they left the Forbidden Quarter and headed for Shredar's lower town, occluding the afternoon sun. The city, never particularly cheerful to behold in the first place, at least in Brakal's eyes, took on a patina of impending gloom even though sunset was still hours away. He noticed Regar staring intently through the rear window and frowned.

"A problem?"

"Perhaps. If I were as paranoid as Mishtak is surely becoming, I would put a *Tai Kan* spy on your tail. One in a vehicle capable of keeping pace with yours."

"And?"

"Nothing catches my eye yet, but we are still in a more salubrious part of the city."

They rode on in silence while Toralk tackled ever narrower streets, dodging refuse piles spilling into the roadway and negotiating blind corners with more verve than Brakal preferred.   He finally stopped near a rundown, two-story stone building that had been old well before the first Shrehari left their home system aboard crude otherspace ships.

A sign depicting an armored, lance-wielding Shrehari hunter from a bygone era impaling an impossibly large *jakarl*, one of Shrehari Prime's most feared predators, hung above a wooden door polished to a deep black over hundreds of turns.

Regar jumped out into the street before Brakal could move, quickly joined by Toralk, so both could scan the immediate area for threats.   When none seemed apparent, the *Tai Kan* officer gestured at his superior to exit on the tavern side, using the car as protection while he entered the establishment.

But the moment Brakal climbed out and stretched to his full height, a muffled crack reached their ears, followed by the sound of metal striking granite less than one hand span above Brakal's head. Small, sharp pieces of stone struck his skull, drawing a muffled curse. He ducked, but no second shot followed the first. Toralk and Regar, guns drawn, took shelter beside him, eyes searching for the shooter.

"Electromagnetic sniper weapon," the latter said. "That was meant as a warning shot. Considering the limited sightlines in this area, an expert would not have missed at such short-range, and common thugs do not use EM guns.'"

"If you are correct, then how would they know to watch this place?" Brakal asked.

"Either Admiral Edronh or someone in his employ betrayed you."

"It cannot be Edronh. He hates Mishtak with the same passion as I do, and he holds the same grievances against both Trage and the council."

"Then you better warn him he has a traitor in his house." Regar holstered his weapon and straightened his back. "I think it is safe to proceed."

— Fifteen —

"A *Tai Kan* spy in my retinue?" Rumbling laughter escaped Admiral Edronh's throat. "You are a strange one, Brakal. Why blame one of mine for allowing those motherless turds to send you a warning via sniper when there is an actual *Tai Kan* officer in your retinue."

Edronh, a middle-aged Shrehari cast from the same mold as Brakal, eyed his colleague with amusement.

"Yet it must be so. On my side, only Toralk, Regar, and I knew about this meeting. Toralk would sooner kill himself than betray me, and I peered into Regar's soul long ago. His oath to me as Lord of Clan Makkar is unbreakable. And since I cannot conceive of you embracing the *Tai Kan*, it means one of yours betrayed this meeting to his true masters."

A thoughtful expression replaced Edronh's mirth.

"If you can answer for your people, then I shall examine mine. Unfortunately, that may not be easy. I made no secret of my destination nor the fact I was meeting you since the idea we of the four hundred might be targeted simply for speaking with each other is inconceivable."

"Someone conceived of it."

"Evidently. But they forget we are made of sterner stuff. Besides, if I harbored any doubts about supporting you before I heard of your encounter with a sniper, they would be gone this very moment, wiped away by anger at such unmitigated gall."

"Then you are with us."

"Of course. Did you ever believe otherwise? Though the idea of asking those damned humans for an armistice pains me, I can think of no other way to staunch the bleeding. Not when Trage is replacing front line senior leaders at an increasingly rapid rate." Edronh took a healthy swig of his ale. "What happens next?"

"Getting those Kraal members who were dismissed by Trage to join us is the easy part. We know in our bones that victory is forever out of reach. However, convincing members who either never served in the Imperial Armed Forces or retired before the war will not be quite as simple. They hear only what Mishtak and his tame *kroorath* whelps deign to tell citizens of the empire and believe our final triumph over the cowardly humans requires just one more successful battle."

Edronh let out a disconsolate grunt.

"Cowardly humans indeed. Whoever sold us that myth deserves decapitation with a rusty ax, one wielded by the most inept low caste butcher."

"Sold us? You mean sold it to the council and the regent. They decided a short, decisive war was just the thing to consolidate their power after the old emperor died." Brakal waved the sidebar away with an irritated gesture. "No matter. We can punish the guilty once we remove Mishtak. Who among those not aware of the true situation do you think you can convince?"

After a few moments of thought, Edronh gave Brakal half a dozen names.

"I cannot promise they will listen and accept a distasteful truth, but at the very least, I will give them reasons for doubting the official story."

"Good. Ask those who accept the truth if they would open doors for us so we may convince others who never fought the humans. I need a majority in favor of forcing the council's hand on the first vote. It will send a message the regent, Mishtak, and Trage cannot possibly misinterpret. We must do everything we can to remove the council without bloodshed."

"But you will spill blood if necessary?"

Brakal allowed himself a fierce rictus.

"Spilling the blood of politicians so I may save military lives has always been a particular fantasy of mine, but it is best if we do not set a precedent for violent regime change."

"Agreed." Edronh drained his mug. "If that was everything, I will find out who sold his soul to the *Tai Kan* before I call on our Kraal colleagues."

"It was." Brakal climbed to his feet. "I will summon the Kraal into session at short notice, so be ready."

"I live in a constant state of readiness, as is required of all good Shrehari warriors."

**

Brakal and his retainers reached Clan Makkar's Shredar estate without further incident, but as they passed through the main gate and entered the walled-in compound, Regar turned to Brakal.

"If I can offer a suggestion, Lord. Conduct further meetings in more refined surroundings, where would-be *Tai Kan* assassins will find less scope to send messages or make a kill. Everyone in this poxed city knows of your intentions by now, making any attempt at discretion futile. Be as open as you dare. That way, should anything happen to you or other Kraal members, it will only further discredit Mishtak in the eyes of the four hundred and make regime change even more imperative."

"That was my intent. I am pleased my thoughts match those of my tame spy."

Regar curled up his lip.

"Tame? Hardly. I merely placed my not inconsiderable skills and ruthlessness at your service for the rest of my natural life."

As the car came to a halt on the inner courtyard's flagstones, Anag appeared in one of the doorways and watched them climb out.

"Lord. A visitor awaits you."

"I see no car."

Anag pointed up. "Aircar. It sits on the pad."

"Ah."

Long before aircars were invented, wealthy families owned vertical takeoff aircraft, and one of his ancestors ordered a special pad built behind the main building. It saw infrequent use these days, primarily because aircar travel over the capital was restricted, though Anag used the estate's to travel between the Shredar mansion and the clan's properties in the hinterland.

"Did this visitor give a name? Or is he a phantom, known only by the marks he leaves behind?"

"She."

Brakal ignored Regar's smirk.

"Who?"

"She who asked no names be used."

"And you let a nameless female into the house even though you knew I was making fresh enemies with every breath I took?"

Anag, clearly unrepentant, made a gesture of assent.

"Meet her, and everything will become clear, Lord. She is in the formal reception room. I offered her the clan lord's hospitality, but she declined any refreshments."

"Now *that* intrigues me." Brakal glanced over his shoulder at Regar.

"Shall I accompany you?" The latter asked.

"Watch from the security room. Unnamed females rarely wish to speak with anyone but the lord."

Regar noted from Brakal's expression he had an idea, perhaps not of the visitor's actual identity, but of who she represented and so he inclined his head, acknowledging the order.

When Brakal entered the reception room, an ornately furnished space overlooking the estate's garden, a tall, slender figure in exquisitely tailored robes turned away from the window to face him. Though she wore gloves, a shimmering head cover, and a full-face veil, making it impossible to get even a glimpse of skin, her voice, although husky, was unmistakably female.

"Lord Brakal. Thank you for allowing me into your home."

He raised both hands in a formal gesture of welcome.

"I am honored by your presence, Lady. How may I serve you?"

"First, please accept my thanks for respecting my anonymity. I commend your retainers for their courtesy."

An amused smile twisted Brakal's face.

"The Lords of Clan Makkar employ some of the finest specimens of our race. Many of them are retired from the Imperial Armed Forces and know how to conduct themselves."

"Surely in large part because of the example you set, Lord Brakal."

"You are much too gracious."

He fought off a sudden surge of impatience. If this lady came from the court, she would expect him to observe the usual forms, replete with endless expressions of mutual admiration.

"I merely act the way any loyal admiral of the empire would."

"As befits your reputation for upholding the honor of the Deep Space Fleet and Clan Makkar."

Brakal acknowledged her compliment with a proper, courtly bow.

"Shall we sit?" He gestured at overstuffed leather chairs.

"Thank you, but since my time here will be brief, I shall remain standing."

"In that case, I am listening. Please go ahead."

"My mistress, who must stay as nameless as myself, understands you will convene the Kraal after many turns of dormancy so it may take the governing council to task over its handling of the war against the humans."

"That is indeed my purpose. The Kraal has shirked its responsibilities for too long while military personnel of both the Shrehari and subject races are dying for no visible gains. In the meantime, our treasury is being drained with no end in sight, and our people groan under the ever-increasing weight of taxation. I fear the council does not know how to extricate itself from the mess it created by invading human space and will keep making the same mistakes until our suffering passes the point of no return. Should that dire event occur, it might make the last dynastic change, during which our current emperor's lineage ascended the throne, resemble a peaceful, routine change of government."

After a brief pause, she said, "Perhaps. However, my mistress fears the Kraal challenging Mishtak and the council will bring about grave political instability at a time when we must join together and focus on forcing the humans to submit."

Bitter laughter rumbled up Brakal's massive chest.

"Forcing the humans to submit? With the greatest of respect, your mistress must stop drinking from the same poisoned chalice as Mishtak. I come from the war, as do many of the Kraal lords. We not only will never force the humans to submit, but at the current rate of attrition in both ships and crews, *we* will submit to the humans on terms your mistress might find onerous."

The mysterious visitor seemed taken aback.

"You should be careful with your words, Lord Brakal. Some might call you a defeatist, and then where will the Kraal be with one of its leading members surrounded by the stench of treason?"

"Is seeing clearly and speaking truthfully considered treason when my goal is ending madness before it destroys the dynasty and perhaps even the empire? Surely your mistress can appreciate the risks of succumbing to political unrest if the emperor's subjects feel he and his regent did not uphold our race's honor against an alien foe."

"The emperor is but a child."

"Nevertheless, he embodies the empire. The Shrehari entrust him with the preservation of their collective honor as a people, even though it is the council under Mishtak's misrule who is at fault. Perhaps your mistress should speak with admirals freshly back from the war zone. They would easily refute the council's propaganda. We cannot win the war. But the empire can still lose it."

Another prolonged pause, then, "Be that as it may. My mistress would rather not witness the Kraal acting against Mishtak and the council. Assemble it by all means. That is your ancient right. Deliberate and vote. But for the empire's sake align Kraal and council, so they present a common front. Do not start a civil war among the noblest branches of our government."

"And if I disregard your mistress' wishes?"

"Then she cannot answer for your continued standing as a Lord of the Empire."

Brakal tilted his head to one side as he tried to stare through his visitor's veil.

"She plays a dangerous game. Perhaps you might encourage her to stay above politics and let events unfold as they must. For the good of the empire. Dynasties were overthrown for lesser reasons than the crisis we will face if we do not end this war."

"Threats, Lord Brakal?" Her voice took on a menacing edge.

"Truth. The enemy is pressing his forces into our sphere and what does Mishtak's tame *kroorath* Trage do? He replaces battle-tested leaders with political sycophants who do not even understand the humans are a species more cunning and adaptable than we ever expected. Another turn, perhaps two, and they will feel bold enough for raids against the homeworld itself. Your mistress surely understands the political consequences of such a development. Tell her from me I will support the dynasty and do everything to keep its rule intact. But she must stay aloof and let Mishtak face the consequences of his fecklessness. If she openly takes the council's side, I cannot guarantee the child emperor will ascend the throne upon his majority.

"And if your mistress or those in her entourage think my death will stop the Kraal from challenging Mishtak, rest assured the events I put in motion can only be stopped by killing every single one of the four hundred. And that *would* mean the end of the dynasty, in an orgy of fire and blood not seen on the homeworld in more generations than the historical records remember."

"I can see your beliefs are indeed passionately held, Lord Brakal. So be it. I have said my piece and heard your response."

"In that case, Lady, unless there was something else, perhaps I can accompany you back to the landing pad. Consider my words and do your mistress a favor by repeating them to her without alterations."

When the visitor vanished into the unmarked aircar, Regar came through the mansion's rear door and joined Brakal. They watched in silence as it lifted off and disappeared over the main building's steep roof, headed toward Shredar and, as Brakal suspected, the Forbidden Quarter.

"Could we be facing problems, Lord?" The *Tai Kan* officer asked.

Brakal made a dismissive gesture.

"Us? No. But I think I gave our regent something to ponder."

"Regent?" A look of surprise came over Regar's angular features. "You mean—"

"No, it was not she, but one of her handmaidens. Probably the principal companion, Adjur of Clan Ruktah. She would hide her face since she accompanies her lady to formal events and is well known. The other handmaidens are rarely seen and could pass as anything they wish beyond the gates of the palace."

"Indeed. Let us hope Adjur whispers your exact words into her mistress' ear."

"I worry not so much about her skills as a messenger, but that Lady Kembri understands her position. And what siding publicly with Mishtak and the council might mean for Tumek's chances of ascending the imperial throne when he comes of age."

— Sixteen —

"**C**aptain Dunmoore." Rear Admiral Kell Petras inclined his head in greeting when the laser link between *Iolanthe* and *Hawkwood* stabilized. Dunmoore sat behind the desk in her day cabin, while Holt occupied a chair beyond the video pickup's range.

"Sir. I'm pleased to announce we put paid to ten of the convoy's fifteen ships. Three *Ptars* and seven freighters. The surviving five jumped into hyperspace without fully cycling their drives, which means they could be anywhere, or even nowhere, depending on how badly tuned the drives were."

"I see. And if you'd waited until we arrived?"

"The convoy would be halfway to the FOB by now. We struck them five hours and forty minutes ago, shortly after they dropped out of FTL. If we'd waited for the rest of the task force, those fifteen enemy ships would have jumped out three-quarters of an hour after arriving. No matter how hard we might have pushed our pursuit, they'd have been sitting under the orbital bases' guns by the time we caught up. Granted, if the FOB is of the same build as the one we destroyed in the Khorsan system, we would probably have been able to take it and the entire convoy out. But we don't know what's waiting for us over there. Yet."

"Yet?" Petras' thick eyebrows crept up.

"I dispatched *Rooikat* to reconnoiter the FOB. We should know more about it in a few hours."

Petras didn't immediately reply, though his eyes slid to one side as if he were glancing at Lena Corto sitting in a corner beyond his day cabin's video pickup range.

"Why?"

"Perhaps it will be similar to the one in the Khorsan system, sir. A wartime construct with no more ordnance than that carried by a pair of *Tol* class cruisers."

"Let me ask you a hypothetical question, Captain. If *Rooikat* sends back evidence the Tyva FOB and its situation are a match for what you found in the Khorsan system, and I wasn't here yet with the rest of the task force, what would you have done?"

She replied without a moment's hesitation.

"Waited for your arrival and your decision whether or not we attack it."

Petras studied her in silence for what seemed like a long time.

"Really?"

"Sir, *Iolanthe* was on detached duty in the Khorsan system. Today, we're part of the Task Force Luckner wolf pack, and that means conforming to your plans."

Another pause.

"I do believe you meant what you just said. Good."

"Sir, if the Tyva FOB presents a target of opportunity, may I suggest we attack it? Losing two bases on top of finding their supply convoys mauled will hit Shrehari pride in the gut. And a wounded enemy will make mistakes we can exploit."

"We will discuss the matter once *Rooikat* tells us what we face. I assume you and Captain Pushkin prepared the usual after-action reports."

"Yes, sir. And ammunition expenditure reports. You should receive them momentarily. Both of us can handle two more heavy engagements before our missile magazines run dry. Or perhaps one attack on that FOB, if we opt for a saturation strike."

Petras rubbed his chin, eyes sliding to one side again.

"Which would mean heading for the nearest base to resupply. I'd hoped we might stay out longer than this."

"Perhaps *Iolanthe* and *Jan Sobieski* could hang back and let the others deal with the FOB's shields. Once they're down, our guns can give it the mercy stroke."

"As I said, let's wait until we know more. The resident strike group might be in orbit, which would shift the odds against us. We're commerce raiders, not a battle group which can seek out the enemy's combat forces and destroy them."

"Of course, sir. But *Iolanthe* is a battlecruiser under the disguise, and we can take on two *Tol* class cruisers simultaneously."

"I know. However, let's not try and prove it unless necessary. The Shrehari can churn out *Tols* at will, but there is only one Q-ship such as yours in the entire known galaxy. I'd rather let *Tol* class cruisers go than risk losing *Iolanthe* to battle damage."

"Understood. For what it's worth, sir, I agree with your sentiment. I've become rather fond of the Furious Faerie, and I'd rather not sacrifice her in a forlorn hope. If the Tyva FOB is too tough a nut to crack, I'll be the first who says so."

Petras dipped his head in acknowledgment.

"We will speak again soon. In the meantime, I'll digest your and Captain Pushkin's reports. Flag, out."

"That went better than expected," Holt said, stretching as he stood. "Though I wonder whether the poor admiral is getting an earful from Lena right now. Judging by his shifty eyes, she wasn't giving him signs of eternal happiness. Truth is, some days I wonder who's running this task force. Good old Kell or our beloved Lena Corto."

"We probably shouldn't speculate, Zeke. Ours not to reason why and whatnot."

"True. The real test will be if *Rooikat* comes back with images of a forlorn FOB ready for the picking. But instead of pouncing, we receive orders taking us back to Atsang and another attempt at making the wolf pack work in space as well as it did in Earth's Atlantic Ocean. But once again without hoisting in the actual lessons from history."

"Don't be so harsh. I'd say this last attempt was an unqualified success. Did you bother checking the statistics from those days? Wolf packs never sunk an entire convoy. A good percentage of merchant ships and escorts always made it to port. Yet they successfully interfered with their opponents' war effort for years, which prolonged the conflict."

"Sure but at what cost, considering how many of those submersible crews never saw home again?"

She smirked at him.

"One which I won't pay, whether we're on detached duty or under the admiral's keen eye. If *Rooikat*'s scans show Tyva well defended, I'll gladly vote we choose another target."

"Last time I checked, the navy wasn't a democracy. The only person who gets a vote around here wears two stars on his collar."

"Also true." Dunmoore climbed to her feet. "And since we won't know for a few hours what that vote will be, I'll grab a plate of something hot in the wardroom, then hit the gym. I've spent entirely too much time in the CIC command chair lately."

**

"*Rooikat* is cruising along the Tyva hyperlimit under silent running right now and transmitting in real-time," Captain Lena Corto announced when Petras gave her the nod.

As usual, apart from Petras and Corto, only *Hawkwood*'s captain was sitting at the conference table in person. The other starship commanders took part via hologram over laser comlinks. The main display across from Petras showed the image of an artificial construct orbiting a reddish, dusty-looking planet.

"No different from the other one," Dunmoore said. "Modular, seemingly thrown together without care for esthetics, and judging by its apparent size, probably no better armed."

Corto turned her icy stare on Dunmoore's hologram.

"Indeed. Its emissions signature is congruent with the signature you and *Fennec* picked up from the Khorsan system FOB. Unfortunately..." She let her words die away as a pair of warships came into view. "At least part of the local strike group is home. A *Tol* class cruiser and a *Ptar* class corvette. There may be more running silent elsewhere in the system, but *Rooikat* picked up only those two in Tyva's immediate vicinity. She paid particular attention to the planet's Lagrangian points and those of its three moons since Captain Dunmoore believes they may have adopted our trick of ambushing any would-be intruders."

Dunmoore successfully stopped herself from uttering a scornful reply to the effect there was no 'may' about it, though she met Corto's gaze with eyes that spoke volumes.

"There are no signs as yet of the surviving ships from the convoy," Corto continued. "Though they may be inbound to Tyva as we speak, which would give the local commander two more corvettes, at least until they leave for Atsang."

In other words, Dunmoore thought, Lena isn't keen on entering the star system, let alone destroying FOB Tyva. No doubt she and Petras had a frank discussion behind closed doors shortly after *Rooikat* opened a subspace channel and sent back images and readings of the Shrehari orbital station.

"One *Tol* and one *Ptar* aren't much against the full strength of our task force," Commander Farren Vento of the Type 330 frigate *Narses* said. "Not if that FOB is a near copy of the one *Iolanthe* destroyed. Especially if we can sneak in and catch them napping. The multiplier effect of forcing the enemy further back into his own space for resupply by taking out these FOBs is worth the price of admission."

"And hitting the boneheads where it really hurts — their damnable pride and sense of honor," Commander Chandra Clar captain of the task force's other Type 330 frigate, *Belisarius*, added. "The admiral based out of Khorsan probably found himself on his boss' shit list, as will the one who owns this FOB if we pull an *Iolanthe* on it. Maybe even removed from command. And whoever's in charge of this sector could find himself under fire from the imperial high command to boot. Anything we can do to cause trouble for their higher ranks will only help the war effort."

Most of the other captains, including *Hawkwood*'s Kirti Midura, nodded. Dunmoore and Pushkin were the only exceptions. Neither wanted to appear as if they were pushing for a particular outcome, even though both agreed attacking FOB Tyva was the right course of action. Dunmoore especially didn't want a clash with Corto in front of the admiral over this decision, lest it push Petras into siding with his flag captain who seemed distinctly unhappy at the possibility he might accept Dunmoore's suggestion.

"We could head for the hyperlimit in packets of two or three ships, which would minimize the hyperspace signature while timing jumps so we emerge in roughly the same area at the same time," Vento suggested. "Stay in silent running until we're within effective weapons range, or they mark us with their sensors, make one pass while we throw everything at them, then head for the hyperlimit and jump out. It seems almost too easy, Admiral."

He grinned at Dunmoore.

"We can't let *Iolanthe* hog every bit of glory."

"I never figured you for a glory hound, Commander," Corto said in a cold voice.

Dunmoore winced inwardly at the unwarranted barb. Vento's fellow frigate and destroyer captains weren't quite as restrained. Even Pushkin gave Corto a look that questioned her common sense. An admiral making a comment of the sort in public might be considered overly critical, but within his prerogative as formation commander. A staff officer doing the same to a starship captain put her in a select category, one where she would find no friends or even comrades in arms, even though she outranked said starship captain.

Petras must have sensed the sudden change in mood caused by Corto's unwarranted sarcasm. He raised his right hand.

"Having been a frigate captain myself, I can well understand Farren's urge to hit the enemy where it hurts.

And I feel the same way. Captains Dunmoore and Pushkin scored their kills a few hours ago. Perhaps the rest of Task Force Luckner should now hit the enemy where, as Chandra so eloquently pointed out, it hurts the most."

Dunmoore and her former first officer exchanged surprised glances. Did Corto's misplaced words tip the balance in favor of an attack? If so, what did it mean for the flag captain's continuing effectiveness as Petras' chief of staff? And for the task force's future?

"You'll receive your orders within the hour. Thank you."

— Seventeen —

"I'm getting a strange sense of déja vu all over again," Lieutenant Commander Sirico said in a stage whisper once *Iolanthe*'s visual sensors locked onto FOB Tyva. Nothing had changed during Task Force Luckner's jump inward from the heliopause. Only two black, wedge-shaped starships were in orbit around the dusty reddish planet, one larger than the other, both trailing the station by a few kilometers.

"Except for the *Tol* and its little brother," Chief Yens replied. "Still no evidence they saw us come out of FTL. You'd think after what we pulled on that other station, they'd be watching their hyperlimit more closely, especially since the convoy sent a warning out."

"Or they're watching, but we were lucky. Space is vast, and their sensors just aren't terribly good compared to ours."

"Can you see the rest of the task force, Chief?" Dunmoore asked.

"Right now, only *Jan Sobieski*, because I knew where to look. She kept perfect station on us. Wait one."

Yens paused as she studied new information on her readout. Moments later, blue icons came to life inside the tactical projection, each accompanied by a name tag.

"Okay. That accounts for every ship. And not because their silent running is deficient in one way or another, but again, they're pretty much where Lieutenant Drost expected them based on the common navigation plot."

Dunmoore left her command chair and studied the tactical projection up close. At its heart, the planet, trailed by three red icons, shone malevolently. Task Force Luckner's well planned and exquisitely timed approach placed the frigates *Belisarius* and *Narses* in the van. They carried the most extensive stocks of missiles and would saturate the three targets from optimal firing range — provided the Shrehari didn't detect them first.

The destroyers *Tamurlane* and *Hawkwood* followed the frigates and would also open fire as they entered optimal range. *Iolanthe* and *Jan Sobieski* were last in the order of march and would take care of the gun engagement once enemy shields were breached. Not only because their missile stocks were lowest, but because they carried the most massive plasma weapons in Task Force Luckner. Both scouts and the armed transport would remain at the hyperlimit, their sensors alert for new enemy units appearing unexpectedly.

Admiral Petras' plan possessed the one characteristic Dunmoore prized above others — simplicity. Simple plans stood a higher chance of surviving contact with the enemy in one form or another. And it was the sort of scheme which, once launched, wouldn't find itself under constant adjustment by a nervous commander or his even more skittish flag captain.

This was to be a raid. One pass by Luckner's six fighting ships pouring out everything they could on targets that were stuck in orbit — at least until the enemy ships got underway — then back to the hyperlimit at maximum acceleration. They either destroyed the station and both ships during that single pass, or they didn't.

Yet it depended on keeping the element of surprise, and that meant remaining undetected until the last moment. Easy with a single ship built for stealth and crewed by unconventional spacers. Not quite as simple with six, especially when four were older models, more prone to leak radiation that might attract an alert enemy sensor technician.

With *Iolanthe* and indeed the entire task force at battle stations, nothing remained but waiting until one side or the other fired the first missile. Which might not happen for a few hours. Rather than brood in the CIC, Dunmoore turned to Sirico.

"You have the chair, Thorin. I'll be in my day cabin wading through the never-ending stream of naval administrivia."

He grinned at his captain, knowing she was retreating into her sanctum so she could fret alone rather than fret where her crew might notice.

"I have the CIC, sir. Slay a few bureaucratic dragons for the rest of us."

Moments after entering her day cabin, the door chime pealed.

"Yes?"

Ezekiel Holt stuck his head through the opening.

"Coffee and a few rounds of chess, Skipper?"

"How is it you always know when to keep me busy, so I don't annoy everyone else with my impatience?"

"A roguishly bearded CIC birdie sang a song that reached the bridge. Since I'm the only one aboard who can legitimately keep you penned in while we creep up on the enemy..."

Holt entered and headed for the urn. He drew two full mugs, gave one to Dunmoore, and reached for the mahogany chess set sitting on a sideboard.

"I'll even give you white."

"Not a chance, Zeke. I'll take black, thank you very much. One of us needs every advantage possible."

As he placed the sculpted chessmen into position, Holt said, "Perhaps we should make you and your nemesis Brakal face each other over one of our chessboards and one of whatever they play to annoy hapless first officers. Whoever wins both games wins the war."

Dunmoore exhaled noisily.

"Would that it could be so easy. We might save many lives on both sides. If I recall correctly, the Shrehari have a strategy board game similar to our Go. Whether I could beat him at that is highly questionable, but when it comes to chess... If I can take you two games out of three, and you're one of the smartest officers around, I don't see how Brakal would stand a chance."

"I'll take the compliment, Skipper, but nowadays it's four games out of seven. I am improving, as you perhaps noticed." Holt moved a pawn. "Much of that is me getting better at picking up your tells because I know you so well. Brakal, on the other hand, wouldn't stand a chance. We humans are inscrutable, and you're more inscrutable than most to anyone other than me — *when* you put your mind to it."

"Tells? Are we playing chess or poker?" When Holt opened his mouth to reply, Dunmoore raised a hand. "Never mind. I don't think I want to hear it."

She picked up one of her pawns.

"I'll take your king in twenty moves."

"Promises, promises."

**

"Either they're truly not seeing us or the bastards are playing dumb, so they can lure us into effective engagement range, because my sensors aren't picking up a damned thing."

"If they spotted us and are playing dumb, you'd think they might power up that *Tol* and its companion, Chief," Sirico replied. "But as you just said, your scans show otherwise."

"Those sneaky boneheads are as quick as us when it's time to wake up and nuke the enemy."

The CIC door whooshed open, admitting Siobhan Dunmoore. Sirico climbed out of the command chair and made for his station.

"Still all quiet on the Tyva front, Captain. *Belisarius* and *Narses* are five minutes from beginning their battle run."

"Oops." Yens raised a hand. "Spoke too soon. I just picked up a power surge from the station. They're actively scanning. Maybe one of the sensor techs saw a ghost he found suspicious." A pause. "They raised shields. The *Tol* and the *Ptar* are also giving off heightened emissions — sensors and shields as well."

"We're not being directly pinged, nor are any of the task force ships going active." Sirico glanced at Dunmoore over his shoulder.

"Yet." She dropped into her command chair and studied first the tactical projection, then the visuals of Tyva and the two Shrehari warships. "If Chief Yens is right, let's hope the nervous sensor tech's officer will wait and see whether the ghosts dissipate instead of calling battle stations and possibly piss off his CO by disturbing everybody for no good reason. We only need four more minutes."

Sirico shrugged.

"The 330s are already within effective engagement range, so the boneheads will shortly swallow a lot of missiles. But yeah, giving them less time to swat our birds away would be a fine thing."

A minute passed in silence, though the tension was palpable. Then another. Dunmoore forcibly stopped her fingers from dancing on the command chair's arm more than once as she willed *Belisarius* and *Narses* on.

She hadn't played a supporting role in a long time — ever since the battle that eventually wrecked the corvette *Shenzen* — and she found waiting for events to unfold rather difficult. But Petras' plan was sound, and *Iolanthe* would do her part in the overall dance of death even if it wasn't during the opening movements.

"The 330s just lit their systems."

"Two minutes early. The boneheads probably pinged them."

Dunmoore and the CIC crew watched with morbid fascination as volley after volley of anti-ship missiles erupted from both frigates' launchers, their drives painting streaks of light across the star-speckled background. For a few moments, she wondered whether the Shrehari would react fast enough to erode the saturation strike aimed down their throats. Then, gouts of plasma fire from Tyva station's multi-barrel calliopes rose to meet the missile flights. The two warships trailing it joined in seconds later.

Warheads exploded mid-flight, but there were more of them than the calliopes could handle. Many came through the defensive fire unscathed and detonated against the Shrehari shields, turning them into ethereal purplish-blue cocoons crackling with energy.

One final volley, as per plan, and the frigates accelerated at full power to slingshot around Tyva and back to the hyperlimit, pursued by a comparatively anemic enemy missile salvo which wouldn't do much more than give the fire control AIs some practice.

Would the Shrehari think *Belisarius* and *Narses* were the only raiders, Dunmoore wondered, or would they look for follow-on attackers? As soon as the thought crossed her mind, it became a moot point.

"The destroyers are active," Yens reported. "And the *Ptar* lost half of its shields. It's rolling on the main axis to present the undamaged side."

"I'd love to be the officer of the watch on that station," Sirico remarked to no one in particular.

"Whoever he is, there's nothing wrong with the duty crew's reflexes, sir. The station launched missiles at the destroyers. I'm counting thirty. No, make that forty-five. The *Tol* is firing its own load. Twelve. Eighteen. Twenty-four."

"Let's hope their stocks are low and we took out the resupply when we wrecked that convoy."

"And another volley of thirty from the station as well as fifteen from the *Tol*. Both *Tamurlane* and *Hawkwood* are firing their missiles."

This time, defensive plasma streams rose from both the attackers' and defenders' calliopes in an attempt to destroy as many warheads as possible before they could go off. But inevitably, a small percentage made it through, and the station's shields flared up with a deep purplish glow that signaled imminent overload. The destroyers fired two more volleys, but their own shields took on a menacing hue as they fought off the energy generated by exploding warheads.

"Wake up," Dunmoore muttered, "time to kick on those sublight drives and accelerate out, people. Three salvos, that's it. Gregor and I will take it from here."

The station's shields seemed to pop soundlessly as their generators lost the battle, exposing its hull to the full fury of the destroyers' guns. But instead of following the frigates out of engagement range so *Iolanthe* and *Jan Sobieski* could deliver the death blow, both *Tamurlane* and *Hawkwood* kept firing, even though they were taking enemy hits in return. And the Shrehari seemed determined to go down fighting, as usual.

Iolanthe's crew watched in horror as *Hawkwood*'s shields wavered and buckled under the onslaught, before the portside generators gave up and quit, leaving the destroyer's flank open to both the station's and the *Tol*'s guns. *Hawkwood* turned one hundred and eighty degrees on her long axis to present the intact starboard shields, but not before enemy plasma dug divots into her hull. Moments later, *Tamurlane*'s port shields flared deep purple, but her captain turned his ship and presented the unharmed, starboard shields.

"Go for God's sake." The entreaty came out in a louder tone than Dunmoore intended as more enemy fire struck both ships' starboard shields, birthing worrisome deep purple auroras. "Are you idiots trying to claim the kill on that station?"

She took a deep breath and let her fist drop on the command chair's arm.

"Bridge. Up systems. Mister Sirico, the moment you're ready, throw everything we can at the station."

"Aye, aye, sir," Holt and the combat systems officer replied in unison.

"Chief Day, call *Jan Sobieski*. Tell them I'd be grateful if they went up systems now instead of waiting for the destroyers to clear. They should concentrate fire on the *Tol* and the *Ptar*. We will take the station."

"Aye, aye, Captain."

Dunmoore silently urged the destroyers to get out of range and felt an unexpected surge of relief when she saw their sublight drives glow brightly.

"At last."

"First salvo away," Sirico announced.

"And *Jan Sobieski* is up systems," Yens added. "She's opening fire."

The sudden appearance of a massive Q-ship and her imposing companion drew Shrehari fire away from the ailing destroyers as they turned their weapons to face a new and more dangerous threat. But even though Tyva station tried its best, without shields, it didn't stand a chance, not under *Iolanthe*'s massive guns.

The *Tol* class cruiser and its smaller *Ptar* class companion shifted their fire from *Hawkwood* to *Iolanthe*, but in vain. *Jan Sobieski*'s heavy guns gave them no quarter, and both ships died hard once their already overstressed shields collapsed in a flare of ethereal color.

"The station is breaking apart."

"Keep firing, Thorin. After this battle run, we're withdrawing to the nearest starbase for resupply. There's no point in hoarding ammo."

"Your command is my wish, Captain," Sirico replied just as a bright flare blanked out the main display. "And it seems both have been granted."

"Confirmed," Yens said. "The station is gone. We hit something vital again, the same as last time. Maybe the design has a fatal flaw."

"If it does, let's not tell them. Bridge, execute the slingshot portion of the plan. We're done here."

— Eighteen —

"**E**veryone is accounted for, sir," Chief Yens said shortly after *Iolanthe* dropped out of hyperspace at the system's heliopause, where Task Force Luckner would regroup and head for interstellar space, as per Admiral Petras' plan. "*Hawkwood* looks to be in bad shape though."

A visual of the flagship appeared on the main display. Her hull was streaked with black marks and dimpled by divots where plasma had eaten into the metal.

"Ouch." Sirico winced when the video pickup focused on a large, ragged hole.

"How is *Tamurlane*?"

"She's not leaking," Yens replied. "Though she took more than a few direct hits. I'll put her on screen."

"Why in heaven's name did the destroyers linger longer than planned?" Holt's hologram, hovering at Dunmoore's right elbow, asked in a sour tone. "Go active, fire three missile volleys and accelerate away at full speed."

"That's what I want to know, Zeke. None of our ships should have suffered so much as a scratch. Hell, between us, *Jan Sobieski* and *Iolanthe* could have done the job, even with the two bonehead ships. This was essentially designed as an exercise to blood the rest of Luckner against an enemy FOB." She let her fingers dance on the command chair's arm. "Signals, open a link with the flag and pipe it to my day cabin. Mister Sirico, the CIC is yours."

Once behind her desk, she composed herself to wait for *Hawkwood*'s response, aware Petras might be dealing with more immediate problems that prevented him from accepting a link right away. But instead of the admiral's square features, Commander Kirti Midura's tired face appeared on the screen.

"What can I do for you, sir?"

"How is your ship?"

"Holding together. It looks worse than it is, but we'll need time in dry dock if only to patch that damned hole and replace most of my shield generators."

"Casualties?"

"No deaths, thank the Almighty. But my sickbay is full." When she saw the questioning expression on Dunmoore's face, Midura grimaced. "The majority of the casualties are from the flag bridge. When they converted *Hawkwood* to a command ship, they shoehorned the flag bridge into a space near the main portside shield generator. That hole in my hull? It's where the generator used to be. Blowback from its failure turned the flag bridge into a giant capacitor, electrocuting everyone in it. Lousy design and even lousier execution, that conversion, if you ask me."

"The admiral and Captain Corto?"

"Still out of it. I was about to call when you opened a link. You're the task force's next senior officer."

"I see. Can *Iolanthe* offer assistance?"

Midura shook her head.

"We're okay, as long as we head to the nearest starbase from here. I can only re-establish partial shields with my spares."

Dunmoore caught her fingers tapping on the desktop as she ran through their options. *Skua* was due for a return to base so she could refill her holds. She and *Hawkwood* — and perhaps *Tamurlane*, depending on her state — could travel back together, leaving *Iolanthe*, the scouts and the three frigates to finish Task Force Luckner's patrol with one more strike. Depending on what the admiral decided once he recovered.

"One moment, please." Midura turned her head to one side as if reading an incoming report. "Sir, my medical officer just placed Admiral Petras in a stasis pod. He suffered secondary complications that are better treated by a shore hospital. Captain Corto is now awake and should be capable of carrying out her duties within a day or so."

And that, Dunmoore knew, left her responsible for Task Force Luckner.

"Fine. I'm assuming command and designating *Iolanthe* as the lead ship. Orders will follow within the hour, but I intend to head for the Torrinos System and Starbase 32."

"Understood, sir. Thank you."

"When things settle, I want to find out why *Hawkwood* and *Tamurlane* lingered long enough to lose their shields instead of shooting and scooting as per plan. Gregor and I were perfectly capable of administering the death blow."

A bitter smile twisted Midura's lips.

"That's no big mystery. The admiral ordered two more volleys once we realized how close the station's shields were to failing. But our portside shields failed first. Or at least I assume it was the admiral. Captain Corto gave the order."

An attempt to claim the kill for the flagship? Dunmoore silently wondered. Or deny it to *Iolanthe*?

"Then I shall discuss the matter with Captain Corto once she's up and about. Dunmoore, out."

She slumped back in her chair once Midura's face vanished and exhaled slowly. It seemed the true glory hound wasn't Farren Vento. But was Petras the one eager to claim coup, or was it Corto?

"First officer to the captain's day cabin."

"Holt here, sir. I'll be there in half a minute."

She mentally counted to thirty. The door chime rang when she reached twenty-nine.

"Enter."

"You seem on edge, Captain," Holt said, examining Dunmoore's face as he sat in his usual chair across from her.

"Admiral Petras is out of action for the foreseeable future. *Hawkwood*'s medical officer placed him in stasis until he reaches a base hospital. That means I'm responsible for the task force."

His eyebrows shot up in surprise.

"Congratulations are in order, I suppose. What does Lena say?"

"I don't know. We haven't spoken yet. She just came out of unconsciousness. Most of the flag bridge crew are casualties. No deaths, thankfully. The main portside shield generator's failure did it for them. A design flaw overlooked by the shipyard when they converted *Hawkwood*."

"Do you think she'll protest?"

Dunmoore shrugged.

"Probably, but she has no choice. Line over staff, as per regulations. I looked it up a few weeks ago, just in case something of the sort happened. An obscure paragraph, sure, but it gives no leeway."

His lips twitched with repressed amusement.

"Figures you'd prepare for every contingency, especially one where a certain flag captain who hates your guts might claim the right to take over. Will you keep *Iolanthe* while acting as the task force commander?"

"I will. We're heading for Starbase 32 when *Hawkwood* and *Tamurlane* confirm they're good to go FTL. Once we're out of the combat zone, HQ will decide on who replaces Admiral Petras, meaning there's no point in my changing current arrangements. Please link all ships with our conference room in thirty minutes, so I can give the necessary orders."

"Yes, sir." A pause. "Can I be a fly on the wall when you tell Lena she'll be *your* flag captain, even if it's only for a week or two?"

A mischievous smile lit up Dunmoore's face.

"I wouldn't deny you that pleasure."

Neither Dunmoore nor Holt waited long. Fifteen minutes after the first officer sent warning of Dunmoore's command conference, an irate Lena Corto demanded to speak with her.

"What do you mean you're taking command of Task Force Luckner?" The incredulous look on her wan, almost ashen face almost made Dunmoore smile. Holt, out of video pickup range, grinned broadly. "I am senior to you by several years. Luckner is now *my* responsibility."

"Sorry, Lena. But under the circumstances, time in rank is irrelevant. Check the regulations. If I recall correctly, it'll be Volume Two, Section One Hundred and Four, Paragraph Fifteen."

"I am senior, and that's an end to it. I will consider any further debate on the matter as insubordination." A cold fury filled her voice, though it still seemed shaky.

"The applicable regulation states that where a formation commander becomes incapacitated for any reason, the next senior officer assumes command. If two or more officers of the same rank are available and they're commanding officers, the most senior by time in rank takes over. Where one is a commanding officer, and the others aren't, the former assumes command, regardless of time in rank. Line over staff. Always. Besides, you're under medical restrictions."

"Bullshit."

"Look it up, Captain Corto. I'm giving you chapter and verse. There is no room for interpretation. A starship captain beats a flag captain under the current circumstances."

If Corto's eyes were deadly weapons, she'd have vaporized Dunmoore.

"We will see about that," Corto replied in a tight voice.

"What we will see is the following. I, Captain Siobhan Alaina Dunmoore, of the Commonwealth Starship *Iolanthe*, am taking temporary command of Task Force Luckner, pending either Rear Admiral Kell Petras' return to duty, or the nomination of a replacement by Special Operations Command Headquarters. Please make the appropriate entry in the flag logbook and promulgate my assumption of command to the task force. Once we're in range of a Fleet subspace array, you will advise HQ of the same. Since *Hawkwood*'s flag bridge is out of action, please plan to join me in *Iolanthe*."

Dunmoore held Corto's eyes and watched her silently weigh the pros and cons of defiance versus obedience, parsing what either choice meant for her career, let alone her chances of ever becoming a flag officer.

"Aye, aye, sir," she finally replied. The words came out as a hiss.

"Good choice, Lena. We can both come out of this looking like future commodores if we work together. Otherwise, we'll grow old together as captains and face involuntary retirement once the war is over. Of course, you'll face it a few years before I do, assuming the war doesn't last another eight years."

A fresh flash of anger crossed Corto's features. After a few seconds, she asked, in an almost normal tone, "What are your orders for the task force?"

"As I intend to announce at the command conference shortly, we will cross into interstellar space as a formation. Once *Hawkwood* and *Tamurlane* confirm they're ready to sail FTL, we will make for Starbase 32 in a coordinated fashion."

"So we're withdrawing earlier than Admiral Petras planned?" Corto wasn't quite sneering with contempt, but her tone gave away her feelings. "I figured you of all people would continue the patrol after sending both destroyers and *Skua* home, seeing as how you're the aggressive commerce raiding expert."

Dunmoore repressed a sigh of irritation. Perhaps it would be better if Corto remained aboard *Hawkwood*. She squeezed the bridge of her nose with her gloved left index finger and thumb.

"Missile stocks are low across the task force, and we need a new flag officer. After accounting for a pair of FOBs and over two dozen enemy ships, I think we can call this patrol a resounding success. The effect on enemy morale will also far outweigh the physical damage we caused. I would be grateful if you drafted our patrol report for HQ over the coming days so we can send it the moment we're within range of a subspace array."

Corto acknowledged the order with a single, silent nod.

"And I want to know why the destroyers deviated from the plan. They shouldn't have suffered any damage."

**

Dunmoore saw approval on most holographic faces around the table when she announced Task Force Luckner was withdrawing from Shrehari space to resupply at Starbase 32. *Tamurlane* hadn't lost hull integrity but still faced replacing over half her shield generators — more than her entire stock of spares.

"We will tack only once when we're back inside the Commonwealth. That will minimize our chances of tripping over marauding Shrehari who pick up our scent. I'd rather not face a running battle with two vulnerable ships and low missile stocks. *Iolanthe*'s navigator, Lieutenant Drost, will synchronize the task force. When we tack, I will transmit the task force patrol report to SOCOM HQ, so please make sure your operational logs are ready to go with it. Hopefully, by the time we reach Starbase 32, we will know who our new flag officer commanding is and when HQ expects us to sail for Shrehari space again. And finally, Captain Corto will shift over to *Iolanthe* within the hour." Dunmoore restrained a smile at the exchange of furtive glances around the table when her words registered. "Questions?"

"Yes, sir." Holographic Pushkin raised his hand. "What about the task force after-action review?"

Dunmoore felt momentarily irritated with herself. She'd held an after-action review with *Iolanthe*'s department heads during the FTL jump to the heliopause but forgot that as acting formation commander, conducting one with the captains was now her duty.

"Thank you for the reminder, Gregor. We will hold it before going FTL. Expect a summons from the flag captain within the next few hours. Anything else." After each of them, in turn, shook his or her head. Dunmoore said, "That's it. Thank you and feel free to call either Captain Corto or me if new questions arise."

After the holographic projections winked out one by one, leaving Dunmoore alone with her first officer, the latter asked. "Will you greet Lena on the hangar deck when she arrives?"

"Certainly. We're stuck together for who knows how long. *Hawkwood* won't act as flagship until she's fully repaired, which means Admiral Petras' replacement will probably use either *Iolanthe* or *Jan Sobieski*. We're the only ships with enough spare room." Dunmoore gave Holt a tired grimace. "And since there's a fifty percent chance of us becoming the new flagship, I suppose we should begin figuring out how and where we set up a suitable flag bridge or command center. Somewhere to park a rear admiral and his staff, so they don't interfere with my fighting the ship or you sailing it."

— Nineteen —

Dunmoore watched *Iolanthe*'s pinnace land on the hangar deck from her usual spot in the control room beside Petty Officer Harkon, the noncom in charge of the cavernous compartment and its giant space doors. When the latter were shut, she gave Harkon a nod of thanks and went out to greet a guest who neither wanted to be here nor was particularly welcome.

The pinnace's aft ramp dropped, allowing Lena Corto to walk out, bag in hand. She stopped just before stepping on the deck and saluted. "Permission to come aboard, Captain?"

Dunmoore returned the salute.

"Permission granted. Welcome." She offered her hand for what turned out to be a perfunctory shake during which Corto avoided meeting Dunmoore's eyes. Two of *Iolanthe*'s spacers emerged from the pinnace, carrying the rest of Corto's belongings. "We've put you in the VIP suite across from my quarters. If you'll follow me."

"Certainly." Corto fell into step beside Dunmoore.

"How is *Hawkwood*?"

"They'll survive. Midura's crew patched the hole to restore temporary hull integrity, but I figure at least two to four weeks in dry dock — if the Starbase 32 facilities are available."

"What about the admiral and his staff?"

"Admiral Petras is stable, though the medical officer figures he faces a few months convalescence after they decant and fix him. The rest of the staff are on light duties for the next week or two. I think we need not bring them across between now and our arrival in the Torrinos system, seeing as how *Iolanthe* has no flag bridge."

"Agreed. Best wait until HQ decides how we move forward under a new commanding officer whose flagship is in dry dock." They entered a waiting lift and stepped aside for the luggage-bearing spacers.

"What will you do if our new admiral decides to sail in *Iolanthe*?" Corto glanced at Dunmoore from the corners of her cold blue eyes when the lift doors closed.

"Build a flag CIC somewhere deep within our hull, far from the main shield generators. Our infantry set up their own command post in an unused barracks compartment. I don't see why we couldn't create something more formal. *Iolanthe* is a big ship with a comparatively small crew. We can carry an entire battalion of Marines for several weeks if need be, though their quartering wouldn't be quite as comfortable as that enjoyed by my single company of Scandia Regiment soldiers."

They emerged from the lift and headed down the passageway where an open cabin door beckoned. When they reached it, Dunmoore pointed across the corridor while the spacers carrying Corto's belongings slipped past them, dropped the bags, and vanished.

"That's mine. And this is yours." She waved Corto in ahead of her. "If you remember from your earlier visits, the wardroom is one deck lower, and the bridge, the CIC, and my day cabin are one deck up. The stairs are just forward of your quarters. I tend to use them instead of the lift. It's not only faster but also gives me a modicum of exercise."

"I'll be sure to follow your example," Corto murmured as she took in the spaciousness of her new quarters. "Impressive. Nicer than what the admiral has in *Hawkwood* and definitely larger than mine."

"I enjoy the same space and layout across the hallway. My day cabin is just a tad superfluous when my sitting room is part office, part lounge. You'll find working from here suitable."

"Just what sort of work do you expect from me between now and our arrival at Starbase 32? Until HQ sends up a new flag officer commanding, drawing up operational plans is rather futile, no? Since you're now an acting commodore in everything but name, perhaps I should take over *Iolanthe*."

"That won't be necessary. I'll carry out my responsibilities as both captain and formation commander in tandem. As you said, until we get a new flag officer, we don't know what the future holds. In the immediate, I want to make sure we can transmit a full report when we drop out of FTL and tack. Our course takes us near one of the interstellar subspace arrays, so it should reach SOCOM well before we dock. With luck, fresh orders might be waiting for us."

Corto raised her pale eyebrows in a way that conveyed deep ennui.

"A day or two of work. Not much more."

"Then you might as well consider the rest of the trip as a mini-vacation and enjoy yourself. I won't be any busier when we're in hyperspace. Other than routine ship's business, you might recall there's not much for a captain except stay out of her first officer's way."

Corto replied with a grudging nod.

"True."

"I'll let you settle in. The wardroom will welcome you for the evening meal at four bells in the dog watch. Perhaps you could join me in my day cabin at two bells, and we can discuss the task force after-action review. We should finalize that today."

"Certainly. It should not be a particularly lengthy or difficult exercise. May I use the CIC duty crew to help organize the AAR?"

"Of course. Lieutenant Commander Sirico is your man. I'll give him a heads up."

"Perfect. Unless our private discussion brings up matters that might influence the review, I suggest we hold it after supper. Say eight bells?"

"Done. Thank you. I'll have coffee ready. See you shortly."

Dunmoore felt Corto's cold stare follow her on the way out. The next few weeks would be uncomfortable, but she could not leave Task Force Luckner's flag captain on an ailing starship, out of touch with the acting formation commander. And not just out of fear Corto might dream up mischief designed to advance her career at Dunmoore's expense. It was equally important she be treated with the respect her appointment deserved, especially for public consumption. Humiliating Corto would only make things worse.

Holt poked his head into the day cabin moments after Dunmoore entered, as expected.

"So? How is our guest?"

"Polite. Impressed by the fact *Iolanthe* can offer better quarters to Task Force Luckner's flag captain than *Hawkwood* could offer Admiral Petras. I'm not sure whether it charmed or disgusted her. She is aware a flag captain is of little use until we reach Starbase 32 and find out what our future holds. But I'm sure she also understands my bringing her here is a kindness. And she probably resents me for it because I've taken away the chance to nurse a fresh grievance."

"No doubt. What next?"

"We treat Lena with due respect. I'll bring her in on every discussion concerning the task force and let events unfold as they will. With any luck, we won't wait long for a new task force commander and then she'll be his or her problem."

"No arguments, Skipper. She gets the freedom of the bridge?"

"Yes. And the CIC. Warn the department heads they're to treat her with courtesy and accommodate her wishes so long as they don't interfere with the ship's operations."

Holt tilted his head to one side.

"If I didn't know you as well as I do, I'd suspect ulterior motives, but you truly are trying to make Lena feel welcome."

"I am. And please make sure everyone understands that."

**

"Come in." Dunmoore rose from behind her desk and put on a smile that felt slightly strained. She waved at the chairs surrounding a low, square table in one corner of her day cabin. "Please sit. Can I offer you a cup of coffee?"

"Thank you. Black is fine."

Though she'd been in the compartment before, during Task Force Luckner's early days, Corto studied her surroundings through expressionless eyes as she sat with her back to one of the bulkheads. Dunmoore noticed Corto's searching gaze and wondered whether she was silently fuming at the fate which had denied her not only command of *Iolanthe* but the task force itself. She handed Corto a mug with the Furious Faerie insignia and sat across from her.

"Anything I should know about the recent operation from a flag bridge viewpoint, Lena?"

Corto shrugged.

"What you witnessed is what we did. The admiral's plan worked, we escaped with minimal damage and no fatalities while the Shrehari lost another FOB and two warships. I don't think there's much worth discussing at the task force level."

Dunmoore took a sip of coffee while keeping her eyes on Corto, who seemed to deal with her circumstances by presenting a facade devoid of emotion.

"I doubt Kirti Midura considers the damage to *Hawkwood* minimal. Tell me what happened. The plan was three volleys and out. Both destroyers stuck around for two more, which cost them most of their shield generators, and us our admiral. Who ordered the extra salvos?"

Corto didn't immediately reply, and though she kept a bland face, Dunmoore saw jaw muscles working under her pale skin.

"Come on, Lena. HQ will want to know why the admiral deviated from his plan, ensuring one ship is headed into dry dock, and the other will be sidelined until she replaces her shield generators."

"It was me, damn you." Corto's reply came out as a low growl through clenched teeth. "A split-second decision. I noticed the station lose its shields and ordered both destroyers to fire twice more before accelerating. We were capable of ending it right there without you and *Jan Sobieski* expending ammunition, something that might have allowed us to stay on patrol just a little longer, considering how low you both are. You know how decision-making can be in the heat of battle. I took a risk, and it didn't pay off as I hoped."

Dunmoore nodded slowly, impressed despite herself at Corto's honesty, though part of her wanted to point out a flag captain didn't make tactical decisions. She merely offered her admiral suggestions. The mistake wasn't one which would leave a black mark on her career, especially since the task force suffered no fatalities, but it made her tactical judgment questionable in Dunmoore's estimation.

Spur of the moment changes to a sound plan which was unfolding as expected could be excused if it brought about a cleaner, quicker victory. But that wasn't what happened. Instead, Corto made the situation worse, and Dunmoore felt a nagging suspicion her reason for doing so wasn't quite as she claimed.

But accusing her of baser motives wasn't something a temporary task force commander who held the same rank could do. Adding confidential observations to the patrol report — eyes only Commander SOCOM — on the other hand...

Either way, Lena Corto's chances of ever wearing a commodore's star were fading by the hour. Petras would probably not receive another command in space after convalescing, and he was her sole patron. Dunmoore couldn't think of any other flag officer willing to take on a bitter, passed over for promotion captain who hadn't held a starship command in over eight years.

"Fair enough. Make sure the report includes mention of your orders and reasoning because HQ will ask what happened once they see *Hawkwood*'s repair bill. Better we're proactive in such a case."

"That was my intention." Not even Dunmoore potentially implying Corto might lie by omission to cover herself seemed capable of breaking through her reserve.

"Are there any other matters you wish to discuss? Or can I convene the after-action review for eight bells?"

"No. Please go ahead."

"Thank you." Corto drained her coffee in two gulps, carefully placed the mug on the table between them, and stood. "With your permission?"

"Granted. I'll see you in the wardroom for supper."

When the door closed behind Corto's back, Dunmoore realized her shoulder muscles were bunched up with tension. She took a few deep breaths, willing them to relax and hoping their interactions over the coming days wouldn't be this painful and tiring.

By and large, *Iolanthe* was a happy ship with a crew that worked and lived well together and coexisted comfortably with the embarked infantry company. Hopefully, Lena Corto's sour mood wouldn't be contagious.

Fortunately, the wardroom's hearty welcome, engineered by Ezekiel Holt, eroded some of her aloofness and the subsequent after-action review with Task Force Luckner's captains proceeded without a hitch.

Dunmoore acknowledged *Hawkwood* and *Tamurlane*'s battle damage stemmed from the order to fire additional salvos, but without implicating Corto in particular. Whether the latter was grateful for escaping censure in front of officers junior to her in rank, Dunmoore would never know since she did not intend to raise the matter ever again.

— Twenty —

Toralk appeared in the day room's doorway and cleared his throat.

"Lord, Admiral Edronh is on the link. He wishes to speak with you. I told him I would see if you were available."

Brakal looked up from his reader and frowned. What did Edronh want at this juncture? They had agreed to minimize communications between Kraal members until it assembled, especially contact via electronic means that could easily be tapped by the *Tai Kan*.

"I am available." The Lord of Clan Makkar climbed to his feet. "And I will take the connection in my office."

Once settled into the carved chair behind a massive desk, Brakal nodded at Toralk.

"Activate."

Moments later, a projection of Edronh's seamed face materialized over the desktop. He appeared older, more tired than the last time they met.

"Edronh."

"Brakal. Thank you for accepting the link. Whether the *Tai Kan* are listening is immaterial. What I wish to tell you is already known at the highest levels of government. I thought it important you were aware as well."

"I am listening."

"The latest news from the war is dire, my friend. Strike Group Base Tyva was destroyed shortly after the humans ambushed a resupply convoy at the edge of its star system, taking ten of the fifteen ships in a matter of moments. Five escaped by going to otherspace before their drives were even half cycled. Three reported back to Atsang. Your phantom battleship was among the human attackers. It appears the hairless apes sent a full strike group of their own to hunt deep within imperial space. Nine vessels, six of which are either as strong as, or vastly stronger than our *Tol* class cruisers. They also destroyed two ships guarding Base Tyva — a *Tol* and a *Ptar*."

Brakal cursed under his breath.

"At this rate, Trage will order half or more of each strike group to guard its base instead of hunting human starships."

"Which would hand the initiative to the humans for good. But this is only part of my news. I brought it up first because of your losses. Surprising no one, Trage has relieved Kerhasi of command. He replaced Kerhasi with a freshly promoted admiral of the third rank who has so far spent the war drawing up campaign plans that remain unused and will do so until the death of the universe."

"Who?"

"Onnak."

"An admiral whose last command in space dates back so many turns no one even remembers him? What a disaster. Trage must be senile to make such an appointment. The moment Mishtak goes, he goes as well."

A bleak look further aged Edronh's features.

"It gets worse. A large human formation — twenty warships of *Tol* size or larger — entered the Cimmeria system several days ago and severely mauled the assault division guarding it. Only after it left did the garrison realize the attack was a cover for the arrival of several armed supply vessels intent on replenishing the human resistance. They captured several containers, but much fell into human hands."

Brakal let out a disconsolate grunt.

"Let me guess, Trage relieved the Cimmeria system commander as well."

"There was no need to do so. Kurrivis led the Cimmeria Assault Division from the bridge of his flagship. The humans destroyed it alongside a dozen others, with the loss of all crew aboard."

When he saw the disgusted look on Brakal's face, Edronh said, "The humans are fielding new ships at a rapid rate. Ships vastly superior to ours. One of them fought alongside your phantom near Tyva, and it is the smaller of the two new designs we know about. The larger version, if the reports from Cimmeria, Nabhka, and Mission are believable, almost match your phantom in terms of firepower."

"Nabhka and Mission as well? Why am I not surprised? Those imps from the deepest circle of the Underworld become bolder with every breath they take."

"They too were struck by marauding human formations boasting examples of the two new ship classes. I expect over the next few tendays, we will hear that each of the star systems we took from them has seen off intruders. Of course, the council will never make this public. At least not officially."

Edronh took a deep breath and exhaled slowly. "The gods are increasingly on the humans' side, it seems. We no longer enjoy the luxury of time if we are to staunch the empire's bleeding before time runs out. When will the four hundred sit in the Kraal?"

"Soon, my friend." Brakal fell silent for a few seconds while he wondered if he should speak freely, considering the *Tai Kan* might be listening, but figured Mishtak already knew the tenor of his plans. "We do not quite have a sufficient majority. The military lords are in step with us, but many civilian lords remain unconvinced we face a dire situation calling for the council to seek an armistice or resign. Your news about our freshest defeats should help with those who know my honor would not allow me to lie."

Edronh's face twisted into a cruel grimace.

"Shoot the ones who would support Mishtak no matter what and the rest will come to their senses."

"If we do not find ourselves with a large enough majority soon, I will consider more forceful methods."

"Propose what you will, Brakal. This must end before the people lose their faith in the empire's leaders. We would not survive the ensuing chaos. By the way, I found the *Tai Kan* spy in my retinue."

"You took his head from his shoulders, I trust."

A burst of grim laughter rumbled up Edronh's throat.

"No. I did even better than that. I fed the miscreant such disinformation he no longer has any credibility with his spymasters."

**

Brakal swallowed a curse when Regar startled him by appearing in the day room without making a single sound. Night was falling over Shredar, and he was enjoying a cup of hot *tvass* while rereading the Saga of Rodek, which recounted the bloodiest dynastic change in recorded Shrehari history.

"What?"

"You might recall my mentioning friends in sensitive positions at *Tai Kan* headquarters. I have just come from a meeting with one of them."

"If you intend to try my patience, you are on the right path."

Regar inclined his head while a sardonic expression twisted his mouth.

"Mishtak has ordered Director Yatron to arrest the military lords of the Kraal if they assemble without his permission."

"So the motherless bastards were listening in on my conversation with Admiral Edronh. Good. Rumors of such a move will ensure the perpetually undecided among the four hundred finally commit one way or the other. Will Yatron comply?"

"Unknown. Arresting lords of the Kraal on spurious grounds could unleash the very tempest we are striving to avoid, and Yatron understands this. He also realizes First Deputy Director Kroesh could use Yatron's act of obeying an illegal order as sufficient cause to relieve him. At gunpoint, if necessary, something Kroesh would do with great pleasure." Regar bared his fangs. "My friend tells me the atmosphere at headquarters is fetid in general and barely breathable on the senior officers' floor."

"Did your friend offer a reason?"

Regar's smile widened.

"Kroesh oversees the Political Branch, which provides *Tai Kan* officers to the Deep Space Fleet."

"You mean it forces them on the fleet, but never mind."

"Those such as I, capable of seeing the same truth as the commanders and admirals they serve, seem in greater supply than we thought, and they report that truth to their superiors in the Political Branch. Those superiors, in turn, keep Kroesh aware of the situation along our frontier with those damned humans."

Brakal put down his reader, leaned back, and studied Regar with discerning eyes.

"Strange that the *Tai Kan*, far from being a monolithic organization serving the council without reservations, is just as divided over our fate as the military and the Kraal. What should I do with this information, I wonder?"

"You are Speaker of the Kraal until the four hundred choose another. Demand a meeting with Mishtak. It matters little what you discuss behind closed doors. The important thing is that those who matter in this city see Brakal, Lord of Clan Makkar, and Speaker of the Kraal, boldly entering the Forbidden Quarter as Mishtak's equal, unafraid of the governing council's *Tai Kan* enforcers."

"Bold. Unexpected. Mishtak cannot refuse me though he will seethe. But my demanding we meet must be public." Brakal thought for a moment, then let a fierce smile curl up his lip. "I will advise the four hundred that I shall confer with Mishtak out of courtesy so I can formally announce the Kraal will rouse from its long slumber and once more take its rightful place as the empire's supreme legislature."

Brakal tossed his reader aside, drained the *tvass* mug, and stood.

"Did Mishtak not boast long ago that the council never sleeps? Perhaps I shall call him now."

"No. Let me contact Mishtak's senior aide. Individuals of your respective statures do not make arrangements themselves." When he saw Brakal open his mouth in protest, Regar raised both hands. "You must trust me in these matters, Lord."

"Very well," Brakal grumbled. "But do not tarry. I want to see that poxed whoreson before this tenday is over."

"It will be done."

"How?"

"With threats, of course." A bloodcurdling grin transformed Regar's gargoyle features.

"Explain."

"I would rather not discuss details, lest you get ideas. There are particular ways of doing things in Shredar, and you are still wholly innocent of them. It would be best if that state of affairs persisted."

— Twenty-One —

"**B**ridge to captain."

Dunmoore reached out and tapped the controls embedded in her desk. "Captain here."

"Lieutenant Drost, sir. I have the watch. We received a text-only message for the acting commander, Task Force Luckner, from Starbase 32."

"Pipe it to my day cabin."

"Done."

She put down her reader and called up the message. *Hawkwood* would enter dry dock at once upon arrival. Admiral Petras' stasis pod and the remaining injured would be transferred from there to the orbital station by shuttle. *Iolanthe, Tamurlane,* and *Skua* would dock with the starbase upon arrival while the rest of Luckner would assume a trailing orbit and dock in turn to resupply. Starbase 32 traffic control would send approach instructions for individual ships once Luckner entered Torrinos orbit. Rear Admiral Mensall wished to see Captains Dunmoore and Corto once *Iolanthe* was docked. SOCOM HQ asked him to hand over orders for Task Force Luckner.

A frown creased Dunmoore's forehead. Tyrel Mensall was the 32nd Battle Group's flag officer commanding and thus in 3ʳᵈ Fleet's chain of command, not SOCOM's. Why would her superiors make him the intermediary when they could just as easily send orders directly to *Iolanthe*? Perhaps because she, or Corto, or both would hear unpleasant news best delivered by someone wearing two stars on his collar? At least this confirmed her patrol report and the confidential notations, including the one about Corto, had reached HQ.

She tapped the intercom.

"Bridge, this is the captain."

"Officer of the watch here, sir."

"Acknowledge receipt to Starbase 32. Retransmit the message minus the paragraph concerning Captain Corto and myself to the rest of the task force, tell Commander Holt, and ask for acknowledgments in return."

Drost repeated the order. When she fell silent, Dunmoore said, "Thank you, Astrid. Please pass the entire message to Captain Corto verbatim and ask if she'd join me in the day cabin."

"Aye, aye, sir."

"Dunmoore, out."

Less than two minutes later, her door chime pealed, and at the invitation to enter, Lena Corto walked in, curiosity writ large on her narrow face.

"Do you know why both of us are reporting to Tyrel Mensall when we belong to a different command?" She asked without preamble or the usual courtesies. Dunmoore and Corto had kept out of each other's way since leaving Shrehari space, and this was one of the few times they met in the course of duty.

"Not a clue, Lena. But I figure the orders from HQ might include bad news, hence the personal touch of a rear admiral."

"It means they received our patrol report."

"Yes. And perhaps something in it gave the brass cause to reassess what we're doing." Dunmoore shrugged. "At least *Hawkwood* is headed for dry dock with no pleading or arguing on our part, and someone drew up a plan to resupply us. They wouldn't be so solicitous if Task Force Luckner were on SOCOM's shit list."

Corto dropped into the chair on the other side of Dunmoore's desk.

"True." The two women examined each other in silence, still visibly uncomfortable, but the tension evident during Corto's first day in *Iolanthe* was no longer palpable. "What do you think is about to happen?"

Dunmoore's lips twisted in a dismissive moue.

"Again, not a clue. The starbase could be resupplying our ships before they head off to other formations and we look for new work, just as it may be preparing us for another patrol deep inside enemy space."

Corto scoffed.

"I might be looking for new work, but you'll still have *Iolanthe*."

"What do you mean?"

A mocking smile twisted her thin, pale lips.

"Line over staff, remember?"

"And you still bear a grudge against me for it."

"Not so much anymore. I realized stoking the fires of resentment is exhausting and a week with little by way of real work allowed me to examine myself and consider my future. I spent a lot of time in the last few months wishing you were one of those privileged, protected officers promoted beyond her ability. You know, the sort who'll eventually show a lack of fitness to command so obvious her next assignment is a remote scientific outpost on the other side of the Commonwealth. But you're not. That realization pained me. Deeply."

When she saw Dunmoore open her mouth to speak, Corto let out a bark of laughter as bleak as it was short.

"It doesn't mean I hold you in any greater esteem than before, though it puts things into perspective. I'm envious of you having *Iolanthe*, I'm envious of your relationship with her crew, and I'm envious of your ability to disregard risk calculations and simply go with your instincts. But that envy is *my* problem, not yours."

A long pause filled the air between them.

"I don't know what to say."

"There is nothing you can say, Siobhan. You and I are remarkably different. We enjoyed different career paths, different opportunities, and different patrons high up the food chain. Whether that's fair, who cares? It's a reality. My seeing you sit there as captain of the Fleet's premier Q-ship makes me feel old and washed-up. Enjoy it while you can. In a few years, you could easily be me, looking back at what was and regretting what might have been. Serving in SOCOM isn't a path to glory. You'll be forever identified with *Iolanthe* and her covert missions, not as the captain of a heavy cruiser with an envious war record, one which, more importantly, will be publicly recognized and celebrated. Yes, I'm bitter, but that makes me no different from a lot of other post captains who realize their dreams of one day wearing an admiral's stars are forever out of reach, war or no war."

Corto stood.

"You and I may face the same future in due course. Let me know when I should join you by the main airlock. I assume Admiral Mensall won't mind if we appear wearing our everyday battledress."

"I doubt he will."

The unexpected tirade left Dunmoore feeling deflated. She spent a long time staring at the map on the far bulkhead after Corto's departure. But the stars offered no answers beyond the truism that human lives were nothing compared to theirs.

**

Dunmoore and Corto made their way down the docking arm that connected *Iolanthe* to Starbase 32 and up to the command deck in silence. Each wrestled with her private thoughts, aware neither could change what would happen next, both knowing they would accept their orders as the professional navy officers they'd been all their adult lives, no matter what.

A middle-aged lieutenant wearing the insignia of a rear admiral's aide and the seamed face of a chief petty officer commissioned from the ranks rose from behind his desk as they entered the executive suite's antechamber.

"Sirs. Admiral Mensall is expecting you." He touched something on his desk, and an inner door behind him opened soundlessly. "Please go in."

Dunmoore allowed Corto to go ahead of her but once inside both captains halted in unison a regulation three paces from Mensall's desk and saluted.

"Captains Corto and Dunmoore reporting as ordered, sir," Dunmoore announced.

Mensall returned the compliment, then waved at the pair of chairs facing him.

"At ease. Please sit."

When they complied, he leaned forward, elbows on the metal desktop, hands joined.

"I realize being summoned by a flag officer not in your chain of command for orders must sound unusual. But since those orders involve next career steps for both of you, Armand personally asked me to pass them along in his stead once he heard Task Force Luckner would make for Starbase 32."

When he saw surprise in Corto's eyes at hearing him casually use the first name of the four-star admiral commanding SOCOM, Mensall smiled.

"Armand and I were Academy classmates back in the dark ages. This was more a favor between old friends than a formal request."

Dunmoore nodded in acknowledgment.

"Understood, sir. I gather it means Admiral Xi received our patrol report."

"That he did, and he sent me a suitably redacted copy. On Admiral Xi's behalf and mine as well, congratulations to the both of you. Destroying Shrehari bases deep within the empire's sphere will hopefully prove irritating enough to make them act rashly. You may not know this since you've been out for several months, but in the last few weeks, regular battle groups carried out fighting raids in almost all of the star systems occupied by the enemy. In some cases, where we knew of active resistance movements on the ground, the raids also covered resupply runs. Perhaps those operations, coupled with your actions behind their lines might make someone in Shredar's Forbidden Quarter think we're gaining the upper hand and look for a way they can end this without besmirching their precious honor."

"We can only hope, sir," Corto replied.

"Now, the reason you're here. With Kell Petras out of action for the foreseeable future, Armand is downgrading the appointment of the flag officer commanding Task Force Luckner to commodore, which is more in line with the formation's size and composition. Commodores, especially those who command in space rather than from a fixed installation, don't rate a flag captain or even much of a staff. As a result, Captain Corto, you're reassigned to the Joint Plans Division at

Fleet HQ as Director, Naval Special Operations Capacity Development."

"Yes, sir."

Corto and Dunmoore kept their eyes on Mensall instead of exchanging glances, though both understood the appointment, important as it might be in the greater context, wouldn't take Corto any closer to a commodore's stars. It was the sort of job undertaken by post captains who would stay at that rank until they retired.

"My flag lieutenant reserved a VIP berth for you in *Normandie*," he continued, naming one of the Fleet's armed transports who spent their lives sailing from starbase to starbase on a regular schedule, moving people and cargo. "She's inbound as we speak and should dock within the next four hours."

"Thank you, sir."

Mensall turned his gaze on Dunmoore.

"Congratulations. You're Task Force Luckner's new flag officer with promotion to commodore, although only acting — while so employed since the Fleet is well over its authorized permanent flag officer quota. But at least the promotion is backdated to the day you took temporary command when Kell entered a stasis pod."

This time Dunmoore reflexively glanced at Corto and caught a brief flash of venom in her eyes before weary resignation replaced it.

"Congratulations, Siobhan. At least one of us made it."

"What about *Iolanthe*, sir?"

"Your first officer is taking her, though his promotion to post captain is substantive as is the appointment." Mensall glanced at the reader on his desk. "He, in turn, is replaced by your second officer, whose promotion and appointment are also substantive. However, your second officer will not be replaced for now, so

Commander Cullop will carry out the duties of both positions."

"And the rest of Admiral Petras' staff?"

"Recalled to SOCOM HQ. Armand figures you're not the type who needs much of a staff. I suppose you can always reach into the ranks of Task Force Luckner and grab a few warm bodies if required." Mensall studied her for a reaction. After a moment he nodded, satisfied by what he saw. "You don't seem unhappy with the situation. Good. I never had much use for flag officers who measured their importance by the size of the staff dancing attendance on them."

"Me neither, sir."

"Armand asked that I formally present your star, so if you'll bear with me." He touched unseen controls on his desk. "Glendan, I'm about to promote Commodore Dunmoore."

"Sir."

Moments later, the aide entered carrying a small box in one hand. A floating silver sphere the size of a baby's fist trailed him at shoulder height. Mensall nodded at the shiny orb.

"I'll send a copy of the recording to Armand, and you'll receive one as well." He rose to his feet, imitated by Dunmoore and Corto, and gestured toward the stand of flags dominating one of the office's paneled bulkheads. "Over there will be a good place. You're welcome to join us, Lena."

"I would rather not. This is Siobhan's moment. Best I stay out of the picture."

"As you wish." Once he and Dunmoore were in position, Mensall took the small box from his aide's hand and pulled out a gold alloy star the size of an adult's thumbnail. "Attention to orders. I hereby promote Captain Siobhan Alaina Dunmoore to the rank of commodore and appoint her flag officer commanding Task Force Luckner."

Mensall reached for Dunmoore's tunic collar and removed the four gold bars of a post captain.

"Hold out your hand." When she obeyed, he dropped the insignia into her palm. "Perhaps you might pass this on to Captain Holt."

"I most certainly will, sir. Zeke and I go way back. This wasn't his first tour as my second in command."

"Good." Mensall reached for her tunic collar again, this time to affix a commodore's five-pointed star. "There. Congratulations."

After they shook hands and posed for the video drone, Mensall invited them to sit and enjoy a cup of coffee with him, however, Corto politely refused.

"Thank you, sir, but I think it would be best if I returned to the ship and packed, so I'm well away before Commodore Dunmoore returns."

"As you wish. Enjoy your trip, and good luck with your future endeavors."

Corto came to attention and saluted.

"With your permission, Admiral?"

"Dismissed, Captain."

When she made to salute Dunmoore, the latter held out her hand instead.

"Fair winds and following seas, Lena."

"You too, sir." Her tone held a slight edge, but she gave the appearance of someone who'd made her peace with the universe. Whether it was feigned, Dunmoore didn't care to find out.

Once Corto was gone, Mensall retrieved a memory chip from his desk and held it out.

"Encrypted orders for your eyes only. I don't know what they say, except you're not to issue them until Task

Force Luckner is beyond the Torrinos heliopause, outbound for enemy space."

"That sounds ominous, sir."

He gave her an amused look.

"Based on Luckner's purpose and your reputation, I'd be surprised if the orders weren't. Ominous, I mean." He waved at the settee group. "If you can spare me a bit of your time, I'm interested in hearing more about how you rampaged through the Shrehari Empire."

"Certainly, sir. It would be a pleasure."

She spent an enjoyable half-hour with Mensall, answering his question about Luckner's patrol behind enemy lines. In return, he gave her nuggets of wisdom on the hidden perils of being a flag officer. When he finally saw her out into the executive suite antechamber, the aide rose from behind his desk and said, "I've informed *Iolanthe* of Commodore Dunmoore's appointment, sir, though I didn't mention who her new captain was."

"Excellent!" Mensall beamed at her. "I'm sure the flagship will receive Task Force Luckner's new commander in style. It'll be the perfect moment to pin those four stripes on your successor's collar."

Dunmoore swallowed a theatrical groan.

"Knowing Captain Holt, I'm afraid he'll overdo things, Admiral."

"Perhaps, but try to enjoy it. Getting piped aboard your flagship for the first time is an experience you'll never forget." He stuck out his hand. "We'll do our best to prepare you for the hunt, but your damaged destroyer might not make it out of dry dock before you leave."

"Thank you for everything, sir."

— Twenty-Two —

Dunmoore thought herself prepared for the welcome aboard after her promotion and appointment became public. But the trill of eleven bosun's whistles and the stamp of thirty booted feet on the metal deck caught her by surprise as she left the docking arm and stepped into *Iolanthe*'s main airlock.

"Luckner arriving. To the flag, present ARMS."

A cramped space at the best of times, it seemed impossibly full with a platoon from E Company, 3rd Battalion, Scandia Regiment to her left and Chief Petty Officer Second Class Anita Dwyn and ten of her mates on the right. A broad pennant, the symbol of a commodore commanding ships in space unfurled from a short, makeshift mast at the airlock's far end.

Ezekiel Holt came up the middle, stomped to attention, and when the bosun's whistles fell silent, saluted.

"Welcome aboard your flagship, Commodore. If we weren't docked, we would give you a bigger welcome on the hangar deck, but I hope this suffices."

Dunmoore returned the compliment. When the soldiers shouldered arms, she said, "It's more than I expected, Captain."

"Sir?" Holt's single eye lit up with an unvoiced question.

"Shall we do this here, or call our Scandians and the ship's company together on the hangar deck?" Dunmoore pulled her former rank insignia from her tunic pocket and held it up for Holt to see. "I wore this until an hour ago. If you accept, I'd be happy for you to wear it."

"No kidding? Of course, I accept. Those stripes of yours are blessed with some sort of magic."

"*Iolanthe* belongs to you, Zeke. My appointment may be acting — while so employed because of the peacetime cap on flag officers, but your promotion is substantive and Emma is your first officer. You won't receive a new second officer for now, but I'm sure she can take care of both her old and new responsibilities."

"And more. I don't know what to say, Commodore."

"Attention to orders," Dunmoore said in a loud voice. "Ezekiel Holt, I now promote you to the rank of post captain and appoint you as commanding officer of the Commonwealth Starship *Iolanthe*. Hold out your hand."

When he complied, Dunmoore reached up, removed his commander's rank insignia, and dropped it into the palm of his hand. "You may want to see Emma wearing your old stripes. Apparently, they're also blessed with magic."

"Absolutely, sir." Unexpected wonderment and delight tinged his voice. "I'm sure she'll be thrilled."

She pinned her old captain's rank insignia on his collar and took one step back.

"Congratulations. I couldn't hand the Furious Faerie over to a finer commanding officer."

"And the Furious Faerie couldn't hope to serve as the flagship for a better commodore, sir."

"Remember our discussions about building a makeshift flag bridge for Task Force Luckner's new commander?"

"Sure."

"Put a second command chair in the CIC, and we'll call it a day. I think between us we can run both *Iolanthe* and the task force with the same crew."

"What about Lena and Admiral Petras' staff?"

"Lena is off to Fleet HQ and the rest recalled by SOCOM. If I want staff, I'm welcome to recruit within Task Force Luckner. And you know me."

"No staff? I'm sure Thorin and his crew will happily serve both of us. But not even an aide?"

"What good would a poor flag lieutenant do me while we raid deep inside enemy space?"

"Point taken, Commodore."

Dunmoore gestured toward the Scandia Regiment soldiers.

"Why don't we dismiss the honor guard and continue this discussion in my — pardon, *your* day cabin?"

"It will stay yours for as long as you wish."

"No. The only thing I'll keep are my quarters. You can take the VIP suite across the passageway once Lena leaves and give Emma the first officer's cabin. Now clear the airlock, will you?"

When the soldiers and Chief Dwyn's party were gone, Holt said, "Lena couldn't run ashore fast enough. I never saw such a thunderous face on a captain before. She barely said a word to anyone. But a flag officer needs her day cabin, surely."

Dunmoore shook her head.

"The sitting room in my suite will do just fine. This is your ship, Zeke. I'm merely a guest using your facilities to coordinate Task Force Luckner's actions."

"If that's what you want. We could still build a flag bridge..."

"Where I would sit alone and unloved. Pass. But if you don't want me in your CIC, please say so."

"Perish the thought. I couldn't think of a better way to harass the boneheads than with you breathing down my neck." He grinned at her. "That was a joke, by the way. I know you'll be a low maintenance flag officer and considering Task Force Luckner's mission, it's the logical approach."

"Glad we still agree on things, Zeke, considering you're also my de facto second in command and chief of my non-existent staff. The promotion and appointment orders from SOCOM should be here by now. Admiral Mensall held them back only so he could act on Admiral Xi's behalf and inform us of our respective assignments. Why don't you log them and read yourself in as *Iolanthe*'s captain?"

"And the rest of the task force?"

"Would you be so kind as to set up a command conference in an hour? I'd rather tell everyone in person."

"Done."

"Meanwhile, I'll remove my personal effects from your day cabin." She gave him a sly smile. "Should I leave you the chess set?"

"Emma's not much of a player, so I won't be using it to browbeat her as my former captain used to do."

"Browbeat? Really, Zeke?"

Holt raised both hands, palms facing outward, in surrender.

"You're the one who considers chess a blood sport, Commodore, not me. And just as a side note, I really enjoy calling you commodore." He glanced around and asked in a low voice, "How did Lena take it?"

"Better than I thought. But if there ever was even an infinitesimal chance of us becoming, if not friends, then at least comrades before my promotion, it'll never happen now. Not even if we live until the end of all things. She's taking one of those staff job at Fleet HQ they give officers whose chances at promotion are over."

"Because of *Hawkwood* and *Tamurlane*?"

Dunmoore made a dubious face.

"I might merely have confirmed what Admiral Xi and the rest of the senior SOCOM staff suspected about Lena. I added a confidential note for Admiral Xi's eyes only to the patrol report, explaining why the destroyers took so many hits when our plan called for them to shoot and scoot. With Petras out of commission, there was probably no one left at SOCOM willing to speak for her."

Holt shrugged dismissively.

"That's what happens when you let careerist ambitions override everything else. Piss enough people off, or simply make them figure you're an asshole behind that insincere smile, and they won't say boo when you really need a friend."

Dunmoore gestured toward the passageway.

"We should move along. Mind you, I feel sorry for her in a way. She didn't distinguish herself as a frigate captain, but very few of us who held commands in the war's early years came across as great naval tacticians. Not when the Shrehari were hammering us with enthusiasm. You may recall the price I paid for losing *Shenzen* because, as the court-martial said, I showed too much aggression."

Holt fell into step beside her.

"And you might recall my testimony at that court-martial absolving you of recklessness."

"Yes, and I've always believed it ensured my exile to Toboso as second in command rather than burial in an obscure staff branch at Fleet HQ, where I'd have spent the rest of the war as a terminal lieutenant commander."

"You give me too much credit, Commodore."

Dunmoore stopped and placed her hand on Holt's upper arm.

"No. I think I've not given you enough credit over the years, Zeke."

A lazy grin spread across his face.

"SOCOM didn't give me *Iolanthe* just because of my rakish good looks. The efficiency reports you wrote praising me to a higher heaven than I deserve surely played a role in Admiral Xi's decision. Think of it this way, your last two first officers were promoted on your watch and given their own commands. What does that say about your leadership? And the way you take care of us?"

"All right," Dunmoore growled. "Let's not get maudlin. Help me move my stuff out of your office and into my quarters. And you will keep the chess set as my promotion gift."

"Yes, sir, Commodore. And thank you." Holt let out a comical bark of laughter. "I still enjoy saying that word. Commodore. Oh and be prepared for Emma's invitation to eat your meals with *Iolanthe*'s officers — once she finds out about her promotion and concomitant appointment as president of the wardroom. She'll make a superb first officer, but I'm sure the efficiency reports you wrote are the main reason she's moving into my former cabin."

"Shall I preside over Emma's promotion?"

"Absolutely. She'll be delighted."

"Then let's get you sorted and decide where and when. But you will pin her new stripes on."

As they entered what was now Holt's day cabin, Dunmoore checked her step so she didn't instinctively sit behind the desk. After a moment of hesitation, she pointed at the captain's chair.

"Try it."

Holt obeyed, smiling with unfeigned pleasure.

"Nice. I'm enjoying the view." He reached for the intercom. "Commander Cullop to the captain."

A few seconds passed, then, "Cullop here, sir. Congratulations. I just heard the commodore pinned on your new rank badge."

"And she told me my old rank badge needs a new home on my first officer's collar. Congratulations, Emma. You're it. Assemble the crew and soldiers on the hangar deck in fifteen minutes. We'll do this properly."

"*Yes,* sir!"

"Captain, out."

Dunmoore pointed at his desk display.

"Read yourself in as *Iolanthe*'s captain, Zeke. Otherwise, you can't promote Emma."

"Of course." He retrieved the orders from SOCOM, logged them, and then said, "Computer, I am Captain Ezekiel Sebastian Holt, NO201553."

"Identity acknowledged," *Iolanthe*'s primary AI replied in its smooth, androgynous voice. "Congratulations on your promotion and appointment, Captain."

"I hereby take command of the battlecruiser *Iolanthe*, hull number BCQ2400."

"I have logged your assumption of command and keyed all functions to your identity. The official notice is posted in every compartment."

Holt sat back and gave Dunmoore a pleased look.

"There. The Furious Faerie is mine now."

"I wish you joy of your time as her captain. She's the finest ship I ever sailed, with the finest crew in the entire Fleet, bar none."

"Thank you." Holt climbed to his feet. "Let's shift your dunnage. Do me a favor for Emma's promotion. Let me enter the hangar deck first and call the ship's company to attention. You received the eleven whistle salute at the airlock, but there are a lot of folks aboard who want to honor your promotion as well."

"Do I have a choice?"

"No. And even if I tried giving you one, Chief Guthren would make me regret it for the rest of my natural life."

Dunmoore snorted. *Iolanthe*'s redoubtable coxswain was a legend in his own right and another old shipmate who'd experienced her victories and defeats in equal measure.

"Understood."

**

"Ship's company, Atten-SHUN."

Captain Ezekiel Holt's command echoed across *Iolanthe*'s cavernous hangar compartment. Several hundred booted feet stomped on metal plates, giving birth to a secondary echo no less deafening than the first.

"Commodore on deck."

That was Dunmoore's cue. She stepped through the inner doors and marched down the heart of the formation. It was composed of two elements facing each other — spacers to her left and E Company, 3rd Battalion, Scandia Regiment on her right. Holt stood in the middle, hand raised to his brow in salute. She stopped three paces from him and returned the compliment.

"Commodore," he said in a voice pitched to carry, "on behalf of my crew and soldiers, I wish to express our pride at hoisting your broad pennant in *Iolanthe*."

"I couldn't ask for a finer flagship, Captain."
Dunmoore dropped her hand and asked in a normal
tone, "May I address the formation?"

"Certainly, sir. They're also your crew and soldiers."

"In that case, please put them at ease."

"Sir." He raised his voice again. "Ship's company,
stand at EASE. Stand easy."

She turned on her heels and let her eyes roam over the
assembled ranks. Everyone present was watching her
with interest, or perhaps examining the single gold star
on her collar, to make sure they weren't seeing things.

"I cannot adequately express my feelings at standing
among you no longer as your captain, but as the flag
officer commanding Task Force Luckner. *Iolanthe* is the
deadliest weapon of war our navy ever commissioned,
and my turn as her skipper was an honor unmatched by
anything in my career. I doubt I shall ever serve with
more professional spacers and soldiers. Captain Holt's
promotion and appointment as my successor are richly
deserved. I know he will keep the name *Iolanthe* shining
brightly among the stars just as I know you will serve him
with the same dedication you showed since I came
aboard. As your former captain, I thank you."

She took a breath before continuing.

"As your new flag officer, I can assure you we will
return to the fight, and soon. Those bloody noses we
gave the boneheads so far are nothing compared to what
we will do now that we've put them off balance. And
we're not alone. While we were raiding deep inside
enemy space, other formations attacked the Shrehari
forces occupying our star systems and resupplied the
resistance movements that are giving their ground
troops not a single moment of respite. The winds of war
are turning, and we will do our utmost to make sure they

turn fully against the enemy, so he cries for mercy under the roar of our guns."

She raised her hand in salute again and spoke the Q-ship's motto, "We strike without warning."

Hundreds of voices shouted back with raw enthusiasm, "*We strike without warning.*"

Dunmoore turned to Holt.

"I believe we have a new first officer to promote and appoint, Captain."

"Yes, sir.   Commander Emma Cullop, front and center."

— Twenty-Three —

"Commodore?" Holt stuck his head into Dunmoore's quarters. "Your captains are present in the conference room."

"Present?" She looked up from her reader. Something about his tone roused her suspicions. She cocked a questioning eyebrow at *Iolanthe*'s new commanding officer. "Why does your pronouncement fill me with dread? What did you do?"

"I'm hurt, sir." Holt placed his hand over his heart. "When I convened the conference, they unanimously asked to come over and congratulate you in person. Since we're orbiting within a few kilometers of each other, it seemed a simple request to grant, especially since there's plenty of parking space on the hangar deck."

Dunmoore shook her head in mock exasperation, though she allowed herself a pleased smile.

"Agreed."

"Emma laid on a little cocktail hour in the wardroom for afterward. It would be a shame if we brought them here and didn't raise a glass in your honor."

"And we're deviating from the path of amicable agreement."

"You'll love it, sir. Were you perusing our orders?" Holt nodded at the reader in her hand.

"Yes, and you'll enjoy them. But they're sealed until we leave this star system, lest the slightest hint of our destination reaches enemy ears."

A piratical grin lit up Holt's face.

"Mystery orders. The best kind. Since you don't seem dismayed, I gather you consider our next mission well within Task Force Luckner's capabilities."

"Not only within our capabilities, Zeke, but an inspired imitation of a raid carried out during Earth's second global conflict, though we will make it a round trip, not a one-shot deal." She placed the reader on her desk and wiped its screen before climbing to her feet. "And you'll have to wait the same as everyone else before finding out."

Holt led her up the spiral staircase and along the command deck passage to the conference room. As they neared the open door, Dunmoore's ears picked up a subdued rumble of mixed conversation, but it ceased instantly the moment Holt entered.

"Captains, the commodore."

He stepped aside and ushered her in. Task Force Luckner's commanding officers were standing at attention behind their chairs, arrayed by order of seniority on either side of the table. Dunmoore saw nothing but pleased smiles, though Gregor Pushkin wore the biggest grin of all.

"At ease. Sit, and thank you for attending my first command conference in person."

"It was the right thing to do, sir," Pushkin replied. "I know I speak for everyone when I express our pleasure at your promotion and appointment. We couldn't wish for a better flag officer now that Admiral Petras is on the injured list."

Vigorous nods greeted his statement.

"Try to remember that sentiment when we face the enemy's guns in a few weeks, Gregor." When she saw the gleam in his hooded eyes, Dunmoore said, "Yes, I received orders along with my promotion. They're the sort that can't be shared until we're well away from prying eyes and intrusive ears. But if our mission meets with success, Task Force Luckner might end up as more than just a footnote in the annals of naval history."

"Sounds interesting," Farren Vento of *Narses* replied. "But I can't for the life of me come up with a mission more tailored to our abilities than what we've been doing so far, Commodore."

"She mentioned something about imitating a pre-diaspora raid," Holt interjected. "Second World War on Earth, if you're inclined to sift through your ship's historical database."

"I might just do that."

Dunmoore cleared her throat to end the sidebar before it went any further.

"Once we cross the heliopause, before our first jump in interstellar space, we will reconvene — via holographic projection this time — and go over those orders. Right now, I want to discuss how I'll run Task Force Luckner."

"Without a flag captain, I hope," Vento said, proving he still smarted at Corto's glory hound comment before the attack on FOB Tyva.

"Without a staff, period, Farren. Commodores running a task force don't rate one. Zeke has kindly offered to provide what support I need and arrange for a second command chair in *Iolanthe*'s CIC. Since I don't expect to direct my ships' actions once the battle is joined, I won't need a dedicated flag crew and bridge."

"Especially if said bridge sits next to one of the main shield generators," Kirti Midura added with a bitter smile. "Given enough enemy fire, they can fail spectacularly, as *Hawkwood*'s new and highly irregular skylight proves."

"Since you broached the subject, did the dry dock's chief engineer give you a sense of how long for repairs?"

She gave Dunmoore a so-so shrug.

"Initial estimate based on my damage report is six days of continuous, around the clock, work. They hadn't begun the physical survey when I left *Hawkwood* just now."

"And can they handle around the clock?"

"So he says."

Dunmoore turned to *Tamurlane*'s captain.

"What about you, Idris?"

"Three days tops. The damage was mostly confined to my shield generators, and we pulled the burned-out units during our jump inward from the heliopause, so it's just a matter of fitting and testing replacements. They promised me delivery from the engineering stores within the next six hours."

"Good to hear."

"Sir, do our orders give you the leeway to wait for the completion of *Hawkwood*'s repairs?" Midura asked. "I'd rather we didn't miss out on becoming more than just a footnote in naval history."

"See her out of dry dock within the next one hundred and forty-four hours, and you'll sail with the rest of the task force."

"I'll make sure it happens, even if it means putting the crew out on the hull in spacesuits so they can push."

A few amused chuckles greeted her heartfelt declaration, not least because of the absurd imagery it evoked.

"Fair enough. About my operating procedures. I will keep most of Admiral Petras' instructions as-is. They make sense, we're used to them, and they leave us enough flexibility. Where I will deviate is in the realm of tactics. Though beyond breaking the wolf pack into individual ships rather than pairs or trios, so we can patrol a larger area, I'm afraid it will be improvisation on the spot, depending on the enemy's tactics or their adaptation to ours. That being said, when in doubt, remember the words of Admiral Horatio Nelson — captains cannot do very wrong if they place their ships alongside those of the enemy." She paused. "Except for our scouts and transport. They should lead the enemy on a fruitless chase and thereby clear the way for our rated warships to seize the day."

Dunmoore waited for the inevitable chuckles to subside before continuing.

"So much for my command philosophy, which will no doubt evolve as I settle into the job. Our next mission, however, which I cannot discuss until we're well away from here, will require us to operate as a regular battle group once we reach the target, but only for a brief period. My own orders will cover the necessary contingencies." Another pause. "The deck is open for questions."

**

"Is everyone ready?" Holt asked, looking around the wardroom where Task Force Luckner's captains had joined *Iolanthe*'s off-duty officers for a small celebration after the command conference.

"We're good, sir," Commander Cullop said raising a stemless glass filled with wine so rich its deep red coloration seemed almost black. "You can go ahead."

"Captains of Task Force Luckner, officers of the gallant Q-ship *Iolanthe*, I propose a toast to our new commander, Commodore Siobhan Dunmoore. Long may her broad pennant fly."

"Hopefully not too long," she said in a stage whisper, triggering a few grins. "I count on raising a rear admiral's flag someday."

Holt winked at her.

"Understood. Commodore Dunmoore. May her broad pennant fly until she gets her second star."

"Commodore Dunmoore," the assembled officers replied in unison before taking a sip.

"Wow," Dunmoore let out an appreciative whistle. "That didn't come from the wardroom stores, Zeke. What is it?"

"Emma has friends in the right places, apparently. When I requested this little gathering, she reached out to a contact on the civilian orbital station and snagged a case of Chateau Pétrus, a prewar vintage no less. From Earth."

Dunmoore put on an air of feigned disapproval.

"Meaning you sent a shuttle to fetch wine?"

A clearly unrepentant Holt shrugged, smiling.

"You're only promoted to flag rank once. I figured we might as well make it memorable."

"Should I ask how much it cost the wardroom?"

"No, but your captains generously reimbursed part of that king's ransom, so your officers aren't quite paupers just yet." When he saw Pushkin make his way toward them, Holt touched her arm. "I'll go mingle and let you speak with Gregor."

"The star looks wonderful on you, Commodore," *Jan Sobieski*'s captain said the moment he was within easy earshot. "And not before time. Admiral Petras is a good commander, but this task force needs someone more flexible, someone capable of throwing doctrine away so she can make things up on the fly. And thank the

Almighty Lena left with him. Given a little luck, you'll come out of this wearing a second star."

A wry smile creased Dunmoore's lips.

"My single star is acting, while so employed, Gregor. The navy is way over its authorized flag officer numbers because of the wartime expansion, which means I can become a captain again with a simple administrative instruction. The names of acting, while so employed commodores don't make the rear admirals' promotion list."

"So?" Pushkin waved away her objection with a dismissive shake of the head. "The way this war is going, you'll move far enough up the list within a year to be among those whose acting promotions become permanent. Admirals are still retiring on schedule, those who hit their level of incompetence are still being made to resign, and some die, whether in battle, by accident or from illness or are invalided out of the service. Admiral Petras being a case in point."

"Perhaps."

"I'm convinced I'll see you wear a few additional stars on your collar in due course. Here," he held up his wine glass, "I know it's not Thursday, but I'll drink to a bloody war or a sickly season anyhow."

"I'd prefer toasting an early end to the war, but sure. A bloody war or a sickly season." They both took a sip. "That is the best wine I've tasted in ages."

"It's also the most expensive I've ever seen." Pushkin's theatrical grimace caused Dunmoore to chuckle. "But for you, nothing is too good. And in that vein, since we'll be at anchor, so to speak, for the next six days or until *Hawkwood* comes out of dry dock — whichever happens first — I want to invite you aboard *Jan Sobieski* for dinner."

"I accept with great pleasure. It'll be nice to see the former Stingrays again."

"In that case, expect Trevane Devall to pull out all the stops. And Chief Foste will make sure you're piped aboard in proper fashion. Perhaps you could bring Chief Guthren along if Zeke doesn't mind. Foste would surely enjoy spending a few hours with her mentor while we eat."

"I'll ask." Her wry smile returned. "You realize each captain in the task force will invite me to supper now. None of your colleagues will accept being outdone by *Jan Sobieski*'s wardroom, meaning I'll have six days to visit eight ships."

"Enjoy the ride, Commodore. You earned it."

— Twenty-Four —

Mishtak, head of the empire's governing council and the most powerful Shrehari alive, remained seated when Brakal entered his office. He was ushered in by an aide whose air of disapproval was finely calibrated to avoid causing overt offense while conveying disdain.

A cavernous, high-ceilinged space, the office showcased exquisitely carved furnishings and gleaming wood-paneled walls. The latter were covered with ancient tapestries made from the finest materials, including precious metals and gemstones. Various antique objects such as pre-spaceflight helmets and weaponry scattered here and there on sideboards and tables tried to add a vaguely martial atmosphere but with little success.

Brakal studied his surroundings rather than look at Mishtak and put on a disapproving air himself at the crass display of wealth while ordinary citizens suffered ever-rising taxes.

"You do not deprive yourself of luxury, Mishtak. Good. Someone in your position needs every bit of coddling and decadence he can get. Does Lady Kembri know your office surpasses her own reception room in opulence or the one which will belong to Emperor Tumek when the child comes of age? If the dynasty survives the next few turns."

Mishtak's eyes widened at Brakal's words.

"Careful, Speaker of the Kraal. Even you are not immune from charges of insulting the empire's rulers, let alone treason by suggesting the dynasty may be in peril."

Brakal met Mishtak's gaze for the first time. A mocking rictus, half contempt, half challenge revealed his fangs.

"Of course. Yet the dynasty may be in peril nonetheless if we do not end this war with the humans. Surely your *Tai Kan* servants bring you word of discontent growing among the civilian population and within the Deep Space Fleet. If it grows sufficiently under the enemy's relentless assaults, who can tell when this mood might shift and become something worse. Our species' sense of honor is a demanding master, Mishtak. Imperial rulers who forget tend to rule no more than a prison cell in the days before their execution. Losing to the humans would strike a mortal blow on our honor." He took one of the soft chairs facing Mishtak's desk. "The Kraal will see this does not happen."

"The Kraal has no say on matters exclusively in the council's remit."

"On the contrary. The Kraal has every right to intervene in the council's handling of matters affecting the empire's wellbeing."

"Why are you here?"

"So it is publicly known we met. As equals. You head the executive, and until the Kraal votes otherwise, I head the legislature."

A mocking rumble shook Mishtak's chest.

"Equals? Hardly. You are but a failed admiral. One among many incapable of winning against an inferior foe."

"You should cut back on your daily consumption of ale, Mishtak. The alcohol is making you believe in your own propaganda. You and I realize by now the humans are the furthest thing from inferior foes. Otherwise, we would have reduced them to vassals long ago. Instead, they enter our realm with increasing impunity, striking blow after blow against our forces. It must end before our fellow Shrehari citizens uncover the ugly truth and demand accountability in a way not seen for many generations. You and I can work together, or we can work against each other. But understand this. Oppose the Kraal, and you will lose power. After that, you may as well spend the rest of your life enjoying your estates. No one will allow you in the capital ever again. Even if you defeat me and silence the four hundred."

"Big words from a small lord."

"Careful, Mishtak. Even you are not immune from a challenge among Shrehari of equivalent social rank."

When he saw a thunderous expression distort his opponent's gargoyle features, Brakal laughed.

"Your sense of honor has suffered under your thirst for power. Ruler of the empire you might be, but the rules still apply, even to one in your lofty position. Oh, and before I forget. I have a second motive for our meeting, a more personal one. If anything happens to me after this, such as injury or death from an assassin's knife, you will be openly suspected of sponsoring the act. And the Kraal, after electing a new speaker, will ensure retribution. As I said, oppose us, and you will retire from public life, whether you want to or not. Work with us and let your name be remembered as the one who saved the empire."

Mishtak made a dismissive gesture, but it seemed forced to Brakal's eyes, just as his next words rang false to his ears. Uncertainty, perhaps even worry, was settling over the empire's most powerful leader.

"If your goal was frightening me, then you failed. The Kraal has no power at a time when the empire's efforts and resources must be focused on our final victory. Did you speak your piece? If so, leave and do not return to the Forbidden Quarter."

"The Kraal's seat is in the Forbidden Quarter."

"The Kraal will not meet without my permission."

This time Mishtak's empty bravado was unmistakable, as were the slight tremors he fought hard to conceal from his visitor.

"We do not need your permission." Brakal stood. "The Kraal exists separately from the emperor and the council and answers to neither. Ponder my words, Mishtak, and see if you can show wisdom at last. The future of our race may depend on it."

"Perhaps I should throw you in the *Tai Kan* dungeon now instead of letting you return home. It seems a wise choice at the moment."

"Your rule would not survive another tenday if that. Many senior *Tai Kan* leaders also understand what we admirals, clan lords, and Kraal members have come to realize. Their front line officers see what we see and come to the same conclusions as us. I would be out of the dungeon before nightfall, and you would lose the last of your supporters within the apparatus of state." Brakal turned on his heels and left without another word, let alone Mishtak's permission.

He walked past the supercilious aide, though not before giving him a dangerous glance promising retribution for his silent insolence.

Once in his ground car, Brakal sat back and exhaled slowly, as if setting his anger at Mishtak's intransigence free to contaminate the Forbidden Quarter.

"May I assume it went as expected, Lord?" Regar asked. "You seem suitably irritated."

"You may. I gave Mishtak fair warning. As expected, he forbade the Kraal from assembling, though he knew the order was as worthless as what passes for his sense of honor." Brakal leaned forward. "Take us away from this cesspit, Toralk."

"We now understand each other's position," he continued. "I gave him a chance to work with the Kraal in finding a way forward and saving the dynasty from an enraged citizenry should our despised enemies prove the council's propaganda has been nothing but a lie. A lie whose sole aim is distracting the citizenry and hiding our rulers' greed and incompetence."

"Will he concede?"

Laughter rumbled up Brakal's throat.

"Never. Mishtak believes in his propaganda as if it was truth handed down by the gods themselves. Absolute power has addled his wits, and there is no cure for such a disease save execution. The idiot even insulted me directly, forgetting he remains bound by custom and would answer for any smear on another's honor." Brakal fell silent as a thoughtful expression replaced his earlier scorn. "Now that I think back on the meeting, Mishtak appeared prematurely aged, as if his soul was decaying along with his body. Perhaps his wits are rotting away as well."

"But you achieved the aim, which is what matters," Regar said. "The idle tongues infesting this den of iniquity will spread the word far and wide across Shredar that Brakal, Lord of Clan Makkar and Speaker of the Kraal bearded Mishtak in his own lair and challenged the council's supremacy on all things concerning the imperial government."

"Huh," Brakal grunted dismissively. "That and three *taklags* will buy me a mug of drinkable ale."

Toralk glanced over his shoulder, spearing Brakal with hard eyes.

"We are not stopping at a tavern, Lord."

Regar made a gesture of approval.

"I agree. Mishtak's first reaction after recovering from the shock of your words might well involve setting his *Tai Kan* assassins on you again, this time with orders to kill rather than intimidate. The estate's cellars are filled with any vintage your demanding palate might desire, and no snipers or other deadly creatures can disturb you there."

Brakal glanced at Toralk and Regar in turn.

"I sense this is a debate I shall not win. Very well. Take us home, miscreant."

"A wise choice," Regar said. "Did you consider calling your closest allies in the Kraal and informing them of your meeting with Mishtak so they may spread the word? Perhaps I could arrange for a conference via comlink upon our return to the estate. The more who are aware you challenged him, the better. It will give those still wavering added courage once word reaches them. You should not wait much past the end of this change of the moons before assembling the Kraal."

"Agreed. Make the necessary arrangements."

— Twenty-Five —

Jan *Sobieski*'s crew received Dunmoore the day after her first command conference as commodore with enough formality to please the most demanding coxswain in the Fleet. Eleven bosun's whistles, a full honor guard on the hangar deck and, since the frigate didn't carry her own band, recorded music for the occasion.

As soon as the arrival ceremony was over, the former Stingrays who now served under Gregor Pushkin's command lined up in the passageway to greet her and Chief Petty Officer Guthren. Dunmoore was pleased she could still remember every name even after all this time.

The last to welcome and congratulate her, just before Chief Petty Officer Foste steered her erstwhile mentor to the chiefs and petty officers' mess adjoining the wardroom was Lieutenant Commander Trevane Devall, *Jan Sobieski*'s first officer.

"The star looks fantastic on your collar, Commodore. Thank you for accepting our invitation to dine with *Jan Sobieski*'s officers." He gestured at the open door. "Our home is your home."

As she entered, trailed by Pushkin and Devall, those officers who hadn't served with her in *Stingray* and were waiting in the wardroom instead of greeting her in the corridor, came to attention.

"At ease, please. I'm merely a guest." She turned to Devall. "Why don't you introduce your messmates, Commander?"

After he'd done so, a young ensign who looked as if she graduated from the academy the previous week shyly offered Dunmoore a glass of wine.

"It won't be as fine as the one Emma Cullop served," Pushkin remarked in a low voice, "but Trevane keeps a good cellar."

She took a sip and smiled at him.

"The wine is excellent, Gregor. Considering your first officer's family origins, I expected no less. *Jan Sobieski*'s wardroom will be hard to top in this task force."

"You mean after *Iolanthe*'s?"

"The flagship has a higher standard to uphold."

Pushkin chuckled.

"I still can't get over the fact you're a commodore, and that behemoth of yours is a flagship."

"Then you and Zeke have something in common. And it's that former behemoth of mine. My promotion and appointment may not be substantive just yet, but Zeke's are."

**

After a pleasant meal, Pushkin invited Dunmoore to join him in the privacy of his quarters for a snifter of brandy.

"This is not top-shelf stuff," he said, handing his former captain a glass half-filled with amber liquid before sitting down across from her, on the other side of a low table, "but it doesn't bite either. Which is more than I can say for what the wardroom serves — at my chief engineer's behest I hasten to add. Trevane knows a battle he can't win when he sees it."

"Like every good first officer." She raised her snifter. "Your health, Gregor. *Jan Sobieski* is an impressive ship, and your officers strike me as more literate and intellectually curious than most wardroom denizens in our beloved Fleet."

"The luck of the draw."

"A captain's influence more likely," she gave him a complicit wink.

"And who did I learn it from?" Pushkin took a sip and sighed. "We've come far since the day you took *Stingray*, haven't we? I never thought I'd get my own command back then, let alone a gem such as *Jan Sobieski*. And I daresay you never figured to wear a commodore's star, let alone take over a raider task force such as Luckner."

"True." She tasted her brandy and nodded. "Nice. From Dordogne?"

"Of course. A commander without friends in low places can't afford the good stuff from Earth. If you thought the Chateau Pétrus dug up by Emma Cullop was expensive, you should see what a real cognac costs." Pushkin shivered in mock horror.

"Pass." Another sip. "We certainly came far. In retrospect I can't quite figure how we turned the mess Helen Forenza left me into a tightly knit, fighting crew, except I couldn't have done it without you."

A bark of laughter escaped Pushkin's lips.

"What I remember most is me being the surliest first officer in the entire navy. I'd not have blamed you for putting me ashore."

"I'd have been a fool to do so. The navy needs senior officers who can work their way through the toughest situations and not lose their professionalism."

"Again, who did I learn it from? You were pretty close to the edge yourself during those early days." After a pause, Pushkin said, "Changing the subject before this becomes uncomfortably mawkish, do you ever wonder what happened to our old foe Brakal? Any idea whether he made it back from that planet of the dingbats — what was it called again? Miranda?"

"Apparently he did. Last I saw his name mentioned in an intelligence report, they thought him to be somewhere in or near our area of operations. We might even have crossed paths without knowing. A few *Tol* class cruisers escaped *Iolanthe*'s guns in the last year or so, and not because we didn't try."

"He always was one of the wiliest bastards on their side. Thank the Almighty there aren't too many of his sort."

"Even if there were, the churn intelligence is reporting among the upper ranks in front line formations will blunt the efforts of even the best among them."

Pushkin gave her an ironic glance.

"Must be nice reading up on the life and times of our favorite enemies. Any chance you could share those intelligence digests with your faithful starship captains?"

Dunmoore gave him an astonished glance.

"You mean Lena wasn't distributing them? But I saw several in recent weeks."

"I'll bet you were the only one, thanks to Admiral Petras bringing you in on his planning sessions. Lena's the sort who figures keeping knowledge close-held increases her power over common mortals. Damn good thing she's gone."

"I'll disseminate everything I received since joining Luckner the moment I'm back in *Iolanthe*."

"Thank you. And did I mention how pleased I am you're our new task force commander?"

She gave him a fond smile.
"Several times, Gregor."

**

"How is *Hawkwood*?" Dunmoore asked the moment Kirti Midura's hologram materialized at *Iolanthe*'s conference table.

"The dry dock did a decent job, sir. We completed the non-essential repairs during our jump outward. She's as good as she'll be short of a full refit, except for the flag bridge. There was no time to start on it, but that can be remedied during the next few jumps."

"Don't bother. I'm fine in *Iolanthe*."

"That's what I figured, sir, which is why I put the flag bridge at the bottom of the priority list."

"Excellent." Dunmoore turned to the virtual Idris Pohlman. "And *Tamurlane*? Did anything shake loose in transit?"

"We're good, Commodore. And ready for battle."

She gave him thumbs up.

"Wonderful."

Once all of Luckner's captains were in attendance — as holographic projections except for Ezekiel Holt, she said, "Good afternoon. The moment you've been waiting for has arrived. Now that we crossed into interstellar space, I can reveal our orders."

Tempted to let the anticipation build just a bit more, she looked around the table and saw eagerness on every face, except for Holt's. He wore the sardonic smile she knew well while he waited for her to speak.

"Task Force Luckner will conduct a raid on the Shrehari Empire's home star system."

Audible gasps reached her ears.

"Though we will attempt to cause havoc by targeting military installations and shipping within sight of Shrehari Prime while ensuring we can escape and return home, the mission's purpose is primarily non-kinetic. Admiral Xi's stated goal is pushing the enemy off balance, causing a loss of confidence in their military leadership, making them consider withdrawing front line units to strengthen core defenses, and most importantly from my point of view, striking a blow at the empire's honor."

"In other words, trigger political instability by proving us weak, cowardly humans can reach out and tickle the imperial regent's royal behind with impunity," Holt said, a sly grin spreading across his face. "Contrary to everything their propaganda has been telling them since before the war."

Dunmoore nodded.

"Just so. The shock of human warships appearing at the home system's heliopause merely to show we can do so will be bad enough on its own. Bagging a few starships, maybe hitting a refueling station or even doing a quick in and out at Shrehari Prime's hyperlimit would be even better from our viewpoint."

Holt's grin broadened.

"If we're going to hit the capital's hyperlimit, we might as well launch a recon drone at the Forbidden Quarter in Shredar with a message suggesting they request an armistice. It'll prove even their precious emperor and his council are vulnerable."

Farren Vento chuckled with glee.

"I do prefer our new flag captain to the old one."

Holt winked at him with his solitary eye.

"We glory hounds need to stick together."

"Just to play the devil's advocate, but won't that goad them into making a retaliatory raid against Earth?"

Commander Pohlman asked. "If they see us risking a task force on such a mission, they'll surely not hesitate. Did Fleet HQ really think this through? Kinetic strikes from high orbit could devastate *our* homeworld."

A smile played on Dunmoore's lips.

"They did. Remember, the enemy has consistently underestimated us, which is why they attacked in the first place. We were, at least in the minds of their leaders, a soft target which would distract political opponents from the uneasy situation when the old emperor died before his heir reached the age of majority. They did not, and mostly still do not consider us courageous or warlike. It means the idea of our forces threatening their homeworld in what some might consider a hopelessly dangerous operation will not have crossed their minds.

"Consequently, the Shrehari did not fortify the planet's high orbitals or the orbitals of the other settled worlds in their native star system. Our superiors and political leaders, on the other hand, harbor no such delusions. A Shrehari raiding force would not make it past Earth's hyperlimit if it even got that far. Besides, as I said, our job is showing the flag and proving we can threaten the very heart of the empire, not bombarding civilian targets and causing needless deaths which would call for brutal retaliation. This mission is psychological warfare at its finest."

Dunmoore suddenly noticed the smug expression on Pushkin's face.

"What?"

"When you said we would imitate, at least in part, an operation from Earth's second global conflict, I spent my downtime scanning the history of those years for anything notable that might parallel our situation."

She arched a questioning eyebrow.

"And?"

"I came across an operation carried out by the United States of America called the Doolittle Raid, targeting the capital of the Japanese Empire, circa 1942. They designed it as a psychological strike rather than a kinetic one, just like ours, to raise doubts about the Japanese military's ability to defend their country."

"Congratulations, Gregor. That was indeed the mission I was thinking about when I first mentioned we had orders which could make Task Force Luckner more than just a minor footnote in history. But contrary to the Doolittle raiders, we will return home instead of ditching our ships on a friendly planet." When everyone other than Pushkin and Holt gave her a strange look, she shrugged. "Check it out. If Gregor found the mission in *Jan Sobieski*'s database, you can find it in yours."

"Though excellent for the morale of the United States, later historians agree the raid's effects on the Japanese empire's psyche was less than anticipated," Pushkin said.

"True, but the Shrehari don't think in the same way as we humans. They believe not only we're an inferior species, but that the heart of their empire is invulnerable, something the Japanese knew wasn't true for their home islands. Their commander-in-chief, an admiral by the name Yamamoto Isoroku even said, before the outbreak of hostilities, *in the first six to twelve months of a war with the United States I will run wild and win victory upon victory. But if the war continues after that, I have no expectation of success.*

"Our foe, however, still believes in a final victory, even after years of stalemate and is therefore much more vulnerable to something which will cause him traumatic cognitive dissonance. And that cognitive dissonance will be signed, sealed, and delivered by Task Force Luckner."

— Twenty-Six —

When the door to Dunmoore's quarters opened at her command, Holt stuck his head in and held up the mahogany box containing the chess set she'd gifted him.

"I thought you might enjoy a little distraction now that we're on our way to give the boneheads a deadly case of existential angst."

She put her reader on the desk and smiled.

"An excellent idea. Here or at my dining table?"

"It would seem strange at the table. I don't think we've ever played on anything other than your desk."

He opened the box, took out the chessmen, and flipped it over before placing each piece on its respective square. While he did so, Dunmoore went to the sideboard and filled two mugs of coffee. She put both on the desk and retook her chair.

"What were your impressions of the conference?" Dunmoore took a sip and watched Holt over the rim of the cup.

He tilted his head to one side as if searching for the most appropriate response.

"A tad zanier than the norm, I think. My fellow starship captains certainly seemed less inhibited now than under your predecessor when it comes to speaking their minds. No one is against the mission, but I figure they're half thrilled at making history and half worried it might turn into a deadly clusterfuck so deep inside enemy space."

"What about you?"

"We've pulled stunts the average frigate skipper can only dream about and never even scratched the old girl's hull. Raiding the enemy's home system is just another wild mission for the good Q-ship *Iolanthe*. One of many."

"So no worries?"

"I'd be lying if I said no. She's mine now, and that means I'll be fretting the same way you did." He nodded at the board. "If you want white, it's yours."

"No. Black is fine. You still need every possible advantage."

Holt made his opening move, then picked up his coffee mug.

"Any idea of how HQ came up with this scheme? I didn't think anyone, even in SOCOM, was bold enough to put such a proposal in front of Grand Admiral Shkadov, or Shkadov daring enough to obtain SecGen approval." When he saw Dunmoore's lips twitch, Holt's single eye narrowed with suspicion. "What did you do?"

"My patrol report included an additional and highly confidential Admiral Xi's eyes only attachment. On top of suggesting Lena was better employed at a desk job, I also proposed we take the deep raid concept to its inevitable conclusion — harassing the imperial capital in a show of courage and strength which would affect enemy morale."

Holt shook his head.

"And once more, it's *l'audace, encore de l'audace, toujours de l'audace et la Patrie sera sauvée!* That's you all right, Skipper. And kudos for getting Corto back where she belongs. Admiral Xi probably walked your proposal directly to the grand admiral's office moments after he read it. This isn't the type of mission that normally gets approved so quickly. Mind you, being daring didn't do Georges Danton, who coined the expression, much good. He lost his head if I recall correctly."

"Quite literally. And if we fail, I might lose mine, but figuratively, though the boss was kind enough to let me decide what I considered success — within the general parameters he set."

They played on in silence for another fifteen minutes until Holt forced Dunmoore into accepting a draw. He sat up, satisfied, and nodded at the coffee mugs.

"A refill."

"Sure. Another match?"

"Of course." As he wandered over to the sideboard, Holt asked, "How will you stay busy during the trip, now that you're no longer running the Furious Faerie? Commodores in hyperspace are about as useful on a warship as a piano tuner."

She began resetting the board.

"Stay out of your way. Read. Spend a few hours per day exercising. See if Tatiana's hand-to-hand combat trainer will accept a private pupil."

Holt chuckled as he returned with full servings.

"Why not ask our soldiers to run you through their boarding party drills as well? You might get fresh ideas after experiencing their techniques, tactics, and procedures first hand."

A thoughtful expression crossed her face as she accepted a mug.

"I know you were joking, but it may not be a bad idea."

Holt raised his hand in a ritualistic manner.

"I give you my blessing, but please avoid injuries. I might be on board with this mission, but I don't possess your mystical ability to take crazy risks and come out smelling like a candidate for promotion."

"Keep playing chess as you've done lately, and I think you might catch up with me. Since you forced the draw, you play white again." Once Holt made his opening move, she asked, "Not that it's any of my business nowadays, but how did your department heads react when you read them my orders?"

"Pretty much as you might expect. After a few moments of delighted incredulity at us taking the war to the imperial capital, Emma immediately began worrying about time, distance, and our fuel and consumable stocks, if I read the gleam in her eyes correctly. I saw her give Joelle a covert glance, indicating they would put their heads together the moment I was done and go through the inventory."

Dunmoore chuckled. "Sounds about right."

"Thorin kept that bloodthirsty grin of his pasted on while no doubt wondering whether we should have crammed a few more missile packs into our holds. Astrid got a dreamy look when she realized that as the flagship's navigator, she'd be plotting the first-ever FTL trip to Shrehari Prime by a Commonwealth Navy unit."

"It'll mean her name ends up in the history books."

"And I'm sure Tatiana was wondering whether there would be anything for her soldiers to do and make the Scandia Regiment proud, though she maintained her usual impassive expression. Only Renny seemed unimpressed, which was reassuring. Starship engineers who impress too easily scare me."

"How about Chief Guthren?"

"Almost as inscrutable as Tatiana and Renny, but he clearly approves." Holt moved a piece. "If you're wondering about the crew's reaction, don't worry. Everyone is excited at the prospect of tweaking bonehead skull ridges within sight of their emperor's palace. I'm sure we'll find rude messages aimed at the Shrehari scribbled on the missiles sitting in our launchers. Our folks live for this sort of stuff."

"At least insofar as you know."

Holt shrugged.

"I had a good sense for the mood in *Iolanthe* as the first officer. Even though I'm her skipper now, the chiefs and petty officers still keep me aware of what's what. Just as they did with you. Besides, hitting the enemy's home system epitomizes the Furious Faerie's motto, and you know spacers. They delight in showing their ship's fighting spirit."

"True."

They played on in silence until Holt moved his queen, sat back, eyes glued to the board and let out a low whistle.

"I do believe you're toast, Commodore."

She studied the chess pieces, frowning, then reached out with a gloved index finger to tip her king over on his side.

"There. Your mystical abilities are growing apace. Soon, the apprentice will outmatch his sensei."

"Never. I scored a draw followed by a win tonight only because your mind isn't fully on the game. Are you perhaps worried about the mission now that we're underway and can't change anything until the task force drops out of FTL to tack deep inside enemy space?"

Dunmoore didn't immediately reply.

"Perhaps," she finally said, looking up and into Holt's eyes. "When it was just us — *Iolanthe*, I mean — heading into risky situations, at least I could directly influence our destiny. Now? I'm responsible for eight other starships and their crews, each under a captain who will act and react in his or her own way, no matter what I might have done in the same situation. I didn't quite understand it in my gut until today, until the moment we went FTL on the first leg to Shrehari Prime, how little control a flag officer has over her formation's destiny once she launches an operation. I have basically no role between now and when we reach the target area. And I don't know how to deal with it."

A sad smile tugged at her lips. "When you said commodores in hyperspace have about as much use on a warship as a piano tuner, you couldn't imagine how close you came to how I feel right now."

"I apologize for that, Skipper."

She waved his words away.

"This is my problem, not yours. I don't know how Petras dealt with it, and it's too late for me to ask. At least formation commanders who run their battle groups from a starbase can always bury themselves in administrative work and forget they can't directly control starships that are light-years away."

"Perhaps he and Lena spent their waking hours playing war games, dissing uppity captains such as *Iolanthe*'s former commanding officer, and planning for a glorious future as the rising stars of SOCOM."

"Or perhaps they no longer remembered how busy they were as captains to notice how idle they became sitting in a flag bridge with not much work most of the time."

Holt raised both hands, palms facing outward.

"Hey, if you want to share the burden of running *Iolanthe* with me, I'll gladly give you the stuff I don't enjoy. Then we can both be at least half busy."

"Sorry. That would confuse the crew. She's yours, the annoying parts included. I'll just find a way to adapt and overcome, as always. I'm sure the stress of making on the spot decisions once we're at the heart of the enemy's empire will more than compensate for my idleness during our passage."

"True. And I for one am glad you'll be dealing with those decisions under fire and not me. Another match? I can't let you retire for the night without a single victory. Your morale might not survive."

"My morale is doing fine, thank you very much. But yes, another match it is, though no more coffee." She righted her king and placed him back in his proper opening position, along with the rest of the black chess pieces.

"You can play white this time around."

"I don't accept charity," she growled. "Let alone pity. Sort yourself out, Captain. And don't you dare make deliberate mistakes to throw the game. Not only will I notice but you'll be stuck here playing until I'm satisfied my wits aren't on vacation."

Holt grinned at her.

"Perish the thought. You've never shown me pity. Why the hell should I show you any? After all, you consider chess a blood sport, and that means no mercy for the weak." He bowed his head respectfully. "Sensei."

— Twenty-Seven —

When the last of Brakal's guests, one of two dozen among the Kraal lords he either trusted the most or absolutely needed on his side, took a seat at the expansive table in the manor's formal dining room, Brakal inclined his head in greeting.

"Since we are all here, it is time to decide. There can be no hesitation and no prevarication once we assemble in the Jakrang. The vote must be swift, it must command a vast majority, and it must be decisive. Any delays will give Mishtak time to act against us. Though he does not command the loyalty of every ground forces officer in and around Shredar, he can count on a number sufficient to make those still uncommitted hesitate."

"The Fourth Imperial Assault Regiment is ours," General of the Third Rank Vagh said. "Its new commander was whelped in my clan. He will deploy around the Jakrang on a training exercise at short notice."

"What about the First, Second, and Third Guards Regiments?" Another of the lords, also a retired ground forces general asked. "Their loyalty to the child emperor and his regent remains beyond reproach."

"So long as we oppose only Mishtak and the council, they will not threaten us," Vagh replied. "Their commanders look to the regent for direction, not the council. Besides, I believe Brakal already let Lady Kembri know we will preserve the dynasty from Mishtak's incompetence, or worse yet, an uprising of the people, should they believe the empire's honor is wounded by our defeats at human hands."

"She knows," Brakal said, recalling his veiled visitor. "Though it would be good if we had ears in the barracks of the Guards Regiments, Vagh."

"I shall endeavor to find some, but hear me. Even Guards soldiers will not fire upon their Assault Regiment brothers unless placed under extreme duress. So long as we stay utterly loyal to the child emperor and his mother, we need not fear them."

"So long as we are also clearly *seen* to be utterly loyal," Admiral of the Third Rank Edronh growled. "We know our goal is ensuring the dynasty's continued welfare, so the empire does not dissolve in fire and blood from within, but some might claim otherwise to brand us as traitors and discredit the Kraal."

"True." Brakal made a gesture of assent. "And therefore, the Kraal will vote on taking a public oath of fealty to Emperor Tumek. That vote will pass by four hundred voices in favor and none against. No one could ask for better."

"It would set an unusual precedent," one of the civilian lords said. He was already sitting in the Kraal when Brakal still ran wild on the Makkar country estate with the other younglings of the clan and was, therefore, the group's wise elder. "The empire is balanced on three quasi-equal legs, with one slightly more powerful than the other two — the emperor. Our swearing a public oath to Tumek, let alone his mother, could make the Kraal seem inferior to Tumek's hand, the governing council."

"Again, true." Brakal acknowledged the ancient lord's intervention with a polite gesture. "But once we achieve our goal, a *kho'sahra* will supplant the governing council, so perhaps the point is moot. No one will consider a dictator named by the Kraal superior to the Kraal."

The ancient graciously indicated his acceptance of Brakal's response.

"Does anyone object to the Kraal taking an oath so we may prove our loyalty?" When no one demurred, he asked, "How many can we count on as of today?"

Brakal turned his eyes on Vagh, who replied, "The forty with whom I spoke will vote with you, but of those, a quarter could still waver if Mishtak threatens their lives or those of their principal clan members."

"They understand Mishtak knows threats against clan lords and their kin will most assuredly precipitate the bloody unrest we fear, and therefore he will not go to such lengths?"

"They understand up here." Vagh tapped his thick skull. "But not with their souls, and as with most of our race, the soul still rules."

"We will strengthen those timid spirits." Brakal turned to Vagh's neighbor. "You."

"The same. Of the thirty-two I brought in, six or seven are not particularly solid, though none demurred outright."

And thus it went around the table until they accounted for all lords of the Kraal. If those who swore to vote as Brakal wished kept their promise, the motion would pass, though not overwhelmingly. Still, if Trage had not removed so many senior officers who were also clan lords from their posts on spurious grounds, Brakal could not have hoped for even that majority. He would take what he could, and if it was insufficient, he would find another way to impose his will.

"We are in agreement? The Kraal can meet whenever I call for it?" None of the lords present dissented. "So it will be done. The precise day and time shall stay secret, even from you, my friends, until the very last moment."

"You will find the Fourth Imperial Assault Regiment ready to move at a few hours' notice," Vagh said. "Issue the call early in the morning and fix the time for midday. When we and our fellow lords enter the Jakrang, it shall be secure against Mishtak's *Tai Kan* minions."

"Then we must ensure all of us live long enough to take our places on the old stone seats and vote." Grunts of approval greeted Brakal's closing declaration. "Ale and other libations are served in the reception room through the door at my back. Join me while I offer the gods a few drops and demand their support."

**

"Satisfied?" Brakal asked Regar when the latter joined him in the reception room after his visitors were gone. Regar had watched the meeting and subsequent reception from the estate's security office.

"Since I do not believe you could have done better in the time available, my answer must be yes. Though I found Lord Unagroth of Clan Ruktah shifty."

"Explain."

Brakal kept his gaze on Regar while the *Tai Kan* officer searched for the right words. Unagroth was an old civilian lord, one who never served the empire other than in the Kraal. His clan, from the hard-scrabble, cold southern continent, was well known for avoiding any activity that did not enrich it.

But because of Unagroth's longevity in the legislature and apparent political neutrality, he could influence over two dozen civilian lords who were of the same mind, hence his presence among a group of mostly military lords anxious for the empire's future across the stars. Convincing him the government's current course led to a disaster which would impoverish everyone proved to be the key. That he and his closest allies cared more about their wealth than the empire's honor, however, made them less reliable.

"An impression, Lord. Nothing more. The others appeared forthright, and even those who might feel apprehension at taking such an irreversible step seemed convinced it must be done. Unagroth? He could still be weighing the risks and rewards, as a true member of Clan Ruktah would."

"We need his vote and those of his allies. They represent a large proportion of the civilian lords and might influence the rest. An outcome which might split us military lords from those who never served will harm the *kho'sahra*'s legitimacy."

"Indeed." Regar tilted his head to one side. "There may be a way of ensuring Unagroth sees the greater risk in sitting on his hands instead of voting with you."

"Speak."

"Did you ever meet First Deputy Director Kroesh?"

"The *Tai Kan*'s second in command? No."

"Then perhaps it might be useful if you invite him here and discuss your intentions. Remember I once mentioned he does not see things the same way as his superior, Director Yatron?"

"I do. Yatron is Mishtak's creature. Kroesh is not."

"Just so. I could arrange for such an invitation. Perhaps even for tomorrow's evening meal."

Brakal studied Regar through suspicious eyes.

"You seem to enjoy extraordinary connections with those surrounding the high and mighty in Shredar. I cannot help but wonder, and not for the first time, why your loyalty to me is greater than the loyalty you give your employer. A *Tai Kan* officer working so wholeheartedly in support of the Kraal's desire to replace the governing council with a *kho'sahra* is unheard of. Do you seek control of the *Tai Kan* as your prize once we remove Mishtak and his allies?"

Regar's upper lip curled back in amusement.

"No. That prize must be offered to Kroesh when you meet with him."

"Then what are your motivations?"

"Turning an idea that has been with me for a long time into reality."

Brakal, suddenly eager to hear what could make a *Tai Kan* officer abandon his service in favor of an admiral dismissed by the council's pet, Trage, gestured at the collection of bottles on a side table, then at the deep, hide-covered chair in front of him.

"Take what you wish and sit. I will hear about this idea of yours if only so I might better understand a warrior I thought to know well already."

Regar took a bottle of ale, uncapped it, and dropped into the seat with a sound of contentment.

"I was wondering when I might finally broach the subject with you." He took a healthy sip of the foaming, purplish liquid. "Ah. You always serve the finest, Lord. That is almost enough to earn anyone's loyalty."

"Do not toy with me, spy."

"And that is the origin of my idea. Everyone calls *Tai Kan* officers spies, though truly we are not. We are the imperial police, entrusted with ferreting out traitors, suppressing disloyalty and banned political movements, of protecting the Forbidden Quarter and more."

Brakal grunted.

"Matters related to the empire's internal security."

"Precisely. And yet, shortly before the start of the war, the council also tasked us with intelligence gathering on matters other than internal security. Such as painting an accurate picture of human capabilities, strengths, weaknesses, intentions, and anything else that might help the empire's military forces win."

"A task the *Tai Kan* singularly failed at, hence our slowly losing to the thrice-damned hairless apes from Earth."

"Therein lies the issue. An internal security agency is ill-equipped to spy on anything but its own citizens. The empire needs a separate intelligence service, one dedicated to ferreting out what it can on our external foes."

"A *Tai Zohl*," Brakal replied in a thoughtful tone, using the ancient term for *Kan*'s opposite. "An outward eye, to complement the inward eye instead of the latter looking in every direction without seeing a thing. Interesting, and well overdue. Strange that a *Tai Kan* spy would come up with the idea."

"I am hardly the only one, Lord. Many of us see what is necessary but are unable or unwilling to speak for fear of punishment. The *Tai Kan* will never voluntarily relinquish its outward intelligence-gathering functions, even though it cannot perform them with any success. But I am fortunate I now serve an admiral known for his open mind and who will soon claim enormous influence within the imperial government. With the council supplanted by a dictator and the *Tai Kan* led by one of the dictator's allies, implementation will be much easier."

"It would indeed take a *kho'sahra* to order its creation. Though a bit late for the war effort."

"This war, yes. But there will be more wars and conflicts we would avoid if we knew about the enemy's strength and dispositions instead of relying on prejudice and wishful thinking. And even when we are at peace with the humans, we will need an outward eye on their activities, so they do not threaten our interests on non-violent battlefields. Commerce, for example."

"True."

Sensing his lord's growing approval, Regar said, "Many good minds serve the *Tai Kan* today which would be better used creating and building a *Tai Zohl*."

"Minds such as yours?" Brakal asked, a sardonic grin baring his fangs.

"It would honor me to help create a new intelligence service."

"And become its first director, no doubt."

"If the *kho'sahra* calls upon me to serve as such, I would scarcely refuse."

"No promises."

Regar made a submissive gesture.

"Of course not."

"It is good you finally spoke of this, spy. I prefer knowing my retainers' motivations beyond selfless service to Clan Makkar. Now that I know yours and approve of them, I can be sure of your loyalty."

"And First Deputy Director Kroesh?"

"I would offer him my hospitality at his earliest convenience."

"Which he will accept. Kroesh has no doubt been following your work to reassemble the Kraal with great interest."

— Twenty-Eight —

To Brakal's surprise, First Deputy Director Kroesh did not resemble a conniving, devious bureaucrat at all. Dress him in an Imperial Ground Forces uniform, and he would pass for a senior combat commander, right down to the Warrior Caste ruff of fur on top of his angular, bony skull.

"Lord of Clan Makkar. Or do you prefer Admiral? Or perhaps Speaker of the Kraal?" Kroesh raised his fist in salute as he entered the manor's reception room where Brakal waited for his guest.

"Brakal will suffice, First Deputy Director. Those who hide behind titles, especially in private, are often hiding something else."

A rumble of amusement rose up Kroesh's broad chest.

"There is truth in what you say. And if I am to address you by name, then I ask that you do me the same honor."

Brakal made a gesture of respectful assent, then indicated the sideboard.

"Would you take a libation before the meal, Kroesh?"

"I would." The muscular *Tai Kan* official turned toward the extensive display of bottles. "Your house serves a fine vintage of the best ale, Brakal. I shall sample it with pleasure."

At Brakal's nod, Toralk, who led the visitor in and now stood silently by the open doorway, stirred into motion and served Kroesh.

After a healthy sip, the latter said, "As if brewed by the gods themselves. Did you know the humans can not only consume this without ill effects, they apparently prize it above many of their own concoctions?"

"Do they now? Fascinating. And does it affect their metabolism in the same way as it does ours?" Brakal accepted a bottle of ale from Toralk.

"So I understand. Perhaps sentient species which evolved to breathe the same gas mixtures and live under similar climatic conditions share more in common than we think. The humans developed a theory they call panspermia," Kroesh mangled the unfamiliar word beyond recognition. "It posits that life at a microscopic level was distributed throughout the galaxy by space dust, meteoroids, asteroids, comets and such things over incalculable periods, seeding planets hospitable to life everywhere. Some even believe an elder race might have seeded planets such as ours, Earth, Arkanna, and more, deliberately with the very building blocks of life. Or if you believe in the legends of the L'Taung civilization, perhaps not our present home world but that which gave birth to the imperial race eons ago, far from here. In any case, the humans also formulated several related theories attempting to explain why our part of the galaxy has such a prevalence of bipedal, bilateral sapient species able to survive in each other's environments and to a certain extent, consume each other's food and drink."

When he sensed Brakal's interest, Kroesh added, "I can ask my aide to send you what we culled from human databases on the subject, if you wish."

"Please do so. Anything that gives me knowledge about our foe is always welcome."

Brakal felt strangely pleased with his guest's display of esoteric knowledge about humans. It made a pleasant change from the average bureaucrat, both military and civilian, infesting Shredar. And, as with Kroesh's warrior-like demeanor, made a lie of the notion all senior *Tai Kan* officers were deceitful, weak creatures who used fear to gain respect.

"Ah, yes. Knowledge about our foe." Kroesh took another sip and studied Brakal for a few moments. "Something that has lacked from the start. When Mishtak first raised the idea of attacking the human empire and thereby gain glory for the child emperor Tumek, my superior, Director Yatron immediately sensed an opportunity to enlarge the *Tai Kan* and his own power. As a result, he demanded we become the empire's outward-facing eyes on top of our traditional duties. A failure, I should think."

"Very much so."

"It also weakened the *Tai Kan*'s internal security capability to the point where those who oppose Mishtak and the ruling council operate with impunity. And I do not speak merely of the Kraal, you understand. That challenge is new. No, there is more happening beneath the surface on the homeworld and on every imperial planet than meets the senses and has been for a long time. Things that could trigger enough unrest to weaken us further in our fight against the humans. Discontent. Feelings of alienation among subject races. Criminal elements. Corruption." Kroesh paused to take a sip. "The sooner we can shed our ill-conceived intelligence-gathering duties, the sooner we can refocus on internal security."

"Will Director Yatron see reason and relinquish them to a new service created just for such a purpose?"

Kroesh's lips peeled back.

"No. It would take someone strong, a Shrehari with the entire power of government in his hand to force such a change."

"One starting with Director Yatron's removal."

"Just so. You are perceptive, precisely as Regar claims."

Something in Kroesh's manner suddenly felt strange, and Brakal tilted his head to one side, studying him with impassive eyes.

"How is Regar known to you?"

"The whelp of a family friend, one whose career I helped along because he is both honorable and intelligent. When you were given command of *Tol Vehar*, he was my choice as your political officer."

"Why?"

"Because you struck me as one of the few Deep Space Fleet commanders who beheld the universe, the humans, and this damnable war with a clear, unsentimental gaze. And it appears my impression was correct."

"So you know about Regar's dreams for a *Tai Zohl*, an outward-looking eye, and you approve."

"Of course."

For a moment, the horrifying notion a faction within the *Tai Kan* was manipulating him overcame Brakal. But they could not have foreseen the human battleship destroying Khorsan Base, which led to his dismissal and his subsequent return home intent on reviving the Kraal.

Then, as if Kroesh could read his mind, he said, "No, we are not using you, Brakal. Watching you, yes. That was Regar's duty. Helping you where we could, that as well. Hoping you would somehow gain enough influence before this war destroyed us, definitely, because you are among those who truly know how disastrous Mishtak's decision to invade human space was since you are one of the few who understand our enemies. Your return to the homeworld took us by surprise, as did your open opposition to the council and the energy with which you are reviving the Kraal. But we are pleased."

"You keep using the plural. Who are the others?"

"Like-minded individuals in the directorates I control. Government officials responsible for security and law enforcement with whom I interact. Palace officials fearful the dynasty might lose the support of the citizenry thanks to Mishtak's intransigence and who whisper in my ear. And many others. Much is bubbling beneath the surface in Shredar and has been while you were fighting the humans on our frontiers. However, the various strands of disquiet need a catalyst to transcend mere words and become facts, something which will unite the disparate anti-Mishtak elements in pursuit of a common goal."

"And I am to be that catalyst?"

"You already are." An air of amusement seemed to cross Kroesh's face. "More is happening in Shredar of late than just the somnolent Kraal awakening to the cries of an empire in distress, though you know it not."

"And who controls these happenings?"

"No one. For now. But unless the Kraal truly rises and challenges Mishtak, things might spiral out of anyone's control when the time comes."

Brakal grunted before taking another mouthful of ale. After swallowing, he said, "And that brings us to Unagroth and others of his sort who might waver under the council's pressure — or its threats."

"The reason why Regar decided it was finally time you and I spoke openly."

"Correct. Satisfy my curiosity, if you will, Kroesh. When would you and I have spoken openly if not for Regar thinking the time was finally right?"

Kroesh made a gesture combining uncertainty with dismissal.

"Perhaps another reason would have arisen, or we would have continued to support you from afar until it became opportune for a formal and public meeting between us."

"Such as when the Kraal would search for a new *Tai Kan* director?"

"The soon to be named *kho'sahra* rather than the Kraal, but yes."

Brakal drained his bottle and held it out for Toralk, refusing a fresh one with a wave of the hand.

"You expect me to become that *kho'sahra*."

"Surely you don't think Mishtak will cooperate with the Kraal and admit his war was a mistake. He will refuse your entreaties. That leaves us with one course of action. Forcing the council's dissolution in favor of a *kho'sahra*. And according to our ancient traditions, the dictator must be a clan lord who is also an admiral or a general."

"There are many of us who are both."

"None with a vision to end this war before the dynasty falls and fall it will if the enemy ever turns our space into his playground. The regent supported Mishtak. His failure will be hers and her son's. Pray no human warships appear in the home system while Mishtak still governs in Lady Kembri's name. His failure to protect the heart of the empire would be more than anyone could bear and instead of a power transition accompanied by a few hundred arrests, we might face a bloodbath on the Field of Honor."

"You ask much of me."

Kroesh's lips curled back again.

"Nothing you do not ask of yourself. Be honest, Brakal. You saw a future as *kho'sahra* the instant you resolved to rouse the Kraal and force Mishtak's hand. You believe no one else could do better in ending the war and healing the empire.”

Brakal made a gesture of agreement.

“No one currently inhabiting the Forbidden Quarter. They would rather hide behind the belief in a final victory we cannot achieve, even if it costs us everything. Some of them would rather the empire perish in fire and blood than admit invading human space was a fatal mistake. Others spent turns drinking at the well of their own propaganda and are utterly blind to reality.”

“Then there is nothing left to discuss. We are in perfect agreement. I will make sure Unagroth and enough undecided Kraal members vote with the military lords, even once you face the necessity of removing the governing council and electing a *kho'sahra*.”

“What if the Kraal, in its wisdom, chooses another military lord for that honor?”

“An unlikely outcome. The military lords know you and the fire you carry within. The civilian lords know of Clan Makkar’s honor, their own losses to the council’s increasing taxes, and not much more. They will gladly hand the problem of our war against the humans to someone else.”

“And what if Mishtak launches a disinformation campaign branding the Kraal as traitors to delegitimize it and its decisions? Or separate the military lords from the civilian lords?”

“No one with a molecule of sense believes what comes out of the Forbidden Quarter any more. Common born or noble, let alone those who labor in the various ministries.”

“Shredar overflows with those who don’t even boast a single atom of common sense.” A thoughtful expression crossed Brakal’s face. “It makes me wonder what hold Mishtak has on Lady Kembri. She is cunning and ruthless in protecting her whelp until he rules in his own right. Surely she knows which way the winds of war are blowing."

"Does it matter? If the Kraal petitions her to dismiss the council and accept a *kho'sahra* named by the four hundred or face a coup which would taint her regency, Lady Kembri will choose wisely." Kroesh tapped his midriff with a clenched fist. "My hunger stirs, Lord of Clan Makkar, and I hear you set a fine table. I should honor it as few would in this city."

"Regar informed you of my table?" Brakal gestured toward the door leading to the dining room.

"No. He is discrete on matters concerning your clan, your house, and your privacy, as befits someone sworn to your service. You did well in accepting his oath. He will serve you as no other if you give him the chance to form a *Tai Zohl*."

"And you will head the *Tai Kan*. If not Regar informing the universe of Clan Makkar's culinary delights, then who?"

Another amused expression curled up Kroesh's black lips.

"That would be telling. We perforce share common acquaintances. Shredar is a big city in area and population, but for our sort, it is a mere village replete with gossips. Fear not. Your friends are loyal, and your supporters have motivations that will keep them honest."

"Our sort?"

"Those concerned for the welfare of the empire, its ruling dynasty, and a future devoid of bloody dynastic change."

— Twenty-Nine —

"**A**ll of Task Force Luckner's ships made it, Commodore," Chief Petty Officer Yens reported once her sensors recovered from dropping out of hyperspace. "And they're running silent. No sign of enemy activity or installations in our vicinity."

An awed hush settled over the CIC as eyes turned to the main display where one star shone brighter than any other.

"So that's the boneheads' native sun, is it?" Lieutenant Commander Sirico asked, his question directed at no one in particular. "Somebody pinch me. I can't believe we're actually here."

"Took us long enough," Major Tatiana Salminen replied from her battle stations post at the rear of the compartment. "And whether that is, in fact, their native sun has long been hotly debated in some corners. Look up the legend of the L'Taung civilization."

"Ah, yes." Sirico turned to grin at the soldier. "That strange story claiming the present-day Shrehari are descendants of an ancient star-faring empire which collapsed a hundred thousand years before our distant ancestors developed the first hints of civilization. Maybe those old boneheads visited Earth back then, leaving us with legends of eldritch gods."

"Not so strange, Thorin. Evidence of its existence has been found in several locations," Ezekiel Holt said, remembering the top-secret report detailing Admiral Corwin's treasure trove on Arietis. He and Dunmoore exchanged a knowing look.

"Ah well, it is an old universe, Captain. Who knows how many species rose to claim interstellar dominance and died away before our own even existed in its most primitive form? Mind you, for an ancient race, the boneheads aren't that smart if they attacked us without being sure we'd fold. And now, we'll make them truly regret that oversight." Sirico let out a contented sigh as he turned his eyes back on the main display. "Lovely view no matter what."

"Give me a few minutes, sir. It'll get better," Yens replied. "The sensors are trying to find Shrehari Prime itself."

Now that they were within reach of the target, Dunmoore felt trepidation at mapping out their next steps. She'd deliberately avoided making plans of action beyond getting here since no one knew about enemy dispositions, activities or anything else useful. The hardest thing would be fighting impatience while they observed.

Though she was intent on a display of confidence by coming as close to Shrehari Prime as possible while remaining beyond the resident assault division's weapons range, destroying a few antimatter cracking stations orbiting the star system's gas giants would do just as well. As would attacking a convoy, a subspace booster array, or any piece of insufficiently protected infrastructure in space.

Dunmoore kept reminding herself their mission was achieving a psychological effect. Physical damage would be incidental to the primary goal of damaging Shrehari morale.

The image on the main display wavered without warning. A small blue and white orb replaced the reddish sun.

"Shrehari Prime. The enemy's homeworld."

"It looks so peaceful, just as Earth does in every picture I've seen," Sirico said. "Or pretty much any of our worlds, actually. Just think about it. The idiots who figured invading the Commonwealth and causing countless deaths would be a great idea live within what? Less than a day's travel from here? Makes you wish for a flight of kinetic penetrators aimed at the imperial capital so you could watch the impact energy turn it into a glass-lined crater."

"An eye for an eye, Thorin?" Dunmoore asked with an eyebrow cocked in amusement at his heated words. A second after she spoke, she realized her mistake.

A broad grin split Sirico's face.

"Sure. Just ask the captain."

She gave Holt an involuntary glance only to see him wearing an amused expression.

"Strictly speaking," he said, "the Shrehari weren't directly responsible for my raffish good looks."

He tapped his eye patch with an extended index finger.

"It was a secondary explosion in *Shenzen*'s engineering section during our damage control efforts *after* the commodore disengaged us. But joking aside, giving them the idea that deliberately targeting civilians is now part of the game would be a huge mistake. The whole city for a city thing almost wiped us out during the Second Migration War."

"I fought the bastards when they tried to take Scandia," Salminen added, "and I'll say this in their favor. The Shrehari sense of honor keeps them from inflicting gratuitous civilian deaths, let alone use mass murder as a weapon against unarmed sapient species. In that respect, if nothing else, they could teach our ancestors a thing or two. I doubt showing them we're so dishonorable we would target cities from orbit will produce the psychological effect we want."

"Indeed." Dunmoore nodded approvingly.

After spending a lot of time with Salminen and her soldiers during their long passage through Shrehari space, safely concealed in hyperspace from any but the most finely tuned sensors, she'd gained a greater appreciation for the Scandian officer's breadth of knowledge and keen insights. The difference between this Salminen and the shaken, disoriented infantry captain who led the survivors of her company aboard *Iolanthe* after the pirate raid on Toboso a few years earlier was striking.

She turned to the communications station.

"Chief Day, please set up optical links with the task force vessels and pipe it to the conference room."

"Sir." A few minutes passed. "Everyone is online. The captains are standing by."

"Thank you." She looked at Holt. "Shall we?"

Holt climbed to his feet. "Commander Sirico, you have the CIC."

"I have the CIC, Captain."

Dunmoore still wasn't used to hearing the combat systems officer exchange the time-honored words with her successor and she was momentarily taken aback, but thankfully no one noticed. Holt ushered her into the corridor, then allowed her to enter the conference room first and sit at the head of the table. Eight holographic projections had already taken their places. Holt sat in the empty spot immediately on her right.

"Can I assume everyone survived that last long jump without issues and is scouring the system on passive sensors?"

A smattering of 'yes, sir' and vigorous nods answered her question.

"Considering we came out of FTL in almost perfect formation, good station keeping, everyone." A pause, then, "You can mark this date in your ship's log. We came out of interstellar space closer to the Shrehari homeworld than any other human warship, not just in this war but in our entire history. And we did so without being detected."

"Now what we need to do is return home and hand our navigation logs to the Fleet historians," Commander Farren Vento said in a droll tone. "Otherwise, it didn't happen."

"Speaking of navigation, as discussed before leaving Commonwealth space, Lieutenant Drost will transmit an emergency jump plot within the hour, so we can escape as a single unit should we find ourselves unexpectedly faced with an overwhelming enemy formation."

Holt, whose eyes were glued on a readout embedded in the table, said, "Already done, sir."

"Thank you. We'll cruise at sublight in this area for a while. Perhaps several days, until I've seen enough to develop a target list. Please send a copy of your sensor log to the flag CIC every six hours. We'll merge your readings with *Iolanthe*'s to build a picture of this star system and the enemy's activities. Needless to say, I expect everyone to maintain strong silent running discipline. Unless we accidentally stumble over a Shrehari surveillance platform or come within visual range of patrolling ships, we should stay undetected. Any questions?"

She looked at each of the holograms before ending with Holt. All shook their heads.

"Make sure you keep the optical comlinks live. The one thing we cannot afford is sending out stray radio waves. Thank you. We will speak again soon."

Eight holos winked out of existence until only Holt remained.

"I'll be in my quarters staying out of everyone's way, Zeke." She glanced at the conference room's primary display time readout. "How about you and I reconvene here after supper, say at six bells in the dog watch? That'll give your threat AI time to digest the first round of sensor logs."

He nodded once.

"Yes, sir. What will you do in the meantime?"

"Continue tinkering with scenarios that'll take us past Shrehari Prime's moons undetected so we can give the folks at their admiralty a collective heart attack when we light up."

Holt chuckled.

"Are you really considering something that — um — bold? They will have seeded their high orbitals with plenty of defense platforms. Perhaps even the moons."

"No. But it keeps me busy and more importantly, amused."

**

After supping in the wardroom, Dunmoore took a mug of coffee up to the conference room and settled in her accustomed chair. Moments later, Holt's day cabin door opened, and he stepped through.

"Sir, you didn't need to bring your own cup. I would gladly serve you from my urn."

"Thank you, Zeke. I was probably operating on automatic when I took it."

"I know you want to make yourself unobtrusive because *Iolanthe* isn't configured as a flagship, but please don't take it to extremes." He settled in beside her. "We enjoy taking care of you and don't want your pennant moving to *Hawkwood*, should they fix that flag bridge and make it functional again. If you want a personal assistant, I'm sure Leading Spacer Vincenzo will gladly volunteer. Chief Dwyn can spare him for such a worthy cause."

She gave Holt a tight smile.

"My personal needs are few. Poor Vincenzo would be bored to tears. If I ever need a steward for a formal supper or a ceremonial guard at my back, he'll still be my first choice." She raised her coffee. "I promise I'll avail myself of the urn in your day cabin next time we meet here. Has the threat AI finished crunching the data?"

"Yes. I hope you didn't plan on turning in early. We face a few hours of analysis already."

"Who can sleep when we're one FTL jump away from the enemy's homeworld?"

"I don't foresee any problems after we plow through the radio intercept summaries and visuals of eleven planets. You probably won't either. In fact, we might wish to stop when we can no longer absorb information and leave the rest for tomorrow. As you said, if we don't break silent running or come across the enemy at really close range, we can take our time."

"Agreed."

"Radio intercepts or visuals?"

"Let's start with the visuals of Shrehari Prime. I doubt we'll go anywhere near it, but who knows?"

"Even if we avoid the homeworld, we could always send them a copy of our analysis before leaving, just to show we mapped out their defensive arrays," Holt suggested, half in jest.

"Not a bad idea, actually. There's nothing quite as worrisome as knowing someone's been taking images of your most intimate domestic arrangements." When Holt raised a questioning eyebrow at her choice of words, she said, "I've been reading old psychological thrillers. Our pre-diaspora forebears were strange people."

"And you think we've improved since then?" When she opened her mouth to reply, he added, "Never mind. Rhetorical question."

"I'll answer it anyway. Leaving the claustrophobic confines of a single planet and settling on new worlds definitely changed us as a species. I can see it by comparing the zeitgeist evident in pre-diaspora literature compared with more recent writings. Whether we've improved?" She shrugged. "I'll let future historians decide. We're different from our ancestors, but different doesn't mean better. In any case, can you pull up the Shrehari Prime analysis?"

Ninety minutes and three coffee refills later, Dunmoore stood, stretched, and wandered around the table to loosen tense muscles.

"We won't be getting through all the data tonight, that's for sure. I haven't done this sort of work since I was a lieutenant and I'll confess it's a tad tiring."

"That's why people who wear stars on their collars surround themselves with dedicated helpers — so they don't suffer from information overload."

"True, but we lowly commodores don't rate much, especially those of us who are acting, while so employed, and living in a Q-ship's guest quarters. You will, however, be glad to know I'm not taking the task force anywhere near Shrehari Prime."

"On behalf of my fellow captains, I wholeheartedly approve. Those orbital stations are seriously big and will carry guns capable of turning the Furious Faerie into the Wrecked Fae. And we probably haven't seen their smaller, automated defense platforms yet. But the intelligence folks back home will love us for this data. I do wonder what they're doing on the moons, though. We never built such large surface structures on natural satellites in our space."

"Maybe the Shrehari don't find it necessary to burrow."

"Could be. If they can put up enough shielding against radiation and deflect asteroids with perfect results every time and at low cost, why dig in? The analysts back home can ponder that one at leisure. In any case, we can rule Shrehari Prime out as a suitable target. What now?"

"Shrehari Minor. The next planet out. The AI calls it habitable but cold. Mostly iced over."

They studied the data in silence for over an hour.

"Could be more promising for a show of force since it apparently lacks Shrehari Prime's massive orbital installations."

"And do what? Burn a few holes in the icecaps? Sure, there are a lot of cities around the equator, where there's no ice, but if it doesn't host obvious military installations, then what? Crossing the sky over Shredar without even firing a shot could produce a massive psychological effect, provided we made it past the defenses. Flying over whatever passes for the planetary capital on that snowball? Not quite. Especially if it has plenty of orbital platforms we can't see at this distance."

Dunmoore squeezed the bridge of her nose with her index finger and thumb.

"Right. I must be getting a little punchy."

"Let's leave it as a possibility for now and look again tomorrow once we've slept for a few hours. I suggest we take a quick glance at the innermost gas giant, say thirty minutes, no more. It probably hosts a few refueling stations and might offer a better military target. And then, bed."

"Okay. Pull it up."

— Thirty —

"**A**pologies for taking so long," Dunmoore said once the last holographic starship captain materialized around the conference table. "But thanks to the amount of sensor data we received, especially from *Rooikat* and *Fennec*'s overpowered eyes, Captain Holt and I almost suffered information overload. I now have a greater appreciation for the usefulness of staff officers."

A few chuckles greeted her quip.

"I'm not sure the advantages outweigh the drawbacks, Commodore," Farren Vento replied.

"You should spend time sorting through an overly eager tactical AI's digests after it's been fed nine times six hours of data four times a day."

Vento inclined his head. "True."

"You'll be glad I've ruled out even a quick swing past both inhabited planets — Shrehari Prime and Shrehari Minor — to trigger their defensive arrays and give them a collective heart attack. The risks simply outweigh the benefits. However, Captain Holt suggested we send a copy of our intelligence report on both places to the Shrehari high command just before going FTL. It should help trigger a nervous breakdown or something equally distressing."

"Sir." Lieutenant Nishino raised her hand. "If I can make a suggestion. Perhaps *Rooikat* and I could each send a recon drone past both planets once they know we're here. The drones will be destroyed of course, but we'll get a closer look before that happens and send the boneheads scrambling since they're small enough to drop out of FTL not much further out than geosynchronous orbit. We can even rig the drones so they emit a corvette's electronic signature. That should get their attention."

"Excellent idea. Consider it part of the plan."

"Yes, sir."

The other scout ship captain, Lieutenant Hauck, gave his colleague thumbs up before acknowledging Dunmoore's order.

"Having eliminated both populated worlds, we're left with two places where we can break a few things of military value without risking civilian lives or stumbling into most of a Shrehari assault division and still make it sting. The two innermost gas giants, Miqa and Hoqa. Each is surrounded by a necklace of twelve antimatter cracking and fueling stations, presumably automated, no different from the ones we destroyed in outlying star systems."

Images of two Jovian planets appeared on the conference room's wall-sized display, one labeled Miqa, the other Hoqa. The outer atmospheres of both were visibly segregated into colorful bands at various latitudes, with storms raging along their interacting boundaries. Small red icons represented the antimatter cracking and fueling stations.

"I plan on attacking them simultaneously using half of the task force for each. *Iolanthe* will lead the attack on Hoqa, with *Narses, Hawkwood, Fennec,* and *Skua. Jan Sobieski* will lead the attack on Miqa with *Belisarius,*

Tamurlane, and *Rooikat.* Captain Holt will command the group targeting Hoqa. I will shift over to *Jan Sobieski* and command the group targeting Miqa."

"We'll be honored to hoist your pennant, sir," Pushkin replied with a pleased grin. "Our CIC can easily accommodate a second command chair."

"My overall intent is for both groups to drop out of FTL at their respective target's hyperlimit, go silent, and coast until they reach optimum firing range. The one tricky bit will be coordinating the respective go live orders. We'll have no choice but use our subspace radios for a microburst. Whoever reaches optimum firing range first will send out a signal. The moment the other one confirms it is also within range, both power up and accelerate for a slingshot maneuver around their respective target planets while firing on the refueling stations. One pass, expend as much ammunition as necessary, then jump for the rendezvous point at the heliopause. Just before jumping, both scouts will launch a pair of FTL recon drones. Because of the relative orbital positions, *Rooikat* will launch at Shrehari Prime and *Fennec* at Shrehari Minor. Any questions so far?"

When no one raised a hand, she said, "*Iolanthe's* navigator is preparing the overall sailing plan and fixing the post-battle run rendezvous. Gregor, I'll expect your navigator to plot our group's course to and from Miqa, then share with Lieutenant Drost, who will plot the other group's course to and from Hoqa."

"No problems, Commodore."

"I expect little more than automated defenses covering each of the stations. Target them along with the fueling stations." She paused. "This will be more of a hasty attack than a planned one. Captain Holt and I will deal with our respective situations on the spot, should we find Shrehari warships in the vicinity, defensive platforms stronger than expected, that sort of thing, so the words of the day are maximum flexibility. You can't go wrong if you engage enemy targets at will, but not civilian vessels, especially passenger ships. Once we reunite at the rendezvous point, always assuming we break clean, I'll shift back to *Iolanthe,* and we'll head for our normal patrol area at top speed. If the enemy puts hunters on our tail, I'll adjust as necessary. That, in essence, is my plan. The deck is open for debate and discussion."

**

"Bloodthirsty bunch," Holt said once the last of Task Force Luckner's holographic captains winked out of existence.

"Better that than too timid. They won't exceed orders, never fear."

"Only because none of them, other than Gregor, perhaps, has your instincts."

She smirked at Holt.

"Which is why I'm riding with him. Just kidding."

"When are you shifting over?"

"Once we've sent out the formal operations orders and finalized the navigation plan. In eighteen hours or so. Pass word to Gregor I don't want full honors upon arrival. It's neither the time nor the place." Dunmoore stood and rolled her shoulders. "I can't pretend I'm not feeling a certain amount of unease at raiding the enemy's home system only a few light hours from his capital, and presumably an entire assault division dedicated to protecting it."

"They're not expecting something such as this, not even in their wildest dreams. If they dream, that is."

"They do, though from what little I've read, the experience carries deeply mystical connotations.

Something about gods or demons communing with the living while they sleep."

"I learn something new every day." Holt climbed to his feet. "I'll check on Astrid's progress with the navigation plan and see what Theo's come up with to cover communications. Why don't you take an hour and work off your anxiety in the gym?"

"Now there's a thought. Maybe Tatiana's soldiers are sparring and won't mind my joining them."

"Even better. Afterward, we can take the evening meal in my day cabin, and I'll update you."

"Sure. You're on."

When Dunmoore entered the gym, aft of *Iolanthe*'s hangar deck, she found two dozen members of E Company, 3rd Battalion, Scandia Regiment training, most of them on the mats, practicing various hand-to-hand combat disciplines.

Major Tatiana Salminen and her second in command, Lieutenant Jon Puro were watching the sergeant major, Talo Haataja, and Command Sergeant Karlo Saari, who led first platoon, circle each other, practicing what they called the Scandian version of aikido. Though how it differed from a barroom brawl, Dunmoore couldn't say.

Saari, striking faster than a Nabhkan desert asp, pulled Haataja off balance, and tossed him over his shoulder. The sergeant major landed with a thump, rolled over and sprang to his feet with nimbleness belying the gray in his short hair. He, in turn, tackled the younger man just above knee level, sending both to the mat in a tangle of limbs. They flailed about in a flurry until one hand slapped the deck with urgency, resigning the bout and ceding it to his opponent.

Haataja was the first one up. He held out his hand to help Saari stand, but the command sergeant ignored it and stood with more vigor than grace.

"You still fight worse than a pregnant ice wolf with degenerative brain disease and two broken limbs, Karlo," Haataja said as he bowed to his opponent. "But that's one limb better than the last time."

Saari grinned at him.

"I'm touched, Talo. Any other sergeant major would call me a weakling and left it at that, but you put effort into your insults." When he caught sight of Dunmoore watching them, he added, "Perhaps you should check and see if the commodore suffers from broken limbs and brain wastage as well."

"I think the commodore will prefer sparring with me than either of you barbarians," Salminen said. "Clear out the ring."

Haataja, incorrigible as ever, winked at Dunmoore before jogging off to one side with Saari for a lengthy and vigorous cooldown session.

"A shame you don't need us to seize an enemy orbital station or something of the sort." Salminen gestured at Dunmoore to enter the circle. "Scandian aikido?"

"These days, I'm not practiced in any other form of hand-to-hand, so yes. And as for boarding party action, sorry. We neither have the time nor the need to capture something we can more easily destroy."

"I know." A wry smile briefly lit up Salminen's face. "But my people feel neglected. We didn't come aboard *Iolanthe* by choice, but until she joined Task Force Luckner, we enjoyed our assignment, especially playing fake mercenaries to bamboozle bad guys."

"There's not much I can do about that right now." Dunmoore loosened her muscles as she took up a fighting stance. "We face a different war these days."

"I understand that. So do Jon, Talo, Sergeant Saari, and the other platoon leaders, but my soldiers become restless from time to time. As you might have noticed when you trained with us during our long trip here."

Puro, watching them size each other up, snorted. "Count me among the restless."

Before Salminen could reply, the public address system sounded. "CIC to the commodore."

"Now what?" Dunmoore murmured. Then, in a louder tone, "Sorry, Tatiana. If you were planning on a round with Jon before I showed up, go ahead. This could take more than a few seconds."

Since she'd left her personal communicator in her quarters, Dunmoore went to the nearest com panel and touched its screen. "CIC, this is Dunmoore."

A few seconds later, Sirico's face appeared.

"Sir, we detected a dozen Shrehari ships dropping out of FTL just over three million kilometers from our current location. They appear on a course to cross the heliopause and head inward. Half are *Tol* class cruisers, the rest naval transports. Sensors confirm Task Force Luckner is running at the tightest level of emissions control. They shouldn't spot us."

"Thank you, Thorin."

Luck, bad or good, was often a factor in war. If the enemy formation had dropped out of hyperspace on top of them, her plans to raid the two refueling station rings and send FTL recon drones past both inhabited worlds would have been for naught.

Three million kilometers were plenty to escape sensors, provided the enemy wasn't carrying out an intensive search. And in the forty-five minutes it would take their hyperdrives to cycle, even the fastest sensors could only search a small section of surrounding space. However, the sooner they headed inward themselves, the better.

"If anything changes, I'm in the gym minus my communicator."

"Understood."

"Dunmoore, out."

When she turned back to the soldiers, she saw both Salminen and Puro staring at her.

"Problems?" The former asked when Dunmoore was back within earshot.

"Enemy ships headed inward passing us at a distance of approximately three million klicks. Nothing to worry about since we're running silent."

"I see. Ready, sir?"

Dunmoore took up a fighting stance again.

"Lieutenant Puro, please call it."

He glanced at both, then raised a hand.

"And — attack!"

— Thirty-One —

Iolanthe's pinnace settled on *Jan Sobieski*'s hangar deck twelve hours after the Shrehari formation jumped back into hyperspace, headed for the imperial homeworld. When the aft ramp dropped, Siobhan Dunmoore saw a single bosun's mate, whistle at the ready, standing beside Gregor Pushkin, who knew better than disobey her order he skip full honors. Travel bag in hand, she walked down the ramp, halting at its lower edge.

"Permission to come aboard, Captain."

He raised his hand in salute. "Granted. Welcome."

The bosun's whistle trilled, Dunmoore stepped off the ramp, and with that, *Jan Sobieski* became Task Force Luckner's temporary flagship.

"The VIP quarters are ready, we installed a second command chair in the CIC, next to mine, and the CIC crew is prepared to work for you as well as me. Trevane also made you an honorary member of the wardroom for the duration of your stay." A repressed smile lit up Pushkin's eyes. "It'll be a treat to sail with you again, sir, even if it's only for a day and a half."

"If everything goes well. You might be stuck with me longer if the enemy chases us out of his home system and *Iolanthe* doesn't have time to send the pinnace back."

"Speaking of which." Pushkin gestured toward the inner door. "We should clear the hangar and let it leave."

He walked her to the accommodations deck and pointed at a door across from the one labeled 'Captain.'

"That would be you. It has the same configuration as my cabin. If you need anything, please let me know. *Jan Sobieski* has amenities our old *Stingray* could only dream about."

"Considering we're halfway between mealtimes, and we're about to spend almost ten hours FTL, I'll try to relax with a little light reading."

"What's piqued your interest these days?"

The VIP quarters opened at Pushkin's touch.

"Anton Kach's *Identity, the Almighty, and the Nature of Evil*, his examination of the Migration Wars' underlying social and spiritual causes."

"That one is on my list, but I've not reached it yet. Kach's interpretation includes an analysis of humanity's spiritual state during the atrocities, does it not?"

"Very much so. And it is cogent, though many might disagree on theological grounds."

Pushkin made a dismissive sound.

"Theologians strive to count the number of angels dancing on the head of a pin, but they can't even define evil in its most primal form. Useless buggers, the lot of them."

"True." Dunmoore dropped her bag on one of the chairs surrounding a narrow table in the VIP quarters' sitting compartment and looked around. "Congratulations, Gregor, *Jan Sobieski* does its guests proud. That coffee urn on the sideboard is a nice touch."

"We strive to please, sir." He hesitated for a moment. "Speaking of faith, do you remember our conversation on the subject during the wild chase aboard *Stingray* which ended with us fighting Brakal in the Cimmeria system and putting his cruiser out of commission?"

"Of course. Every moment is seared into my memory. You stated the view that religion was awe at what we can't explain."

"I still consider it a valid point. But what I remember as well is you saying words to the effect that a crew which doesn't believe in itself or its ship cannot fight and survive for long."

She smiled at him.

"Sounds like me."

"You need not wonder about my crew's belief in itself. Ever."

Dunmoore reached out and grasped Pushkin's upper arm.

"I've known that for a long time, Gregor. Crews are a reflection of their captains. It's one reason I chose *Jan Sobieski* to lead the group against Miqa."

Pushkin glanced away, clearly embarrassed by her praise.

"I learned from the best of the best, Commodore."

She released his arm.

"I'll settle in and let you prepare your ship for departure."

"Yes, sir. I would be pleased if you'd join me in the CIC when we go FTL in ninety minutes."

"Certainly. I wouldn't miss it."

Once she was alone, Dunmoore dropped into a chair and exhaled slowly while butterflies fluttered in her stomach. Her first combat mission as a flag officer was about to kick off in earnest, and it would be the most daring in this war to date. As the old proverb said, be careful what you wish for, you just might get it. And HQ gave Dunmoore her wish, with the implied message of put up or shut up. Or so it seemed.

She glanced at the coffee urn but after a few moments decided against a cup of the black, heavily caffeinated stuff that kept the navy going as much as antimatter did. Her nerves didn't need a booster shot. Dunmoore retrieved her reader and tried to focus on Kach's treatise, yet she kept rereading the same passages over and over again.

Eighty minutes passed in a fog of irritation and anxiety before she put the reader down and stood. Perhaps entering the CIC with one of *Jan Sobieski*'s mugs in hand might not just project the right image, but also keep her nerves under control.

Gregor Pushkin already sat in his command chair when the CIC's door slid aside to admit her. An empty copy of it waited to his right while officers and ratings, focused on their respective readouts, occupied the remaining stations.

"Commodore on deck," a petty officer sang out, though Dunmoore was relieved no one sprang to attention.

"At ease," she replied, nodding at Pushkin. "How are we doing?"

"Luckner Group Miqa is synced and ready, sir. *Iolanthe* reports Luckner Group Hoqa is also ready and synced. The countdown timer is running. No noticeable enemy activity which might be aimed at us."

Dunmoore dropped into the jury-rigged command chair. Part of her noticed a certain hardness compared to her usual seat in *Iolanthe*'s CIC, but it would do.

She studied the three-dimensional projection of the Shrehari home system dominating *Jan Sobieski*'s CIC. The target gas giants glowed with the red of marked targets, while the remaining planets gave off a more sedate hue. No wedge-shaped icons were pulsing to show Shrehari warships closing on their position, meaning they remained either undetected or still beyond the range of any enemy patrols closing in on them. So far, so good.

Dunmoore turned her eyes on the countdown timer in the main display's lower right corner. Five minutes before her task force jumped past the heliopause and entered the enemy's home star system to make history. Or died trying.

When the timer hit one minute to jump, a klaxon resonated throughout the frigate, followed by the first officer's verbal warning. Precisely sixty seconds later, she felt her stomach turn inside out as the universe twisted, propelling Task Force Luckner into hyperspace.

When her innards settled, Dunmoore heard the usual notice to set the ship at FTL cruising stations. She glanced at Pushkin who leaned forward and stood.

"Could I interest you in a game of chess, Commodore, seeing as how we're spending the next ten hours in hyperspace?"

"With pleasure. I've become used to Zeke's manners and know his weaknesses. Facing you again will be refreshing."

"Mister Jokkainen, you have the CIC."

Jan Sobieski's combat systems officer, a dark-haired, youthful-looking lieutenant, stood in turn. "I have the CIC, Captain."

Once in Pushkin's day cabin, he pointed at the samovar sitting on a sideboard.

"My preferred tea blend, but if you'd rather not, I can call the wardroom for coffee. Please sit. I'll serve us."

"Tea is fine. In fact, it'll make a change from the usual. With a coffee urn available twenty-four hours a day, either in my quarters or the wardroom, every cup has been remarkably consistent to the point where I can't quite recall the taste anymore."

Pushkin chuckled as he pulled two mugs with *Jan Sobieski*'s emblem, a winged hussar, from the rack above the samovar.

"A professional peril in the navy, I think. We run on antimatter and caffeine."

"So long as we remember which goes where."

She took the visitor's chair by Pushkin's desk.

"I'm sure a starship's engines can survive a bit of tea in her fuel feed. Humans and raw antimatter might be a little messier." He handed her a steaming cup. "Not something I want to witness, let alone try."

Pushkin retrieved a mahogany box similar to the chess set she'd given Holt.

"White or black?"

"I always give Zeke white."

"Would it annoy you if I chose black?"

He sat behind his desk, opened the box, and withdrew the carved pieces before flipping it over and setting up the board.

"It's your ship, Gregor."

With the chessmen in place, he spun the board.

"Yours is the opening move, Commodore."

Three hard-fought bouts later, each of which ended in a draw, Pushkin glanced at the time.

"We're expected in the wardroom for the evening meal, sir. If you don't mind, I suggest we call ourselves matched opponents."

"Agreed."

Pushkin returned the chessmen to their slots and stowed the box in one of his desk drawers.

"Shall we?"

Jan Sobieski's officers received Dunmoore with the élan of polished hosts. But she thought their conviviality seemed a little forced, perhaps even overly bright, as if masking the tension they felt at jumping into the Shrehari home system without quite knowing what perils waited when their ship would come out of hyperspace.

Perhaps the enemy had spotted them and deployed his ships to cover vulnerable points, such as the antimatter fueling station necklaces around the two inner gas giants, turning what Dunmoore intended as a fast, destructive raid into a pitched fight with a dozen *Tol* class cruisers.

Yet they also exuded a quiet pride at being not only chosen for the most daring mission of the war but serving as flagship for Task Force Luckner's Group Miqa. The latter would be a brief honor yet one which could cement the frigate's place in naval history.

This close to full battle stations, the drinks were non-alcoholic, though the meal itself was fresh and warm, not made from reconstituted rations or consisting of a self-serve cold food buffet. Trevane Devall, as befit the scion of a wealthy and politically connected family, was in his element at the head of the wardroom table, presiding over the meal and making brilliant conversation with his guests and fellow officers.

A veteran of *Stingray*'s adventures under Dunmoore's command, he appeared calmer than the rest, though she sensed he was repressing the same thoughts and worries as everyone else.

At the end of the meal, Devall tapped his knife against his glass to call for silence. Once it fell, he turned to Dunmoore and said, "Commodore, we should never call upon guests of the wardroom to perform for their meal, but considering the circumstances, I wonder if you'd care to say a few words."

"It would be a pleasure."

She let her eyes roam around the table and smiled. The frigate's officers stared back with the intense fascination of those convinced they were about to hear a flag officer produce words of ineffable wisdom. Or bore them to tears with platitudes.

"As some of you might remember from your academy days, the greatest naval battle in the era of sailing ships on pre-diaspora Earth was fought off Cape Trafalgar on October 21, 1805. It will always be remembered as Admiral Horatio Nelson's greatest and last victory — the Battle of Trafalgar. For centuries, Nelson's service, the British Royal Navy observed the battle's anniversary with ceremonies, dinners, and speeches. The Commonwealth Navy has other traditions, stemming from more recent wars and it's been long since anyone commemorated Trafalgar Day. But since we are descended from Earth's greatest naval forces, it still forms part of our history."

She paused and watched for eyes lighting up, hoping she wouldn't see dull stares of incomprehension. None of Pushkin's officers seemed to have forgotten their naval history, or at least not the names Nelson and Trafalgar.

"One custom for Trafalgar Night dinners was saying grace, or if you wish, praying to the Almighty for those of faith, before and after the meal. I still remember one after dinner prayer I read long ago — it dates back to wet navy days on Earth, in fact — and I think it might serve us with a few changes."

She paused for a few seconds, then,

"To do what's right, when others' feet get cold
We pray for courage strong to make us Bold
To Faithf'lly serve our Spacers and Marines
Our Captain, each other, and our species
And so that we our hurting galaxy may bless
To fight for Peace and Justice with Success."

After taking a breath, Dunmoore continued, "A few of you may recall Admiral Nelson's signal just before his fleet engaged the enemy read 'England expects that every man will do his duty.' I need not make a similar signal when we drop out of FTL in a few hours, because I know you and everyone else in Task Force Luckner will do their utmost to claim coup against the enemy and leave him reeling."

She climbed to her feet.

"Thank you for your warm hospitality and keep in mind that when we return home, you'll be able to dine out on this mission for the rest of your lives. With luck, you'll even tell your grandchildren about it."

"And mightily bored they'll be," Trevane Devall replied, grinning broadly as he gave the traditional reply, eliciting chuckles and smiles from the entire wardroom complement.

For a second, Dunmoore could feel the tension, never far from the surface, ease just a bit. After one last smile and a wink at Devall, she turned on her heels and left with Pushkin in tow.

When they were beyond earshot, the latter asked, "Tell me you prepared that story and prayer in case Trevane put you on the spot, and didn't pull it out of thin air right there and then."

She glanced at him with amusement dancing in her eyes.

"I was ready for your first officer's polite ambush, Gregor. Although my memory is better than that of most people, even I can't keep a million obscure details in my head. But I can share another amusing fact if you'd like. At Trafalgar, Nelson broke with doctrine and separated his fleet into two columns, a bit like I've done with Luckner, though we'll be attacking orbital installations, not cutting across the enemy's line."

They stopped outside their quarters, and Pushkin turned to face her.

"I'm sure you realize that little speech will become part of *Jan Sobieski*'s history, right? I don't think anyone present will ever forget it. They're a little scared, though they hide it well, but they're also proud and determined. Your words gave them just enough spirit to reinforce the latter. As you no doubt intended."

She met his eyes and said, "If it worked, I've done my duty. Goodnight, Gregor."

— Thirty-Two —

Soldiers of the Imperial Ground Forces' Fourth Assault Regiment wearing black combat armor did not try to pretend they were anything other than a protection detail surrounding the Jakrang ruins when Brakal passed through the weather-worn main gate. Though Vagh's reassurances still rang in his ears, the paranoid living deep within Brakal's mind could not help but wonder whether the stoic troopers would turn around and aim their weapons at the lords once they were assembled.

Mishtak and his supporters had been suspiciously quiet of late, as had the *Tai Kan*, even Brakal's newest friend Kroesh. Nor had Lady Kembri or anyone else from the imperial palace reached out to him. Still, Shredar felt as if it sat on top of a rapidly waking volcano. The capital's entire population, from the highest officials to the lowest of beggars, seemed to hold its collective breath while waiting for the dramatic political explosion once the Kraal voted to oppose the governing council's handling of the war effort.

Would Lady Kembri accept a vote of non-confidence, as per tradition? Or would she anger the four hundred most powerful lords in the empire, Shrehari who commanded the loyalty and obedience of countless millions, including most of the Imperial Armed Forces, by refusing? And would such a refusal, in effect a violation of ancient custom, be deemed dishonorable by the empire's ordinary citizens and see them revolt against the dynasty?

The questions chased each other in ever-tightening circles as Toralk drove Brakal and Regar through the dun-colored sandstone ruins of what was once an intricate religious, political, and entertainment complex long before the first starships lifted from the planet's surface.

Sitting among untended meadows and woods some distance from Shredar's city limits, it still belonged to the imperial government but was rarely used anymore. The odd operatic production might play in the open-air amphitheater, and the odd religious rites were performed in temples so old they had been rededicated to different gods over the course of a thousand generations.

Time had worn down most of the statues, fluted columns and wall-sized carvings, leaving little of what were once artistic masterpieces in stone. Anything that once gave the complex a bit of color was also gone, washed away by rain, wind, and harsh sunlight.

Yet the Jakrang retained an eerie majesty that always left Brakal with a vague sense of awe. If his people were able to build something this beautiful with nothing more than muscle-powered tools, why could they not defeat a species younger than the imperial race, one deemed beneath a Shrehari's contempt?

To his surprise, uniformed *Tai Kan* troopers stood guard outside the amphitheater where the lords of the Kraal would shortly assemble to salvage the empire's honor and ensure the dynasty's continued existence.

"What is this, Regar?" He gestured at the figures in white armor.

"First Deputy Director Kroesh deployed a battalion loyal to him. They are under the control of the Fourth Assault Regiment's commanding officer."

"Why?"

"Kroesh decided the presence of uniformed *Tai Kan* loyal to him would help serve as a deterrent should Mishtak deploy his own *Tai Kan* battalions. There is no love lost between my service and the military, but never in the *Tai Kan*'s history has one uniformed unit fired on another."

"Why was I not informed of this change?"

"A late decision, Lord."

"Yet you knew."

"I knew of the possibility, but thought it best not to say a word unless Kroesh acted on his decision."

Brakal let out an irritated grunt.

"You did not wish a protracted argument with me, is that it? Miscreant. However, provided Kroesh's troops are indeed here to help protect the Kraal and not arrest us the moment I declare it in session, the idea has merit."

"You will find soldiers of the Fourth Assault Regiment standing guard within the amphitheater's walls. Kroesh's troops will not pass them unscathed."

"Good. It would pain me if the next *Tai Kan* director proved false."

"Is the appointment confirmed?"

Brakal's lips curled back.

"No. I am the only Kraal member who knows. For now. One step at a time."

As the car entered the amphitheater's outer gate, the two *Tai Kan* troopers standing guard on either side raised their gauntleted fists in salute upon recognizing the Clan Makkar emblem. Once through, they passed a pair of soldiers in black armor who did the same.

"See," Regar said. "Three cordons. Soldiers, *Tai Kan* and again, soldiers. Mishtak would be crazy to force the issue."

"Who designed the array?"

This time, Regar curled back his lips in a smile.

"Kroesh, the Fourth Regiment's commander, and I."

"Well done. We will make something useful of you yet, my tame spy."

Toralk took them across a cobblestone plaza to where the theater's south wall still stood. An underofficer indicated they should park closest to the entrance, in the place of honor, after saluting them.

As planned, Brakal was first on the scene. Or at least the first of the lords. Chief Keeper of the Kraal's Records Gvant and his aides would already be inside, preparing the place, though their vehicle would be parked elsewhere, out of sight. Perhaps alongside the Fourth Regiment's transports. The plaza itself was reserved for the lords.

As they climbed out of the car, Regar pointed upward.

"The regiment put surveillance floaters aloft. Nothing will approach from the air without being seen, and if necessary, destroyed."

"Let us hope Mishtak and his minions know about these precautions and keep away. I would rather not shed blood on the first Kraal assembly in many turns."

"They know. Kroesh has made sure of it. As has General Vagh through his friends at the admiralty. Officially, the Fourth Imperial Assault Regiment is on an unplanned training exercise, but carrying live ammunition, and will answer if anything threatens one of the empire's oldest and most venerated institutions. Mind you," Regar gave Brakal a sly glance, "if Mishtak decides on the strongest of measures, there is little anyone can do to prevent the Jakrang's destruction via a kinetic strike from orbit."

"He is not that stupid. Neither is Lady Kembri. Wiping out the four hundred would trigger a mutiny in the Armed Forces and revolution in the streets. That would ensure the dynasty's overthrow and his swift death."

Brakal stepped off toward the entrance tunnel cutting under the seats, leaving Regar and Toralk to wait by the car. Only the lords and the record keepers were allowed into what was now effectively the legislature's hallowed grounds.

The amphitheater was as he remembered it. Thirty tiers of stone polished by generations of Shrehari backsides rising in a semi-circle to face an immense stage, empty on this occasion, though Brakal had seen Shrehari Prime's largest land animals paraded across it during operatic performances.

At the foot of the stage, Gvant and five of his assistants were fussing around the speaker's rostrum, moved here from the Forbidden Quarter a few hours earlier. Brakal saw no evidence of voice amplification gear though he knew such modern devices would not be needed in a space designed and built to support performers with perfect acoustics.

Gvant noticed him and warned his people. All six, formally robed and wearing chains of office around their necks, turned toward Brakal and stiffened to attention.

"Good afternoon, Speaker." The Chief Keeper of the Kraal's Records bowed his head. "Everything is ready."

"Excellent. My thanks for making the necessary arrangements so we could meet here instead of in the Forbidden Quarter."

"It is good the Kraal assembles again after so long, whether it be there or in the Jakrang."

As if on cue, a thickset, robed figure walking with a stately pace came through the entrance tunnel.

"General Vagh." Gvant bowed his head again. "A pleasure to see you again."

"And you." Vagh bowed back politely. He turned his attention on Brakal. "You approve of the security arrangements, I trust?"

"They are satisfactory. Any sign Mishtak might move against us?"

"None, but that does not mean the poxed whoreson will let us disavow the council with impunity."

"Bah. In the end, it will be Lady Kembri who decides. If she accepts our vote of non-confidence and dismisses him when he refuses to cooperate with us, then Mishtak and the rest of the council go into retirement."

"And you become *kho'sahra*."

Brakal made a gesture of indifference.

"We name someone *kho'sahra*."

"If you wish an added sense of menace hovering over the proceedings, a friend at the admiralty who keeps me apprised of interesting events contacted me just before I left my estate. Convoy *Morak* Five Three reported sensor ghosts at the home system's heliopause while it was between otherspace jumps."

Brakal's head whipped around.

"Sensor ghosts?"

"Home System Command dispatched a patrol ship to the area but found nothing. The ghosts were probably gas clouds or artifacts of ill-tuned equipment."

"I wonder. Often, in recent times, when such things were spotted in my patrol area, it meant humans were preparing mischief."

"Surely they will not come this deeply into imperial space. At least not yet."

"Perhaps. But the motherless apes' most defining characteristic is their unpredictability."

"True."

They fell silent, each mulling over the incident in his own way while watching their colleagues arrive, singly or in small clusters. Most gave Brakal no more than a polite nod, though his closest colleagues joined him and Vagh for a few quiet words.

None of them wore anything other than a solemn expression that gave no sign of their leanings. He could not tell whether the waverers had chosen, those opposed had experienced a change of heart, or, the gods forbid, avowed supporters were turning against him.

When the lower tiers clustered around the entrance tunnel eventually seemed to overflow with dark-robed Shrehari, Gvant approached Brakal.

"Lord Speaker, the four hundred are here. You may call the Kraal to order."

"Thank you."

Gvant bowed and withdrew to one side, where two of his record keepers waited. The retired officers standing with Brakal left wordlessly to take their places, leaving him alone at the rostrum. Once they were seated, he raised both hands.

"Lords of the Kraal, I ask for your attention."

His words resounded with the force of a starship lifting off on full military power. The amphitheater acoustics did their job and stilled every last shred of conversation. Black within black eyes turned toward the Shrehari standing before the stage in sober robes marked with the emblem of Clan Makkar.

"You know me. I am Brakal. Under the Rules of the Kraal, I am the speaker because I summoned this noble assembly when no other would. I, therefore, call it to order. If you consult your displays, you will find this session's agenda."

Robes rustled as the lords retrieved their personal devices and linked them with Gvant's network.

"Our first order of business is the election of a speaker. Under Kraal Rules, my appointment ends the moment the speaker's election is called. I so call it. Enter your nomination for speaker." Brakal fell silent. Unlike his fellow lords, he did not pull out his device to vote.

After a short wait, Gvant consulted his device, then stepped forward.

"The votes are tallied. A majority of two hundred and fifty lords nominate Brakal, of Clan Makkar as Speaker of the Kraal. The assembly remains yours."

Pretty much the expected number. Brakal and his core allies had not bothered forcing the speaker issue. It paled beside the more important vote of non-confidence in Mishtak's governing council.

Brakal stepped up to the rostrum and let a challenging gaze encompass the assembly in silence for long enough to discomfit many of those whose heart was not set on forcing the council's removal.

"You know why I invoked the ancient laws and called this honorable Kraal back from the dead. The empire's future is at stake in a way it has never been before. The war, out there," he raised an arm and pointed at the clear blue sky above, "is not going the way Mishtak and his council pretend. It has never gone the way Mishtak and his council claimed. We are losing it, slowly but surely, to an enemy Mishtak tells us is contemptible, weak, unworthy of existing. An enemy without honor. Something has gone wrong, my lords of the Kraal. That contemptible enemy is not only pushing us out of his sphere, he is attacking Deep Space Fleet installations and convoys within the imperial sphere with near impunity.

This is dishonor on a level the empire has never before faced in its history."

Mutterings of disbelief reached Brakal's ears. They came mainly from civilian lords who opposed Brakal and his allies and preferred things as they were. Apparently, some thought his openly stating what was already whispered among Kraal members crossed a line of sorts. One of them stood.

"You speak too freely of dishonor, Brakal. A dishonored empire always endures upheaval, unrest, and dynastic change. Promoting such ideas in a time of war is tantamount to treason."

"Perhaps, Kevek, but so is losing a war we should never have started in the first place. Mishtak and the council lied. They lied to the regent, to the Kraal and to the people of the empire. If we do not correct our course, we will suffer, as you say, upheaval, unrest, and possibly dynastic change. I do not wish to see these come to pass, and neither does anyone else in this noble assembly. We are loyal citizens. That is why we must deliberate on a solution and do so quickly. This solution would ideally include the council, but if Mishtak refuses his cooperation, we lords of the Kraal will act alone."

Growls of approval rose from the military lords, most of whom were experienced in battle against the humans.

General Vagh rose to his feet. "What do you propose, Speaker Brakal?"

— Thirty-Three —

The critical moment had arrived. Brakal gave his friend a respectful gesture of acknowledgment.

"What do I propose, Lord Vagh of Clan Najuk? I propose we end this war. Now. Before it ends the dynasty and permanently harms our species."

"Since we did not yet vanquish the humans and will probably not vanquish them in the foreseeable future, how would you propose the imperial government act?" Having asked the second part of the question, as planned, Vagh took his seat again.

Brakal let his eyes roam over the assembly.

"We offer the humans an armistice. A cessation of hostilities. We withdraw from the star systems we took, and they withdraw their ships from our space. We return to our respective spheres as they were the day before Mishtak and the council took the irrational step of attacking a species which is anything but weak."

Kevek rose again.

"What you propose can be interpreted as defeatism, Brakal. And defeatism is treason."

"You speak too freely of treason, Kevek. Take care you do not cause insult or worse. Some things cannot be forgiven, even here. Yet the truth may always be uttered, and the truth is we are being defeated. In detail, if not yet in general. Peace with honor is what I propose this Kraal advocate. A peace which will preserve civil order and the ruling dynasty and end the useless slaughter."

Brakal raised his chin in defiance.

"The council claimed we faced a weak, cowardly, and dishonorable species. Lady Kembri believed the council's word and sanctioned Mishtak's war. But the humans are not weak. Or cowardly. Or dishonorable. They are cunning. Strong. Capable of building ships which surpass ours. And they are stubborn, unrelenting. How do I know this? I have been fighting them as a starship commander and admiral for almost the entire war. My lords, forget Mishtak's propaganda. Forget the nonsense peddled by the information channels. Our reality is this. The humans are the opposite of weak and cowardly. They are a worthy foe, one which even now roams at will within imperial space. Surely I need not remind this assembly there is no dishonor in ending the war against a worthy foe when victory becomes impossible. Our traditions demand it."

"Humans a worthy foe?" Kevek demanded in a voice shaking with barely suppressed rage. "You say too much, Brakal. Humans are nothing but clever animals, meant to be crushed. If you and the other ineffective admirals could not manage, then perhaps the fault is with the Deep Space Fleet and its selection process. And since you personally proved ineffective against them as well, I think you may in fact not be the best choice as Speaker of the Kraal. What say you, my fellow lords? Shall we hold another vote?"

Kevek looked around the amphitheater with a triumphant air.

"What say my fellow lords?"

Vagh climbed to his feet once more.

"Simply repeating Mishtak's lies about the humans in this sacred place does not make them true, Kevek. And we will not take a new vote for speaker."

"We will if the majority demands it."

Brakal and Vagh exchanged glances. The former turned to Gvant.

"What are the rules in such a case?"

"You may put the question to the lords if it is proposed."

"Then I propose it," Vagh thundered. "Will the Kraal hold a second vote for speaker?"

Gvant raised both hands to attract attention, then said, "Using your devices, please vote now."

Brakal barely had time to consider how he would bring the discussion back on track when Gvant looked up from his tablet.

"Speaker, the assembly has decided. There will not be a second vote."

"Thank you." Brakal stared at Kevek who finally took his seat, murder blazing from his black within black eyes. "We will discuss the matter at hand. The Kraal must force the council to end this war while we can still demand honorable terms from a worthy foe."

Angry muttering came from the nucleus of civilian lords around Kevek. One of them stood to be recognized.

"Yes, Dazk?"

"What terms?"

"A return to our respective spheres as they were the day before Mishtak and the council triggered hostilities. Peace without penalties between our species."

An air of stunned incredulity twisted Dazk's angular features.

"You would give conquered star systems back to the hairless apes without a fight?"

"Indeed. It is the only way they will accept an armistice."

"Yet giving up what we gained leaves us with an obscene expenditure of wealth, the loss of countless lives, and nothing to show for it." The civilian lord made a dismissive gesture which bordered on the insulting. "Unacceptable."

"Sunk costs. We will never recover those losses, even if we fight the humans until the end of the universe. But limiting the losses to what we expended so far, that is now our sole and overriding duty. As is ensuring the dynasty does not lose favor with the gods and find itself rejected by the people. We need political stability now more than ever. Letting things continue as before, that is unacceptable. When one concedes a war is unwinnable, then one is honor-bound to end it."

"*If* one concedes the war is unwinnable."

Brakal's lips curled up, revealing his yellowed fangs.

"A plurality of lords present today fought against the humans in one capacity or another. Shall we hold a vote on whether they believe final victory is a fantasy dreamed up by Mishtak's fevered brain? They will tell you we can only bleed treasure and lives until there is nothing left."

Dazk glanced at his military peers sitting stone-faced in a great cluster to his right.

"Why should the word of those dismissed by the admiralty carry any weight with this noble assembly?"

Brakal's rictus widened at the logical trap yawning in front of those who refused to see the truth.

"Because they faced a worthy foe and could not contain him. It led to their dismissal by Admiral of the First Class Trage on Mishtak's orders. Their replacements cannot do better and never will. Do you think an enemy capable of besting so many senior officers can still be cowed?"

When he saw Dazk's mouth open for what would no doubt be a scathing retort, Brakal added, "Take care you do not accuse your peers of incompetence. They were among the best of our Deep Space Fleet's leadership, honed to a keen edge by the war, Shrehari who served the empire with honor. If they were truly incompetent, Trage would have relieved them long ago and not in recent times. War has a way of culling peacetime officers promoted beyond their ability during the earliest stages. Now answer me. Do you want a vote on whether this assembly believes we can still force the humans to bend?"

Instead of replying, Dazk took his seat and pointedly stared over Brakal's head.

"I thought not. My lords, if a majority agrees we must seek an armistice before it is too late, then let us put forward a motion for debate and a vote."

Brakal stepped back to the rostrum and picked up his device. Its screen displayed the text of the motion, one carefully composed with Gvant's help and approved by his closest backers, such as Vagh. It left little room for interpretation.

"The Shrehari Empire has been at war with the human Commonwealth for half a generation and has not achieved victory beyond seizing and occupying border star systems which remain, to this date, in a state of irregular warfare against occupying forces. Moreover, the humans are gaining in material superiority to the point where they raid us with near impunity within imperial space and the occupied star systems, while the empire's treasury is bankrupt. The Deep Space Fleet, though courageous and aggressive, cannot match the increasingly superior human starships which destroy ours faster than we can replace them. It is necessary to admit we cannot win this war with honor. We can only

end it with honor. The Kraal, therefore, enjoins the
governing council to work with it under the guidance of
the imperial regent in seeking an armistice which will see
the occupied systems returned to the Commonwealth in
exchange for peace without penalties. Should the
governing council refuse, it will face a vote of non-
confidence by the Kraal."

He took a deep breath.

"The text of the motion is now on your devices. I open
the floor for debate."

Most of the lords glanced down and read the words
with their own eyes. Those who helped draft the motion
kept their eyes on Brakal. After a while, Kevek, who
seemed to have appointed himself the leader of the
opposition, stood.

"This is fine and well, Brakal. But leaving aside your
contention our only choice is seeking an armistice—"

"There are other options," Brakal replied. "One of
them is keep fighting and watch the enemy raid deeper
and deeper inside the empire, turning everything the
council has done with the regent's blessing into a deadly
lie. Seeking an armistice is a lesser evil because it will
allow us to disengage on our terms."

"What if the humans ask for harsher terms than we are
willing to give since they apparently surpass us in
strength by such a great margin nowadays?"

"I have studied them. They will accept a peace that
returns their star systems and nothing more because
they too are tired of fighting. But you were about to ask
something else, Kevek."

"I was. What if the council refuses to join us in seeking
an armistice? What if the regent herself supports
Mishtak in rejecting our demand? They hear only what
Admiral Trage tells them, whether or not it is the truth.

Whenever the Kraal and a council supported by the dynasty are at odds, the empire suffers."

It was the point Brakal wanted someone to raise and that it came from a lord who proved himself recalcitrant instead of coming from a known supporter made it that much better.

"A fair question. In that case, tradition says the Kraal takes a vote of non-confidence against the council and petitions the regent to dismiss it. Should the regent ignore the Kraal's petition, it may then vote to censure her and precipitate a schism between the imperial government and the four hundred highest-ranking lords of the empire. No emperor or regent has ever ignored or refused a Kraal's petition and lived to see the dynasty survive. Lady Kembri knows this. As I warned Mishtak — work with the Kraal or retire for good."

Kevek acknowledged Brakal's answer with a polite gesture.

"What replaces the council after Lady Kembri dismisses it?"

"Another council named by her and hopefully made up of those willing to work with us, though it will probably be composed of career politicians rather than Shrehari capable of making painful decisions so we avoid any further destabilization. Or the Kraal nominates a *kho'sahra* who will rule in the regent's name. One of us who holds or held an admiral or general's rank in the Imperial Armed Forces."

And there it was, laid out for everyone to hear and consider. Nothing less than the government's removal, hopefully with the regent's blessing, but if she demurred, a *kho'sahra* elected by the Kraal could theoretically act on his own. That, however, would ensure her dynasty was stripped of power and faced replacement in due course.

"A far-reaching proposition," Kevek replied. "Fraught with peril."

"But nonetheless necessary. Even though you doubt our conclusion that we can no longer hope for victory, surely you agree Mishtak and his council must go. They are tired, bereft of ideas, and will ultimately bring disaster to the empire."

Many in the assembly, even on the civilian lords' side, silently signified their approval of the sentiment. Perhaps the lords of the Kraal were remembering the power they once wielded in governing the empire and could feel renewed energy coursing through their veins at the thought of taking back what was theirs by ancient law. Even Brakal could sense something undefinable stirring in the amphitheater. An awakening of sorts.

Kevek inclined his head.

"It seems you and I can agree on at least one thing, Brakal."

When Kevek sat, Brakal let his gaze roam over the assembly.

"This is the time to speak, my fellow lords. If we wish to save the empire from further harm, we must be as one in our thoughts and actions. We must reclaim our power and exercise it for the common good."

"Let us stop talking and vote on the motion," one of the military lords said without standing to be recognized. "The longer we delay, the more will die out there."

Dozens of voices shouted out their assent and Brakal inclined his head.

"So be it. Gvant, do your duty."

The Chief Keeper of the Kraal's Records acknowledged his order and raised the tablet in his hands.

"My lords, please use your devices to vote on the motion put forth by Speaker Brakal."

A few minutes passed before Gvant turned to Brakal.

"We have recorded the vote. Three hundred and five for, eleven against, and eighty-four abstentions."

Brakal felt a savage joy rise up his gorge. Over three-quarters of the Kraal in support! Even if Mishtak held a threat over Lady Kembri, she could not ignore the motion. His scheme to save the empire from the council's folly was unfolding as he hoped.

"Gvant, please send the approved motion along with the vote results to the regent and the head of the governing council."

"Immediately, Speaker."

A rumble of approval echoed across the amphitheater.

"And now, my lords of the Kraal, I propose we vote on declaring our loyalty to Emperor Tumek, so he and everyone else in the empire may know our quarrel is with the council and not the dynasty."

Vagh stood.

"I demand a vote by voice."

"I second the motion." Edronh joined his comrade in staring at the last recalcitrant civilian lords.

Brakal looked at Gvant, who nodded.

"The motion is valid and has been seconded, Speaker. You may call for a vote by voice."

"Then, I do so. Chief Keeper of the Records, call upon each lord in order of seniority to declare for or against."

The final tally was four hundred in favor, no votes against, and no abstentions.

— Thirty-Four —

Half an hour before *Jan Sobieski* and the rest of Group Miqa's planned drop out of hyperspace, Dunmoore finally gave in to her impatience and entered the CIC. As she expected, every station was crewed, and Gregor Pushkin sat in his command chair, tablet in hand, distracting himself with administrative work.

"Good morning, Commodore." His face lit up when he saw her. "I trust you slept well."

Technically, it was still the middle of the night watch, which ran from midnight to four in the morning, and Pushkin's cheerful greeting almost triggered a weary yawn.

"Quite well, thanks." Though in truth, Dunmoore's short spell in the VIP cabin bunk had been fitful and beset with inexplicable dreams. "And you?"

"Tolerable." The twinkle in his eyes told her he knew they were both lying. Few slept soundly on the eve of a raid as daring as this one. "The ship is at battle stations and everything is ready."

"Thank you."

She settled into the second command chair, wishing there was a way she could reach out to the other ships in her group and especially to Ezekiel Holt, who would

282

shortly come out of FTL several light-hours away. Too far for conventional radio or an optical comlink. And as for using subspace radio before revealing their presence in the Shrehari home system by opening fire at point-blank range...

Being a spectator until they engaged the enemy was the price Dunmoore paid for the star on her collar. But it made her wish she was back in *Iolanthe* as captain where she could control her and her crew's destiny. Right now, she was only a passenger with CIC privileges.

The three-dimensional tactical projection at the heart of the CIC showed their last view of Miqa and its antimatter cracking and refueling stations. A blurry blue icon showed where the navigation plan saw them come out of hyperspace and, at her last-minute orders, it was as close to the gas giant as even the emergency safety rules allowed. The strain of leaving hyperspace so close to a gravity well would take a few years off her ships' lifespans, but increase their chances of surprising the enemy. Since this might be the navy's one and only chance of successfully raiding the enemy's home system, it was worth the added risk.

Pushkin must have sensed her mood because he didn't engage in small talk or otherwise break through her thoughts with irrelevant observations. The CIC's atmosphere was palpably tense though the crew spoke in subdued tones. Otherwise, they worked in silence.

Dunmoore wondered whether *Iolanthe*'s CIC watch was engaged in its usual pre-battle banter, or whether the enormity of the occasion also led to an unusual solemnity in these final minutes before dropping out of FTL on the enemy's doorstep.

Lieutenant Commander Devall's voice over the public address system came as a startling surprise.

"Now hear this. Transition to sublight in five minutes. That is all."

Her eyes automatically searched out the countdown timer on the CIC's main display. Five minutes until she knew whether she'd taken Task Force Luckner into a trap from which they couldn't escape.

"Five minutes to death or glory, eh, Skipper," Pushkin murmured in a voice pitched only for her ears. "Reminds me of old times."

"That it does." Dunmoore kept her eyes glued to the timer while one part of her wished it would reach zero faster and the other that time would slow to a crawl so she could gain control over her nervousness.

With sixty seconds left, a klaxon sounded three times throughout the ship, warning everyone aboard they were about to shift from hyperspace back to sublight. Then, the last moments flashed by, and familiar nausea gripped Dunmoore's innards as her body reacted to the transition.

Almost half a minute passed before *Jan Sobieski*'s sensor chief said, "The ships of Group Miqa are where we expected and running silent. If fact, they're clean enough I wouldn't detect them if I didn't know exactly where to look. Damn boneheads won't see us."

The gas giant Miqa filled the CIC's central display moments later, its colored bands and storms more awe-inspiring than ever this close.

"That's zero magnification, incidentally, sir," the combat systems officer said in a matter of fact voice. "A view as live as can be."

Small red icons appeared, both on the main display and in the tactical projection, marking artificial satellites one by one as the visual sensors registered them. Some quickly turned into representations of the antimatter warning symbol, while others became orbs with lines radiating from them, indicating defense platforms.

"I'm not picking up anything other than automated navigation instructions on the usual channels," the signals petty officer reported. "No alerts on Shrehari routine and emergency regular or subspace radio.

"No sensor pings either besides standard search patterns for natural hazards. The orbital defense platforms are on low power."

Pushkin turned to Dunmoore.

"I think we achieved step one — getting close without being detected."

"Now, we just need to get closer." She glanced at the signals petty officer. "Are we linked with the rest of the group, PO?"

"Aye, Commodore. Everyone is connected via laser."

"Captain Pushkin, please ask your combat systems officer to designate targets for Group Miqa."

"Mister Jokkainen."

"Sir?"

"You may indulge yourself."

Dunmoore gave Pushkin an amused glance, aware she'd just heard the first bit of humor in his CIC.

"Indulging myself, aye."

Jokkainen's fingers danced over his console, assigning orbital platforms and cracking stations to the group's starships so that when they collectively lit up and opened fire, the Shrehari wouldn't know what hit them. Hopefully, that devastating first salvo would suffice to warn the Shrehari their inner core was no longer safe from an implacable enemy.

"Targets assigned, sir," the combat systems officer finally said. "Once the commodore orders up systems, the refueling stations and orbital platforms currently visible will come under sustained fire."

He gestured at the three-dimensional tactical projection, where pulsing blue icons, the ships of Task Force Luckner's Group Miqa were connected via dotted lines to red symbols representing the sum total of enemy installations within initial engagement range on this side of the gas giant.

Dunmoore studied the target assignments and could find no fault with Lieutenant Jokkainen's work. It covered, in every detail, what she'd laid out in her orders and would allow them to throw devastating firepower at the gas giant's necklace of artificial satellites within a very brief period.

"Nicely done," she said, smiling. "That'll hurt them for sure."

"I'm amazed they're not picking us up, sir," Jokkainen replied. "Us stalking a wartime FOB such as Tyva is one thing. This, however, is a bit surreal."

"We're not within optimal range yet, Lieutenant. They might still realize four human warships plan on ruining their day. Mind you, since most orbitals in that necklace are probably automated, with maybe one crewed node to oversee them, we're at lesser risk of tickling a nervous duty officer's instincts or making a bored sensor tech wonder why he sees ghosts this close to Miqa."

"You'd think after we took out two of their FOBs without losing a ship they would be more alert."

"We're not supposed to be here. Or anywhere near this star system. We're just hairless apes to them, not dangerously unpredictable fighters who've achieved technical and tactical superiority."

The sensor chief chuckled.

"Hairless apes. Nice. I'll remember that one. Mind you, if they saw a few of my old messmates, they might look for another nickname."

"It's not actually an exact translation, Chief," Dunmoore replied. "There's a species of non-sapient primate analog on Shrehari Prime which the boneheads consider contemptible. Their term for us is a hairless version of that particular animal. We simply translated the actual name of the species for our Anglic word ape since the original Shrehari is hard to pronounce and sounds like someone expectorating."

Pushkin allowed himself a smile at the exchange between Dunmoore and his CIC crew. It felt as if he was back on *Stingray*'s bridge. And the banter was having the same effect now as it did then — it took the edge off the crew's evident pre-battle jitters. Funny she should bring up Admiral Nelson at the end of last evening's meal.

The historical text he'd read in the early hours of the night watch when, unable to sleep, he searched for something to occupy his mind, called the admiral's leadership style the 'Nelson Touch.' Perhaps what he'd witnessed so many times before and was seeing again in his own CIC was the 'Dunmoore Touch.' A way of putting people at ease, of fostering trust and mutual respect. It was indeed working if the amused grins on most faces were any indication.

"*Jan Sobieski* is entering effective gun range now. *Belisarius* is at extreme gun range. *Tamurlane* and *Rooikat* are still out of useful range." The sensor chief reported. Then, after a moment of hesitation, he said, "Can I ask you a question, Commodore?"

"Sure."

"Do you speak bonehead?"

"Some. Probably just enough to get myself knifed in a Shrehari tavern for insulting someone's honor."

"Can you say their version of hairless ape?"

Almost immediately, a strange guttural sound exploded from Dunmoore's throat, stunning the CIC crew.

"Was that it?" The chief asked after a brief moment of silence.

"Supposedly, though I can't vouch for my pronunciation or accent."

Pushkin, who'd been watching his people with growing amusement caught the look in Jokkainen's eyes.

"No, Tupo. Don't."

"But it's our species' nickname in bonehead, sir. We should know how to say it."

"No."

Jokkainen turned a pleading look on Dunmoore.

"Sir, if I buy you a drink in the wardroom once we're done here, would you teach me?"

She and Pushkin exchanged a glance.

"We'll see how perfect a score you run up with your fire plan."

"Deal."

Time seemed to stretch until Dunmoore felt as if they were crawling along, even though she knew *Jan Sobieski* and the three starships following her in a single line were closing in on the planned firing window at best possible speed. And still no reaction from the enemy orbitals.

Finally, "*Jan Sobieski* is entering the engagement window."

A few more minutes passed, then, "*Rooikat* is about to enter the firing window." Since the scout was last in line, that meant it was time.

"Signals, ping Group Hoqa and let them know we're ready."

Another minute passed. "Sir, Group Hoqa is ready too."

"In that case, let them know we're going active, then make to Group Miqa, up systems, execute the fire plan."

"Group Miqa, up systems, execute the fire plan, aye, Commodore," the communications petty officer replied. A few seconds later, he said, "Message sent and acknowledged by all ships and Group Hoqa."

Dunmoore could feel *Jan Sobieski* come to life as the shield generators and gun capacitors powered up.

"I'm locked onto the assigned targets," Jokkainen reported. "Firing missiles."

Faint vibrations coursed through the soles of her feet as the launcher bays opened and ejected the first salvo into space. Almost immediately, automatic feeders pushed a fresh flight into the now empty tubes.

Tiny blue icons came to life in the tactical projection as the frigate's sensors tracked both its own and the rest of the group's missiles. First, she saw only a few dozen, then countless more joined them until the space between the ships and the targeted orbitals, both refueling and defense, turn almost a solid blue.

Dunmoore kept one ear open for Jokkainen's running report to Pushkin while she watched with morbid fascination as the defense platforms belatedly lit up and open fire at the oncoming missiles. Many of them winked out of existence, both in reality and in the tactical projection, but the Shrehari designers hadn't planned for a saturation strike such as the one she'd unleashed.

The first antimatter cracking station turned into a miniature nova with such suddenness it momentarily robbed the CIC crew of breath. Then, a second and a third exploded, and the sensor chief let out a bloodcurdling whoop. Defense platforms were dying as well but without quite as spectacular a release of antimatter.

Feeble return fire struck their shields, but once the task force's plasma guns opened up, it was over for almost half of Miqa's artificial satellites. The rest died one after the other as the planet's gravitational pull swung the ships around it and onto the planned return heading.

"There's a *Tol* class cruiser refueling," the sensor chief said as a new target came into view.

"Make that station a priority, please, Mister Jokkainen."

Pushkin glanced at Dunmoore, who nodded with approval. If they could trigger an antimatter explosion with the cruiser still connected to the orbital, it would be wrecked far more quickly and easily.

"Excellent idea, Gregor. Signals, to all ships, concentrate fire on the fueling station nearest to the *Tol* class cruiser."

"Concentrate fire on the fueling station nearest to the *Tol* class cruiser, aye."

"The *Tol*'s shields are up, and I see an emissions spike. She's powering weapons." A pause. "And she's cut the magnetic fuel line loose."

Fresh missile volleys erupted from the frigate's launchers one after the other, but the Shrehari captain understood his precarious position, so close to a volatile antimatter reservoir. He concentrated his fire in a defensive pattern which took out many before they were halfway to the target. More missiles joined *Jan Sobieski*'s flights as *Belisarius* and *Tamurlane* switched targets at Dunmoore's command.

"Seems a little unfair," Pushkin muttered for Dunmoore's ears only. "Two frigates, one of them a pocket cruiser, and a destroyer ganging up on a single *Tol* caught with its fuel lines open..."

"If you're in a fair fight, you didn't plan properly."

"The *Tol* is trying to put some distance between it and the station—" A bright flash stilled the sensor chief.

"Was it?" Jokkainen turned to the main sensor board between him and the chief. "That was the target station, sir."

"And the *Tol*?"

The main display wavered for a fraction of a second as the visual sensors obeyed Jokkainen's orders before settling on a mangled black mass venting columns of freezing gases from various hull breaches. As they watched, a stream of large-bore plasma from *Jan Sobieski*'s main guns struck the wreck, eating through its unprotected shell until one of the rounds hit a vital spot, triggering a final explosion which blew the hapless ship apart.

For a moment, Dunmoore expected to hear 'That never gets old' from the sensor chief's station, but she wasn't in *Iolanthe,* and he wasn't Chief Petty Officer Yens.

The rest of the group's swing around Miqa passed in a blur and before long, they were heading back to the hyperlimit at maximum acceleration.

"Sir, from *Rooikat*. She launched the recon drones. They went FTL for Shrehari Prime moments ago."

"Thank you. A shame we'll be in hyperspace when they make their pass. I'd love to see the Shrehari reaction to their appearance."

"Icing on the cake, sir," Pushkin replied. "We broke enough of their toys just now to make the emperor and his council rage at the heavens."

"We most assuredly did."

Dunmoore knew the moment they jumped into hyperspace, her stress-fueled adrenaline spike would crash. And that, coupled with a short, disturbed night's sleep meant she would start yawning uncontrollably.

"I'll be in my quarters, Captain. Once we're FTL and stood down from battle stations, I would be grateful if you'd allow me to walk through the ship with you."

"It would be my honor, sir."

Pushkin didn't need to ask why. He already knew. Speaking with individual crew members after a battle was one of her longstanding habits. It had become one of his too.

— Thirty-Five —

"I would raise my drink to our Speaker of the Kraal for a grand success this afternoon." General Vagh, a foaming mug of ale in hand, stood. "And I invite you to join me."

The rest of Brakal's inner circle, assembled in the Makkar estate's formal dining room to celebrate, followed suit. As Vagh raised his drink to his lips, a strange look came over his face, and he placed the mug down again so he could pull a small personal communicator from his robe's inner pocket.

"What is it?" Admiral Edronh asked.

"My friend at the admiralty. He would not call me tonight of all nights on a trivial matter. My apologies."

As Vagh read the message on the device's small display, his face seemed to lose its dark coloration.

"No. No. No. This cannot be happening *now*. Maybe the gods do exist and are taking away the dynasty's mandate to rule."

He turned his eyes on Brakal.

"Those thrice-damned human imps attacked the home system earlier today. Our antimatter cracking and refueling complexes in Miqa and Hoqa orbits are gone along with their defense platforms. Destroyed by two strike groups, one of four ships and the other of five. They also wrecked a *Tol* class cruiser refueling at Miqa as well as two *Ptars* and an armed transport at Hoqa. The enemy ships escaped via otherspace virtually unscathed and are presumably heading for home. Trage has ordered one of the system's assault divisions to hunt them."

"We no longer have antimatter fueling capabilities in this system?" Edronh asked.

"Not until replacements are towed out from Shrehari Minor's orbital yards. But there is more. Both Shrehari Prime and Shrehari Minor were targeted by enemy otherspace automated reconnaissance craft. Two per planet. They were destroyed, but not before they triggered both planets' close-in defense arrays." Humorless laughter escaped Vagh's throat. "And presumably not before they sent back extensive intelligence."

"This changes things," Brakal said. "Once word gets out among the population, we could face civil unrest. That may lead Lady Kembri and Mishtak to panic and impose martial law."

"Which will only make matters worse," one of the admirals dismissed by Trage said. "We cannot wait on Mishtak to accept the Kraal's demand for cooperation in ending this war, or for his and the council's resignation."

"Or for Lady Kembri to see reason by herself. You know what must be done, yes?" Another forcibly retired senior officer asked.

"Indeed." Brakal took a sip of ale while he sorted through his thoughts. "We must stay ahead of events so that when word of the enemy attack reaches the streets, a new government has taken over by command of the regent. A government untainted by Mishtak's council. One who can point at Mishtak as the author of our empire's dishonor, thereby saving the dynasty from a bloody overthrow."

"In that case, call Lady Kembri now and offer to save her and Tumek's lives by taking over as ruler. She will dismiss Mishtak without hesitation and appoint a replacement who will serve pending the Kraal's approval if it means her son becomes emperor upon his majority." Vagh put his communicator away and raised his mug again. "An emperor guided by someone wiser than every governing council in living memory. All hail *Kho'sahra* Brakal."

"We should put the question to the Kraal," Brakal replied, eyes looking for the reactions of his inner circle at Vagh's impetuous toast.

"Nonsense." Edronh climbed to his feet. "Yes, the Kraal can appoint one of its own as *kho'sahra*, but the emperor or his regent can also put forward a dictator, provided he meets the requirements and is endorsed by the Kraal. If our goal is outrunning bad news, it must be done in the latter way, and I can think of no better candidate than the current Speaker of the Kraal. I promise you our fellow lords will endorse such a nomination by the regent."

"Leaving you to choose a new speaker and me to find a member of Clan Makkar who can take my place."

"Your cousin Hradeq would be most suitable. Is he not a ground forces general currently serving out on the frontiers somewhere?"

"Every family has its strange ones, but yes, Hradeq would be acceptable to the clan and the Kraal," Brakal replied. He studied the two dozen Shrehari military lords around the table. "Are we, therefore, agreed on this course of action?"

"If Lady Kembri dismisses Mishtak and his council," Edronh said, "and appoints you *kho'sahra*, I can speak for everyone present when I say we will serve the new government to the best of our abilities. Provided your aim is ending the war with honor. The dynasty cannot survive another raid on the home system, and we know what happens when ordinary citizens believe a dynasty is no longer favored by the gods."

Brakal slapped the tabletop with an open palm.

"Then let it be done."

He drained his mug of ale and stood.

"If my lords of the Kraal will excuse me, I must speak with Lady Kembri about the hairless apes' latest outrage."

**

To his surprise, Brakal faced Mishtak seconds after the imperial palace accepted the comlink from Clan Makkar's estate.

"What do you want?" He growled.

"Your resignation and that of the other councilors before the news of this infamous human attack on our home system spreads."

"Never. It is I who demands you resign as Speaker of the Kraal after adopting a motion that is nothing short of treasonous."

"I will speak with Lady Kembri."

"No," Mishtak snarled.

"Then I will come to the Forbidden Quarter with an escort from the Fourth Imperial Assault Regiment and enter the palace at their head."

For a moment, Mishtak seemed robbed of his ability to speak by the sheer ferocity in Brakal's tone. When he recovered, he said, "You wish to precipitate a fratricidal uprising? Are you that addled by your thirst for power?"

Brakal put on an exasperated expression.

"Enough posturing. You know what will happen once word gets out. Rumors of the gods withdrawing their favor will stir up anger and fear, which in turn guarantees unrest capable of toppling the dynasty. *That* will precipitate a fratricidal uprising. There is only one solution. Resign along with the rest of the council. Let Lady Kembri appoint a new government untainted by the decisions you took, decisions which culminated in the hairless apes striking at our empire's heart."

"A new government which will surrender to the damned creatures?" Mishtak sneered with contempt, but Brakal sensed growing uncertainty in his tone and expression.

"No. We will offer them an armistice and a return to how things were the day before you unwisely chose war as a way of consolidating your power."

"Perhaps it would be safer if I ordered your arrest and that of those who support you, then declare martial law until this blows over. Maybe even launch an attack on their home system and show we can do anything they can, only better. Send a few dozen ships, perhaps."

Brakal let out a sharp bark of laughter which echoed off the stone walls and carried back to the dining room.

"The humans will expect retaliation and prepare accordingly, you fool. No matter how many ships you send, they will be destroyed. And we cannot afford losses of such magnitude. The only way we can save the dynasty is through a change of government sanctioned by the regent. Arresting the four hundred and imposing martial law will merely precipitate the disaster you wish to prevent. Now let me speak with Lady Kembri, or you will next see me over the barrel of an assault trooper's weapon. The Speaker of the Kraal is allowed unfettered access to the regent under our laws and traditions."

The sound brusquely cut off when Mishtak turned to one side, lips moving as he spoke with someone beyond visual range. Then, without warning, Mishtak vanished, his tired face replaced by that of a richly bejeweled female. As he had every time he met Lady Kembri, Brakal wondered what the old emperor who could have any mate he wanted, saw in her.

"My Lady Regent." He inclined his head in a respectful gesture.

"Lord Brakal. You find me discussing this latest outrage with Mishtak. How you heard of it even though Admiral Trage was ordered to keep the news secret is something I will not ask."

"Then you understand what will happen once word reaches the ears of the common people, Regent. And it will. One way or another and within a matter of days."

"That sounds curiously close to a threat."

"A fact. If I found out within mere hours, then others will know by now. As I told Mishtak—"

"I heard everything you said."

"Then I urge you to heed my advice, Regent. For the sake of Emperor Tumek, you must replace the government which allowed the enemy to desecrate our home system by one which will make sure the war ends with honor. Otherwise, your son might no longer have a throne when he comes of age. Place the fault on Mishtak's governing council, dismiss it, and install a new government with the mandate to seek an armistice. It is the only way we will get through this without seeing Shrehari spill Shrehari blood. Any scheme Mishtak might devise to keep power will imperil your dynasty."

"What would you do if I refuse and instead sanction your arrest, the imposition of martial law, and aggressive continuation of our fight against the humans?"

Brakal's lips curled back.

"You know the answer to that question, Regent. It would mean your dynasty does not survive."

"You would remove Tumek?"

"Not me personally. But the people will, once they see how you insist on supporting a government which has brought dishonor on the empire. Do not expect the Imperial Armed Forces to spill civilian blood so you can keep the throne for Tumek. The *Tai Kan* might open fire on ordinary citizens, but I would not rely overmuch on them either. Many, if not most in both services, will share the people's views."

Kembri tilted her head to one side as she studied Brakal through black within black eyes.

"You would see me replace the current leadership with who or what, Lord Brakal?"

Did he sense the regent's support for her governing council waver?

"Whatever or whoever you choose, if that choice is a clean break with Mishtak and his disastrous policies, and is committed to ending the war instead of seeking a final victory which will forever be out of our reach."

"Should I punish Mishtak?"

The unexpected question took Brakal by surprise. Perhaps Lady Kembri understood the precariousness of her position and saw the current governing council members as potential sacrifices which might appease an angry citizenry. But he knew better than cornering a *kroorath* without leaving it an escape route.

"No. Let him and the other councilors retire and live on their estates, never to set foot in Shredar again."

Kembri turned her head to one side.

"And you, Mishtak. If I dismiss the governing council, will you go into retirement without causing trouble?"

"Of course, Regent. We serve only at your pleasure."

Did Brakal hear a note of relief in Mishtak's voice? Perhaps he had finally concluded it would be better for his continued health if someone else dealt with the fallout of the human attack.

"Then you are dismissed. I expect you and the council to leave the Forbidden Quarter within the hour."

"As you command, Regent."

Kembri's attention turned back on Brakal.

"Now tell me who I should appoint to rule in my son's name."

"Not who, Lady. What. In troubled times such as these, naming a *kho'sahra* with full powers is the best choice, an individual who will cleanse the imperial administration and keep the dynasty safe."

"The *kho'sahra* must come from among the military lords of the Kraal, must he not?"

"That is the tradition. Though you can name him and ask the Kraal to ratify his appointment after the fact. I suggest you do so quickly and announce the change of government in response to the day's events."

Amusement seemed to radiate from Kembri's eyes as she asked her next question.

"Who would you suggest? You know the military lords better than I do. Or will you serve the empire as *kho'sahra*?"

"If you wish me to do so, Regent, I could scarcely refuse."

"Then you are my son's *kho'sahra* from this moment on. Save the empire, save my dynasty, and find peace with honor."

Brakal bowed his head.

"I pledge my life to your son, Lady Kembri, and to the empire's welfare."

She acknowledged his oath with a regal gesture before saying, "I will publish the proclamation momentarily.

Lady Adjur, who has heard everything we said, is even now drafting it for me. I expect to see you in the palace tomorrow morning at the ninth hour with a preliminary plan of governance. You may nominate whoever you want to whichever position you wish, but I will ratify your choices."

"You understand I will change most of the administration's senior officials, starting at the admiralty."

"I expect you to dismiss Mishtak's people, *Kho'sahra*. Replace them with competent, honest, and honorable Shrehari. That is all I ask."

"I will."

"In that case, begin your task. Goodnight."

Kembri cut the link leaving Brakal with his thoughts. A victory for him and his supporters. Brakal took a few moments to regain his calm. The speed at which he achieved his aim left him somewhat dizzy. And more than a little daunted by his new responsibilities. No one thought Lady Kembri would dismiss the council so quickly. Perhaps he had misjudged her intelligence and ruthlessness.

When he re-entered the dining room, everyone present jumped to their feet while Vagh called out, "The *Kho'sahra*" and saluted him with a clenched fist.

"We stand at your orders, Supreme Commander."

"So the proclamation is out?"

"Delivered to our devices moments ago."

"Lady Adjur is remarkably efficient."

"Perhaps you should steal her away from the regent," Edronh suggested, grinning.

"Instead of making facetious proposals, Admiral of the First Rank, start thinking about who you want as your senior command team."

"Trage is out?"

"He will be when I see him tomorrow morning, before meeting with the regent. She wants my initial governance plan, and we have but one night to draft it."

"Then call on your servants for *tvass*, lots of it," Vagh said, to the general approval of his fellow military lords. "There is much we must discuss and many of us you must nominate so we can throw out Mishtak's familiars before the sun sets tomorrow."

— Thirty-Six —

Dunmoore entered Pushkin's day cabin and headed straight for the samovar under the latter's amused gaze.

"Your Lieutenant Jokkainen will never speak Shrehari understandably, but he sure is trying. Don't be surprised if he uses his newfound knowledge of bonehead insults on his messmates."

"Tupo's shooting score was almost perfect, and you promised..." She handed him a mug of tea. "Thank you."

"He did well." Dunmoore dropped into the chair across from Pushkin and sighed. "I hope Zeke's group was just as successful. Not knowing feels as if I have a tiny pebble in my boot, one digging into my foot with every step."

"We could have tried to raise him before jumping out."

"No. It was better we kept radio silence, just in case. A nervous commodore's need for reassurance doesn't count as a reason for breaking it."

"Meaning it's my job to soothe a frazzled flag officer." Pushkin cocked a questioning eyebrow. "Should I break out the chess set?"

"No. And I shouldn't be drinking this black stuff you pass off as tea either and try to sleep instead."

"Why? We're in the middle of the forenoon watch."

"Right." Dunmoore took a tentative sip. "The tyranny of time. That's my reward for starting a fight in the middle of a starship's night."

"If you're that tired, may I note we're facing eight hours in FTL before we drop out at the rendezvous point? I seem to recall a certain commodore pointing out she was of no use while her flagship traveled in hyperspace, cut off from the rest of her command."

"Point taken. Perhaps I should get out of everyone's way and pretend I'm not here." She stood, yawning.

Something in her tone caught his attention.

"Post-battle blues taking hold?"

"Yes. I was probably tenser than usual, what with spending most of my time as a spectator while the operation I planned unfolded before my eyes. It makes for a harder adrenaline crash. Teaching Jokkainen a few words in Shrehari just delayed the inevitable."

Pushkin winked at her.

"Then we definitely don't want you moping around the ship as if you're Banquo's ghost at the banquet while we're celebrating a victory."

"Ooh... A reference to the Scottish play. Are you expanding your literary horizons?"

"Hardly. It's just an expression I picked up somewhere."

"Read Macbeth when you find an hour to spare. Shakespeare's works are a wonderful source of quotes for every occasion. Maybe instead of talking about Nelson last evening, I should have whipped out the St Crispin's Day Speech from his *Henry V*. Do you know it?" When Pushkin shook his head, she said, "I'm too tired to remember every line right now, but if you're curious, it'll be in the ship's database. See you in a few hours."

"Enjoy your rest."

After she left him to his thoughts, Pushkin called up the play in question and searched until he found the king's speech. One part, in particular, struck him.

Crispin Crispian shall ne'er go by,
From this day to the ending of the world,
But we in it shall be remembered;
We few, we happy few, we band of brothers.

Pushkin smiled at his faint reflection in the display. We happy few, indeed, he thought. A shame today wasn't October 25th, the day of St Crispin's feast. But that would have been too much of a coincidence.

**

"What's the word, Zeke?"

Dunmoore asked the moment Holt's face stabilized on her quarters' main display. Group Hoqa had shown up at the rendezvous point twenty minutes after Group Miqa.

"No fuel for the boneheads. A clean sweep, including two *Ptars* and one armed transport which was sipping pure antimatter when we unleashed a storm of nuclear-tipped warheads on them. They fought back, I'll give them that. *Hawkwood*'s replacement shield generators screamed a little. Her chief engineer figures hastily built wartime units with poor quality control. But Hoqa won't be feeding any starships until they put replacements into orbit. *Fennec* shot off her drones at Shrehari Minor, as per plan. One thing you should know. *Fennec* picked up four dozen Shrehari warships breaking out of orbit from both Shrehari Prime and Minor shortly before we went FTL. I'd call that a revenge posse."

"And they'll have figured out your and possibly my vector to the heliopause, which makes it an easy triangulation. I think it's safe to assume they'll arrive shortly. By the way, we also made a clean sweep. You can ask Gregor for a copy of his log if you want."

"Since the enemy's on his way, will you stay in *Jan Sobieski*?"

"No choice. You need thirty minutes to cycle drives and sending a shuttle to fetch me will take forty. I'd rather not find myself on the wrong end of a stern chase with four dozen furious Shrehari starship captains."

"They do say a stern chase is a long one."

"Yes, but I'd still rather break clean, and that means jumping out before the boneheads show up. You'll need to do without me for a while."

"I'm sure Gregor won't mind."

"For some reason, he enjoys having me around. Besides, adding skipper of Task Force Luckner's flagship to his official record won't hurt come promotion board time."

"I'm sure he's not thinking of it that way."

"No. He's not. But that's the situation. I'll stay here so we can jump the moment your ships cycle their drives and leave the enemy guessing at our escape vector."

"Understood. Do you still want Astrid as the task force chief navigator? Or will *Jan Sobieski*'s sailing master do the job?"

"Did she plot a single jump for our regular patrol area?"

Holt glanced to one side, then nodded.

"Yes. We can sync the task force at your command."

"Then make it so." She put her reader aside, stood, and slipped on her tunic.

"All ships confirm," Holt said.

"*Iolanthe* will control the transition into hyperspace. Set the countdown. I'm heading for the CIC."

"Aye, aye, sir. Countdown sync coming through now. As is my report on the raid against Hoqa."

The moment she entered *Jan Sobieski*'s CIC, Pushkin glanced up from his command chair's display.

"We're locked in and ready to go at *Iolanthe*'s signal, Commodore. I understand you're staying with us for now."

"Sorry for the imposition."

"No apologies necessary. We're glad you're staying with us a little longer."

To occupy her mind, Dunmoore called up Holt's message and watched the video portion of his destructive raid on Hoqa until the jump klaxon sounded three times, startling her.

"All hands, now hear this. Transition to hyperspace in sixty seconds. That is all."

"Sir." The signals petty officer raised his hand. "*Rooikat* reports a large cluster of hyperspace bubbles headed in our direction."

Dunmoore felt her shoulder muscles tense. The pursuit, already. She glanced at the timer and forced herself to relax.

By the time the Shrehari dropped out of FTL, Task Force Luckner would be long gone. Sure, the boneheads could figure out their general heading, but space was vast enough even the best guess would spit them out on the disputed frontier several light-years distant in any given direction.

If she were the enemy commander, she wouldn't even bother pursuing. Not if it meant stripping the home system of an assault division just when their human foes were showing a surprising degree of daring. Nausea gripped her innards as soon as the countdown timer dropped to zero.

"We are FTL, Commodore," Pushkin said while she mentally shoved her guts back into place. "And won't exit hyperspace for a good long time. I'm placing the ship at cruising stations."

Dunmoore shook herself and stood.

"In that case, I'll place myself at left-handed spanner stations."

"Perhaps you could acquaint the wardroom with the St Crispin's Day Speech at some point," he suggested. When he saw the questioning glance in her eyes, he added, "We few, we happy few."

"There is a time and a place for that sort of thing, and I missed my chance. But if the invitation to dine in the wardroom still stands, I'll gladly bore anyone to death with my fund of ancient trivia, should they be foolish and sit at my table."

"It stands, and I'll be the fool, Commodore, so I may better protect my impressionable officers."

"Like any good captain would."

— Thirty-Seven —

Trage was busy packing his belongings when Brakal and Edronh entered the office assigned to the head of the Imperial Armed Forces. Though Brakal wore nothing to denote his new status, Edronh was clad in an admiral of the first rank's robes.

When he spied them out of the corner of his eyes, Trage straightened his back and bowed respectfully.

"*Kho'sahra*. As you can see, I am clearing the way for my successor, since I cannot see you keeping me on active duty, even if I wanted to remain. After reading the regent's proclamation appointing you as the one who would rule in her son's name, I understood my tenure was over, and in truth, I felt nothing but relief. Leading our military forces throughout this war prematurely aged me." As he spoke, Trage pointedly ignored Edronh who wandered around the room, studying its lavish furnishings and decorations. "Did you see the videos of the attack we received from Miqa and Hoqa before the orbitals were destroyed?"

"No. But I would watch them now."

Trage reached for a control surface embedded in the desktop, and a display on the far wall came to life.

"I watched them over and over since it happened, incapable of comprehending what insanity drove the humans to attack our home system."

Brakal scoffed. "Insanity? Hardly. But I would not rule out their understanding of our thought patterns as a cause or maybe even the sole cause. This was not random. Their high command knew that striking at the heart of the empire, even if the only thing they destroyed were easily replaced targets such as antimatter cracking and fueling stations, would cause more political turmoil than the annihilation of ten assault divisions."

When he saw the look of outraged disbelief on Trage's drawn features, Brakal chuckled.

"They know us better than you think. Certainly much better than we know them. And judging by the fact Mishtak and the council are gone, replaced by the first *kho'sahra* in countless generations, they succeeded. Perhaps beyond their most fevered dreams. Now let us see the ships our enemies deemed worthy of this mission."

"This sequence is from Hoqa."

Brakal watched with sick fascination as five Commonwealth Navy ships suddenly appeared above the gas giant and launched enough missiles to saturate the ring of defense satellites. One caught his attention, and he reared back with a low growl.

"That battleship. It is the one which bedeviled me for so long on the frontier. It destroyed Khorsan Base, Tyva Base, and countless supply convoys."

"Your phantom?" Edronh asked, speaking for the first time since they entered what was now his office.

"The very same. Its commander is a demon spawn, sent to drive me mad. Let me see those who attacked Miqa."

When Trage called up the sequence, Brakal grunted.

"That cruiser is one of their newest models, capable of destroying a *Tol* class in a matter of moments. I think those nine ships come from the strike group that has been hunting in the Atsang sector since earlier this turn. Remarkable. I would meet the admiral who led them here, thereby ensuring my appointment as head of government, charged with ending the war. You sent an assault division after them?"

"I did. The Shrehari Prime and Shrehari Minor monitoring stations determined both groups' vectors when they transitioned to otherspace and calculated where they would emerge to reunite and cycle their engines before entering interstellar space. Our ships should be there soon."

"And the humans will be gone by then. Their commander has surely planned on a quick escape, knowing we would pursue to punish them. Edronh, you may decide whether chasing these impudent creatures back to their own sphere is a worthwhile use of your ships. Since I will end the war before the close of this turn, retribution for tweaking our skull ridges within sight of the imperial palace would be senseless."

"If they come across the humans upon emerging from otherspace, I will allow them to attack. But if the humans are no longer there, the chase will end." Edronh dropped into the high-backed chair behind the desk and grunted. "Soft. It will need replacing. As will most of the furniture. In fact, take anything you wish, Trage. Someone who has served the empire as long as you did deserves a bountiful retirement gift."

Trage gave his replacement a baleful look, aware Edronh, whom he had personally relieved of duty, was mocking him.

"You may do as you wish with the contents of your office. I want nothing other than the items I already placed in this box. Do you need a handover briefing or am I free to go?"

"You are free to go. The empire thanks you for your service and bids you a pleasant retirement."

After one last look around, Trage picked up the box and walked out without saying another word.

"He was a capable admiral when he still commanded a strike group, long ago," Edronh said. "But his best days were behind him even before Mishtak took us to war."

"And he knows it, deep within, which is why he spoke of relief at being dismissed. Lady Kembri expects me momentarily. Enjoy cleansing the admiralty of its stench."

**

Brakal bowed upon entering the imperial palace's small reception room. Lady Kembri and a youth of barely twelve turns, both sitting on throne-like chairs adorned with precious metals and rare woods, acknowledged his gesture with regal nods.

The young emperor took after his late father more than his mother and was already showing hints of growing Emperor Ahikar's sharp skull ridges as well as his robust musculature.

"*Kho'sahra* Brakal. Welcome," Kembri said.

"My lady, my lord Tumek. I am honored to be in your presence."

"And we are honored to meet he who will rule in our name," Tumek replied in a steady, though still somewhat high-pitched voice.

Kembri raised a hand, and Lady Adjur entered via a side door with a small box under her arm.

"The palace staff needed most of the night to find it."

"Lady?"

"The ancient and revered *kho'sahra* badge of office, last worn by a lord named Tawdek long ago."

Kembri took the box from Adjur and opened it. Within, resting on a bed of faded material, was a disk of steel no bigger than the palm of Brakal's hand. The imperial dragon emblem was engraved on the disk, but this version held a sword in each of its six claws, signifying the *kho'sahra*'s sacred duty to defend the empire and the dynasty.

As badges of office went, the simplicity of its design pleased Brakal. No precious metals, no gems, and no extraneous artwork to detract from the message it conveyed. An adornment suitable for a member of the Warrior Caste who became admiral on his own merits.

She turned to Tumek.

"It would be proper if you presented this to your *kho'sahra*."

"Of course." Tumek took the badge from the proffered box. "Approach, Lord Brakal."

When the latter complied, Tumek stood and reached out to pin the badge on Brakal's chest, just below the right shoulder. "It suits you, I think."

Kembri made a gesture of assent.

"I agree."

A pair of servants brought a chair for Brakal, and he sat, facing regent and emperor at the latter's command.

"Tell us your plans, *Kho'sahra*."

"Certainly. I hope you understand I formulated them overnight and they need refinement."

"I do. But the emperor and I want a sense of what you intend."

"Certainly. My first purpose will be to offer the enemy peace, bring our occupying forces back within the empire, and relieve your people of the crushing tax burden imposed by Mishtak. We will no longer shed treasure and blood for no gain. Better we trade with the humans. They proved most conclusively their technological prowess now outstrips ours."

"Many will consider ending the war short of victory a shameful act."

Brakal turned his eyes on Tumek.

"No doubt. And they will be the ones who made no sacrifice and paid no price. But there will never be a victory because there was never a possibility of beating the humans. In fact, had your father lived, we would not be fighting them. He knew better than to believe stories about cowardly hairless apes who would surrender after a single devastating strike. Yes, we captured the star systems abutting our sphere, but only because we achieved surprise. Once the human warriors were roused, we advanced no further. They even defeated us on a planet called Scandia and seized one of our regimental standards as a war trophy before chasing our troops out of the star system."

"I did not know we lost a precious sacred standard during the initial conquest."

"Mishtak did not wish it known. Such incidents contradict his narrative on human weakness. More importantly, in the intervening turns, we lost too many equally precious lives, my lord. Sending the best of our race out there and watching them die needlessly, *that* was truly shameful."

"Strange words from an admiral and military lord," Tumek replied, though his tone conveyed wonder rather than censure.

"But words that must be spoken. We wish what is best for the empire and its people. Recognizing the humans as a worthy enemy, one with whom negotiating an armistice would not be dishonorable under our sacred traditions, is best for the empire, your people, and your dynasty, my lord."

"Agreed," Kembri said. "Let us now speak of more immediate matters. How do you propose organizing the government?"

Brakal spoke until his throat ran dry. When a servant brought him water, he revived it and spoke again just as long. Lady Kembri asked pointed and intelligent questions and in the end, appeared satisfied she had given the *kho'sahra*'s badge of office to the right lord. But convincing her was the easy part. Carrying out his ambitious program would be a very different matter, and there were plenty in the Forbidden Quarter who might try to stymie him.

"You have our approval, *Kho'sahra* Brakal," she said when he finally fell silent. "What do you need from us?"

"Right now, the order to seek an armistice which will include withdrawing from occupied star systems."

"Lady Adjur will draft it before the end of the day."

"Thank you, my lady."

"If that was all, you may go."

Brakal stood, bowed, and left the small reception room, feeling both buoyed and strangely weighted down by the badge of office he now wore.

— Thirty-Eight —

Holt greeted Dunmoore at the foot of the pinnace's aft ramp, along with a single bosun's mate who piped her aboard *Iolanthe* after the long hyperspace jump returning them to their regular hunting grounds.

"Welcome back, Commodore. How was the trip in *Jan Sobieski*?"

"Boring, if truth be told. And after the amount of chess I played with Gregor and his officers, I won't be challenging you for a while."

"Thank the Almighty!"

"She's a nice ship, but she's smaller than *Iolanthe* and that made life for an idler such as me a tad claustrophobic. I wrote the part of my mission report covering the Miqa attack, but I still need access to your logs so I can finish it."

"Already written for you. I know your style so it'll simply be a matter of integrating my part with the overall narrative." He gestured at the inner door. "Shall we?"

Dunmoore fell into step beside Holt.

"Thank you, Zeke, but I was actually hoping for useful work."

"Never fear. Plenty is waiting for you. Such as looking at the task force's overall ammo situation and deciding whether to redistribute some of it, leave things as they are, or head for the nearest starbase and replenish."

"I would rather we stayed out a little longer. What's your ammo state?"

"Enough for at least one saturation strike against a FOB with a convoy attack thrown in. The rest of Group Hoqa have somewhere between one third and a half of their initial loads left."

The door to Dunmoore's quarters opened at their approach.

"The same as Group Miqa. We'll stay out. Perhaps hang around one of the major star systems and see if we can track a convoy to a forward operating base. But first, we'll take a few days and stay here where the Shrehari won't stumble over us and give our ships a good once over. Extended jumps will degrade more than just the drives."

"That was my next recommendation. Renny has been grumbling for days about the strain we've put on the old girl. He'll be happy when he hears you're giving him the time he needs to baby her."

"And I need to hold a general after-action review with my captains. I just realized I can't complete my report to HQ until that's done."

"See." Holt grinned at her. "There's plenty of work for the next few days. Should we invite the captains to shuttle over and take part in person, followed by supper in the wardroom?"

She shook her head. "Since we're still in enemy territory, I'd rather not take them out of their ships, even if the chances of a Shrehari formation finding us in interstellar space are minuscule. After giving us a clean run at the boneheads' home system, Fate might use her fickle finger and remind us we are but mortal by dropping an assault division out of hyperspace within sensor range of this area. Or if they didn't pursue, another bunch alerted by their high command to be on the lookout for underhanded human raiders."

"Feeling unlucky?"

"No. Just overly lucky for far too long." She sat behind her desk and sighed. "It's nice to be home."

"And it's good to have you back." He nodded at the urn on the sideboard. "Shall I pour you a cup?"

"Please. Gregor prefers tea and *Jan Sobieski*'s wardroom, though otherwise pleasant, only serves indifferent coffee. Take one yourself and sit if you can spare a bit of time."

"A bit and more. Emma is a superb first officer. I don't even notice I'm short a second officer. It makes me wonder why the position even exists."

"Because not every first officer has her breadth of experience and her work ethic."

"I know. And I also realize I'm fortunate to have her." Holt handed Dunmoore a mug decorated with *Iolanthe*'s Furious Faerie insignia and dropped into the chair across from her. "What effect do you think our raid will end up having, beyond forcing them to replace two extensive refueling constellations?"

Dunmoore shrugged.

"Probably less than what Admiral Xi hoped for when he took my idea to his boss. But if it riles them up enough to make mistakes we can exploit, then it'll have been worthwhile, especially since we came back with barely a scratch."

"The element of surprise will work wonders every single time." He took a sip. "If we're really lucky, they'll pull starships off combat patrols to reinforce vital areas across the empire in case we broaden our raids. That should help us take the initiative."

"We already took the initiative some time ago. It just wasn't a big enough shift to be noticeable until recently. While we were commerce raiding under Admiral Petras, our conventional navy colleagues struck at the occupied star systems in force for the first time, remember."

"True. Sad to think we might never find out how our raid on Miqa and Hoqa affected the enemy other than by inference."

"Though it'll cheer our side up when and if Fleet HQ publicizes the raid."

"If? You mean there's a possibility they'll keep it a secret?" Holt asked in an incredulous tone. "The most daring operation this war has seen, and they'll sit on the news of its complete and utter success?"

"Who knows? SOCOM has strange quirks."

"And even stranger people. Present company included. Speaking of which, since HQ is waiting with bated breath on your report and we're a little too far from the nearest subspace array, will you use one of the scouts or *Skua* to get within range and send it? If we empty her while we're here, she can head for Starbase 32, send your report along the way, stock up again and rejoin us. Or stay there and wait for us to come in when we're running low."

Dunmoore thought about the suggestion for a moment.

"I'll send *Skua*. But she'll stay at Starbase 32. We won't know where we'll be by the middle of next week, and I'd rather not play Marco Polo over the subspace channels in case the enemy picks up a stray transmission and figures someone's plotting mischief in their backyard. Especially now that they'll be extra paranoid. Besides, I never quite figured why we needed a supply ship permanently attached to the task force, other than as a space-faring warehouse. And that's wasteful considering we're not bound to a permanent patrol route and can come in without asking HQ whenever we run low on ammo or other consumables."

"One of Lena's bright ideas, no doubt. Mind you, if you're ever in the mood to bait the enemy, *Skua* will make a perfectly tempting target."

"Pass. I prefer pursuing my victims rather than enticing them into my parlor."

Holt gave her an amused look.

"An interesting choice of words."

"I'm a little stir crazy after all that time trying to avoid bothering Gregor and his crew."

"Don't try that here. We are your flagship, and being bothered by you is part of the job. I certainly don't want you becoming even crazier. Think of how someone such as Thorin will react if you use words like enticing within earshot. He wouldn't be able to help himself, and then I'll have a disciplinary issue on my hands."

Dunmoore made a face.

"True. Our Mister Sirico does forget himself at times, especially when off-color jokes are involved."

"I thought he watched himself around you."

"Every so often, when I'm in the gym quietly doing my thing while Tatiana and her bunch are exercising, he'll come in and train with them. When he's hanging around soldiers in an informal setting, Thorin can become rather ribald. Even Tatiana surprises me sometimes."

Holt's eyebrows shot up.

"Tatiana? The things I learn now that I'm *Iolanthe*'s captain."

"Everyone watched their language around you back then because spacers know you never annoy a first officer and the soldiers learned quickly from them."

"But captains are okay?"

"Didn't you enjoy the usual round of banter in the CIC while waiting for the show to begin?"

"Sure. But nothing that would make me take someone aside for counseling, though Thorin does sometimes exaggerate his bloodthirsty pirate act."

"That's what a captain gets. For the real deal, you need to make folks forget you're around, and the gym is pretty much the only place aboard unless you're deliberately eavesdropping, which isn't a good idea." Dunmoore drained her cup and glanced at the old clock with the gaunt knight's silhouette on its face. "Real coffee is such a pleasure when you've not tasted any for a long time. How about we call the captains together for a virtual after-action review in two hours? Then I can complete my mission report and prepare it for *Skua* once her holds are empty."

"Two hours it is, Commodore." Holt climbed to his feet. "I'll make sure they present their ammo and critical stores status so we can discuss who gets what from *Skua*."

"Excellent. Thank you for shouldering some of the flag captain duties."

"As always, it's my pleasure, sir. But you should know there is self-interest involved."

"Oh?"

"A close and personal look at the inner workings of a task force will stand me in good stead someday. Or at least I hope so."

"I'm sure it will."

**

"So, Commodore, did you draft the Encyclopedia Galactica entry for our historic raid on the Shrehari home system?" Commander Farren Vento, or rather his hologram asked the moment Dunmoore entered *Iolanthe*'s conference room.

"No. Can't do that until we discuss what happened. Good afternoon, everyone. I hope you and your crews survived that epically long jump without suffering hyperspace jitters and your ships don't show excess wear and tear on the drives." When no one spoke up, she said, "Good, because we won't return to base right away. I gather from your reports everyone has still at least one-third of the initial ammo load left. That being the case, I'll run one more wolf pack operation while the enemy is still having conniptions at us desecrating the heart of their empire."

None of them seemed taken aback by her announcement.

"What we'll do is empty *Skua*'s holds, after which I will send her back to Starbase 32. Along the way, she can ping a subspace array and send my report to SOCOM HQ."

Dunmoore turned her gaze on Lieutenant Jubinville, the transport's captain and, like Emma Cullop, a merchant spacer serving in the navy for the duration.

"You'll stay there and wait for us. With any luck, we'll find suitable prey, give them a bit of Luckner love with the rest of our ammunition, and then join you. Two weeks if we're lucky. No more than a month, I'd wager."

Jubinville nodded once.

"Understood, sir."

"Now, let's talk about the raid. Captain Holt, would you please start with Group Hoqa."

"Certainly, sir."

An hour later, Dunmoore had what she needed. Task Force Luckner's captains were proud of their accomplishments and eager to say so, conscious that mention of their names and the names of their ships in the commodore's mission report might mean a lot when the next round of promotion boards sat.

She also sensed a sort of giddiness, as if surviving a stab at the enemy's heart made them, if not invulnerable, then capable of surviving commerce raiding's lesser risks.

"Thank you for your candor." Dunmoore met each of her captain's holographic eyes in turn. "What we accomplished might not appear to be much in the grand scheme of things, but I'm sure we made a difference. The wolf pack hunts again in forty-eight hours. If you won't be ready by then, please let me know soonest."

— Thirty-Nine —

"**Y**ou'd think they would be more circumspect these days," Holt remarked as he and Dunmoore watched video transmitted over an encrypted subspace channel by one of *Rooikat*'s FTL drones. It showed a Shrehari convoy leaving Toksang, one of the sector's major hubs.

Since she planned on only one quick wolf pack operation before heading back to base, Dunmoore figured the risk of the Shrehari picking up a drone's weak subspace signal was minimal. But it would allow her to position ships more effectively along the heliopause and intercept a target.

"How would you change things if you figured human commerce raiders were watching?" Dunmoore asked.

"Randomly send individual ships to various points within the system and reform the convoy at a predetermined spot instead of jumping together on a measurable vector from Toksang's hyperlimit to the heliopause. We wouldn't know where to look. Those fifteen ships, if they did what I just proposed, would leave us with at best a one in fifteen chance of figuring out a given vector. By the time we sorted ourselves out, they'd be away on an interstellar jump."

She nodded with approval.

"A good thing the Shrehari aren't innovators. At least not in the tactical realm."

"They jumped," Chief Yens said. "I'll figure out their probable course in a moment."

"Signals, tell *Rooikat* she can recover her drone."

"Aye, aye, sir. *Rooikat* to recover her drone."

The holographic tactical projection lit up with a representation of the Toksang system. An ever-widening red line connected the Shrehari colony with a spherical blob at the system's heliopause while a forlorn blue icon a quarter of the way around the heliosphere represented Task Force Luckner.

"They'll emerge somewhere within that area."

"Magnify." She stood and walked over to the projection, studying it as she decided how her ships would be best deployed, and how long it would take. After a few minutes, Dunmoore glanced at Sirico.

"Ready to copy deployment orders, Thorin?"

"Go ahead, sir."

Dunmoore touched the blob's periphery eight times as she called out ship names until eight blue icons covered the side facing interstellar space. She examined the result for a while longer before nodding.

"That should do. Send the deployment plot. They can leave as soon as they're ready."

Less than ten minutes later, *Iolanthe*'s jump klaxon sounded its warning. Shortly after that, Dunmoore's stomach twisted as they transitioned to hyperspace.

**

"Bridge to the commodore."

Dunmoore put her reader on the desk. It was too early for the convoy's appearance, Task Force Luckner was

Eric Thomson

under radio silence as per standard operating procedure, and she took no part in the ship's routine.

"Dunmoore."

"Lieutenant Kremm, sir. I have the watch. We received an encrypted subspace message eyes only for the flag officer commanding Task Force Luckner. I'm piping it to your quarters."

Her eyebrows shot up in surprise.

"How did it reach us here?"

"Via aviso. *Skua* told HQ approximately where we were operating. The aviso jumped into our general area and began broadcasting on the emergency channel in the hopes of our catching its message. I acknowledged, but they're waiting for your confirmation and would rather not hang around longer than necessary."

A frown creased Dunmoore's forehead. What could be significant enough to risk one of the Fleet's lightly armed courier starships, used to carry data which shouldn't travel over the subspace net along with small, valuable cargo items, or people for whom speed was more important than comfort? The message must be incredibly urgent if the aviso was under orders to transmit continuously inside enemy space.

"Thank you, Theo."

"Bridge, out."

She glanced at her reflection in the mirror and cocked an eyebrow. Encrypted, always, especially if transmitting where the enemy could intercept. For her eyes only? That was unusual.

Her desktop chimed softly, announcing the message's arrival. She called it up and let the ship's computer match her biometrics to her authorization level as the flag officer commanding Task Force Luckner. The encryption faded away in a matter of seconds, leaving her with text in plan Anglic.

She read the message three times before its import finally sank in. Hands trembling with unexpected emotion, Dunmoore stood and walked over to the coffee urn for a mug, wishing she could spike it with something a little stronger. She took a few calming sips, then returned to her desk and read the message a fourth time. It still said the same thing.

Dunmoore stroked the intercom.

"Flag to the CIC."

"Sirico here, sir. What can I do for you?"

"All ships will join *Iolanthe* at our current location. They will not, I repeat, not engage in any hostile act from the moment they receive this order. I'm canceling the planned wolf pack operation against the enemy convoy."

Deep silence greeted her words. Then, "Does that mean?"

"Apparently so. I will speak with Captain Holt at once and the rest of the task force captains as they arrive. Captain Holt will surely gather his department heads when we finish."

"I'll let him know, sir. Anything else?"

"Negative. Dunmoore, out."

She closed her eyes with a deep sigh. The door chime yanked her back to the present only a minute or two later.

"Enter."

Holt, anticipation writ large on his face, burst through the door.

"Thorin said you just issued a most peculiar order and canceled the wolf pack."

She pointed at the chair across from her.

"Sit. This is news you don't want to hear standing." When he'd obeyed, she said, "It's over. This damned war is over. The Shrehari asked for an immediate armistice. Earth granted it."

A low whistle escaped Holt's lips.

"Unbelievable."

"But true." She glanced at the message. "Commonwealth Armed Services units will cease hostilities against the Shrehari Empire immediately. Those operating inside the prewar imperial sphere will withdraw to our current sphere and wait for instructions. If a Shrehari unit offers battle, assume they did not yet receive word of the armistice and do your best to disengage without causing further loss of life."

"Does HQ say why they threw in the towel?"

"Apparently, there's been a coup d'état. Members of what passes for a legislature in their political system overthrew the governing council that triggered the war. This legislature put forward a *kho'sahra* who will rule on the emperor's behalf. I understand it's a sort of military dictator, akin to feudal Japan's shoguns. Three days ago, a Shrehari ship showed up in the Scandia system and surrendered so the envoy it carried could hand over the *kho'sahra*'s message."

"What?" Laughter rumbled up Holt's throat. "The first bonehead ship to surrender since the beginning of the war and it's the one carrying the entire empire's surrender? Karma on a cosmic level."

"Oh, it gets better. The Shrehari are pulling their ships back inside the empire's prewar sphere and promise they would evacuate the occupied star systems as quickly as possible once the armistice is in place. They wish to negotiate a peace treaty once our respective forces have disengaged."

"Unbelievable," Holt repeated. "Over ten years of fighting, countless dead, thousands of ships destroyed, planets ravaged and without warning, they're walking back to the status quo ante, giving up everything they bled for. I guess those who figured the Imperial Armed Forces weren't particularly enthusiastic about the war from the start might have been on to something. If the military sponsored or supported that coup, it means many, perhaps even most of their senior officers finally figured out they couldn't win. They might even have picked up on the fact we've been operating at will within imperial space for almost a year. And allowing such a thing would mean dishonor of the sort no imperial dynasty could survive. From what I read, when a dynasty falls, it falls hard."

A mischievous smile tugged at Dunmoore's lips.

"There's more. You'll really enjoy this little tidbit."

Holt cocked his head to one side.

"Yes?"

"You might recognize the Shrehari dictator's name. I certainly do, and I doubt there are two admirals of the same name and fame in the Imperial Deep Space Fleet."

"Dragging this out comes under the heading of torture, something not even flag officers can inflict with impunity."

Her smile turned into a broad grin.

"Brakal."

"What? Your Brakal? The one you faced in *Victoria Regina* and *Stingray*?"

"I won't know for sure until I see an image of this *kho'sahra*, but overthrowing the council to end a war they can't win strikes me as something he'd do."

"No doubt. What's next?"

Dunmoore shrugged.

"We assemble the task force as quickly as possible and, since Luckner doesn't have an assigned patrol area, we head to the nearest starbase. One jump." She thought for a few seconds. "Let's make that Starbase 30 in two jumps. We might as well get out of 3rd Fleet's way and place ourselves at Admiral Singhal's disposal until SOCOM figures out what they want from us. *Skua* will join us there. I'll let each captain know about this the moment their ship shows up. You can inform *Iolanthe*'s crew now. But make sure everyone understands that until Fleet HQ confirms the enemy has fully disengaged, we remain on a war footing. Nothing changes other than we stop hunting and go home."

"Of course."

"And now, if you'll excuse me, I must draft a reply confirming I received the orders, understand them, and will comply."

Holt jumped to his feet.

"I still can't believe it's finally over. And more importantly, that we survived. I'll put Astrid to work on the navigation plan so that thirty minutes after the last ship arrives, we're out of here, hopefully never to return."

"Thank you. But let's wait until we're orbiting a human colony, safe under the protection of a starbase's guns, before breaking out the champagne. I'd hate for us to go down in history as the last casualties of the war because we came across a Shrehari strike group that didn't hear about the armistice."

"Pessimist."

"Amateur historian. Over the centuries, plenty of battles were fought after peace was declared simply due to a delay in communications. Considering we still don't know how well the Shrehari can disseminate orders, I won't celebrate just yet."

"Point taken, sir."

**

Gregor Pushkin reacted much in the same way as Holt when Dunmoore told him the news after *Jan Sobieski* dropped out of hyperspace at the rendezvous point several hours later. But he took greater delight in hearing Brakal's name.

"It just occurred to me that half of my crew never served in a peacetime navy, Commodore. I daresay it'll be the same for the other ships. I'm not sure how well those who joined up since the Shrehari invaded will adapt. If war is long periods of boredom interrupted by brief moments of sheer terror, how will the youngsters deal with long, uninterrupted boredom with no moments of sheer terror at all? I can barely remember patrolling for months on end, hoping an adventurous pirate will cross your bow, and what I recall involves a lot of drills and self-directed professional development. Not that pirate-chasing does much to raise the adrenaline level."

She gave him an amused smile.

"Trust you to think of everyone else first. Never change, Gregor."

"I wouldn't know what I might change into, so no worries. What about you? When the navy returns to a peacetime footing, Task Force Luckner won't be kept on the order of battle. You'll be a commodore without a command, and since Zeke's appointment as *Iolanthe*'s captain is permanent..."

Dunmoore replied with a shrug.

"Whatever happens will happen. I'll worry about it when the time comes, and that won't be tomorrow or the next day. Demobilization takes months, something which won't even start until the armistice is signed and the Shrehari evacuate every star system they took from us. You won't be rid of me as your flag officer that quickly."

"No complaints, sir."

"Let your crew know. Since *Jan Sobieski*'s the last to show up, we leave in half an hour. That should allow us to clear out before the convoy gets here. Your navigator should have received the plot for our trip to Starbase 30 by now."

Pushkin glanced away, then nodded.

"Got it."

"In that case, we'll speak again when we drop out of FTL at our destination."

He gave her thumbs up.

"Here's to making it more or less intact."

Before she could caution him, his image dissolved.

With the task force assembled and preparing its withdrawal from Shrehari space, she was once more left with little to do, other than bringing Luckner's operations log up to date.

Dunmoore glanced at the clock with the silhouette of a gaunt knight on its face, a decommissioning gift from the crew of *Don Quixote*, her first command, now long consigned to history. She still vividly remembered sitting in her command chair on the scout ship's tiny bridge with her coxswain, then Petty Officer First Class Guthren, the day Fleet units received notice of the invasion which started more than a decade of war.

Dunmoore had been a keen, ambitious lieutenant in her late twenties back then. Now she was a forty-year-old commodore with the thousand light-year stare of someone twice her age and enough silver in her hair to exude a flag officer's gravitas.

She stared at the clock for a long time, lost in memories of past ships, of crewmates both dead and alive, and the moments of sheer terror which punctuated every encounter with an implacable enemy. The jump klaxon startled her and brought her thoughts back to the present.

They were going home.

— Forty —

"**I**'m not sure I understand, sir. Why is HQ assigning my task force the mission of escorting the armistice delegation?"

Dunmoore gave Admiral Alok Singhal's image on the display in Holt's day cabin a questioning gaze. The flag officer commanding 3rd Fleet smiled at her apparent puzzlement.

"The new Shrehari leader has asked that the ship which destroyed his forward operating base and then impudently raided the imperial home system be included in the official escort. He credits your action against the FOB for triggering a chain of events culminating in his becoming the imperial shogun, or whatever the title is in Shrehari. Never could manage the language. Your raid on their home system apparently triggered the regime change and convinced the imperial regent to seek an armistice.

"HQ decided, as a gesture of good faith, they would grant the request since Task Force Luckner is available since it's not tied to a specific patrol area and is of approximately the right size and composition. The mission and the honor of representing us falls to you.

Privately, I also think HQ chose you because you tweaked their skull ridges in such a spectacular fashion."

"The FOB in the Khorsan system was Brakal's? Unbelievable. It means we've been fighting him for a long time without knowing. That area was *Iolanthe*'s hunting grounds."

How many times, she wondered, did their missiles and gunfire cross?

"And he seems to think your attack was the proverbial flap of the butterfly's wings which caused a storm half a world away." Singhal paused. "If they developed their own version of chaos theory, that is."

"I see." The idea of finally meeting her old foe in the flesh felt more than a bit outlandish.

"The Secretary-General and his delegation will travel aboard the Space Control Ship *Terra*, one of the carriers reconfigured a few years ago."

"I know *Terra*, sir. For a brief time, before I came to my senses, I was a pilot in her fighter wing, long before the war."

The rueful expression on her face turned Singhal's smile into a delighted chuckle.

"I gather you discovered human-controlled non-FTL attack craft were good only for giving our Marine Corps brethren air support and therefore better flown by experienced Marine noncoms who can tell their own troops and the enemy apart."

"Within a month. My wing commander took almost a year before deciding it would be better if I served in another capacity on another starship. Sorry for the digression. So the SecGen and his delegation are traveling in *Terra*. What is the rendezvous point and our destination? And when?"

"The armistice will be signed on Aquilonia station, a mining operation dug into one of Thule's moons in the Cimmeria system."

Dunmoore nodded.

"I know the system well. That's where I gave Brakal his first bloody nose when I had *Stingray*."

"Which won't be lost on him once he finds out who destroyed his forward operating base, I'm sure. The Shrehari are withdrawing from Cimmeria and should be clear by the time you arrive. The rendezvous point will probably be in interstellar space and its coordinates communicated in good time. For security reasons, it'll be at the last minute. The date on which *Terra* will depart Earth is also still up in the air."

"Makes sense. Confusion is probably the order of the day pretty much everywhere right now."

"No doubt. Fleet HQ said I should warn you that your crews and Marines will be called upon to provide ceremonial guards on Aquilonia. *Terra* is bringing its own contingent, but the SecGen and Grand Admiral Shkadov want to put on a show."

"My Marines are a company of soldiers from the Scandia Regiment, many of whom stared at Shrehari infantry through gun sights during the empire's unsuccessful attempt to invade their homeworld."

"Even better, though I wouldn't parade the Shrehari battle standard the Scandians captured."

"No worries. It's sitting in an armored display case in the regiment's headquarters."

"Good. If you need to refresh your ceremonial attire and equipment, I'm sure we can help."

Dunmoore made a face.

"In that case, I suppose I'll need a commodore's dress uniform."

"Done. Tell your staff to speak with mine." Singhal contemplated her for a few seconds. "I envy you, Commodore. You'll witness one of the most momentous events in human history. Peace between our species and the Shrehari after more than a decade of war."

She thought about it and put on a dubious air.

"I'm not sure it's that remarkable compared to the negotiations which ended both Migration Wars. The casualties were at least an order of magnitude greater, as was the devastation. We humans inflicted greater harm on each other than the Shrehari ever did."

"Indeed." Singhal inclined his head to acknowledge her point. "Civil wars are always among the most vicious of conflicts. In any case, those are your orders. Why HQ funneled them through me, I couldn't say, since you still belong to SOCOM. Nevertheless, my supply warehouses are yours. Take whatever you need and ask us to order it if it's not in stock. Should any of your ships need a turn in the dry docks, they're yours. Even if HQ hadn't ordered me to support you with everything Starbase 30 can offer, I would have done so anyway, seeing as how our hopes for a peaceful future go with Task Force Luckner."

Dunmoore inclined her head.

"Thank you, sir."

"One more thing, Admiral Xi asked me to congratulate you on his and the grand admiral's behalf for the success of your raid in the enemy home system. Task Force Luckner will receive a Commonwealth Unit Citation for the operation. Now, if there's nothing else, I'll leave you to it and let HQ know you're ready for one last mission."

"Can I mention the nomination for a unit citation to my captains?"

"Sure. Admiral Xi said it's about to land on the Secretary General's desk and Lauzier most certainly will sign it."

"Excellent."

"Before Task Force Luckner leaves, I wish to entertain you and your officers in the starbase mess. If you let my flag lieutenant know when you plan on sailing, he'll arrange things. We'll give you a traditional send-off."

"Much appreciated, sir. I look forward to raising a glass with you."

"Until then. Singhal, out."

**

Stunned silence greeted her announcement when she told the assembled captains, for once sitting around the conference room table in person, of their next mission, why Luckner was chosen, and the soon to be announced award. With all nine ships docked at the huge, spindle-shaped station, a first in the task force's history and a rare event for a ship *Iolanthe*'s size, getting everyone aboard was simplicity itself. However, Holt had made sure his colleagues were piped aboard in style by a bosun's mate and a quarter guard from E Company, 3rd Battalion, Scandia Regiment at the main airlock.

"Are you telling us our actions are what ended this damned war?" Commander Vento asked. "If so, we should get more than just a Commonwealth Unit Citation. How about a victory parade on the Palace of the Stars' ceremonial plaza in Geneva? Or a lifelong free drinks allowance in any Armed Services mess for every spacer and soldier in Luckner?"

"I'm afraid the citation, and the honor of escorting our armistice delegation is it, Farren. Sorry. You'll need to keep buying your own drinks."

Vento put on a disconsolate air and shook his head. "Sad."

"Keep in mind the unit citation comes with a nice, shiny device you can pin to your dress uniform," Holt said. "Wear that in an officer's mess and steer the conversation in the right direction. With any luck, someone might consider buying you a glass."

"Consider the notion, take one look at your ugly mug, and reject it," Pushkin added, grinning at his friend. "Tell you what, Farren. Come eat supper in *Jan Sobieski* tonight and I'll feed you as much questionable booze as your stomach can handle."

"Knowing the sort of bar your lot keeps, pass."

"All right, folks." Dunmoore raised a restraining hand. "We'll be tasked with ceremonial duties as well, so make sure you have enough crew members with presentable dress uniforms to form an honor guard of, say, seventy-five under a lieutenant commander. Zeke, it's a given E Company will parade alongside *Terra*'s Marines, so I need it ready. If we're short of anything, Starbase 30's supply section will help us."

"Such as making you a commodore's dress uniform, I hope?" Holt asked.

"Already on order. Replenish your ammo and ship's stores. We're heading for Cimmeria ready to fight if necessary. Until that armistice is signed, we are still technically at war. Anything requiring dry dock time is a priority since I don't know when we'll get the order to sail."

"That would be *Hawkwood*," Commander Midura said. "Those long crossings in hyperspace shook a few of our earlier repairs loose. We could do them ourselves, but it would be faster if we let the engineering section handle it."

"Call the chief engineer directly. He'll have received Admiral Singhal's notice we're a priority."

"Yes, sir. I'll do so the moment we're done here."

"Does anyone else need dry dock time? No? Good. You may put your crews on liberty rotation, one third at a time until you've replenished and completed necessary maintenance tasks. After that, you may allow liberty to anyone not standing harbor watch. But no one leaves Starbase 30. I don't want your coxswains chasing crew members all over the place if we receive sailing orders on short notice. And please warn them about getting into trouble. We've been on the go for so long, some might overdo the recreation part of R&R."

"If you'll allow me, sir," Holt said. "What the commodore means but doesn't wish to say in crude terms is anyone overdoing the intoxication part of I&I will be on her personal shit list. Our people will have drinks pushed on them because our raid on the Shrehari home system is now common knowledge. We don't want those with insufficient self-control ruining Task Force Luckner's good name. Make sure your coxswains hammer it home."

As Holt looked around the table, his fellow commanding officers nodded one after the other saying, "Understood, sir."

**

The first week docked to the starbase quickly stretched into a second. By then her ships were ready to sail, *Hawkwood* included, and Dunmoore was feeling restless to a surprising degree. With her reports sent and no fresh orders, she found herself at loose ends. Since she wasn't the sort to enjoy the various entertainment facilities offered by Starbase 30, her sole social outings were dining in each ship, at the base officer's mess and, for old times' sake, in *Iolanthe*'s chiefs' and petty officers' mess at Guthren's invitation.

But if the daily digests published by 3rd Fleet were correct, the Shrehari had ceased hostilities and were evacuating the occupied systems with commendable speed. A small number of shooting matches, quickly ended by the human ships withdrawing, were reported in the first couple of days, but since then, everything was quiet on the Shrehari front. Evidently, their communications network was reasonably efficient or had suddenly become so under Brakal the military dictator.

Her captains reported a few minor disciplinary incidents during the first rotations ashore, mostly alcohol-related, but nothing that the respective first officers couldn't deal with after their coxswains collected the defaulters from the base brig. Thankfully none of them came from *Iolanthe*, though she heard unconfirmed rumors Sergeant Major Haataja inserted himself into a shouting match between his soldiers and Marines from the local garrison before fists flew and successfully prevented a brawl.

After fifteen days alongside, the orders to sail, complete with coordinates in interstellar space and a time-date group for the rendezvous came as a relief, not only to Dunmoore but just about everyone in the task force. Liberty on a starbase became stale quickly and until peace broke out, real furloughs, long enough to visit a planet with breathable air or even go home and visit families they only half-remembered after years in space wouldn't be granted.

The night before Task Force Luckner left Starbase 30, Admiral Singhal hosted a formal reception for Dunmoore, her captains, and the officers who weren't standing harbor watch in the officer's mess.

Simultaneously, 3rd Fleet's coxswain hosted Luckner's chief petty officers in the senior enlisted mess. By all accounts, the chiefs had a better time, but everyone appreciated the sincere effort.

An abstemious Dunmoore felt no pain the next morning when her ships released moorings and moved off, though some officers standing watch seemed worse for wear. How Luckner's chief petty officers fared after their reception would forever remain a mystery.

— Forty-One —

"What the hell is *that*?" Holt stared at the image of a sleek civilian starship trailing CSS *Terra*.

Both vessels had emerged at the precise coordinates a little over three hours after the given rendezvous time.

"Transponder has it as the liner *Equinox Nova*, of the Black Nova Shipping Company," Yens replied.

"Damn space brothel," Sirico muttered in a disgusted tone. "Let me guess, his nibs the SecGen and his posse prefer traveling in luxury instead of the Commonwealth Navy's flagship."

Holt gave him an amused look.

"Might I infer you don't enjoy fancy passenger ships, Thorin? I thought you were a man of the galaxy, with a taste for the finer things in life."

"I am, but I lost the urge to travel in high-end civilian liners. Back when I was a freshly promoted sub-lieutenant, I hitched a ride on one of Black Nova's fancy oversized yachts so I could reach my new ship before it left on a three-month patrol in the badlands. Paid by the navy, of course, since it reassigned me after my ensign cruise and there was no other transport available. How shall I put this politely? The crew included some of the most arrogant, snobbish sods I've ever met. Looked down their noses at the navy and treated me as if I was an annoyance rather than a valued passenger. And don't get me started on the people who travel in those space brothels."

"Why do I think your trip included a love affair gone wrong?" Major Salminen asked in an innocent tone. "Rich older woman. Young, impressionable, and penniless junior officer. It's an old story."

"I was neither impressionable nor penniless. Just so you know."

"All right, folks." Holt raised a hand. "Save it for the wardroom."

He glanced at Emma Cullop's hologram, hovering by his elbow.

"You can cancel battle stations now."

"Shall we open a link with *Terra* or wait for them to call us?"

Holt turned to Dunmoore, sitting in the CIC's second command chair.

"Commodore?"

She was saved from having to answer by the signals chief.

"Sir, *Terra*'s commanding officer is calling for Commodore Dunmoore."

"You want to take it in my day cabin?" Holt asked.

Dunmoore stood. "Sure. Why don't we both do that?"

"You have the CIC, Mister Sirico."

Seconds after Dunmoore settled behind her former desk, the primary display came to life with the face of a dark-complexioned, heavy-set, bald man in his late forties. Intelligent eyes beneath thick brows met hers.

"Commodore Dunmoore. I'm Oliver Harmel, *Terra*'s skipper. I'm placing *Terra* and *Equinox Nova* under your command." He spoke in one of the deepest voices she'd ever heard.

She inclined her head to acknowledge his words.

"Welcome. This is Ezekiel Holt, my flag captain, as well as *Iolanthe*'s commanding officer."

"Captain Holt. A pleasure to meet you."

"Likewise."

"Why are you traveling with a civilian liner?" Dunmoore asked.

For a moment, it seemed as if Harmel wanted to roll his eyes but restrained himself at the last second.

"After the SecGen's aides inspected my VIP facilities, they decided a more suitable starship would transport the civilian delegation. The government, therefore, chartered *Equinox Nova*. Her captain, Steffan Ricker, is a reasonable fellow and understands the concept of taking navigation orders from a naval vessel. I did, however, put a company of Marines aboard, along with three of my officers and a handful of enlisted, to make sure there are no misunderstandings."

"Is either ship carrying Armed Services flag officers?"

Harmel nodded once.

"I have Grand Admiral Shkadov, Lieutenant General Daetor Pelc, the deputy commandant of the Marine Corps, Lieutenant General Macmillan Devereux, the Army's assistant chief of staff, Vice Admiral Kallie Bogdan, the deputy chief of naval operations, and Commodore Janya Lemmone, the grand admiral's senior aide-de-camp. The deputy service chiefs also brought their own senior aides."

"Admiral Shkadov left the service chiefs at home?" So much for seeing Admiral Nagira again. "I suppose he figured it would be best, just in case things go pear-shaped. And they're in *Terra* you said?"

"Yes, sir." Harmel hesitated for a fraction of a second. "Just between you and me, none of them wanted to be cooped up with a bunch of politicians and civil servants in what General Pelc's aide calls a space brothel."

Holt snorted with amusement.

"That's precisely what my combat systems officer called it just now."

"I've been aboard, to meet the SecGen and Captain Ricker. The term is apt, though only if one compares it with the most expensive establishments. Not that I know what they look like on the inside. Not on a captain's pay and certainly not on an ensign's pay, which was the last time I was looking for adult entertainment."

"Are your passengers—" She paused, searching for the right word. "Unobtrusive?"

"Very much so. The flag officers' section is separate from the rest of the accommodations, with its own dining, entertainment, and physical exercise facilities, as you'll shortly see. The grand admiral invites you and your flag captain to come aboard *Terra* at two bells in the dog watch for a meet and greet, followed by a supper in the flag officers' dining room. I'll be there as well. Dress of the day is fine. Our guests have been wearing shipboard uniforms since we departed Earth."

Dunmoore chuckled.

"Out here, our daily wear is battledress, but Zeke and I will change into shipboard uniforms."

Harmel let out a rueful sigh.

"One of the many things I miss from my days chasing boneheads. *Terra* is a magnificent beast, but frigates are more fun. What I wouldn't give for command of a Voivode class right now."

"When we reach Aquilonia, you should talk with Gregor Pushkin while the diplomats are discussing the shape of the negotiation table. He has the first of them, *Jan Sobieski*, and considers her a pocket cruiser."

"Since I plan on inviting your captains to dine aboard *Terra* at least once while we're there, I'll ask him about his ship and live vicariously for a few moments. But back to business. I assume your flagship navigator will be giving us instructions?"

"That would be Lieutenant Astrid Drost and yes she will, within the hour as a matter of fact," Holt replied. "Along with the commodore's orders which are quite simple. We will adopt a spherical formation with you and *Equinox Nova* at the center. I trust the civilians can keep in formation."

"No complaints so far. I'll say one thing for Black Nova. They don't stint on maintenance. That liner's engines are perfectly tuned."

"Excellent." Holt glanced at Dunmoore. "Anything else, sir?"

"No. You, Captain?"

Harmel shook his head.

"I've said my piece, and we'll see you in a few hours. Cheers!"

"Until then." The display went blank.

"I would hate his job right now," Holt remarked. "Even though he says his passengers are unobtrusive, that many stars in my ship would keep me as wary as a Sister of the Void in a tavern."

"At least he's not burdened with the politicians and bureaucrats."

"Small mercies. But we're now burdened with their protection."

Dunmoore shrugged. "A very minor thing. Captain Ricker will respect my orders with absolute precision because his employers do not want the Secretary-General of the Commonwealth mad at them."

"Indubitably." He jumped up. "I'll see that the hangar deck crew prepares the pinnace. Any preference for pilot?"

"None whatsoever. I'd fly us myself, but apparently, commodores can't get away with it the way captains can."

"I won't say a word."

"*Terra*'s hangar deck NCO will notice, and unlike yours, he answers to a captain who's not under my command."

"Harmel technically is for this mission."

"Assign one of your pilots, Zeke. If I feel an irresistible urge to take the controls, we'll do it far from the prying eyes of our head of state, our commander-in-chief, and the deputy chief of naval operations."

**

Fifteen minutes before the appointed time, *Iolanthe*'s pinnace, with Petty Officer Third Class Gus Purdy at the controls, nudged through the force field keeping *Terra*'s shuttle deck pressurized and settled at the center of a lit circle. The space doors closed and a Marine quarter guard under the command of a natty lieutenant in full dress uniform marched out, followed by a bosun's mate with a silver call in hand.

While they formed in good order perpendicular to the pinnace's aft ramp, Captain Oliver Harmel appeared to greet his guest in person. He was as massive as she'd imagined, a tall, broad slab of a man, easily bigger than Chief Petty Officer Guthren. His physique matched his deep voice and more.

The pinnace's ramp dropped, and when its upper edge touched the deck, the bosun's mate raised his call to his lips, and a trill filled the air just as the Marine officer ordered his troopers to present arms. Dunmoore walked down the ramp, raised her hand to her brow in salute, and asked, "Permission to come aboard?"

"Granted," Harmel replied, returning her salute. "Welcome, Commodore."

With the formalities concluded and the guard shouldering arms, Holt followed Dunmoore and saluted as well.

"Captain Holt. Welcome aboard."

"Thank you." He looked around at the cavernous hangar and nodded appreciatively. "Almost as big as ours."

"This is the secondary, for administrative shuttle movements only. The combat hangar is one level down. You'll find it much larger."

Dunmoore nodded.

"I remember it well. We flew fighters from the combat deck when *Terra* was a carrier."

Harmel noticed Dunmoore's pilot wings for the first time.

"You were part of *Terra*'s fighter group?"

"For a brief time, long ago. Turned out it wasn't what I wanted as a naval career."

"Would you enjoy visiting the officer's accommodations deck and see what's become of your former cabin?"

Dunmoore shook her head with a rueful smile.

"Thanks, but no."

"Then I'll take you to the flag officer's section for your meeting with Grand Admiral Shkadov."

"Does that include me?" Holt asked.

"It certainly does."

After walking along a bare corridor and up spiral stairs, they passed through an open airlock giving onto a part of the ship with a very different atmosphere. One of quiet contemplation and genteel comfort rather than the austere functionality of a warship's working sections. The bulkhead paneling and decorations weren't overstated but conveyed that this was a place reserved for the Fleet's top leaders.

Harmel stopped at a door bearing a blue insignia with five gold stars joined in a circle at its center.

"Grand Admiral Shkadov's day cabin."

He touched the gray panel to one side, and the door slid open without a sound.

"Please enter."

— Forty-Two —

Dunmoore, with Holt at her side, marched in and stopped a regulation three paces in front of a large desk dominating the compartment. Both saluted in unison while she said, "Commodore Dunmoore and Captain Holt, Task Force Luckner, reporting to the grand admiral as ordered."

"At ease," a low, raspy voice replied. "And sit."

When she relaxed, Dunmoore caught her first glimpse of the Commonwealth Armed Services' commander-in-chief. He was a man in his late seventies with iron gray hair. Hooded eyes beneath black brows and an aquiline nose dominated his narrow face. Those eyes studied them with an almost eerie intensity as they complied.

"So. You are the masterminds behind the mission that resulted in this Brakal becoming the Shrehari dictator and suing for peace. Or perhaps I should say the missions since he claims his rise to power started when *Iolanthe* destroyed his strike group's forward operating base. Well done. Well done indeed."

"Thank you, sir," Dunmoore replied.

"Admiral Xi informed me you proposed the attack on the Shrehari home system, Commodore. And while you were only acting as Task Force Luckner's commander.

Surprisingly bold, both the idea and voicing it even before you knew you would take over from Kell Petras. Admiral Nagira speaks highly of you, and I can see why."

Since his statement did not call for an answer, she merely inclined her head.

"And you, Captain Holt. Your commodore's reports are full of praise for your work in both commanding *Iolanthe* and acting as her flag captain. Your promotion and appointment seem well deserved."

"Sir."

"You're probably wondering why I summoned both of you here, and while we must discuss arrangements, most of the details will wait until we reach Aquilonia. What I really want is to hear your story first hand, starting with your raid on Brakal's FOB and ending with that spectacular attack on his empire's home system. Call it an old man's conceit. I want to know how a young commodore and her raiders accomplished what my entire fleet couldn't do in a decade of war — make the enemy ask for terms."

Dunmoore spoke for more than an hour, nudged along here and there by Holt who remembered minor facts that escaped her and prodded by Shkadov's penetrating questions.

"So you know this Brakal from long ago and spoke with him on a few occasions. Interesting. That your paths would cross so often and in such a manner almost makes one believe in karma or the intervention of divine beings. I will be interested to see his reaction when you enter the meeting room as head of the SecGen's military escort. Considering we've not told him the name of the officer responsible for both raids, it will be a surprise." He checked for her reaction, then asked, "Do you speak Shrehari?"

"Some, though my accent probably grates on Shrehari ears."

"I'm more interested in Brakal's unfiltered reaction when he sees you. Let me know what it is."

"Of course." She hesitated. "If I may ask, sir, Admiral Singhal informed me Admiral Xi nominated Task Force Luckner for a Commonwealth Unit Citation, and we were curious whether that went anywhere."

A faint smile softened Shkadov's ascetic features.

"That was the next item on my agenda. Secretary-General Lauzier approved the unit citation. He asked that I present it in his name before we arrive in the Cimmeria system, so your people may display the device on their dress uniforms when you escort him to meet Brakal. Congratulations. It is well deserved."

"That's good news, sir. My spacers and soldiers will wear it with pride. When, where, and how would do you wish to make the presentation?"

"The when is once we're done here, which is in a few minutes. The where is in the flag section's common room and the how is simple. Captain Harmel is even now linking *Terra* with your ships so we can broadcast my giving you the citation in front of the deputy service chiefs and *Terra*'s senior officers. That way, your crews can witness the presentation, and we can be on our way to the armistice talks once you're back aboard *Iolanthe*. I'm sure your onboard fabricators can make enough copies of the device for everyone."

"Yes, sir."

A soft chime sounded, then one of the day cabin's doors opened to admit a stocky, black-haired, middle-aged woman wearing a single star on her collar and an aide-de-camp's twisted gold braid on her left shoulder. Her brown eyes briefly rested on Dunmoore before turning to Shkadov.

"Sir, the deputy service chiefs, and *Terra*'s senior officers are assembled in the common room. The video pickups are live, and we're linked with Task Force Luckner."

"Thank you, Janya. Commodore Dunmoore, Captain Holt, meet Janya Lemmone, my long-suffering senior aide."

Both stood, and Dunmoore extended her hand.

"Pleased to meet you."

"Likewise." Lemmone's grip was firm, almost testing. She turned to Holt. "Captain."

"Sir."

"If you'll follow Janya, I'll be along in a few moments."

Lemmone led them down the paneled passageway and through an open door into what resembled the main room in a starbase officer's mess. All conversation ceased when the aide announced them.

She introduced Dunmoore and Holt to the assembled flag officers and their aides one by one, after which Captain Harmel did the same with his department heads. Moments after they took their assigned positions in front of a rostrum bearing *Terra*'s insignia, Lemmone called the room to attention.

"Grand Admiral Shkadov."

The commander-in-chief of humanity's military forces entered with an energetic stride that belied his age.

"At ease."

He stopped beside the rostrum and let his eyes roam over the assembled officers.

"I hope everyone in Commodore Dunmoore's ships can see me."

Harmel nodded once.

"Yes, sir. I spoke with each captain myself from this room moments ago."

"Then let us go ahead."

He held out his hand, took the tablet proffered by Lemmone and, after another look around the room, turned his eyes on its screen.

"Task Force Luckner, made up of the Commonwealth Starships *Iolanthe*, *Jan Sobieski*, *Hawkwood*, *Tamurlane*, *Narses*, *Belisarius*, *Rooikat*, *Fennec*, and *Skua* is cited for extraordinary courage and outstanding performance of combat duties in action against the Shrehari Empire by raiding the imperial home system on September 12th, 2471, shocking the enemy into suing for peace and ending our decade long war. The officers, non-commissioned officers, ratings, and soldiers serving in the above-named ships displayed daring, determination, and esprit de corps in accomplishing their mission under extremely hazardous conditions and by their achievements they brought distinguished credit on themselves, their ships, and the Commonwealth Armed Services."

Polite applause greeted Shkadov's reading of the actual citation as it had been gazetted before *Terra* left Earth.

"Commodore Dunmoore, front and center so you can accept the Commonwealth Unit Citation on behalf of Task Force Luckner."

She snapped to attention.

"Yes, sir."

As the assembly watched, Shkadov pinned the device, a small gold-edged metallic oblong bearing the colors of the three services, Navy blue, Marine Corps red, and Army green, on Dunmoore's chest, above her name tag.

He offered her his hand.

"Please accept my congratulations and pass them on to your people. What you did was extraordinarily gutsy, especially since no one knew whether the raid would have any effect whatsoever on the war effort. Or how well the Shrehari home system was defended. Or even whether you would find targets you could attack without risking the lives of everyone in the task force. Fortune does indeed favor the bold. Come to think of it that would make a great motto for Task Force Luckner, don't you think, Commodore? *Audaces Fortuna Juvat.* Since you don't have a motto, consider it yours from now on."

"Yes, sir. Thank you, sir."

Another round of applause, this time a shade more enthusiastic, punctuated Shkadov's statement.

"I've also taken the liberty of authorizing a formation crest to mark the occasion."

He gestured toward the display at his back. It lit up, revealing a stylized black eagle on a white background surrounded by an equally black circle. Wings and legs outstretched, the eagle clutched an anti-ship missile in each claw. The name *Task Force Luckner* and the motto *Audaces Fortuna Juvat* were inscribed in white on the black circle, proving without a doubt Shkadov prepared his words well in advance. Just as Dunmoore did in *Jan Sobieski* for her supper with the frigate's officers the evening before the raid.

"This is a representation, suitably updated, of the emblem at the center of the ensign hoisted by your task force's namesake, Count Felix von Luckner moments before attacking enemy vessels with his commerce raider, *Seeadler.*"

"An inspired design, sir," Dunmoore replied after a pause to search for the proper words. "I don't quite know what to say."

"You needn't say anything. A formation which proved its worth deserves an emblem of its own. I expect to see you wear and display it by the time we reach Aquilonia."

"We will, sir."

"In fact, why don't we start on that right away? Janya?"

Lemmone gave him two cloth disks the size of an adult's palm embroidered with the eagle badge. Shkadov carefully placed one on Dunmoore's right sleeve, just below the shoulder seam and activated its auto adhesive layer, then did the same to Holt, who wore the Furious Faerie emblem on his left sleeve.

"There."

It finally dawned on Dunmoore that this ceremony had been well prepared and rehearsed for reasons beyond simply honoring her task force. Politics? Propaganda? To show the Shrehari who was boss? Probably that and more. She figured a visual record of the proceedings would find its way into the hands of the Fleet's public relations branch before they even reached the Cimmeria system and made available to civilian news organizations.

"That," Shkadov said with a clear air of satisfaction, "concludes the proceedings. Commodore Dunmoore, Captain Holt, I would be honored if you consented to dine with us before returning to your flagship."

"It would be a great pleasure, sir."

**

"Did the last few hours feel a tad surreal to you as well, Skipper, or is it just me?" Holt asked once the pinnace's aft ramp closed and they settled into adjoining seats immediately behind the cockpit.

"No, it's not just you. I felt as if we were props in a propaganda play, but we got our unit citation, a crest, and a motto out of the whole staged ceremony. And the flag officer's mess serves a fine meal. Dining with the deputy service chiefs won't harm our careers either, especially since neither of us overindulged on that fine Dordogne grand cru or showed bad table manners. But if I never again tell the tale of how Task Force Luckner won the war, it won't be too soon."

"The Fleet's official historians will want their turn at some point, and the War College, the Academy and various HQ directorates concerned with planning the next war."

"Thanks for cheering me up, Zeke."

He grinned at her.

"That's why we flag captains, official or unofficial, exist."

Emma Cullop greeted the pinnace on *Iolanthe*'s hangar deck with an enthusiastic quarter guard from E Company and the bosun herself piping them aboard.

"That was spectacular, sir," she said after saluting. "The grand admiral really put on a nice show. We fabricated the citation devices and Luckner crests already. The other ships should be doing so as well since *Terra* helpfully sent us the necessary specifications. Everyone is waiting to hear how you want them distributed."

Dunmoore glanced at Holt.

"Zeke?"

"Since we should be on our way within the hour, how about virtually presenting the citation badges and the eagle crests to your captains and let them take care of their people? I'll do my department heads and chiefs. They'll take it from there."

"Good plan."

"I'll set up the conference room and link them in."

By the time the armistice delegation and its commerce raiding escort went FTL, Grand Admiral Shkadov's orders had been carried out. Every last member of Task Force Luckner sported a Commonwealth Unit Citation and an eagle crest on his or her uniform tunic.

Whether they would mean anything to the Shrehari remained doubtful, but Dunmoore felt more than ever that the grand admiral's *mise-en-scène* was mainly for propaganda purposes.

— Forty-Three —

"**A**ll ships had a successful transit," Chief Day reported shortly after the armistice delegation and its escort dropped out of FTL at Thule's hyperlimit, "and are standing by for navigation orders."

"There are twelve Shrehari ships in orbit, all *Tol* class cruisers," Chief Yens said. "Their shields are down, and I'm not picking up any signs that their weapons are up and ready. We're being scanned at low power, but there's no targeting component to their sensor beams. I'd say they're more peaceful than any imperial ships we've seen in over ten years."

Dunmoore nodded.

"Good. Let's make sure we're equally peaceful. Pass the word to stand down from battle stations."

"Sir?"

Something in Day's voice caught her attention, and she turned to the communications chief.

"Yes?"

"The Shrehari are broadcasting at us, text only, in Anglic. It is addressed to the human admiral commanding the escort strike group."

"Well then, it's obviously not for you, Commodore," Holt said in a droll tone.

"Nice try, but you know my equivalent in their fleet is an admiral of the fifth rank, so yes, it is for me. Put it on screen."

Human commander, welcome to your star system.

A guffaw escaped Sirico's valiant attempt to stay quiet. "Damn right it's our star system."

We are here in peace to discuss peace. Kho'sahra Brakal is aboard his flagship Tol Radaq, which sends this message. Admiral of the Third Rank Kaalak commands his escort. We bid you enter into orbit around the moon you call Aquilonia at an altitude above ours as proof of our peaceful intentions. We evacuated the moon's colony and left it in the care of its human owners who await your arrival. Please take possession and do with it what you will. Chief Imperial Negotiator Surgh wishes to communicate with your chief negotiator and discuss preparations for the meeting between Kho'sahra Brakal and Secretary-General Lauzier as soon as possible. We beg acknowledgment of this message.

"Not a bad effort at Anglic, if a bit comical," Holt remarked.

"Too bad my Shrehari isn't as good. Otherwise, I'd reply in their language and give their flagship's combat systems officer a little laugh. Chief Day, send the following via text. Shrehari commander, on behalf of the commander, Task Force Luckner, aboard *Iolanthe*, I acknowledge your message. We will enter orbit around Aquilonia fifty of our kilometers above your ships. I will notify Ambassador Januzaj, the head of the Commonwealth Armistice Commission that Chief Imperial Negotiator Surgh wishes to communicate at the earliest opportunity."

Day read back her words.

"Perfect. Transmit." She turned to Holt. "Although every ship has read their message and is now reading our reply, I think we should still contact *Equinox Nova* and let them know the ambassador can start his thing the moment we arrive."

He nodded.

"Good idea. Some of the civilian top brass might get snooty if we unwashed spacers don't respect the proper forms. Let me do it for you. And I'll ask Astrid to draw up the orbital parking assignments."

While Holt busied himself, Dunmoore studied Thule's image on the main display. The next planet out from Cimmeria, which was home to almost every human in this star system, it boasted a breathable oxygen-nitrogen atmosphere but was stuck in an interminable ice age which left it as nothing more than a white ball hanging in space. Yet the pure surface she remembered seeing when she passed through before the war was liberally covered in black smudges. What had the Shrehari done? Used it as a firing range? Tried to kick-start terraforming with nuclear or kinetic strikes from orbit? There was no way those massive volcanic eruptions dotting the planet occurred naturally in only the last ten years.

"Show me Aquilonia please, Chief."

The visual sensors shifted aim and zeroed in on a small gray ball outlined against its brilliantly white primary. Once the image grew and sharpened, Yens helpfully marked the dozen Shrehari ships in Aquilonia orbit with blurry red dots.

As Dunmoore knew from the mission briefing, a mining colony called the moon home before the war, established in part to help the Cimmerians terraform Thule. The habitat dug into the moon's crust was still relatively crude. But in keeping with every station built on an airless world, it was solid enough to resist direct meteor strikes.

And as a mine, had plenty of airtight spaces suitable for large groups, such as a few infantry battalions in parade formation facing each other across a floor polished by mining lasers.

If the Shrehari suggested Aquilonia in good faith as a meeting place, it meant someone had maintained the habitat during the war. Perhaps even its human owners. A squadron-sized security detail from the Marine Corps' 1st Special Forces Regiment traveling aboard *Terra* would confirm everything in due course before anyone else landed.

And since they were responsible for the Secretary General's physical security as well as that of the Armistice Commission members, the grand admiral, and the deputy service chiefs, they were neither under Dunmoore's command, nor her responsibility. The major in charge answered directly to the SecGen's principal assistant and would declare Aquilonia ready after a thorough inspection.

"*Equinox Nova* acknowledges, Commodore," Holt said, cutting through Dunmoore's study of the moon, "and advises future communications not of a strictly military nature concerning relations between both naval escorts should be referred to Ambassador Januzaj and his delegation. Why is it once we military folks clean up the diplomats' mistakes, they push us aside without as much as a by your leave and go right back to messing things up?"

Dunmoore shrugged.

"It's been the same since our primitive ancestors stopped throwing stones at each other when their arms got tired. The war is over — dogs and uniformed humans, keep off the grass."

"Sorry, sir," Sirico said. "But I think the expression was dogs and soldiers, keep off the grass."

He gave Major Tatiana Salminen a significant look as he spoke.

Holt shook his head in despair.

"Has anyone ever mentioned correcting commodores to tease majors could be detrimental to a lieutenant commander's career, Thorin?"

"I apologize, sir."

The contrite air on Sirico's face was so obviously false, Dunmoore couldn't hide a smile.

"I forgive Thorin for his attempt at teasing the commanding officer of my sole infantry unit. Flogging, keelhauling, or any other form of traditional punishment will not be required."

"If you say so, Commodore," Holt replied in a grave tone.

"How about we study Aquilonia station?"

"Coming right up," Chief Yens said.

The image on the CIC's main display wavered again as the optics focused on a small chunk of the airless moon. A broad, flat area surrounded by flashing navigation lights came into view. It was bisected by a low, rectangular structure, almost a kilometer long and one-third of that wide, with space doors at regular intervals, the sort capable of extruding bulk loaders to feed refined metals into the holds of waiting cargo shuttles or small bulk haulers. Landing pads surrounded the structure at regular intervals, each defined by glowing yellow markers.

"Charming."

"Functional. Austere. Hasn't been inspected by the technical standards authority in years." Dunmoore glanced at her flag captain. "Fortunately, checking it for trouble isn't our job, even though I'm sure Chief Guthren and a hand-picked crew of boarding party specialists, backed by Tatiana's soldiers could do as good a job as the Marines from the 1st Special Forces Regiment."

"Don't let them hear you, Commodore." Holt nodded at Yens. "Give us a high power scan of the place, Chief. Pound it with the best our sensors can manage. Ask *Rooikat* and *Fennec* to do the same and merge the data."

"Aye, aye, Captain. Between us, we'll paint you a detailed three-dimensional picture in the tank." Yens jerked her thumb at the holographic tactical display.

"Excellent. With life signs?"

"Of course."

While Task Force Luckner approached Thule and its moons, *Iolanthe*'s sensors scanned Aquilonia at full strength. Soon, the shimmering image of an underground warren filled the virtual space where representations of star systems, orbital bases, and enemy formations usually held pride of place. Bright spots appeared, indicating the presence of living beings clustered on the two levels immediately beneath the above-ground loading docks.

"Pass the data to *Terra* for the Special Forces folks," Holt said. "I'm sure she's scanning as well, but we're newer with better gear and are backed up by two sharp-eyed scout ships."

A few minutes passed in silence until Chief Day said, "*Terra* thanks us for the data. They'd appreciate it if we kept the same sharp eye on Aquilonia Station until they put boots on the ground."

"Tell them we will do so."

Dunmoore barely heard the exchange. Her mind was shifting from what lay beneath the landing area's surface to what the Shrehari in orbit aboard those twelve *Tol* class cruisers were thinking as they watched a formerly hostile task force approach. Were their trigger fingers itching? How many knew the ships they saw were the same who shamed the empire by desecrating their home system several weeks earlier?

Was Brakal watching and did he recognize *Iolanthe* as the phantom who'd been plaguing his hunting grounds for so long? The Furious Faerie was in her battlecruiser mode, hiding the fact she sometimes appeared as nothing more than a large freighter — slow, vulnerable and ripe for the picking. Until the hunters became the prey and died in an uncontrolled release of antimatter before they could warn their HQ that a Q-ship was trolling the sector, looking for victims.

"Astrid worked out the orbital assignments, Commodore." A side display came to life, showing the moon, the Shrehari cruisers, and the human ships' proposed orbits.

She examined the schematic, then said, "Approved. Please disseminate."

**

"There. That battleship." *Kho'sahra* Brakal pointed at *Iolanthe*'s image on the large display dominating *Tol Radaq*'s flag bridge. "It is the phantom which bedeviled me for so long on the frontier. It and the others, save for the largest and the one seemingly unarmed, attacked the home system, and destroyed Tyva base."

"The battleship appears to be the human's flagship."

"Appropriate, considering its power and battle prowess, even if it is not quite as large as the one in the middle of their formation. Did they identify their admiral or the phantom's commander?"

"No, Lord," Admiral of the Third Rank Kaalak replied. "They merely named the one who will speak with Surgh and begin negotiations once their ships are in orbit."

"Then I will wait until we meet face-to-face. They promised the officer responsible for Khorsan and the raid on the home system would form part of their supreme leader's escort."

"I could ask for a visual link with that battleship." Kaalak thought about trying to pronounce *Iolanthe* but knew nothing more than a mangled gurgle would come out.

Brakal thought about it, then made a gesture of refusal.

"This is a delicate time. Best if we let Surgh carry out his duties so that events unfold as planned."

Though the Chief Imperial Negotiator was a career bureaucrat, he did not carry the stench of the former council's misrule. On the contrary. Most in the Forbidden Quarter and beyond respected his wisdom, even temperament, and talent at ending the most bitter of disputes. And he spoke the humans' barbaric language thanks to time spent in their Commonwealth on trade missions long before the war.

"As you command."

Brakal wished Regar was with him. Peacefully sharing an orbit with a human strike group was strange and left him uneasy. The spy's cynical view of the universe would have provided a certain measure of relief. But as promised, Brakal gave Regar his reward and left him on Shrehari Prime to form the empire's outward-facing intelligence service, the *Tai Zohl*, with the help of the new *Tai Kan* director, Kroesh.

Instead, he settled into his throne-like chair and studied the human warships with keen interest. One of the *Tai Zohl*'s first assignments would be uncovering the secrets of human naval architecture. The empire's had stagnated for so long, its designers and engineers barely remembered the meaning of the word innovation.

That one they called a frigate, for example. A class of ship which would have eventually eroded the Deep Space Fleet's ability to keep human raiders at bay once sufficient numbers roamed the disputed frontier. And praise the gods they only ever encountered one vessel such as that battleship which could vanish and reappear at will.

"Who commands you?" He murmured, remembering his defeat, many turns ago, at the hands of the flame-haired she-wolf close to where his flagship now orbited. Would it not be poetic if...?

"The first human ships are entering orbit, Lord. Those they classify as seekers."

Brakal marveled again at the hairless apes fielding so many designs instead of concentrating on a few models that could be modified and adapted to any mission. Perhaps part of their success in improving ships so quickly stemmed from this propensity. That strike group included no more than two ships of the same configuration among the eleven now on final approach. Three pairs. The other five were as different from each other and the matched pairs as demons and gods. Especially the one with unusual markings which was surely no warship.

"What is that?" He indicated the space liner.

"A civilian luxury transport used by wealthy and powerful humans to travel among the stars," *Tol Radaq*'s gun master said after consulting his ship identification database. Taking his cue from Admiral Kaalak, he decided it would be best to avoid speaking a human name which would only come out of his Shrehari throat like the grunts of a choking *kroorath*.

"Is the human supreme leader traveling in that instead of the flagship?" Brakal sounded incredulous.

"Perhaps it carries entertainers for the delegation and its escort. We know so little about their customs beyond those purely related to war."

"Strange."

— Forty-Four —

Iolanthe's pinnace, bearing a commodore's single star on a blue rectangle, entered one of Aquilonia's large cargo hangars five days later. It carried Siobhan Dunmoore, accompanied by Lieutenant Commander Thorin Sirico, Major Tatiana Salminen, Chief Petty Officer Guthren, and Sergeant Major Talo Haataja. Shuttles from the rest of Task Force Luckner's ships, except for the scouts and the transport, already sat in a neat row to one side, waiting for her arrival.

The pinnace's pilot, Petty Officer Knowles, gently parked her craft on the spot closest to the inner airlock, deliberately left for Dunmoore's craft. When the space doors closed, the smaller of the two internal airlocks opened, and a tall, muscular man in Marine Corps battledress stepped through. He wore a major's four-pointed star and oak leaf wreath at the collar, and the 1st Special Forces Regiment's winged dagger on his sky blue beret.

All six shuttles dropped their aft ramps and disgorged Task Force Luckner's reconnaissance team come to scout out the facilities ahead of tomorrow's formal meeting between Secretary-General Lauzier and *Kho'sahra* Brakal. Grand Admiral Shkadov wanted a display of military perfection from the SecGen's ceremonial escort headed by Commodore Dunmoore.

She had, therefore, ordered the officers who would command the various ships' guards and their chief petty officers to join her in walking Aquilonia's corridors to the former warehouse which was even now being furnished with a table, chairs, flagpoles, banners and more.

When he saw her, the Special Forces major snapped to attention and saluted.

"I'm Alois Tucker, sir. Welcome to the hind end of the galaxy."

"That bad?"

"The place is a former mining colony which has seen little love in the last ten years, not the Palace of the Stars. But I suppose it's the closest thing to neutral ground we can find. Secure neutral ground. The Shrehari didn't leave any nasties behind."

"The contrary would have surprised me. Once a Shrehari of the Warrior Caste gives his word, it is inviolable."

"True."

Dunmoore indicated the officers behind her.

"Each of my six major warships is forming a seventy-five strong guard under a lieutenant commander and a chief petty officer. The SecGen's ceremonial bodyguard will be provided by E Company, 3rd Battalion, Scandia Regiment under the command of Major Tatiana Salminen. Chief Petty Officer Guthren, my flagship's coxswain will play battalion chief."

After Tucker shook hands with each as they introduced themselves, he gestured toward the large inner airlock which was slowly sliding open.

"One of the advantages here is the size. Everything is huge. Your entire battalion will be able to march comfortably from this hangar through the corridor to the central warehouse which will serve as meeting space, then take up a normal parade formation when they arrive. There's only one hitch. I wouldn't bring *Terra*'s band with you. The acoustics are abominable."

"I was planning on a silent evolution, Major. Since the Shrehari wouldn't understand human music, let alone the sentiments it's supposed to evoke, the effect will be better with just verbal orders and clicking heels. We'll keep time via ear bugs."

"And I understand *Terra*'s Marine contingent won't be joining you."

She shook her head.

"No. Admiral Shkadov decided he wanted only tunics with the Task Force Luckner crest and the Commonwealth Unit Citation on parade."

"That simplifies things, sir."

"Why?" Dunmoore gave him a curious look.

"*Terra*'s embarked contingent is from the 1st Marine Regiment. They're rather peculiar about their ceremonial protocols. Especially if they're parading with an Army unit."

"Understood."

The 1st Marines, stationed on Earth, were known as the Palace Guard because of their duties in the Commonwealth capital, Geneva. The nickname, when used by someone from a front line regiment such as the Special Forces, was undeniably pejorative.

They spent an hour pacing back and forth between the hangar and the cavernous space which once held stacked containers of refined metals ready for shipping while going through the plan for tomorrow's performance. When Dunmoore declared herself satisfied, Tucker showed them the cargo hangar which would be used by the Shrehari contingent, and their path to the place where history would be made. The visit ended in the passenger shuttle hangars next to their larger cargo siblings.

"Still hard to believe we'll be in full dress uniforms and facing a battalion of Shrehari in less than twenty-four hours, isn't it?" Dunmoore remarked as they returned to their shuttles.

"No kidding, sir," Tucker replied. "I'll need to watch my itchy trigger finger. Unlike your guard, my folks will carry live ammo. Not that I expect any problems, but when you're working close protection on the Commonwealth's head of state, it's lock and load all the time. Good thing we're only doing it for this mission. I'd probably catch a bad case of cafard if I were babysitting him full time on Earth."

Tucker's use of the Marine Corps slang for depression momentarily caught her out, but she quickly remembered what it meant. And where it came from.

"I wouldn't blame you, Major." When they reach the line of shuttles, she stuck out her hand. "Thanks for playing tour guide. We'll see you tomorrow morning."

After shaking hands, Tucker came to attention and saluted.

"Until tomorrow."

**

Dunmoore felt unaccustomed nervousness as she buckled on her sword belt and stepped off the pinnace with Chief Petty Officer First Class Guthren. He also wore a sword belt but carried a silver-tipped black rosewood cane, a coxswain's symbol of authority, tucked under his left arm.

Contrary to the previous day, her pinnace had landed in the smaller personnel hangar next to the cargo hangar where her people were forming up by guard, ready to receive the Secretary-General and his retinue whose shuttle would also use the personnel hangar.

Though the navy blue tunic with a commodore's broad gold stripe topped by an executive curl on the cuffs fit as if tailor-made, she nonetheless felt as if she was wearing someone else's uniform. Even the white crest with the black eagle on her upper left sleeve seemed strange. But strangest of all was carrying a ceremonial sword on an airless moon which had been, until a few weeks earlier, occupied by the same enemy she was about to face as head of an honor guard rather than fight them from her flagship's CIC.

As she came through the airlock connecting both hangars, Dunmoore heard Major Salminen call Task Force Luckner to attention. She found them arrayed in facing ranks, three ship's guards to a side, with E Company between them, ready for the SecGen.

"Task Force Luckner, to your flag officer commanding, present ARMS."

Weapons came up, swords swept down, heels stomped, and Dunmoore raised her hand to her brow in salute.

After a suitable interval, "Task Force Luckner, shoulder ARMS."

Standing behind Dunmoore, Chief Guthren ran a critical eye over the makeshift battalion, then let out a satisfied grunt.

"Not bad," he muttered in a voice pitched only for Dunmoore's ears.

Once Salminen put the troops at ease, she asked, "Is everything ready, Major?"

"Yes, sir. We made one practice run from here to the meeting room. We might be a bit rough changing from column to line, but the Shrehari won't notice. Nor will the VIPs since my troops will surround them."

Dunmoore let her eyes roam over the assembled spacers and soldiers and was struck by the pride in their bearing, the neatness of their uniforms and the determined look in their eyes as they met her gaze without embarrassment. If the other ships had selected their guards in the same manner as *Iolanthe*, these would be the best of the best, those deserving the honor of witnessing history.

Not far from where she stood, in another hangar, a Shrehari admiral was probably doing the same — making sure his guard didn't dishonor the empire by appearing sloppy in front of the damned hairless apes from Earth.

Major Tucker's voice in her ear bug gave Dunmoore a start.

"Commodore, the VIP shuttle is entering the main personnel hangar. *Kho'sahra* Brakal's shuttle is on final approach to the secondary personnel hangar."

Dunmoore glanced at Guthren and nodded to say, we're on.

"Task Force Luckner." Her voice echoed across the hangar, making everyone stiffen for the order to come to attention. "The VIP shuttle is landing. In a few minutes, we will escort our Secretary-General to meet the Shrehari supreme leader and formalize the armistice between the Commonwealth and the Empire. I know you will do our task force, our fleet, and our species honor."

She paused.

"Task Force Luckner, atten-SHUN." She turned to face the airlock and drew her sword while Guthren took position behind her and to her right.

When Lauzier, trailed by Grand Admiral Shkadov, Ambassador Januzaj, and the deputy service chiefs appeared, she called out, "Task Force Luckner, to your Secretary-General, present ARMS."

Her sword came up until the crossbar above the hilt was level with her lips, then swept down and to the right until its tip was mere centimeters above the hangar deck's scarred floor. Hands slapped weapons, feet stomped in unison, and Guthren raised his hand in salute.

Lauzier, a lean, sixty-something with wavy black hair and deep-set eyes on either side of a patrician nose, placed his hand above his heart in a solemn gesture and inclined his head. He wore a dark gray suit with a high-collared tunic made from a material which shimmered like real silk under the hangar's harsh lighting.

"Task Force Luckner, shoulder ARMS." She raised her sword and took a step forward. "Sir, we are ready to escort you and the delegation."

"Please proceed, Commodore."

Dunmoore and Guthren spun on their heels in a perfect parade ground maneuver. "Task Force Luckner will form in column of route. To the left and right, in column of route TURN."

She and her coxswain marched through the ranks of E Company followed by Lauzier and the VIPs. When the latter were engulfed by Salminen's soldiers, Dunmoore called out, "Task Force Luckner, by the center, quick MARCH."

The entire battalion stepped off on the left foot, six hundred heels coming down at once, but eerily without a drum to set the pace.

Dunmoore led the formation through the cargo airlock and into the large corridor, Guthren keeping everyone in step by softly calling cadence via a quasi-invisible throat mic which fed six hundred ear bugs. Any onlooker would think the formation marched in dignified and menacing silence, arms swinging. Her ears eventually caught the faint sounds of alien voices far ahead shouting commands in a guttural tongue, though she could not, at this distance, make out the words.

When she entered the warehouse, the naval guards on either side wheeled to the left and right forming ranks facing the far wall, while E Company coalesced into a square protecting the human VIPs.

"Task Force Luckner, HALT."

Six hundred feet stamped with a loud thud which echoed off the walls.

After briefly studying the table, chairs, and banners set up halfway between the two cargo doors, Dunmoore took several steps forward until she stood alone in front of her troops. As prearranged, Secretary-General Lauzier, Grand Admiral Shkadov, Ambassador Januzaj, and the deputy service chiefs left the soldiers' protective cocoon and took position on either side of her to wait for the Shrehari. Around them, hidden but active video cameras were recording every moment of the ceremony and had been since the moment Lauzier entered the main cargo hangar to receive Dunmoore's salute.

The first bare-headed Shrehari assault troops wearing black armor emerged from the corridor leading to the other cargo hangar, marching with the same silent precision as Task Force Luckner. Dunmoore knew Shrehari were generally larger than humans, but she was surprised at how imposing they appeared, even across a broad expanse of polished stone.

They too formed ranks facing their erstwhile foes, but instead of carrying power weapons, each wore a long, sheathed knife at the waist. The blades and the strips of fur on their skulls meant they were Warrior Caste, every single one of them, the elite of their military forces.

The Shrehari silently stared at their human counterparts through expressionless black within black eyes and Dunmoore couldn't help but feel a shiver run up her spine at the sight. That such an enemy ended a war they started was a good sign the navy was hurting them. Badly.

Then, a familiar Shrehari emerged from the corridor, trailed by a wizened civilian she knew to be Negotiator Surgh and an officer wearing the uniform of an admiral of the third rank who could only be Kaalak. Brakal, in formal court robes with what Dunmoore assumed was a *kho'sahra's* badge of office on his right breast seemed older than when she last saw him above Miranda, but he exuded the same powerful aura as his troops. He stopped and stared at the human VIP party around Dunmoore. When their eyes met, she knew he recognized her as clearly as she recognized him.

— Forty-Five —

Without a word, Brakal, the one Dunmoore believed to be Kaalak, and Surgh resumed walking toward the center of the space, stopping near the negotiation table to wait.

Lauzier glanced at her.

"Commodore, the officer with Brakal, is it their grand admiral or whatever they call him?"

"No, sir. He's what we would call an admiral of the third rank in Anglic, roughly equivalent to our vice admiral. He's probably the commander of his escort battle group, a Shrehari by the name Kaalak."

"In that case, you're with Ambassador Januzaj and me," SecGen Lauzier said before stepping off to meet his Shrehari counterpart.

Dunmoore sheathed her sword and marched in step behind Lauzier and the ambassador, halting when they did.

The three Shrehari raised clenched right fists to their chests in what Dunmoore recognized as their formal greeting. Lauzier and Januzaj replied by inclining their heads in a courtly gesture. After a moment of hesitation, Dunmoore raised her hand to her brow in a proper parade ground salute. It made the moment seem more fantastic than ever. But she knew paying a former enemy the appropriate military compliments due to someone of his rank was well within protocol.

"I am pleased we finally meet, *Kho'sahra* Brakal," Lauzier said. "Our respective ambassadors have done good work over the last five days."

He paused while Surgh translated for Brakal and Kaalak's benefit. When Surgh fell silent, Brakal made a gesture of assent and spoke in his language, though he articulated each word with care so that Dunmoore could understand.

"They did so indeed, Leader of the Humans Lauzier." The SecGen's name came out as a mangled jumble. "I hope you are as satisfied as I am, so we may conclude the armistice and live side by side in peace from now until the end of time."

Surgh translated in his halting Anglic, making Dunmoore happy her own version of Brakal's statement mostly matched it.

"I am indeed satisfied," Lauzier replied, gesturing toward the table. "Shall we sit and formalize the armistice agreement?"

Brakal listened to Surgh, then laboriously pronounced the Anglic word 'yes.' But when Lauzier, Januzaj, Kaalak, and Surgh headed for their seats, he remained rooted to the spot and turned his unnerving stare on her.

"Dunmoore. I knew it was you who destroyed Khorsan Base, Tyva Base, chased my strike group across the sector, and attacked my home system," he said slowly in Shrehari, allowing her time to translate mentally. "We met many times after the battle at the planet of the lost humans without knowing. I owe you my thanks for having been an efficient enemy. Without your boldness, I would not have lost my command and found myself on

Shrehari Prime where thanks to your daring raid I was able to seize power and end the war."

She inclined her head in acknowledgment, then replied in rough, badly accented Shrehari, "I did my duty as best I could, *Kho'sahra*."

"Your best was good enough. If more of your commanders resembled you, the war might have ended earlier. I am honored to have fought a foe of your ability." He raised his fist to his chest again.

"I am equally honored I faced you in battle." This time, saluting her former enemy didn't seem strange, it felt right, as if their brief, private exchange made the armistice a reality between combatants in a way diplomats could never manage.

After one last long stare into each other's eyes, both made their way to the table. Brakal sat across from Lauzier while Dunmoore stood behind the latter, imitating Kaalak who loomed over his leader.

Januzaj opened his attaché case and withdrew two sheets of what appeared to be paper but were copies of the agreement printed in Shrehari and Anglic on an almost indestructible polymer. He placed one before Brakal and one before Lauzier.

The actual signing of the armistice instruments took only a few moments because the agreement hammered out between Surgh and Januzaj over the previous days was simplicity itself and its words were by now well known to everyone.

The Shrehari Empire evacuates all occupied star systems, returns to its prewar borders and enters into a perpetual and mutual non-aggression pact with the Commonwealth. In return, the Commonwealth agrees to waive reparation claims.

The parties agree they will negotiate a formal treaty and deal with trade agreements, resolution of disputes, and the future of the unclaimed star systems in the area adjoining both spheres of control. They shall sign said treaty within one Earth year on the imperial border world of Ulufan.

The leaders made their marks on both copies of the armistice agreement after which Surgh and Januzaj each took one.

Lauzier and Brakal stood, exchanged farewells, and, with their respective ambassadors and escort commanders in tow, left the table. Dunmoore wondered whether she would ever meet the mysterious Shrehari *kho'sahra* again or whether this was indeed the last time their paths would cross. When they approached the cluster of VIPs, Grand Admiral Shkadov gave her a significant look, promising questions about her private interaction with Brakal at a later time.

Dunmoore led the escort back to the cargo hangar with due formality, gave Secretary-General Lauzier another general salute and, once the VIPs vanished into the passenger hangar, placed the spacers and soldiers at ease.

"That was a splendid showing," she said in a voice which carried to the farthest corners of the vast chamber. "You did our species honor. And I know you'll always remember the day we stood facing our mortal enemies and made peace with them so that no one else dies in the name of vain ambition. Thank you. You are dismissed to your ships. Guard officers take over."

After a final exchange of salutes, Dunmoore, followed by Chief Guthren, left the cargo hangar to rejoin *Iolanthe*'s pinnace. Grand Admiral Shkadov intercepted her on the other side.

"What was that with Brakal, Commodore?" After she repeated the conversation, if not word for word, then close enough, he grunted. "Interesting fellow. In any case, well done, both for apparently being the catalyst that propelled him to power and for giving our SecGen a finer escort than the Palace Guard could have managed. I'll let Armand Xi know."

"Thank you, sir."

They saluted each other, then Shkadov hurried aboard *Terra*'s imposing and luxurious VIP shuttle while Dunmoore and Guthren joined Petty Officer Knowles in the pinnace.

"Impressive ceremony," the noncom said over her shoulder from the cockpit as they settled in. "You and the top bonehead seem to have a past, sir, if I may inquire."

"You may." She sat back and closed her eyes. "I spoke with Brakal for the first time minutes after taking over as acting captain of *Victoria Regina*, the Fleet's last true battleship, a little over six years ago, when Captain Prighte was killed by one of Brakal's gun volleys..."

**

"The Shrehari left without even saying farewell," Holt reported when Dunmoore joined him in his day cabin after shedding her ceremonial finery. "As Yens would say, good riddance. You made us proud, Skipper. Everyone up here was watching. We even saw you and Brakal skip down memory lane. What did he say?"

For the second time in less than two hours, she recounted their conversation.

"You should have recorded his statement for your service record, sir. It would have done wonders to convince the promotion board you're more than fit to be an admiral."

She served herself a cup of coffee and dropped into the chair facing Holt's desk.

"The video of us having a sidebar will have to suffice. Has anyone sent us instructions about what happens now?"

He nodded.

"I just got word from *Terra*. We're paying Cimmeria a visit. The SecGen wants to meet with the provisional government that sprang up hours after the last Shrehari shuttle lifted off and see the damage left by the occupation with his own eyes. After that, *Equinox Nova* is heading back to Earth solo on a long jump while we're staying here with *Terra* until HQ sends a permanent battle group to set up a new garrison."

"Makes sense. If some rogue Shrehari commander decides on a revenge strike, we'll fend him off. It's not as if Task Force Luckner has any other missions lined up anyway."

"You think they'll keep us together as a formation? There are plenty of pirates needing a speedy death in the badlands."

Dunmoore gave him a sad smile.

"Do you think they'll keep us together? We're not on the permanent order of battle."

"We can always hope, considering the grand admiral gave us a snazzy crest."

"Mostly for propaganda purposes, Zeke."

He sighed.

"True."

"Deliberately changing the subject, did Astrid compute the jump to Cimmeria?"

"On it as we speak. She'll let me know when everyone is synced and we can break out of orbit." He looked into his coffee mug and exhaled noisily.

"What?"

"Now that they signed the armistice, I feel exactly as I do when my adrenaline crashes after a battle."

"Getting the blues, eh? For what it's worth, I'm about to crash as well, now that I've done my job. We face major adjustments, Zeke, especially those who never served in a peacetime navy, or those who have forgotten what it was like — such as us two."

"Or those who lived for the thrill of danger and the relief that comes with the realization they were still alive and the boneheads were dead."

He looked up at her.

"Can I interest you in a few rounds of chess?"

— Forty-Six —

They remained in the Cimmeria system for almost a month before a regular battle group showed up and took over. Fittingly, it included the Reconquista class cruiser *Cimmeria*, allowing Dunmoore to reconnect with a few more old Stingrays, such as Kathryn Kowalski.

But a day after she handed control of the system to the battle group's commander, Dunmoore received the message from SOCOM HQ she'd been both expecting and dreading.

It was for Dunmoore's eyes only, and after digesting its contents, she sat on the news a little longer so she could regain full control of her inner turmoil. Too many changes, too much on the verge of becoming nothing more than memories. Dunmoore eventually summoned Holt to her quarters, and when the door chime rang, she prepared herself for what would inevitably happen.

"Enter."

The cabin door slid aside with a sigh. Captain Ezekiel Holt took one step in and came to a sudden halt when he caught sight of her uniform collar.

"What—"

She held up a restraining hand. "Before you say a word, you'd better listen to the orders from SOCOM. Sit."

Surprised at her harsh tone, Holt obeyed out of reflex although his eye never left her face. "I'm listening, sir."

"With the Fleet returning to its peacetime strength, Task Force Luckner is officially stood down. I'm sure this won't be a surprise for anyone. The ships are reassigned to regular battle groups, except for *Hawkwood*. She's headed to the Fleet reserve instead of undergoing a full refit since the powers that be plan on reducing the number of ship types. The navy's focus will be on Voivode class frigates and Reconquista class cruisers, a bit like the Shrehari with their *Tols* and *Ptars*. *Iolanthe* remains under Special Operations Command and will head for the badlands to clean up a piracy problem that's been plaguing us since the beginning of the war."

When she saw the question in Holt's eyes, Dunmoore nodded. "Yes, you're keeping her. Your promotion and appointment are permanent. If Emma wishes it, she can stay on as a career naval officer instead of returning to merchant ships, keep her commander's stripes, and remain your first officer."

"She does."

"You should expect individual reassignments now that we can afford to send people on longer training courses and resume the ship to shore rotation cycle, but most of the crew will stay for the next few months. However, Tatiana and E Company are going home to Scandia, and they won't be replaced by a Marine Corps contingent unless a particular mission profile calls for infantry or Special Forces. You'll drop them off on your way out of this sector."

"It's what we expected. I doubt any of them will be unhappy their tour in *Iolanthe* is over."

A faint smile relaxed Dunmoore's tense features.

"I think you might see a few requests for component transfer from the Army to the Corps cross your desk in the next few days."

"And you?" Holt asked, unable to wait any longer for an explanation of why she once again wore a captain's four bars on her collar. "Why did they take your star away?"

"We discussed this before, Zeke," she replied in a gentle tone. "There's a ceiling on the number of flag rank officers the peacetime Fleet can have on active duty at any given time. And the regulations governing a reduction in force stipulate the most recently promoted commodores will revert to their previous rank should that ceiling be breached. I'm among the most recently promoted, if not *the* most recent. Besides, I've not punched my ticket by doing staff duty tours as a commander or a captain, so my qualifications for a permanent flag position are a bit thin. Not to mention I only have three years seniority as a post captain, which isn't quite enough time in rank."

"That's bloody bullshit, Siobhan." Holt's voice quavered with tightly controlled fury. "If Nagira wants you as a commodore, he can make it happen. Hell, even Grand Admiral Shkadov praised you in person, and he's the guy who can give just about any legal order in this damned navy, including one to make you an exception to the rules. A fine way of rewarding the officer who, by *Kho'sahra* Brakal's own admission, triggered the cascade of events that ended this war."

Dunmoore raised both hands.

"Stop, Zeke. Think for a few moments. If Nagira or Shkadov pull strings and take another commodore's star away, one who wore it longer than I wore mine, instead of following regulations, how do you think I'll be perceived as the beneficiary? Or ignore the ceiling and keep me on the books as a commodore, acting, while so employed until enough flag officers retire while others ahead of me revert to captain? It would follow me for the rest of my career and pretty much make sure I never wear a second star, let alone get decent assignments because Shkadov and Nagira will retire in two or three years, leaving me exposed. We, the officers who survived the war, don't deal well with favoritism anymore after seeing how useless a lot of the peacetime captains and admirals were when the Shrehari invaded."

She watched Holt's nostrils flare, then he seemed to deflate as his anger evaporated. He exhaled noisily.

"I suppose you're right."

"There's no suppose about it." She took a deep breath. "Look, the orders taking away my star were a dagger thrust to the heart, which is why I didn't summon you until I dealt with my disappointment in private. Chances are I'm far from the only shiny new commodore to wake up as a captain this morning. I'm probably one of three or four dozen. And I won't be the only officer to drop one rank because of the Fleet returning to its peacetime configuration. A lot of ships will be mothballed and most of those who joined up for the duration plus six months are on their way back to civilian life. This is what happens after every war. It's just my bad luck I didn't make it above the cut-off line before the government ordered us to demobilize."

Holt scoffed. "We should have let the damned boneheads stew another ten or twelve months, so you were no longer among the most junior one-stars."

"Heavens, no! I'm glad the war is over, even if it means a reduction in rank. Compared to most of my classmates, I can't complain. I not only survived relatively unscathed, but I also held four warship commands in just over ten years, a record of sorts I suppose, even if I wrecked two of them. It's time for others such as you to get their turn."

A mischievous smile unexpectedly crossed Holt's face.

"Perhaps they should stuff you into a stasis pod marked *decant in case of war*."

Delighted laughter burbled up Dunmoore's throat.

"Are you saying I'll make a lousy peacetime staff officer? Then you can rest easy. I'm not headed for a job as flag captain or worse, sailing a desk in a large headquarters. Now that would make me go bonkers."

"Oh?" He sat up. "What then?"

"Meet the first head of unconventional naval warfare studies at the Armed Services War College. I'm hitching a ride to Caledonia aboard *Terra* when she breaks out of orbit tomorrow since that's where she's headed." Dunmoore gave Holt a rueful smile. "*Terra* will be mothballed when she gets there, meaning I can commiserate with Captain Harmel. But he's becoming a battle group flag captain, so that's a step up for him, and a staff ticket he can punch on the way to his first star."

"Instructor at the Armed Services War College *and* setting up a new curriculum? Does Fleet HQ know what they're about to unleash?"

"If not, they'll find out soon enough. It's a two-year assignment. Hopefully, I'll return to a battle group as flag captain when I'm done, and maybe after another two years, I'll put up my commodore's star again."

"It better not take the brass more than four years to return what they should never have taken away." A thoughtful expression erased Holt's air of indignation. "When will you leave *Iolanthe*?"

"*Terra* wants me aboard by eight bells in the afternoon watch tomorrow. If you can arrange a shuttle for, say, six bells, I'd be grateful."

"Oh, I think *Iolanthe* might do better than that. When will you announce Task Force Luckner's disbandment to the others?"

"As soon as we're done here. I wanted you to hear it first so you could get everything out of your system while we were in private."

"You know Gregor will have an apoplectic fit when he sees you're wearing captain's bars again."

Dunmoore shrugged.

"There's no way around that, though in the presence of his peers, he'll feel more constrained than the last time he thought Fleet HQ gave me a raw deal. In any case, it's done, and I'm now nothing more than a guest aboard your ship, Zeke."

"Bullshit. Until the moment you step off *Iolanthe*, I will consider you my flag officer commanding, orders be damned."

"Then could you please link up the former Task Force Luckner ships and prepare your conference room?"

"Certainly." Holt sprang to his feet. "With your permission?"

"Carry on. I'll send the captains their ships' assignments ahead of the meeting."

**

"You'll have received your orders by now and know that with the war finally over, Task Force Luckner is disbanded and its constituent ships transferred to permanent battle groups."

Dunmoore turned her gaze on each captain in turn. Everyone except Holt was present around the conference table via holographic projection.

"Save for *Hawkwood*. Sorry, Kirti. I hope the additional bar on your collar makes up for the transfer to a shore assignment."

"It does, sir. Thank you."

"I'm sure we'll spend the rest of our lives dining out on the fact we escorted the Commonwealth delegation to the armistice ceremonies. And if the Shrehari *kho'sahra* wasn't lying, we also played a role in setting him on the path to power. No one else in the Fleet can claim anything of the sort."

She paused for a moment so she could gather herself.

"Captains, it has been an honor and a privilege to serve with you. No flag officer in the Fleet could have wished for better crews and starship commanders. Please pass my thanks and my best wishes to your people."

Gregor Pushkin's hologram raised a hand.

"If I may, sir. Where is your commodore's star?"

Dunmoore repeated what she'd told Holt earlier almost word for word.

"A damn injustice, if you ask me," Pushkin said when she fell silent. "Captain Holt, I trust *Iolanthe* will see the commodore off in style."

"Of course. And you're invited. In fact, perhaps we can share a glass with the commodore in our wardroom before she leaves and toast her future success. Shall we say four bells in the afternoon watch tomorrow?"

Every hologram around the table nodded enthusiastically.

"Full dress uniform, I presume?" Pushkin asked.

"I wouldn't want it any other way."

Dunmoore turned her head and speared Holt with a hard stare. "What are you planning, Captain?"

"Just making sure you don't sneak off on us, Skipper. Believe it or not, many people around here would be crushed if we didn't give you full honors."

— Forty-Seven —

Dunmoore took one last look around her cabin when the door chime rang. Stripped of her personal effects, which were already aboard the shuttle, it held no more warmth than any transient senior officer's quarters. For reasons she couldn't explain, Dunmoore fancied this may well have been her last cabin aboard a starship as anything more than a passenger.

"Enter."

Holt, in full dress uniform, poked his head through the opening.

"The Task Force Luckner captains are aboard and waiting for you in the wardroom, sir."

"Coming."

Dunmoore glanced at her reflection in the full-length mirror affixed to the bulkhead, glad she'd kept her old tunic with a post captain's four gold stripes and executive curl on either cuff. Perhaps she never truly believed they would let her stay a flag officer for long, not with only three years' seniority as a captain, not now that she served in a peacetime navy. But the commodore's uniform with its Task Force Luckner crest on the right sleeve was packed away with the rest of her things, in case fate smiled on her again.

Holt led Dunmoore down the passageway, and as he entered the wardroom, he called out, "Ladies and gentlemen, the commodore."

All conversation ceased as those present snapped to attention.

"At ease," Dunmoore said. "Thank you for coming."

"We wouldn't have missed it for all the gold in the galaxy," Pushkin replied.

She went around the room, shaking hands and saying a few words to each of the captains who, until yesterday, were under her command. Meanwhile, the wardroom steward passed out stemless glasses filled with ruby red wine. When everyone held one, Holt cleared his throat.

"Captains, I want to propose a toast to our commanding officer, and it won't be the toast of the day, since it's Thursday, the war is over, and I'd rather we didn't experience a pandemic."

A few chuckles greeted Holt's quip.

"Instead, I will wish our departing commodore the following."

He raised his glass.

"May the winds of fortune sail you,
May you sail a gentle sea.
May it always be the other guy
Who says, this drink's on me."

"To Siobhan Dunmoore!"

The assembled officers raised their glasses and called out, "To Siobhan Dunmoore."

Her eyebrows shot up at the first sip of wine. Where Holt found such an excellent vintage at short notice, she didn't dare ask. The Chateau Pétrus was long gone, it certainly wasn't from *Iolanthe*'s stocks, and after ten years under the Shrehari thumb, it wasn't from

Cimmeria either. When Dunmoore glanced at him, he put on a roguish smile and winked, as if he knew exactly what she was thinking.

"I owe Oliver Harmel a big one, Skipper. When the brass shifted over to *Equinox Nova*, they left the good stuff behind."

"Oh."

Their time in the wardroom passed at a dizzying speed, and it came as a surprise when Holt touched her elbow.

"Sorry, Skipper, but your shuttle is waiting."

"Of course. Please lead on."

"No, sir. As your last duty, we, your captains, ask that you lead us to the hangar deck."

She gave him a curious stare.

"If you wish."

When the wardroom door opened, she found two pipers and two drummers from *Terra*'s Marine band in the passageway, facing aft, toward the hangar. The pipers inflated their instruments, then one of the drummers muttered a command, and as they stepped off, they began playing a traditional military march, *The Crags of Tumbledown Mountain*. Since she had no choice, Dunmoore followed them at a brisk pace, trailed by her captains marching two by two.

The hangar deck's inner doors opened at their approach, and Commander Emma Cullop called the ship's company to attention. When she entered the cavernous compartment, Dunmoore immediately understood that orders be damned, Holt was giving her an admiral's farewell, both to honor her and flip HQ the bird.

As she approached the formation, the spacers arrayed in three ranks on her left and the soldiers of E Company, 3rd Battalion, Scandia Regiment arrayed on her right presented arms with a thunderous crash. Their officers and command noncoms saluted with drawn swords while the rest of the Marine band joined their four comrades.

The pinnace, still wearing a commodore's flag on its sides sat at the far end of the formation, its open aft ramp facing Dunmoore, waiting for her. She knew her role, having participated in just such a ceremony years earlier and raised her hand in salute as she marched between spacers and soldiers.

She stopped at the foot of the ramp and made a precise about-turn, only to see Holt and the other eight captains standing at attention in a single row, closing off the far end of the formation. Then, Dunmoore noticed a short white mast, flying a commodore's broad pennant in one corner. Cullop gave the shoulder arms command, and the music died away.

Holt took one step forward.

"Lower Commodore Dunmoore's pennant."

A familiar voice, belonging to newly-promoted Petty Officer Third Class Vincenzo, called out, "Flag party, quick march."

Six spacers emerged from the shadows and headed for the mast, heels clicking on the metal deck.

When they reached the mast, Vincenzo took hold of the cords, and the band began playing *Auld Lang Syne*. He lowered her pennant with care while his mates gathered the material.

Once the pennant was free, they folded it into a small triangle which Vincenzo tucked under his left arm. When the flag party stepped off toward Dunmoore, the band segued into *Will You No Come Back Again*. After the first few bars, the spacers and soldiers broke out into song.

And will ye no' come back again?
Will ye no' come back again?
Better lo'ed ye canna be
Will ye no' come back again?

A sudden rush of emotion forced tears into the corners of her eyes.

Vincenzo stamped to a halt in front of her, saluted, and held out the folded pennant. His voice came out as a hoarse croak when he said, "Sir, it's been an honor serving under your command. Fair winds and following seas."

She accepted the pennant. "Thank you for everything, Petty Officer Vincenzo."

"Sir."

He took a step back and saluted again. She returned the compliment, then watched him and his party march away to vanish among the spacer ranks.

Chief Petty Officer Second Class Dwyn stepped forward with ten of her mates, each carrying a silver bosun's call. Eleven calls met eleven sets of lips, and the farewell trill to a flag officer echoed across the deck.

"Ship's company, present ARMS."

Holt, voice pitched to cut through the noise, said, "Luckner, departing."

Dunmoore knew it was her cue. She raised her hand to salute her ship, her crew, her captains, and her soldiers one last time. As the calls fell silent, a lone piper began to play the traditional lament for the occasion, *Sleep Dearie Sleep* as he stepped away from the band and slowly marched across the hangar deck.

Dunmoore pivoted on her heels and marched up the ramp. Once inside, she turned around and looked back while the ramp slowly rose, taking one last gaze at what she knew had been her final starship command.

The shuttle lifted off, pivoted, and then slipped through the force field keeping the deck pressurized while the space doors were open.

They closed moments after the pinnace cleared *Iolanthe*, cutting off her view of the assembled crew and the lone piper through one of the aft portholes. Now that she was alone, save for Petty Officer Gus Purdy, the pilot up front, she let tears stream down her cheeks without shame.

Leaving *Iolanthe* was more heart-wrenching than leaving any of her other ships had been and for one reason only — the Furious Faerie would continue to sail, fight, and live on without her.

Where Dunmoore had been *Don Quixote*, *Shenzen*, and *Stingray*'s last captain, she was *Iolanthe*'s first. The Q-ship still had a long career ahead of her, longer perhaps than Dunmoore's, while she faced life without being surrounded by a crew for the first time in a decade. It would be a difficult adjustment.

Many long service starship captains never manage the transition. If she was one of them, perhaps early retirement from the navy to work in the merchant service might be an option. Although with the current demobilization, there would be plenty of experienced wartime officers looking for work in shipping companies large and small.

But Dunmoore knew she would eventually come across many of those with whom she'd sailed for so long. The navy was about to become a small family again, and perhaps, if fate smiled on her, some might even serve under her command once more. If they gave her another command.

Yet leaving them behind still ached and would for a long time, especially since she wouldn't be able to bury herself in work until one of *Terra*'s shuttles dropped her off at the Sanctum spaceport on Caledonia.

By the time her former command faded in the distance, Dunmoore's eyes were once again dry, though her voice still held a tinge of sadness.

"Fair winds and following seas, my friends."

About the Author

Eric Thomson is the pen name of a retired Canadian soldier who served more time in uniform than he expected, both in the Regular Army and the Army Reserve. He spent his Regular Army career in the Infantry and his Reserve service in the Armoured Corps. He worked as an information technology executive for several years before retiring to become a full-time author.

Eric has been a voracious reader of science fiction, military fiction, and history all his life. Several years ago, he put fingers to keyboard and started writing his own military sci-fi, with a definite space opera slant, using many of his own experiences as a soldier for inspiration.

When he is not writing fiction, Eric indulges in his other passions: photography, hiking, and scuba diving, all of which he shares with his wife.

Join Eric Thomson at www.thomsonfiction.ca
Where you will find news about upcoming books and more information about the universe in which his heroes fight for humanity's survival.

Read his blog at www.blog.thomsonfiction.ca

If you enjoyed this book, please consider leaving a review on Goodreads, or with your favorite online retailer to help others discover it.

Also by Eric Thomson

Siobhan Dunmoore
No Honor in Death (Siobhan Dunmoore Book 1)
The Path of Duty (Siobhan Dunmoore Book 2)
Like Stars in Heaven (Siobhan Dunmoore Book 3)
Victory's Bright Dawn (Siobhan Dunmoore Book 4)
Without Mercy (Siobhan Dunmoore Book 5)
When the Guns Roar (Siobhan Dunmoore Book 6)
A Dark and Dirty War (Siobhan Dunmoore Book 7)
On Stormy Seas (Siobhan Dunmoore Book 8)

Decker's War
Death Comes But Once (Decker's War Book 1)
Cold Comfort (Decker's War Book 2)
Fatal Blade (Decker's War Book 3)
Howling Stars (Decker's War Book 4)
Black Sword (Decker's War Book 5)
No Remorse (Decker's War Book 6)
Hard Strike (Decker's War Book 7)

Constabulary Casefiles
The Warrior's Knife (Constabulary Casefiles #1)
A Colonial Murder (Constabulary Casefiles #2)
The Dirty and the Dead (Constabulary Casefiles #3)

Ashes of Empire
Imperial Sunset (Ashes of Empire #1)
Imperial Twilight (Ashes of Empire #2)
Imperial Night (Ashes of Empire #3)
Imperial Echoes (Ashes of Empire #4)
Imperial Ghosts (Ashes of Empire #5)

Ghost Squadron
We Dare (Ghost Squadron No. 1)
Deadly Intent (Ghost Squadron No. 2)
Die Like the Rest (Ghost Squadron No. 3)
Fear No Darkness (Ghost Squadron No. 4)

Printed in Great Britain
by Amazon

46772882R00225